OPERATION SALAZAR

Dan Lawton

Also by Dan Lawton

Deception

For more information, contact:
info@danlawtonfiction.com
or visit:
www.danlawtonfiction.com

Cover designed by Samuel G. Wilson
http://designskills.samwilson-online.com

ISBN: 978-0-9964076-4-9

First Edition: December 2015

This book is for my wife, Elizabeth – My number one fan and greatest supporter.

CHAPTER ONE

It's half past midnight and the streets are filled with blackness. It's been dark for hours. The single family homes in the upscale Stoneham neighborhood in the suburbs of the Back Bay of Boston are quiet. There are no street lights and no police presence in this area. Only shadows line the pavement. The target is a 1941 Victorian, and there has been no movement inside since just before midnight. Marco Salazar is accompanied by Antonio Esposito inside of his Cadillac, which is parked outside on the street. Its lights are off, but the engine is still idling, humming gently. Warm air fills the cabin, which helps to neutralize the crisp October chill. Marco's hands are frozen, in spite of the two air vents that are angled directly on him.

"Remember what Uncle Sal said," Marco says as he kills the engine with a flick of his wrist. "We're in and out." He pulls a dark ski mask over his face, a pair of gloves over his hands, and waits for his best friend and roommate to do the same. The cotton tugs on his chapped skin, suddenly making him itchy all over.

"Got it," Antonio says, as he too pulls a mask over his face.

Marco steps out. The near-freezing temperature sends a chill down his back and goosebumps crawling up his arms. On a silent count of three, he and Antonio close their doors together, making almost no sound. Being quiet is key at this time of night, as they've learned over the past few months. Anxious, Marco waits for Antonio to join him on the driver's side of the vehicle. A white cloud of moisture crystallizes in front of his face as he breathes into the chill. With a peek over his shoulder, Marco is reassured that they're alone for this one final job. When Antonio approaches, Marco holds out his closed fist, which Antonio bumps with his own, just as they always do. Without looking first, they creep across the empty street and head up to the concrete stairwell.

Still knowing its exact location, Marco bends down and reaches for the loose brick that lines the base of the stairs. Even through the darkness, he finds it quickly, yanks it out, and reaches his fingers inside and feels for the key. He pinches it between his covered fingertips and slides the brick back into place. Back on his feet, he slides the key into the deadbolt first, then into the door key lock and turns. The front door unlocks and the two men slide inside like they own the place. Marco enters first. Antonio follows behind and closes the door.

The hardwood floors are the originals, although much of the oak is covered with overflowing moving boxes. Marco's first thought is that the new owners don't have enough stuff to fill up the house. The house is more spacious than it looks. Marco remembers it well. Without hesitation, Marco heads up the stairs that are to his left. Antonio follows once Marco reaches the top.

There are three bedrooms and two bathrooms upstairs, the second of which is only accessible through the master bedroom. The only bedroom that has the door closed is the one at the end of the hallway. Marco slides into the first bedroom on the right, which only has more moving boxes. He quickly moves out. The next bedroom adjacent to the first is much of the same. Antonio meets Marco in the hallway, and Marco shakes his head at him. They both know there's only one place left to look.

Time for stealth mode.

The last bedroom at the end of the hallway has some faint snoring coming from behind the door, but the job must go on. Marco reaches behind his back and removes the pistol from his belt. Antonio does the same, except his is in the front. Gripping the door handle like a vise, Marco turns the knob with caution, hoping that it doesn't creak too loudly. The Victorians in this region of the country are well-kept and many of them modernized, but the old frames and foundations do still tend to make a lot of undesired noise. The door does squeak when he opens it, but not loud enough to cause a stir from inside.

Step one is complete.

There's a man and a woman in the bed, and neither one of them react to the sound of the opening door. Marco can't tell which one of them is snoring. Maybe it's both. Squinting through the black, Marco scans the room the best he can, trying to force his eyes to adjust. The goods are somewhere in this room, as Big Sal had told them, but he doesn't know where exactly. There's no logical hiding place readily obvious, but that's to be expected.

There's a matching set of nightstands on either side of the bed, both made of vintage wood. On the wall directly parallel to the bed, now behind the open door, is a dresser with a wide vanity mirror hanging on the wall above it. Next to that is an open door leading to the attached bathroom. Marco slides along the left side of the wall, Antonio the right, and he listens for any subtle movement of the floorboards as they glide. What they're looking for is likely somewhere behind one of these nightstands, although he's unsure which one. As Marco steps toward the nightstand in front of him to investigate, the floor beneath him creaks when he puts his feet together. The sound echoes in the bedroom, seemingly refusing to end, and he tenses up.

The man in the bed grunts when the loud creak sounds, and he releases the woman's torso from his grasp and begins to stir. He turns his head in Antonio's direction and appears to be staring, unmoving, like he sees something. Marco tries to make himself small on the other side of the room by pulling his arms in close to his torso, but it's no use.

"What the hell?" the man whispers under his breath.

Marco can sense that the situation is quickly about to spiral out of control.

The man reaches across his body and turns on the lamp on the nightstand. Although dim, the light from the bulb almost blinds Marco, and he's forced to look away. When he's fully adjusted, he looks back over to Antonio, who's now standing just a few feet away from the man in the bed with an outstretched arm.

"Don't move," Antonio says with a menacing tone as he steadies the gun in his hand. He looks up and across the room to Marco, who now has no choice but to draw his own weapon. He hadn't planned to use it, ever, but the dealer has shuffled the deck and he's been dealt some new cards. Folding is simply not an option.

The man, whose mostly hairless chest protrudes from underneath the bedspread, thrusts his back against the wooden headboard with a thud at the acknowledgment of Marco, a second gunman. With a look of sheer terror on his face, he reaches for the woman next to him and shakes her. "Jen, wake up," he says with a stammer.

She groans at him but doesn't do much else.

"Jen, wake up!" he repeats, shaking her more violently this time. He switches between the eyes of Marco and Antonio and refuses to blink.

Marco's heart is thumping with anticipation, the muscles in his legs threatening to spasm from the tension. He keeps his eyes on the woman, Jen, while he tries to figure out their next move.

"Jen-" the man pleads.

"What are you doing?" Jen finally mumbles as she tries to swat away the man's hand. "Turn off the light."

"Lady, listen to the man," Marco says in Jen's direction, his voice much deeper and more awake than that of the trembling man next to her, ready to take control of the situation.

Her eyes are suddenly wide open and alert. She sits up and turns her head, notices Marco pointing a gun in her face, and she screams. Then she spots the second gunman, Antonio, on Peter's side of the bed, and she screams again. Marco can see the horror starting to set in on both of their faces.

"What do you want from us?" the man asks as he wraps his arms around Jen so that they can both shudder in place as one. His forehead is soaked in a panicky perspiration. "Please don't kill us."

Jen buries her face into the man's chest and grabs a handful of the wrinkled bedspread with her hand. Tears stream down her face as she braces for the pain that's about to come.

Marco shifts his eyes from Jen's to Antonio's, and they connect. Antonio gives a subtle nod, which Marco takes as his queue that they're on the same page. This isn't their first rodeo, so they both know what to do.

They silently count to three.

CHAPTER TWO

Marco's Cadillac glides through the streets of the Back Bay, heading toward Arlington Street. Marco is still a little shaken up by the whole event, but he needs to pull himself together before they arrive at Big Sal's. What just happened was not part of the plan, and he hadn't anticipated it. The ski masks and gloves that they wore are in a plastic bag on the floor under Antonio's seat, hidden from view and readily available in case they need to go back. Marco drives in silence while the spare key to the Victorian is kept securely in his hip pocket. The teeth on the key dig into the fatty part of his thigh.

"What are we going to tell Big Sal?" Antonio asks with a slight hesitation.

Marco doesn't respond right away. He tries to think. He speeds up through the amber light before it turns red. "We're going to tell him the truth. Let me do the talking though, okay? I know how to talk to him."

Antonio nods.

Big Sal's Pizzeria is on the corner of Arlington and Boylston, just past the commuter rail. His business does well, and he stays open late so that the stragglers from the last subway run can eat. The crowd at night isn't the most pleasant, but he's a tough guy who doesn't put up with any bullshit. Plus, there's a Boston police station about a mile from the pizzeria, which, although ironic, helps to ease his mind.

There's a small parking lot outside of Sal's place, plus a few other spots in the back, most of which are empty at this time of night. Sal's Lexus rests in the corner of the lot by itself, so Marco pulls up next to it and kills the engine. Marco can see the rust on the underside of the Lexus, and it reminds him of his Cadillac. Sal has mentioned numerous times how he just hopes that the car will pass inspection in the spring, but Marco doubts it'll even survive the winter. The Cadillac's in better condition than that, but not by much. There's a studio apartment above the pizzeria that Sal calls home, so he hardly ever leaves. When he does, the Lexus usually gets him to where he needs to go without much trouble. But winter is approaching, and that's a different animal.

Winter in New England.

Marco steps out of the car and approaches the front door of the pizzeria. The temperature has dropped even a few degrees further below freezing as the night has gotten later. He zips his coat up to his chin to keep the heat in. Sal closes shop at half past midnight seven days a week, so Marco doesn't even bother trying to pull on the door. He knows that it'll be locked. He presses the call button on the buzzer that's wired next to the mail slot beside the door, and he waits.

"Who is it?" Sal's voice is scratchy through the buzzer unit.

"Uncle Sal, it's me, Marco. I've got Antonio here with me too."

The buzzer goes off and the door's lock disengages. Marco pulls on the handle and walks inside, being sure to wipe his hand on his pant leg to eliminate any bacteria that may have been left behind. Antonio follows behind, dragging his feet. They walk around the counter, which is freshly cleaned and still smelling of disinfectant, and head into the backroom. An industrial oven rests against the back wall, and there's a door just to the left of it that leads up to Sal's apartment. The kitchen still smells of pepperoni, which makes Marco's mouth moisten. The door swings open as they approach.

Amelio Salazar, or Big Sal as most people call him, is a heavy-set man who only wears black slacks with a black undershirt in which he tucks into his belt when he's not working. He thinks that taking off his t-shirt with the pizzeria's logo on the breast is considered changing clothes. His pants are dirtied with flour and pizza dough, as he spends much of his day making pizzas special for his best customers.

"Boys, how you doin'?" Sal says with a smile on his face.

Marco approaches first, and Sal places one arm on each of his shoulders. They lean in and kiss cheeks, one for each side. Sal releases his grip from his nephew and goes through the same routine with Antonio.

"How'd it go, boys?" Sal continues. "Do we have the goods?"

Antonio backs away and looks for Marco to take the lead, which he does.

"No, Uncle Sal, we don't have the goods."

Sal shows no emotion, doesn't say anything, and waits for Marco to continue.

"Something happened."

"Did you get inside okay? The key should have been under the stairs," Sal says.

"Yeah, I remembered. We got in okay, but they woke up before we could locate the item."

Sal looks between his nephew and Antonio, then he nods. "I didn't think they had moved in already. Did they see your faces?"

"No, we were wearing our masks."

"Good boys."

"We were able to look around a bit, but we didn't see anything that stood out. It was dark though, so maybe we missed something."

Sal looks away to belch and rub his belly, so Marco takes the opportunity to shift his eyes to Antonio. Antonio looks on edge, but things seem to be going fine so far. Marco has it under control.

"Okay, boys, things like this happen. We'll just go back another night."

Sal puts his arm around Marco's shoulder and squeezes, then pulls Antonio in and does the same. Antonio is still tense, but now looking more relieved, while Marco is relaxed and had been expecting nothing less from his uncle. Sal is a reasonable man.

"Come on upstairs and grab something to eat," Sal says. "I got a freshly made pie. Pepperoni." Sal leads Marco and Antonio through the door and up the stairs to his studio apartment. "About those people that were inside," he says, "tell me what happened."

CHAPTER THREE

Peter and Jen Winston sit at the rustic wooden table that rests in the corner of their mostly empty kitchen. Moving boxes are scattered all over and the table is covered with dust. Jen has a baby blue colored bathrobe draped around her, and her eyes are swollen from crying. Her head is pounding – a migraine. Peter is wearing flannel bottoms and a solid white t-shirt, and he tries to comfort his wife as they talk with the two police officers.

"Let me get this straight, Mr. Winston," begins Officer Dale of the Stoneham Police Department, who sits across from them at the table. "You and your wife were sleeping in your bed upstairs, and you woke up to two men standing in your room?"

"And they were both holding guns, that's right," Peter says.

"And they were pointing them right at us!" Jen exclaims. Peter pulls his wife closer to him to comfort her.

"Did they assault you?" Officer Dale asks.

"No," Peter says.

"Did they take anything?"

"No, I don't think so."

"Officer Harris and I didn't find any sign of forced entry anywhere on the property."

Officer Harris nods in confirmation from where he stands in the corner of the room.

"We're telling you the truth!" Jen blurts. She's struggling to understand why there seems to be no urgency from the officers. It's almost like they don't believe that it actually happened or something.

Officer Dale holds up his hand to stop her. "Listen, ma'am, we never said you were lying. But neither one of you saw the perp's faces, no one got hurt, nothing was taken, and there are no signs of forced entry. There isn't much we can do in a situation like this."

"So that's it? You're not going to help us then?" Peter asks, sounding defeated.

Officer Dale retrieves a small notepad from his breast pocket and flips open the cover. He pops the cap off his pen and looks to Peter. "Tell me again what happened. We'll do what we can."

Peter sighs. "Fine, when we woke up-"

"No, after that."

"One of the guys told Jen to listen-"

"After that too."

Peter pauses and thinks back before continuing. He's already repeated himself three times, and now these guys finally want to take notes. Typical. "Fine. After that, the two guys looked at each other and didn't say anything. Maybe three or four seconds later they put their guns down and ran out of the room. Jen and I hugged and cried, then we heard a car peeling away outside. A few minutes later we called you guys."

"Did you see a license plate?"

"No, I already told you. We were too scared to do anything. We couldn't move for a few minutes after they left. We just froze. Are you even listening to me?"

Officer Dale scribbles some notes on his pad and places it back in his breast pocket. He rises to his feet and hikes up his pants by the belt. "We'll see what we can do. I just want to warn you now, don't expect much. Unless someone else saw something, the vehicle maybe, we don't really have anything to go on. Don't count on it though, as not many people are up at this time of night around here."

Officer Dale motions to his partner and they head for the door. Peter and Jen stare at each other in bewilderment at the lack of concern shown by the officers.

Officer Dale stops and turns back to Peter and Jen before disappearing down the hallway. "Oh, and one more thing," he says. "Welcome to the neighborhood. You might want to start locking your doors at night."

CHAPTER FOUR

Sal's studio is compact and smells of melted cheese and spicy tomato sauce. The garlic hits Marco's nose like a clove is being shoved in his face. It's overwhelming, but he loves it. In the background, the TV is on and the volume is low, and Sal's bed is unfolded from the wall.

"Sit down, boys," Sal says, motioning to the table in the middle of the room. "Have a piece of pie, yes?"

Marco and Antonio sit around the rounded table and help themselves to the half-empty pizza box. Sal stays standing and watches the boys with satisfaction.

"Pretty good, isn't it?" Sal says. "It's a new recipe I'm trying out."

"It's really good Uncle Sal," Marco says mid-bite. He really thinks there's too much garlic, but he would never actually say it. Sal will figure it out on his own in time.

Sal nods and smiles and waits for the boys to finish their slices. "Do you have any idea about the location of the goods?"

Marco looks to Antonio and shrugs. "Not so much," he begins. "We checked all of the rooms upstairs and we didn't find anything."

"I told you to look in the bedroom at the end of the hall, that's what your pop's told me," Sal offers.

"Yeah, I know that. We saw that door was the only one that was closed though, so we were hoping to get lucky without going in there. We didn't want to wake them up."

"But you did wake them."

"I know, Uncle Sal, but we didn't mean to. We were being quiet, I swear. It was those damn floors."

Sal looks to Antonio, who nods nervously in confirmation. He pulls up a chair and sits between the boys. One of the legs of the chair is missing a floor protector pad, so it digs into the checkered linoleum and screeches when Sal slides it forward. "Okay, boys, I believe you. But we have to go back. We don't have much time."

"How much time do we have left, Uncle Sal?"

"What's today?"

"Tuesday," Antonio says.

Sal looks at his watch. "It's 1:30 A.M. now. We have to be down at Old Man Willy's at eight o'clock. Why don't you boys stay here tonight? One of you can take the couch and the other can take the chair. We can get some sleep and head down there in the morning."

"We?" Marco says, confused. It had always been just Sal going to see Willy, alone, while he and Antonio played their own part. He had thought their roles were pretty well defined at this point in the game, but apparently not.

"That's right. Willy was expecting the goods first thing on Tuesday, and if you boys say that today is Tuesday, then we have to go down there and explain what happened."

Marco can see that Antonio is starting to get panicky by the outline of his jaw that continues to flex, so he offers him a reassuring smile, telling him that everything will be alright. But at the end of the day, Marco doesn't offer any resistance to Sal's idea. He needs to help his father, and if this is what needs to be done, he has to do it. He has to be a man about this. "Okay," Marco says, "we'll stay."

"Good then," Sal says, then rises from his seat and makes his way across the room. He flops himself on his bed, belly first, and flips off the TV. Antonio waits until Sal turns his back to them before approaching Marco.

"I can't stay here," he whispers.

"Why not?"

"I can't go with you to Willy's. That old man gives the creeps."

"Don't worry about him. We've been doing business with him for quite a while now. My uncle will take care of it."

"I don't know, Marco, I have a bad feeling about this."

"Listen, you don't have to be involved anymore if you don't want to, but I do. I need to do this for my dad. He's counting on me." Marco takes a breath and pauses for a beat before continuing, "But I do really need you. I can't do this alone. One more job and we're done for good. Please, Antonio."

Marco makes a fist, holds it out, and waits. Antonio looks between it and Marco's pleading eyes. Despite his obvious reservations, Marco knows that he won't leave him hanging and let him go after this alone. Antonio is too good a friend. Marco has always been there for him, and although he would never actually say it to his face for the fear of upsetting him, he feels deep down that Antonio owes it to him to repay the favor. Antonio eventually makes a fist and knocks it against the top of Marco's. Then they reverse roles and Marco knocks his fist on top of Antonio's. Marco grins, impressed with himself for how well he knows his best friend.

"Brothers?" Marco says.

"Brothers."

CHAPTER FIVE

The front door closes and Peter and Jen watch the unhelpful officers walk back to their car through the bay window in the living room. It's nearly 2:00 A.M. and Peter has to be up in five hours, which he's dreading. Jen starts in on him before the officers even get into their car.

"You need to call a locksmith and have our locks changed," she demands.

"I will first thing."

"There must be someone available on-call for twenty-four hours. We're in the city now."

"I'm not dealing with this right now. My alarm is going to go off in five hours and I need to get some sleep. I'm going back to bed."

"Bed? How can you go back to bed right now? I'll never be able to sleep again until you have those locks changed."

Peter sighs. "Jen, I said I'll make a call tomorrow. Some of us have to get up in the morning."

The subject is a sensitive one, and they've had the conversation a hundred times over. Jen crosses her arms and stares at her husband in disappointment.

Peter sighs again. "I'm sorry, I didn't mean that. Listen, it's been a long night and I'm just exhausted." Peter leans in and kisses Jen on her forehead. She doesn't lean in, but she doesn't fight it either. She just stands there and takes it. "I'll call first thing in the morning, okay? Whoever was in here, whatever they want, they won't come back tonight. There's nothing else we can do right now. We'll deal with it in the morning."

Jen looks away. She doesn't respond and Peter doesn't wait for her to as he climbs up the creaky stairs and disappears into the hallway upstairs. When the door to their bedroom closes, Jen sits in the one chair that rests by the window. She wraps her favorite throw blanket around her shoulders and gazes into the darkness. It's the first night in the new house and she misses her home back in the woods of Maine already.

PETER AND JEN HAVE been married for eight years. They have no children, no pets, and have never wanted either. Jen is adventurous and woodsy, Peter is not. Jen is an introvert who prefers a quiet life of solitude. Peter is an extrovert who enjoys social gatherings and spending as much time out of the house as possible. He's always wanted to live in the suburbs and commute into the big city, while Jen works out of the house and loves it. What once was a typical case of opposites attract has morphed into something different. Something without romance. Something almost toxic at times. They've been slowly drifting apart and their marriage has been failing for years because of it. They can both feel it.

Peter is in the fine jewelry business. He was offered a major promotion and substantial salary increase to oversee a handful of retail locations in the Boston area. He accepted without consulting with his wife and took the position nearly three months ago. He's been staying in the area during the week and making the commute back to their apartment in the woods on the weekends since then. He does well and was able to grab a house larger than he had ever dreamed on foreclosure. He's been bringing boxes in for the past couple of weeks now, and Jen has just finally made the move with the rest of their belongings after tying up some loose ends up north.

Jen is a wildlife blogger for a local outdoor magazine in Maine. She grew up in the state, went to the University of Maine, and has been working at her dream job for the last five years. She can work remotely from just about anywhere, so she had agreed to make the move the city to try and save their marriage. Peter has been unhappy living in the woods for years, so he feels that it's her turn to suffer for a while. It's only fair that way. Their therapist had agreed with Peter, albeit in different terms, so here they are. Jen's hates it already.

PETER'S ALARM GOES OFF at 7:00 A.M. He stirs quickly at the startle and dismisses the buzzer before his wife wakes up. He already has a headache from the lack of sleep and knows it's going to be a long day before he even rolls out of bed. He notices that his wife isn't in the bed as he drags himself out of the room, down the hall, and into the bathroom.

He thinks back to the previous night's events as he prepares himself for the day. He remembers with a high degree of certainty that he had locked the front door. He and Jen were unpacking some of the kitchen items before they went up to bed. He stopped at the door, checked both the deadbolt and the key lock, and followed Jen up the stairs. He knows with certainty that the house was secured, yet the police said there were no signs of forced entry. That means that the intruders found another way in somehow. That disturbs him.

Peter freshens up, tightens his necktie in the mirror, and heads down the stairs. Jen is sleeping with her head leaning forward in the chair next to the bay window. Peter walks over to where she sits and tucks the sagging blanket back around her torso. Her breaths are quiet and rhythmic, and he watches her for a moment. He hopes this move will bring them closer together as she'll be forced to lean on him for guidance more than ever before. She's out of her element here, so he's hopeful it'll help break her out of her shell.

There are two windows in the living room aside from the bay window, so Peter checks them all. All three are locked securely, just as he had thought. He makes his way down the narrow hall and into the kitchen, where the aroma of the coffee pot nearing its brew captures his attention. He checks the sliding glass door that leads out back again, but the lock is still jammed. Being a foreclosure, the house has some minor deficiencies in certain areas, and this busted sliding back door is one of them. There's nothing major, luckily, and he's confident that he'll be able to fix most of it over time. He checks the other four windows along the back and right side of the house, and they too are all secured. He knew they were. Before heading back down the hall, Peter takes a second to watch a couple of blue jays fight over some seeds in the feeder out in the yard. Some of the seeds fall to the grass, so the bigger of the two jays backs away from the feeder and tends to that. Peter wonders if the two birds are married, with the one eating from the feeder being the woman, obviously. He can't help but smirk thinking about a couple of animals getting hitched out in the woods somewhere.

Neither of the doors and none of the windows appear to be tampered with, so the intruders didn't force their way inside. That much is clear. The slider seems to make the most sense as the entrance point, but it looks fine. Peter would have thought that the door would be destroyed if someone tried to force their way inside. How they would have got it open from the outside is a mystery, as that's something Peter's been unable to accomplish for weeks. The busted lock pretty much confirms that the slider was not how the intruders got inside.

Peter knows that he and Jen are lucky to be alive, but the way those guys acted has him feeling uneasy. And a little less macho. He admits that he didn't handle himself very well last night, although he doubts that anyone else would have reacted much differently. He's still a little embarrassed, though. What kind of intruder breaks into a house, doesn't take anything, runs away, and doesn't kill the witnesses? It just doesn't add up. He won't say anything to Jen, of course, but he fears that they might be back at some point. It might not be today and it might not be tomorrow, but they'll be back. He just knows it. It's something in his gut that makes him feel so confident, something instinctual. Maybe they just wanted to check out the place and to see what they're up against the first time around. What it is that they want is the biggest mystery of them all. Peter doesn't think that he's been here long enough to make enemies yet.

Peter grabs his keys from the ceramic bowl on the counter and fills his travel mug with coffee before heading back down the hall. He quietly approaches and kisses his wife lightly on the cheek before leaving. He whispers his love for her in her ear, but she stays asleep. He decides that he'll call a locksmith on the way to the office, just as he promised he would.

Jen wakes up when Peter kisses her, but she keeps her eyes closed and tries to pretend to still be sleeping. She doesn't want to look at or talk to him right now. It was he who brought her here, and it's his fault for not keeping her safe.

CHAPTER SIX

7:00 A.M. comes quickly. Sal gets up first and wakes up the boys. They each take quick showers and head down the stairs into the back of the pizzeria. Sal grabs a brown paper bag from underneath the counter in the front and leads the trio into the parking lot. They all pile into Sal's Lexus and head east toward Willy's Pawn.

Old Man Willy has run a successful pawn shop for fifty years. Sal and Willy have been friends for years, but business is business. Pawn is not a business that offers the flexibility of backdoor deals based on trust. It's a simple model really - tangible goods for cold hard cash. Willy is a loyal friend, but a better businessman, and he won't make any exceptions. That's part of what Sal likes about him. Willy's Pawn closes for a few hours each morning, but the shop stays open for a total of twenty hours a day and 365 days a year. Even at his age, Willy is good for twelve hours every day, except for Sunday.

The traffic is heavy, so Sal doesn't pull into the empty parking lot until five minutes before eight. He parks his Lexus near the front door and leads the boys inside. No words are spoken. Glass cases line the perimeter of the shop and contain vintage weapons, jewelry, and lots of pieces from American history. Much of the wall space is covered with signed memorabilia from various entertainment industries, including professional and college sports, music and movies, and an occasional rare piece from Warhol, Picasso, or van Gogh. Although he's a regular visitor to the shop, Sal's always impressed with the collections. Today's no different.

Sal heads directly toward the rear of the shop and waits for Willy to make an appearance. He taps on the glass lightly with his fingertips and clears his throat in the direction of the employee-only cutout behind the counter. Marco and Antonio wait a few steps behind Sal and concentrate on looking around the shop and being careful not to stare at any one item in particular. Willy is a sucker for those who stare, and he rarely lets the customer leave without buying the item. He's a heck of a salesman. Buying is not the purpose of the visit today, though, so they know better than to be reckless.

At 8:00 A.M. sharp, Willy emerges from the back. His frizzy beard is whiter than ever, and he walks with a slight limp. He's seen a multitude of merchandise in his day, and his mind is filled with endless knowledge because of it. He's like a portable walking and talking museum. He spots his friend of many years immediately and makes his way in Sal's direction.

"If it isn't my old friend, Sal," Willy says. "Right on time as always."

Sal leans across the counter and they each plant courteous kisses on one another's cheeks.

"Good morning, my dear friend," Sal says as they finish up their greetings. "I brought along my nephew, Marco, and his buddy, Antonio, this morning." Sal steps to the side and shows the boys behind him. "You remember the boys, don't you?"

"Of course I do. Good morning, Marco. Good morning, Tony," Willy says.

Marco returns the pleasantry. Antonio waves but doesn't say anything. Willy keeps his eyes on Antonio for an extra second before returning to Sal's attention.

"Is it Tuesday already?" Willy asks.

"Time flies, my friend," Sal says.

"Well let's get down to business then, shall we? Do you have what we discussed?"

Sal bites his lip. "Not exactly. That's why we're all here. Before you say anything, let me explain. The boys here ran into a little bit of trouble while trying to retrieve the goods, you see? But it's no problem, because they're going back." Sal turns to the boys. "Isn't that right, boys?" He doesn't wait for them to respond before turning back to Willy.

"That's no good for me, Sal. My guy is coming by this afternoon and he has high expectations."

"I realize that, but we need more time."

Willy shakes his head. "Listen, my guy isn't going to wait around forever. He's got cash in hand and is ready to pull the trigger. We need the merchandise now, Sal."

"You think I don't know this? My brother's life is at stake here, alright? The boys are going back and will get the goods. I just need you to buy me some more time, just a little. Can you do that for me?"

Willy pauses and sighs. His beard bounces around as his chest exhales a heavy breath. "That's not really up to me, you know that. I'll see what I can do, but I can't guarantee you he won't walk."

Sal holds up the paper bag that he's been holding and places it on the counter in front of Willy.

"What's this?" Willy asks.

"Let's just say it's a little gift from me to you, for being such a good friend." Sal grins.

Willy opens the bag, reaches inside, and pulls out a vintage pistol. The handle is wooden and in pristine condition. The long barrel is a smooth black, and Willy looks it over in awe. He inspects every square inch of the weapon with wide eyes. "Where did you find this? I haven't seen one of these in a decade."

"You know I can't tell you that," Sal says.

Willy looks to Sal. "How much?"

"Nothing, it's a gift."

"This is a big time weapon. Not many of these made it back to the states after the war. I'll be able to sell it to one of my collectors by noon. Let me give you something for it."

"No, really, it's-"

"Take it." Willy hands Sal three folded one hundred dollar bills from his pocket. "I can probably get $5,000 for it, just take it."

Sal looks at his friend, then he pockets the money. He can up with at least ten things right off the top of his head that he could use the money for, the first being a new cheese grater for the pizzeria. "So do we have a deal then?"

Willy pauses. "I think I can buy you some more time, but not much."

"Thank you," Sal says with sincerity. He leans over the counter and he and Willy exchange cheek kisses again. Sal can smell his old friend's musky aftershave when he gets close.

Before leaving, Marco waves to Willy, and Willy returns the gesture. Sal turns to leave and motions for the boys to follow. Willy yells to them before they get to the door.

"Hey, Tony," he says, capturing Antonio's attention, "sticky fingers?"

Antonio raises his hands and wiggles his fingers around. He opens his coat and spins, showing Willy that he's clean. Willy nods, then Antonio leaves with Marco and Sal.

Antonio was caught trying to swipe something from Willy's shop when he was fourteen, and Willy almost beat him to death because of it. It was a minor thing - a Pedro Martinez Expos rookie card - but Willy has never let it go. To avoid the inevitable awkward confrontation, Antonio rarely goes into the shop anymore, except for when he has to. Unfortunately for him, today was one of those have to days.

With a tick of encouragement after his barter with Willy, Sal drives back to the pizzeria and drops off Antonio. Marco gives his friend his keys to the Cadillac so that he can go back to their shared apartment to freshen up. When done, he'll drive the three miles back to the pizzeria to open the restaurant for 10:00 A.M.

Once they drop Antonio off, Sal and Marco head west toward Massachusetts Correctional Institute at Concord. Sal's brother and Marco's dad has been an inmate there for nine months, and visiting hours end at noon. It's imperative that they see him today. They need to figure out how much more time they have left.

CHAPTER SEVEN

To clear her mind, Jen changes into yoga pants and an athletic top and decides to go for a run. She's feeling up to it physically today. She doesn't know the area at all yet, so she uses the GPS on her phone to plan out her route and track her distance. She's going to do five miles this morning, she decides, and that will give her a good start on familiarizing herself with her new surroundings.

The city around her is bustling and everyone seems to be in a hurry. She hears more horns and sees more spilled coffee than she has in all of her adult life in Maine. People stare at her as she runs in place at crosswalks and quietly sings to herself. They don't seem to understand why she's not in business attire or why she's chosen to run for pleasure. She sticks out like a sore thumb here, and that's no surprise to her. She knew she wouldn't fit in with these people. She tries to ignore the stares and concentrates on her breathing, but she has a difficult time putting what happened last night behind her.

She wonders if any of the people on the street are watching her, or if the intruders are going to go back to the house again. She wonders who they were and what they wanted. She imagines what it would have been like if they'd attacked her and Peter instead of running away. She wonders what they would have done to her. Just the thought of the possibilities sends a little tremor down her spine. These thoughts consume her mind, but she pushes through and speeds up the final leg of her loop and arrives back at the house in less than an hour. A light blue painters van is parked in the driveway when she returns home.

She stops in her tracks when she spots it. Is she expecting someone?

She wonders if it's them again, the guys from last night. Neither she nor Peter had seen what type of vehicle they were driving, and she admits that a van is a reasonable choice. It's always the ones who drive vans that creep around people's neighborhoods.

Jen doesn't know what to do. She's exhausted and timid and has no energy to fight off a would-be attacker. And she has nothing to defend herself with either – no pepper spray, no air horn, no rape whistle. Those are the types of things that women carry around in the city, right? She's still learning. Her face is beet red and her breathing increases in intensity with each pump of her rapidly pulsating heart. She looks around the neighborhood and sees no one else around.

No witnesses.

Realizing she can't avoid it forever, Jen decides to approach the van. Maybe it's just a delivery driver, she hopes. Gray smoke is pouring out of the exhaust of the vehicle as she approaches, so she makes a wide loop around the side to take a peek inside. She's relieved when she sees a key lock emblem printed on the side of the van, although she doesn't recognize the logo or the company name. Then she remembers. The locksmith. She had asked Peter to call a locksmith. She didn't actually think he would so soon.

Jen approaches the van and knocks on the window with a single knuckle. The glass is chilly on her finger and it leaves a little bit of moisture residue on her skin. The driver inside is startled, but he offers her a casual smile. The window rolls down.

"Hi, are you Mrs. Winston?" the man in the van says.

"Hi, yes," Jen says. "Sorry, I didn't know you were coming so soon. I hope you haven't been waiting long."

"Your husband called and said you have an urgent need for our locksmith services?"

"Yes, thank you for coming."

The man in his forties or fifties rolls the window back up and gets out of the van. Jen watches him and is pleasantly surprised that her husband actually did something she asked for once. She doesn't know what to make of that. Once he gathers all of his tools from the back of the van, Jen leads the locksmith into the house and shows him the locks in question.

Jen walks with the locksmith and tells him the reason for him being there while he works. He doesn't say much, and it takes him around an hour to complete the repairs. He replaces both the deadbolt and the key lock on the front door, and he repairs and rekeys the lock on the slider in the back. He gives Jen two keys for each of the new locks after he finishes up.

Before he leaves, he finally says something to her. "You know, I've been in this business for twenty-five years. I've heard of every reason you could imagine why someone may want to have their locks changed. I'm not here to judge, and I know it may not be my place, but in my professional opinion, something is going on here. Whoever broke into your house knew what to look for. They didn't bother going to the back door, as I can tell it wasn't tampered with, so they must have known it was broken. Neither of the locks in front have any damage either, so these guys didn't use any tools to break the locks or anything. It seems to me that whoever you saw last night had a key and let themselves in. It's a good thing you had me come out here today, as I don't doubt they'll be back. I'm not a cop, I'm just a locksmith, but I know keys and locks. Take it for what you may, but that's just my opinion." The locksmith gathers his tools and nods to Jen before heading toward the front door. "You have a good day now."

Jen is taken aback. She watches out the bay window as the locksmith gets back into his van and backs out of the driveway. He honks the horn once, his arm waving out the driver's side window, as he drives out of site. His words are chilling, and she doesn't know how to react to the man's comments. Everything he had said makes sense to her. She fears he may be right. Those guys are definitely coming back. With that all but certain conclusion, a knot of anxiety forms in her chest.

Inside the house, Jen decides to forego working or unpacking today. She heads down the hall and into the kitchen instead. She grabs Officer Dale's business card from behind the magnet for Chinese take-out on the refrigerator and dials the number on the front. Her second call will be to ADT Home Security, and her third will be to her husband.

CHAPTER EIGHT

Massachusetts Correctional Institute at Concord is typically a forty minute drive from the pizzeria, but it takes Sal an hour today. Marco stays quiet for most of the ride while he and Sal listen to sports talk on the radio. He hasn't been to visit his dad in a couple of months, and he feels guilty about that. He hopes he doesn't get chewed out for that, as he's not in the mood for an argument. Not today.

Bartolo Salazar was arrested just after Christmas last year for a crime that he claims he did not commit. It was all a big misunderstanding, he said, although he refused to go into many details on what actually happened with any of the members of his family. All anyone knows is that it involves a dead body, no alibi, and no bail. The state seems confident they have a strong case against him, but Bartolo insists that he's innocent. But don't they all? Maybe the truth will finally come out during the trial, which is supposed to start in mid-December.

Bartolo's incarceration has been tough on the entire family. His brother, Amelio - Big Sal - has had to run the pizzeria by himself, and even though it was always called Big Sal's Pizzeria, it was never a one-man operation. Bartolo had lost a friendly bet when they were preparing a business proposal for the bank, so Sal got his name on the sign. Truthfully, Bartolo never minded not having his name on it, as it was really always his brother's dream anyway. Sal has always been a chef at heart, and Bartolo has always been a businessman. The combination of the two skill sets made for a successful pizzeria, although it was only open for a short time before Bartolo got locked up. Sal has adapted as well as he can and he's making it work, but he's just as eager as anyone to have his brother back in the fold to handle the finances again. But to have that happen anytime soon is going to require some good fortune.

The whole situation has especially put a lot of strain on Bartolo's relationship with Marco. His only child has gone through a lot of changes in his life by necessity because of it, but he tries not to be bitter about it. That can be difficult sometimes, though. Shortly after the incarceration, Marco's mother filed for divorce. She had claimed that their marriage was on the rocks to begin with, and Bartolo's arrest was the final straw for her. Whatever that means. The proceedings took place quickly and she and Bartolo were divorced within thirty days of the paperwork being filed. She moved to Montana to live with her sister and Marco hasn't spoken with her since. Nor does he intend to. He never has accepted the idea that their marriage was failing to begin with, and from his perspective, she gave up on Bartolo. Family doesn't just give up when times are tough; they're supposed to stick together during times of turmoil. That's a lesson he learned directly from her.

So much for the idea of practicing what you preach, right?

Marco started working full-time at the pizzeria to try and save the house, but it was all for naught. The bills were just too much for Marco to handle, especially with him being on his own for the first time. The house got foreclosed on in August and was auctioned off in September. He moved in with his lifelong friend, Antonio, shortly thereafter, and they still share that arrangement to this day.

INSIDE THE CORRECTIONAL FACILITY, Marco and Sal wait to be ushered into the visiting center. They both go through the metal detection system without incident and pass the visual exam from a member of the prison staff. A page goes out across the intercom for someone to notify Bartolo that he has a visitor. It's an unexpected visit, so Sal hopes he doesn't cause his brother to worry. When everyone is in position, a uniformed correctional officer leads them through a doorway and into a separate room where other inmates are already deep in conversation with their law-abiding loved ones. Marco sits in one of the two empty chairs and waits for Bartolo to be escorted out to them. Sal sits next to him. The entire sequence makes Marco feel uneasy – everything from the strange uniformed black lady monitoring the metal detection system and glaring at him with her cunning eyes, to the echo of his father's name ricocheting off of the walls of the prison - and it's one of the many reasons why he doesn't come around very often.

The chairs are jammed close to one another and the booths lack any privacy. A thin sheet of glass separates them from the empty chair on the other side, and a single phone hangs on the right side of the barrier. One-way conversations can be heard with minimal effort from the surrounding booths.

Through the glass, Marco spots a bright orange jumpsuit walking slowly toward the empty seat across from him and his uncle. His heart leaps when he sees who it is. The man in the jumpsuit wobbles toward the empty chair with both ankles chained together, the steel clanking as he steps. His wrists are cuffed together in the front too, and the escorting officer helps him sit into the chair before backing away a few steps.

Marco makes eye contact with his father and barely recognizes him. He looks beat down and has dark bags under his eyes, like he hasn't slept in days. He has clearly thinned out and his once curly hair has since been buzzed off. Some skin art peeks up from underneath his collar that wasn't there the last time Marco saw him. This is most definitely a converted man, Marco decides, and he's not sure that he likes the looks of it. Bartolo almost looks like he belongs.

Marco accepts his father's smile, then watches as he struggles to grab the phone that hangs on his side of the booth. He fights to grip it between his cuffed hands, but he eventually does and finds a comfortable position to hold it. He pinches the phone between his shoulder and his ear and slides it up so that he can look straight ahead. He does it like a pro. Seeing his father this way makes Marco hurt more than he thought it would. He can't find it in him to pick up the phone, so he backs away.

Sal picks it up. "It's good to see you," he says.

"It's so good to see you too, Amelio," Bartolo says, still smiling.

"How are you holding up?"

Bartolo shrugs. "I'm just taking it day by day. Do you have good news for me?"

Sal pauses. "I don't know how to tell you this."

Bartolo drops his head and holds the position for a moment. Marco can tell that his father knows that it's bad news.

"I don't have all the money yet," Sal says, "but I've explained the situation to Willy and he thinks he can buy us more time."

"We don't have more time, Amelio. That's the problem."

"I know, but-"

"How much are we up to?"

"About $80,000. Willy has a guy who is guaranteeing us another $25,000 once we make the exchange. That'll give us enough to cover it, plus a little extra."

"Where is it?"

"It's in the bank. It's safe."

Bartolo nods. "Can you get it?"

"When?"

"He told me he needs the money by tomorrow or he's out. Do you still have his number?"

"Yeah, I have it."

"Maybe you should give him a call. If you give him the $80,000 now and promise him the rest in a day or two, maybe he'll stay. Just explain the situation to him. This is my last chance, I really need him."

"I know. I'll get the money, I promised you I would. Have I ever failed you?"

Bartolo doesn't respond. He looks away and blinks rapidly, like he's trying to fight back some tears. Once he gets rid of whatever foreign material he had pretended was stuck in his eye, he looks back up to his brother. "Just call him when you leave here, okay? And put Marco on the phone."

Sal hands the phone to Marco, who looks at it with reluctance. Bartolo mouths his thanks while he waits for Marco to hold the phone up to his ear.

"Hi, Marco."

"Hi."

"How are you doing?"

"Okay."

"That's good. Have you heard from your mom?"

"No." Marco stares at his father, wondering when it became so awkward between them. They used to be inseparable, and now it seems as if they barely know each other. "Listen, dad," Marco continues, "Antonio and me tried to get the stuff-"

"Shut up, Marco. Don't say another word. These calls are monitored," Bartolo demands. He quickly changes the subject. "Your birthday is coming up this week, the big two-one. Are you and Antonio going to go out and celebrate?"

Marco shrugs. "Probably not. We'll probably just work at the pizzeria or something."

Bartolo nods slowly, looking unsure of what else to say. "I'm really sorry about all of this, Marco. Between me and your mom, and the house, and everything else that's gone on, you've stayed really strong. I know it's been tough on

34

you. When this is all over, you and me, we'll start over. It'll be like it used to be, okay?"

Marco looks away and doesn't say anything. He tries to stay positive about the situation, but deep down he doubts if any of this will even work at all. Sometimes he feels like it's all hopeless.

The same officer who had escorted Bartolo into the visiting area earlier approaches him from the back and tells him to wrap it up.

"I've got to go now, son," Bartolo says. "But I just want you to know that I'm really proud of you. I love you, buddy."

Marco drops the phone, pushes his chair out, and turns his back to his father. He wipes tears from his eyes when no one is watching and waits for his uncle. It's all just too much for him to handle today - the wild rollercoaster of emotions.

Back in the car, Marco is distant and in no mood to talk about his feelings. He thinks it's a sign of weakness to show emotion, so he does the best he can to bottle them up and avoid talking about them. For the most part, it works, but seeing his father always seems to open the lid a bit, and some of that bottled up emotion trickles out for the world to see. That's another reason why he doesn't visit very often - he doesn't like to be judged. Men don't cry, especially in prison. The same rules apply for visitors as they do for inmates. Crying is for sissies. But he misses his father desperately and would do just about anything to have things go back to the way they were between them. He thinks he's proven that. Maybe someday, he hopes, everything can just be forgotten. He thinks it, hopes it, dreams about it, but he doesn't have much confidence about the realistic prospect of it.

Thankfully, Sal recognizes that Marco needs his space, so he lets him be - no bombardment of questions about how he feels or why he acted the way he did in there. Marco appreciates that. Sal never had any children of his own, but he thinks of Marco as a son – he even told him as much one time. Once on the road, Sal dials the number that his brother had given him during a previous visit.

Stan Brothers picks up on the first ring.

CHAPTER NINE

J en debriefs Officer Dale about the locksmith's theory, and he begrudgingly agrees to swing by the house again later in the afternoon. She makes an appointment with ADT Home Security, who will be over tomorrow to do a full home security installation. Peter doesn't answer his phone, which doesn't surprise her in the least, so she leaves him a message asking him to call her. It's been two hours, and he still hasn't returned her call yet.

Jen tries to work for a bit, but she struggles to get into the zone. The cursor on her laptop blinks at the beginning of the blank page as she stares at the white screen in front of her. She doesn't typically get writer's block, but everything about her new environment is distracting her. Every time a car drives by or an unfamiliar creak sounds from somewhere in the house, she's startled. She's completely on edge, completely preoccupied, completely uneasy.

She gets up from her seat in her isolated office that's tucked away in the corner of the house and begins to pace. A single window allows her to monitor the activity on the street, which makes her feel less vulnerable. Moving boxes are piled up along the walls with a small space carved out for her desk. She considers starting to unpack the clutter, but she doesn't even know where to begin. She can't stop thinking about what the locksmith had said earlier.

On her desk, her phone rings and the chime makes her jump. As she's finding out, she had forgotten to turn down the volume on her phone after her run earlier in the day, so the melody is louder than expected. The high decibel level pierces her eardrum a bit, and she cringes. She walks over to the desk, picks up the phone, and looks at the screen. It's finally her husband calling her back. It's about time.

PETER'S HAD A LONG morning. For starters, there was an accident on the freeway, so he was over an hour late for work. His inbox was and still is overflowing, and his voicemail had five urgent messages in it. To make matters worse, one of his stores was robbed at gunpoint last night, and the store manager in another gave his resignation notice. He's been on the phone with his boss and the police all morning, and he's on his way to the store that was robbed now. He's not sure that he was prepared to deal with this type of responsibility that comes with the new job, but it's a little late for that. Jen had called him a while ago and he hasn't even had time to listen to her message yet. He dials her number and waits for her to pick up.

"Peter, where the hell have you been all day? I called you two hours ago. Did you not get my message?"

Peter sighs and wants to tell his wife what his day has been like, but she cuts him off and continues before he can even begin.

"Do you know what happened to me today? The locksmith came this morning, thanks for telling me by the way, and he said that he thinks that someone had a key last night. He said that in his professional opinion there's no other explanation to how they could have got in. The policeman from last night is coming back over soon to talk and I'm having a security system installed tomorrow."

"A security system, Jen? Jesus Christ, how much is-"

"I don't care how much it costs and you shouldn't either. Moving to this place was your idea and I don't feel safe in the house by myself. Do you not remember what happened last night? What if those guys didn't run away? We could have been killed, Peter!"

Peter sighs again. "Listen, can we talk about this when I get home? I've had a really shitty day, okay?"

"What about my day? I'm stuck here in this place that I don't feel safe in and it's all your-" Jen stops herself, as if reconsidering saying something that she may regret.

"Go ahead, say it," Peter urges.

There's a pause as Peter waits for Jen to say something. The awkwardness between them is at an all-time high. Or low, depending on one's perspective.

"Officer Dale is here, I've got to go," Jen finally says.

"Fine. Let me know what he has to say."

"I'll tell you tonight. You won't answer your phone if I call anyway," Jen says, then she hangs up.

Peter hangs up the phone and tosses it on the seat beside him. He shakes his head in frustration as he as pulls off the interstate and merges into traffic.

JEN OPENS THE FRONT door before Officer Dale can even reach for the doorbell. His arm is extended when she opens it, and he slowly lowers it to his side and steps back when he sees that it's no longer needed.

"Come in," Jen says as she moves herself to the side. She's a little frazzled from her argument with Peter.

Officer Dale removes his hat and walks past her and into the hallway.

Jen leads Officer Dale to the kitchen, where they sit at the table. Officer Dale sits in the same seat that he had just hours earlier. Jen recaps everything that the locksmith had said to her, repeating it nearly word for word. Officer

Dale takes notes as she speaks, and something in her tone seems to change his attitude. When she finishes, he flips his notepad closed and puts it back in his breast pocket.

"Who was the locksmith?" Officer Dale asks. "What was his name?"

"He said his name was Dave, that's all I know."

"Which company did he work for?"

"I think he said he works for himself."

"But you didn't get his last name?"

Jen shakes her head. "I remember the van had a logo of a key lock on it though, and it was blue. He did say that he's been in business for twenty-five years too. Does any of that help?"

"Maybe. It might help me narrow things down a bit, although that probably does describe ninety percent of locksmiths in this area." Officer Dale stands up and hikes up his pants by the belt. He pushes the chair back in before heading for the doorway.

"Where are you going?" Jen asks, surprised at his quick visit.

"Home. But first, I'm going to go find this Dave guy and figure out what he knows."

Jen starts to rise from her seat, but Officer Dale holds his hand out to stop her. "It's okay," he says, "I can let myself out. If anything else comes up, you let me know, alright? Otherwise, I'll call you when I find something out." Officer Dale walks down the hallway and exits out the front door.

Jen waits until she hears a slamming car door outside before she gets up from her seat and heads down the hallway herself. She looks out the bay window and watches as Officer Dale drives out of site, leaving her alone and unprotected. She goes to the front door and pushes it to make sure that it's closed, then she engages the new key lock and deadbolt. After the deadbolt clicks when it locks securely into the wooden doorframe, Jen presses her back against the door and sighs. She wonders to herself if she's ever going to feel safe in this house. Or in this city. Or in this state. And now, more than ever before, she longs for her old life back in the woods of Maine. Times were so much simpler when the only real worries she had were if there were enough candles in the house to enable her to read if the power went out during a nor'easter, or enough lumber to keep the woodstove running so that her feet wouldn't get cold during those frigid winter nights. She misses that life. She misses her life.

CHAPTER TEN

"Stan Brothers speaking."

"Stan, it's Amelio Salazar. We talked a couple of months ago about my brother, Bartolo," Sal says.

"Yes, I remember. I thought I might hear from you today."

"Are you at your office? I'd like to swing by to discuss something with you."

"I can probably fit you in for fifteen minutes or so in an hour. Just tell my secretary your name when you arrive. I'll tell her I'm expecting you."

"Thanks, see you soon," Sal says, then he hangs up. He puts the phone in the center console and grips the steering wheel tightly with both hands. He sneaks a peak to Marco, who is staring out the window and shielding his face with his shoulder, as if not wanting to be bothered. Sal flips on the radio and cranks the volume. It only takes a moment for Marco to turn it back off. So they ride back into the city in complete silence.

Before heading to Stan's office in Brookline, Sal makes a detour and swings by the Bank of America on Beacon Street. He tells Marco to wait in the car, and he does so without resistance. Sal brings an empty drawstring sack inside with him, and the eyes of the tellers light up when they see it. It's not long before the branch manager approaches him, pulls him to the side, and cautiously questions his motives. Sal's response is not as the manager had been expecting, considering his wide grin and suddenly touchy-feely persona.

It takes a little while for the bank to gather everything, and after a firm handshake from the manager, Sal exits the bank with a full sack and mixed emotions. Back in the car, he tosses the bag at Marco's feet and takes off toward Stan's office. Marco refuses to even look at it.

Stan Brothers' name is plastered all over the glass walls inside the spacious third floor office building. His headshot hangs behind the reception desk and the smirk on his face tells it all. Stan is a highly successful defense attorney with an impressive track record. He's taken on and won a handful of high-profile cases in the last few years, and his reputation of getting his clients' cases dismissed despite what seems like overwhelming evidence against them is growing, or so he claims.

Stan had approached Bartolo a few months back after reading about his case in the *Globe*. He sat in the back of Bartolo's preliminary hearing and listened to all of the details of the case, then he visited him at the correctional facility the same day. He believes that Bartolo is innocent, and he convinced him that he can win the case and have all charges against him dropped. He's a good salesman and a great businessman, and he has the entire Salazar family eating out of the palm of his hand. And he wouldn't have it any other way.

It takes Sal a moment to find a receptionist since no one is behind the desk when he enters the office. After yelling out for one, a young woman no older than college-aged appears from the hall. With her blonde locks out of place, she readjusts her skirt and asks Sal to have a seat in the lobby. Sal waits there, alone, with the drawstring sack on his lap. The weight of the contents is starting to strain his shoulders a bit, so the shifting of the weight is a relief. The floors in the waiting room are clean and newly carpeted, and the entire place smells like scented candles. It reminds Sal of a massage parlor, and he wonders if the blondie behind the desk is responsible for providing happy endings. Is that even a real thing? All of the furnishings are top notch - everything from the chrome door handles to the crown molding on the walls to the Italian leather chairs, which his rump is especially enjoying the presence of - and the entire office reeks of wealth.

A few minutes later, the blonde secretary finally calls Sal's name and leads him down a narrow hall to a glass door which has Stan's name engraved on the frame above it. She knocks twice and opens the door, then she stands to the side. Sal enters the office and the door closes behind him. The sound of heels clicking away in the corridor echoes in his ears.

"Amelio, it's nice to finally meet you in person," Stan says as he shakes Sal's hand. "Please sit."

Sal sits in the leather chair - also Italian - across from Stan's desk and glances around the room. It's magnificent. There's a huge window behind Stan's desk that overlooks the city in the horizon. A tall bookshelf lines the wall to Sal's right, and dozens of law books are organized alphabetically on the shelves. There's a card table with a crystal pitcher holding a dark liquid to the left, which illuminates with triumph.

"Thank you for meeting me," Sal says, unsure of where to look. "There's something we need to discuss."

Stan puts his feet on the top of his desk and places his fingers together in a pyramid and nods his head. He spins his chair a bit so that he can see Sal's face. "I think I know why you're here."

"You do?"

"The money for my retainer is due tomorrow for Bartolo's case. That's what you want to discuss, I assume."

Sal pauses and isn't sure whether it's good or bad that Stan is prepared for the conversation. "How'd you know?"

"Just a hunch," Stan says, then he smiles.

"Well, we don't have all the money yet," Sal says.

Stan loses the smile and pulls his feet off the desk. He crosses his arms and waits for an explanation.

"But we have most of it," Sal offers. "We need just a little more time to get the rest."

"How much are we talking?"

"We're $20,000 short."

"That's not good enough. My time is more valuable than that. I could have any case I want. I took this one because I believed in it, but I need to be compensated for my time. Do you understand that?"

"I get it, but-"

"I'm sorry, but I'm out. Tomorrow is the deadline. You've known about it for months, and you've failed to fulfill the agreement. I have a business to run here."

Sal stares at Stan but doesn't say anything. He grabs the drawstring sack, stands, and drops it on the center of Stan's desk.

"What's this?" Stan asks. He stands from his seat and loosens the drawstring. He looks inside the bag, then at Sal, then back inside the bag. He reaches his hand in and feels around.

"$80,000 in cash," Sal begins. "Cash, not a wire transfer or a check, but cash. So it can go undetected. There's no record of the transaction ever taking place, no paper trail, so you don't have to claim it come tax time. Add around thirty percent that you're saving by paying no taxes, and you're grossing more than the $100,000 you asked for. Just don't let the IRS find out."

Stan looks to Sal and is obviously in deep thought as he considers what Sal has proposed.

Sal continues, "We give you the final $20,000 as a standard transaction so it doesn't raise any red flags in accounting. It looks like you took a retainer of $20,000, but you actually get more than five times that. We just need a little more time to get you the rest."

Stan pauses for a moment, but Sal can tell that it's all just for effect. He's trying to make him sweat it out.

"You have one week," Stan says. "You said it yourself, there's no paper trail, so there's no proof that you gave this to me. I'll spread it out over a hundred accounts so no one will even notice the deposits. You make the transfer of

$20,000 in one week, and I'll take the case. If you don't, you just wasted $80,000."

Sal stares at Stan and considers the offer. It's a no-brainer. He's already put months of his time and energy into this, and he can't give up now. He'd agree to just about anything to help save his brother. Sal takes a step closer to the desk. He opens his hand and holds it in front of Stan.

Stan looks deep into Sal's eyes - Sal can almost feel the heat - and waits for another moment. Sal wonders if Stan had expected him to negotiate more. But Sal has nothing to offer in return, no leverage, nothing to barter with. He knows that. Any deal will do.

Stan grasps Sal's open hand and shakes it firmly.

"Deal," Sal says.

CHAPTER ELEVEN

Officer Dale leaves the Winston's house and heads back to the station. He should be going home to get some sleep, but if what Mrs. Winston had said was true, he really needs to see this Dave guy first. He picks up his phone from the center console and dials his partner, who had stayed back at the station to fill out the paperwork from their earlier traffic stops.

"Hey, Gerry, what's up?" Jamaal Harris says from the other end of the phone.

"Jamaal, are you still at the station?"

"Yeah, I was just getting ready to pack up though. What's going on?"

"Hang out for a bit, will you? Mrs. Winston told me something that we should look in to."

"What is it?"

"I'll tell you about it when I get there. In the meantime, can you get Shultz to start doing some digging? Have him look into every locksmith within a thirty mile radius of here. We're looking for a guy named Dave. Last name unknown. He might work for himself and he drives a blue van with a key lock logo on the side."

"That describes just about every locksmith in town."

"Yeah, that's what I said too."

"What's all this for?"

"Tell Shultz to get on it right away and to bring me the results as soon as he can. I'll tell you everything when I get there. I'll be there in twenty."

"Okay, Gerry, see you soon."

JEN CONSIDERS CALLING HER husband and telling him that Officer Dale is going to look into the case further, but she decides against it. He had sounded busy earlier when they spoke, plus she doesn't really want to talk to him right now. She's still a little heated. Instead, she goes back into her office and tries again to get some work done. She has a column due to her editor by Friday, and so far she hasn't gotten any work done at all.

Jen does feel a little better having new and functional locks on the two doors, but it hasn't helped her productivity any. After spending an hour in her office, she still only has a couple of sentences typed out. She probably writes a total of fifteen or twenty, but getting started is always the most difficult part for her. She typically spends a good chunk of time writing and scrapping the beginning until she finds an introduction that she loves. There has to be a hook, an attention grabber, a reason for a potential reader to spend their precious time reading it. Without that, she simply can't go on. She's particular like that, and it may be her Achilles heel sometimes.

It's not long before she realizes that she's not going to get anything done today, so she closes her laptop and retires for the day. This one can be marked down as a failure.

After having a late lunch, she decides to spend the rest of the afternoon cleaning up the house. She's more productive than she had expected, as she unpacks and organizes a bunch of the moving boxes, and she gets her entire office plus the master bedroom upstairs entirely unpacked. She puts on some music while she works and turns it up louder than she normally would. Although unpacking is a chore, the distraction is welcome and it helps to keep her mind occupied. Having two good sweats in the same day is an added bonus too.

GERRY DALE AND JAMAAL Harris have been partners for eleven years. They have grown to be quite close in that time. So close, in fact, that they typically spend most holidays together with their families instead of their own relatives. They've participated in the others' kids' birthday parties, Baptisms, and general ups and downs that come with life. Despite their obvious cultural differences, the two officers are more than partners; they're best friends.

Gerry arrives at the station and heads right for his partner's workstation. He tells him all about what Jen had said the locksmith told her and how he has a plan of attack going forward. Gerry can tell that Jamaal is surprised by his sudden interest in the case, considering their combined lack of conviction earlier in the day, but he knows that Jamaal will go along with it. They've been through a number of cases in which the other doesn't fully understand the urgency of the situation, but it always seems to work out the way it should. Trust in the other's judgment is key. They balance each other out like two people in a successful marriage.

Gerry summons for Ben Schultz to discuss his findings.

Ben Schultz is a young guy, just recently out of the academy, and he's the go-to guy for time-critical research. Many of the officers in the precinct are in their mid-forties and older, so having a young guy with twenty-first century technology skills has been a major plus for the department. Mr. Schultz is in high demand.

Ben approaches the table that Gerry and Jamaal await at and sits across from them. He tosses a thin stack of documents that are on police letterhead on the table. The documents primarily consist of photos with descriptive text blurbs underneath them, all of which are of locksmiths within a thirty mile radius of the Winston's residence.

"Shultz," Gerry begins, "it looks like you've found something for me. What do you have?"

"I did indeed," Ben says as he separates the photos and lays them across the tabletop. The ten photos almost line up perfectly across the table and he spins each one of them so they face his superiors. "These are the locksmiths in the area that meet some or all of your search criteria. As you can see from the photos, each of these vans has some sort of key lock reference logo on the side. The three guys on the top row have blue vans, but none of their names are Dave and they don't work for themselves. The four in the middle row work for themselves but don't have blue vans. The three in the bottom row are the closest matches. They're all named Dave and are self-employed. The one on your left has been in business for five years, forty for the one in the middle, and the one on your right has been in business for twenty-five years."

Gerry studies the three photos on the bottom row and looks for a logo that best matches the description that Jen had given him earlier. They all look about the same to him and none of them separate themselves from Jen's description, but the one on the right makes the most sense. He points to that one. "This guy, tell me about him?"

Ben looks at his notes and reads the details, "Dave Carson, age forty-nine, owner of Carson's Lock and Key since the late eighties. He lives and works in Dorchester and he drives a blue van with his company name on the side."

Gerry looks to his partner. "This is our guy," he says with excitement before looking back to Ben. "Do you have his address?"

"Home and business," Ben says, then he hands Gerry a sheet of paper containing the addresses in question.

"Good work, Shultz, that'll be all for now."

Ben nods and gets up from his seat. He leaves and heads back to his desk with a youthful swagger that Gerry admires. He and Jamaal rise to their feet simultaneously.

"Want me to go with you?" Jamaal asks.

"That's okay, you can get out of here. Doesn't Jayla have a recital tonight?"

Jamaal looks around for a calendar. His youngest daughter, Jayla, has a dance recital with other six and seven-year-olds from her class on the eighth. Gerry finds it hard to believe the Jamaal can't remember these things, yet he can, even though Jamaal had only mentioned it in passing a few weeks back.

"What's today?" Jamaal asks.

"Tuesday the eighth."

"Then yeah, I guess that's tonight then. Are you sure you don't need me to come along?"

"I'll be fine. I'm just going to head over there and confirm what Mrs. Winston told me, ask a few questions, and then I'll be going home myself. Go home before Shauna makes you sleep on the couch."

Jamaal chuckles, then playfully smacks his partner on the back of the shoulder. "Okay, if you insist," he says. "See you tomorrow then?"

"Yeah, tomorrow. We'll reconvene then and decide the next steps after I talk to this guy."

PETER ARRIVES HOME AROUND 7:00 P.M. after a long day and rough commute. He's exhausted and hungry and really just wants to go to bed early after another stressful day at the office. All of the lights are on downstairs when he arrives, but his key no longer fits in the front door, so he's unable to get inside. That pisses him off. He rings the doorbell and pounds on the door with his fist. He yells out to his wife, but he gets no response. Frustrated, he walks around the side yard and heads toward the back deck. The darkness from the sky above makes him feel like he's walking blindly.

On the sliding door on the back deck - the one with the broken lock - the curtain is pulled to the side slightly, so Peter's able to see in to the kitchen through the glass. There are a couple of pans in the sink and a plate on the counter under the microwave with food on it, but no sign of Jen. He tries the slider, but it doesn't budge. It's either still broken or now repaired and locked, so he can't get in that way either. He heads back out front.

Standing in the grass near the entryway, Peter looks up at the second floor window and sees another light on, this one coming from the bedroom. He pulls out his phone and dials his wife. He hears her phone ringing through a cracked bedroom window upstairs, but he doesn't spot Jen. After a few rings and no answer, he's directed to her voicemail. He hangs up, knocks on the door again, and calls for his wife, but there's still no response.

His frustration has reached its boiling point now, and he's close to losing it.

Ready to smash in a window with one of the bricks from underneath the stairs on the front stoop, Peter tries ringing the doorbell a few more times. When his yells to his wife go unanswered yet again, he heads back toward the driveway and gets into his sedan - an Audi. He sits sideways with his legs hanging out, barely making contact with the pavement, and lays on the horn. He doesn't even care if it disturbs the neighbors. His only goal is to get his wife's attention. He doesn't understand why it requires so much effort on his part.

CHAPTER TWELVE

S al leaves Stan Brothers' office and makes his way back to the parking lot where Marco is waiting. He opens the driver's side door and hops in, the seat letting out a poof of air as he flops hard into it. Marco looks at him and gives him a look of uncertainty.

"Where's the bag?" Marco asks.

Sal glances at Marco out of the corner of his eye but says nothing. He starts the engine and they head back toward the city in the direction of the pizzeria.

Sal pulls into the parking lot in front of his home and business and gets out of the car. Marco does the same and the two of them make their way toward the entrance. Marco's Cadillac is in its customary position at the far end of the parking lot, which means that either Antonio has already left and come back, or he never left at all. It must be the latter. Sal enters a combination on the dial pad next to the door and the lock disengages. He leads Marco inside.

Sal hollers into the empty storefront as he enters the building, "Antonio, you in here?"

There's some commotion in the back, then Antonio appears front and center just moments later. He's equipped with a fresh outfit, including a clean t-shirt with the pizzeria logo on the breast, which confirms that he left and has already returned, as instructed. For Sal, seeing others wearing his logo never gets old.

"Hey, Big Sal," Antonio says. "What's going on?"

"We need to talk, boys," Sal says.

Antonio makes his way around the counter and finds a seat in one of the booths next to the door. Marco sits next to him, and Sal sits across from them both. There's a bit of tension forming all around them.

"Is everything okay, Uncle Sal?" Marco asks, now seeming to finally get it after yet another long ride of complete silence.

"Boys, we really need to get the goods, and fast," Sal says. "The situation is becoming urgent."

"How much time do we have?" Marco asks.

"The lawyer said we got a week, that's it." Sal waits for a reaction, but gets none. "So I need you boys to go back to the house tonight."

"Tonight? But—"

"This is not negotiable, Marco. Just go there tonight and watch them for a day or two. We need to find some kind of pattern. They must work, right? Figure out when they both leave for work and get inside and get the goods then. I'll do some digging on my end and see what I can find out about who these people are."

Sal ignores Antonio, who has started his panicky habit of looking between Marco and the table in front of him again.

"So you just want us to watch them for now?" Marco asks. "What if they do leave?"

"There's no need to report back to me," Sal says. "If you see an opportunity to get inside, take it." He pauses. "Why don't you both go home and get some shuteye? I'll take care of business here and make some phone calls, do some digging. You two head over there tonight and start checking the place out. Capiche?"

Antonio waits for Marco to nod, then he does so himself. They both slide out of the booth.

"Okay, Uncle Sal, I'll call you later if we find something."

Sal catches the eye of his nephew and holds it for a while in an effort to show him the importance of what he's asking him to do. He wants Marco to feel the same desperation that he does. "Marco, this is really important. We're counting on you."

"I know, I understand. I'll get it done."

OLD MAN WILLY'S PAWN shop is bustling. There have been lots of tourists in the area recently, and Willy can't seem to figure out why. It's not the typical time of year for them - the summer months are long gone in the rearview. Maybe it's the leaf peepers making their way north to the Granite State. Although crowded with browsers, most tourists don't buy much, so Willy spends most of his time just watching them to make sure they don't try to swipe anything. Theft can be an issue at times, so he keeps a fully loaded shotgun under the register in the back of the shop, just in case.

The front door chimes, just as it always does when someone enters, and inside walks the man that Willy has been expecting. The man supports an average frame that's solid, and he wears wrinkle-free slacks and an expensive blazer over his shirt that buttons up the chest. His snakeskin shoes complete the look. He's impressive.

The man brushes his way through the crowd with complete disregard for anyone else and darts toward the back, kind of like he's been here before. Which he has. Willy makes eye contact with the man, then he walks around the register and opens up the break in the glass cases. The glass separates and opens up into a walkway, and the man walks through it without hesitation. Willy closes it up again and he and the man disappear into the backroom without speaking. Willy motions to one of his workers to watch the shop.

The backroom is an open space with cement floors and metal shelves lining the walls, much like in an industrial building or a garage. Willy stores his duplicate items in the back, plus any items that he doesn't have room for or those that he doesn't think are salable. Each item has a price tag somehow attached to or near it since Willy determines the initial sale price upon the receipt of the item. Willy has a small, enclosed office in the corner near the front of the warehouse, and he leads his guest in that direction.

The man sits down in the single chair that's across from Willy's desk, and Willy sits on the opposite side, behind it. In the corner, file cabinets are bursting with copies of receipts and tax documents for the IRS, and a small black and white TV with a live feed of the activity in the storefront rests on the edge of Willy's desk.

"Enrique," Willy says to the man across from the desk, "how are you?"

"Let's cut out all these formalities, shall we?" Enrique says. "I think you know why I'm here."

Willy swallows hard once. "Fine then. I spoke with my guy earlier today, and there has been a slight change of plans."

Enrique burns his eyes into Willy's, forcing him to look away for a second.

"Go on."

"My guy hasn't gotten his hands on the merchandise quite yet, but he assures me that he'll get it soon. He needs some more time, but he promises he'll get it."

Enrique gets to his feet and reaches inside his jacket pocket. He pulls out an envelope and shows the contents to Willy. "Listen, old man, I have a lot of cash in my pocket, right now, and I ain't walking out of here empty handed."

"I know, and I'm sorry, but-"

Enrique raises a finger and points it in Willy's direction. "You listen to me, and you listen to me good. I've got people calling the shots above me, and they've got people to answer to themselves. You not having the artifact when you said you would is fucking up the whole chain of command. Do you get that?"

"I said I'm sorry. I don't know what more you expect me to do. My guy didn't have it, it's out of my hands."

Enrique shakes his head and starts to pace the room, which makes Willy nervous. He doesn't know what to expect from this guy that he barely knows and doesn't trust. Searching for a distraction, Willy remembers the gift that Sal had given to him earlier, so he reaches under his desk for it. He hasn't even had a chance to price it and tag it yet, as he was going to call his collectors this afternoon to gauge their interest. He places the paper bag on the top of his desk and waits for Enrique to notice. He hopes that it'll satisfy his needs for now.

"What's in the bag?" Enrique says when he notices it. He stops pacing.

"Take it. You said you weren't going to leave here empty handed, so take it. It's yours."

Enrique approaches the desk and looks inside the bag. His eyes pop and he looks between Willy and the weapon inside. "Whoa. Where did you get this?"

Willy shrugs. He's never willing to share who or where he buys his stuff from. It's bad business. "It's an 1882-"

"I know what it is."

"How's that to buy us some more time?"

Enrique pauses as he studies the weapon. "Get the artifact," he says after not very much time passes. "I'll be back on Friday. If you don't have it by then, someone will have to pay. You got that?" Enrique plays with the gun and pretends to shoot Willy with it, as if to forecast the future. "I'll show myself out." Enrique wraps the gun back in the bag, puts it under his arm, and leaves.

Willy takes a moment to gather his wits as he watches Enrique leave through the live feed on the TV. His heart is pumping too fast, so he sits down to catch his breath. He's getting too old for this shit. Once self-diagnosed to be deemed close enough to a normal heartbeat again, he reaches for the phone and dials Big Sal's Pizzeria. His hand trembles as he fights to select the correctly illuminated digits.

Sal picks up on the second ring. "Willy, how are you doing, my friend?" he asks from the other end of the receiver.

"Sal, I just met with the buyer," Willy says with shallow breath. "We have a problem."

MARCO AND ANTONIO ARRIVE at their apartment complex and head up the stairs to their studio. Antonio leads the way while Marco waits a few steps behind him as he finds the key to the door. A marching band sounds from inside Marco's pocket and he fumbles around to retrieve the source.

"Hello?" he says, answering the phone.

"Marco, where are you?"

Marco can sense the panic in his uncle's voice almost immediately. "We just got home. Is everything okay, Uncle Sal?"

"There has been a change of plans. I just talked to Willy, and we need the goods by Friday."

"Friday?"

"That's right, Friday. I need you and Antonio to head over to the house as soon as you can. We need to get this thing moving before it gets ugly. We have less than three days."

CHAPTER THIRTEEN

J en is upstairs toweling off after a long, scalding, well-deserved shower. The dirt and grime from the moving boxes had covered her in filth, so she couldn't relax before cleaning herself of that. A bellowing horn sounds in the background, so Jen stops the hair dryer to listen closer. When she does, the echoes increase in intensity and don't appear to be stopping. She tightens the towel around her upper torso to avoid exposure and makes her way to the window that faces the front of the house to investigate. She pinches the blinds open and peeks outside. The coolness from the night air that seeps in through the cracked window gives her the chills when it hits her exposed skin. Goosebumps are sent crawling to the surface from underneath her skin. In the driveway is her husband's black Audi, and Peter is sitting inside with his legs hanging out the door.

Jen knocks on the window with a knuckle to try to capture Peter's attention, but he's not looking in her direction. She sighs, frustrated, and wonders why he's making such a commotion.

Then she remembers.

She bites her lip and hopes that he won't be too upset, although she can already tell by the disgusted look on his face that it might be too late for that. Back in the bathroom, she drops her towel to the moistened tile floor, grabs her robe from the back of the door, and wraps it around her damp body. The feel of the cotton on her still wet body makes her grimace, but she tries to ignore it. She hustles down the stairs, being careful not to slip with her clammy feet, and rushes to open the front door. She unlocks the door and steps onto the front stoop.

Peter lets off the horn and the night turns silent. He slides out of the car and slams the door before making his way up to meet his wife. Jen clenches her teeth in anticipation of his upcoming wrath.

"I'm so sorry," Jen says as Peter approaches, "I totally forgot that the locks were changed today."

"Why'd you lock the doors?" Peter snaps as he brushes past Jen and into the house. "You knew I was coming home."

Jen follows behind him and closes the door. She locks the deadbolt and key lock before turning to her husband. "I said I was sorry, Peter. I was upstairs taking a shower, I didn't hear you trying to get in."

Peter doesn't say anything as he glances in a few rooms, hopefully to admire the progress that Jen has made with unpacking. Although he doesn't say anything, he offers a nod of approval before heading down the hall. In the kitchen, he grabs his dinner plate from the counter and pops it in the microwave. Jen follows and retrieves a set of her mother's old silverware from one of the drawers and places it on the counter for Peter.

"It's okay, you're right. I'm sorry," Peter finally says. "I had a long day." Peter walks over to her and pulls her into an embrace. Jen doesn't contribute much or give anything back, but he still kisses her on the forehead anyway. She can still faintly smell what's left of his cologne.

"It looks like you were busy today," he says.

"I couldn't concentrate to get much work done," Jen admits, "so I figured I might as well be productive around here at least."

Peter nods. "I had one hell of a day."

"Do you mind if I go first?" Jen interrupts.

Peter retrieves his meal from the beeping microwave and places it on the counter in front of him. He looks up at Jen before shoving the first fork full of carbohydrates into his mouth. "Go ahead."

GERRY DALE LEAVES THE station a few minutes after his partner does. He heads in the direction of the address that is neatly written on the paper that Ben Shultz had provided to him. He tries Dave Carson's place of business first, which is just an office on the ground level of a two story small business colony. He finds the complex without any issue, but the actual locksmith office only has a small sign on the door once inside, so he spends more time than he expects weaving through the building in search of the number written on the note. When he does find it, the secretary at the desk tells him that Dave Carson is out on calls all day and that the rest of his week is fully booked up too. After getting little helpful information from the old lady, Gerry leaves just as quickly as he arrives and decides to head home. He'll try again tomorrow.

Gerry's house is on the other side of town and in the opposite direction of Dave Carson's, plus his shift has been already over for hours with another one starting sooner than he would like to think about. Both he and Jamaal are on the graveyard shift for the next couple of months, it being their turn in the rotation, and he's been struggling to get anything done during the night. Because of that, his hours have been extended significantly over the requirement, and not a day goes by without his wife reminding him of that.

Gerry goes home, gets some sleep, and wakes up in time to eat dinner with his wife and two sons. It's actually breakfast for Gerry, but he forces himself to eat the same thing as everyone else to avoid the confrontation with his overzealous wife - she's firm about everyone eating the same meal so that she's not forced to come up with more than one at a time. She's always been that way. The schedule adjustment is a difficult transition for Gerry's family, but it's all just part of the call of duty. Although the rotation of schedules is just temporary, it never gets any easier when it does come around every other year. Neither Gerry nor his wife is sure how much longer their marriage can handle it.

When the day has turned dark again, Gerry heads back to the station - or the place that his wife refers to as his second home - and meets up with his partner. They mostly discuss the Winston case and the events of Jayla's dance recital during their late night patrolling. Gerry hopes the night is quiet so that they can get back to concentrating on the Winston's in the morning, and it's just that. Once the morning hits, they agree to head over to Dave Carson's house together around 6:30 A.M. with the hopes of catching him before he leaves for the day. The guy is a busy man, as it turns out.

PETER FINISHES UP HIS dinner while Jen rattles off the details of her day. She tells him again about the locksmith and about Officer Dale's afternoon visit, and she casually reminds him that ADT will be over in the morning to install a complete home security system. Peter thinks better of bringing up the price issue again, as he understands he has no leverage and realizes that it's an argument he's bound to lose. He decides to let it go.

After he eats, Jen goes back upstairs to finish drying her hair and to try to get some work done on her laptop, and she leaves without allowing Peter to tell her anything about his day. He's convinced that she did it on purpose, as a way to get back at him. He's still trying to figure out what it is that he even did wrong. Later on, he joins her upstairs and slips into the bed next to her.

"The first project I want to tackle is the sanding and repainting of this room when this is all over," Jen says as she types away on her laptop. "I might start the sanding tomorrow actually, and maybe we can go out and get some paint tomorrow night when you get home."

"What about your column? Isn't that due by the end of the week?" Peter asks.

Jen shifts her eyes from her laptop to her husband and gives him a look of dissatisfaction. "I've never missed a deadline and I won't start now. You know I hate it when you say stuff like that."

Peter rolls his eyes. "Just trying to help."

There's a long pause before Jen changes the subject. "If you don't want me to, I can-"

"It's fine. We can go get paint tomorrow."

"Are you sure?"

"Yes, I'm sure."

Jen pauses for a moment, but Peter offers nothing further. "Okay," she says, "I should be able to finish unpacking in here once ADT finishes, then I can pull the bed out and start sanding that one area. What are you thinking for a color? I was thinking maybe a plum or a pistachio, or maybe we can do a-"

"I don't know, Jen," Peter snaps. "We'll figure it out tomorrow."

Jen folds the lid on her laptop and whips her head in Peter's direction. He recognizes it as her way of trying to be combative.

"What's the matter with you?" she asks.

"Just tired, it's been a long day. I'll see you in the morning, okay?" Peter leans across the bed and lightly kisses his wife on her cheek before killing his light and turning his back to her. He's not in the mood for another argument.

An hour or so later, once Jen saves her draft and shuts the machine down, she kills her own light. Complete darkness fills the room, which, for Peter, is a long time coming. Jen leans in close to him and whispers her love for him in his ear, then she spoons with him. Peter clenches his eyes closed and slows his breathing, pretending not to hear his wife whisper in his ear so that he doesn't have to respond. He's been unable to sleep with the light on and the repetition of the keys from Jen's keyboard being smashed. He's still pissed that his wife didn't even give him a chance to tell her about his day and that she seems to have completely forgotten about his wanting to talk about it. Either she forgot that he had tried, or she doesn't care. Either way, Peter just wants his wife to put forth the same level of effort that he is. Their therapist had said that they need to work on listening better to what the other has to say. But the thing is, Peter feels that he's the only one that's doing any listening around here. He feels like he's marching down a one-way street by himself.

CHAPTER FOURTEEN

Marco informs Antonio of the news that Sal had shared with him, and Antonio deflates. It's a wrench in their plans, but they agree that they need some sleep before they can stake out the place for a while. Once they go to the house there's no sleeping on the job, so a few hours each is the best path forward, they agree. Marco disappears into his bedroom, Antonio his, and he closes the blinds to block out the light. He forces himself to shut down his brain for a while, and as it turns out, it's not very difficult to do. He falls asleep almost immediately once his head hits the sunken, feather-filled pillow.

His alarm buzzes at exactly 5:00 P.M., waking him. Feeling refreshed, he meets Antonio in the living room, where he too looks refreshed and ready to take on the night. Marco had gotten more sleep than he had expected to, so he hopes that the extra energy will keep him up through the night while they watch over the house in Stoneham. He and Antonio take turns heating up a couple of slices of meat lovers pizza in the microwave, and they eat mostly in silence at the table. Marco contemplates his next move.

He thinks of his dad and how badly he wants to recapture the bond that they once had. He wishes that he could go back and see him and have a real conversation with him - a conversation without the glass in between them and without being eavesdropped on by a correctional officer. He doesn't know why he acted the way he did earlier, but he hopes that his dad forgives him when he gets out. Everything he's done is for his father.

Beginning a few months ago, he and Antonio had started out on small jobs, hitting random houses around the suburbs of the city. Once the owners left for work, they would break in and swipe jewelry and art primarily, plus whatever else stood out that looked like it may have value. They're not experts, so they've done the best they could. When considering the amount of cash earned by selling the items to Willy with the effort that had been required to obtain the said items, it's mostly worked out so far. They haven't hit the same neighborhood twice, and they've been careful to always strike during different times of the day so that the police can't connect all of the break-ins to them if they were ever to get caught. Sometimes Marco finds it hard to believe that they haven't been caught yet. And he's been shocked to learn how many people still leave their front doors unlocked during the day. They've practically been invited it at times. Although he and Antonio have always brought weapons with them, just in case, they've never had to use them. The other night was the first time the guns were even pulled out.

Antonio never liked it from the beginning - he had told Marco that directly - and Marco doesn't much care for it either. He doesn't get a thrill from it like most criminals do, and he doesn't crave the adrenaline rush that he gets while doing it. In fact, he dreads it. He dreads the way it makes him feel afterward, dreads that he has to ruin the victims' lives, and he dreads that he and Antonio have to keep doing this in the first place. But they do. Just until they get what they need from that Victorian in Stoneham. Then they can stop for good.

The first time he saw a family photo on a bookshelf it became real for him. Seeing the faces of the victims made it difficult, but the thought of them only taking material goods helped to ease his mind. It's not like they've taken family heirlooms or destroyed photo albums or anything - everything they've taken can be replaced. At least he hopes so. He tries not to think too much about the collateral damage that they've caused. The little devil on his shoulder keeps telling him that it's not that bad. The logic is probably flawed, but it's the only thing that keeps him going. That, and the fact that it's all for a good reason; it's all for his father.

So far, the local police don't seem to have any leads on any of the houses that he and Antonio have broken into, and he hopes it stays that way. Obviously. Antonio's older sister is getting married next month in Baltimore, so one of Marco's secondary goals here is to ensure that Antonio is around to attend. Antonio's family has never been supportive of his friendship with Marco, as they've always seen him as a bad influence and accused him of having bad intentions. Marco's never understood that. He's always wondered why they feel the way they do, but he's never been able to work up the courage to actually ask anyone, not even Antonio. If they were to find out what he and Antonio are up to, they'd fly Antonio south to live with them in a second. Marco knows deep down that they'd throw him under the bus without any hesitation too, if it meant saving Antonio. He supposes he doesn't blame them for that. Although what he and Antonio are doing may look ugly from an outsider's perspective, Marco's just trying to do the right thing. He always does.

Antonio stayed in the Boston area when his entire family up and moved to Maryland after he graduated from high school. He had received a full ride to Johnson and Wales University to enter the Culinary Arts program - Marco was so genuinely happy for him when it happened - but he had thought that he would gain more real-life experience by working at Sal's. He had told Marco all about it one night. Sal had been pressuring him about it too, but Marco knew that Antonio was strong enough to make his own independent decision. Marco tried to stay neutral. Sure, he had wanted his best friend to stick around and work in the pizzeria with him and his family, but he fully understood why Antonio might not want that. He had a lot to look forward to in Maryland. Ultimately, Antonio decided to stay in Boston - his parents disagreed, of course - but it was his decision in the end and no one else's. Marco sometimes wonders if Antonio made the right decision or not, and he can't help but think it's partially his fault. Looking back on it now, maybe Antonio's parents were right about him. Maybe Marco did have some part in persuading Antonio to stay instead of pursuing his dreams - whether it was done intentionally or not is irrelevant. Marco still feels a heavy burden of guilt because of that, especially now that he has involved him in this mess.

WITH ANTONIO IN THE seat next to him, Marco pulls the Cadillac outside of the Stoneham house and waits for a moment. He scans the area to make sure that they're not being watched. He sees nobody. It's just shy of 7:30 P.M. and the street is completely dark already. There are two cars in the driveway: a green Subaru is close to the house and a dark colored Audi is behind it, closer to the street. There are lights on inside the house on both levels, so Marco keeps moving.

He loops around the neighborhood a couple of times and finds a spot toward the end of the street to park the Cadillac. He adjusts his rearview mirrors so the house is in view, then he turns off the engine. It rumbles to a stop, sounding exhausted. Marco unbuckles his seatbelt and reclines the seat a bit, then leans back and crosses his arms. They're going to be hanging around for a while, so he needs to get comfortable. His eyes rotate between the two mirrors.

"What do we do now?" Antonio asks.

"We wait."

"For what?"

Marco shrugs. "I'm not sure yet."

SAL'S ALONE TO OPEN the shop today since Marco and Antonio are busy attending to other business. More important business, perhaps. He has three other guys that work for him besides Marco and Antonio, but no one will join him today until it gets closer to the dinner rush. That's nothing new.

Sal prepares the pizza dough with the homemade sauce - his late mother's recipe - in the morning before opening and will pop the pies in the oven with the desired toppings once ordered. He has a tendency to prepare too much dough when he's by himself, and that's something that Bartolo used to rag on him about when he was around. He used to hate it when his brother rode him about wasting supplies like that, but he misses him dearly now that he's not around to bother him. Sometimes you don't know what you have until it's gone.

Sal opens up shop around 11:00 A.M., and a steady stream of people pile in until midafternoon. Being busy is good, he realizes, and he loves that he has so many regulars from the nearby business district, but he was really hoping today would be a slow one so he could do some research. He sells pizza by the slice and as a whole pie, but he's still forced to toss out some extra dough once it dries out by late afternoon.

Once dinner approaches, two of Sal's employees arrive to relieve him, although he never tends to stray too far away. He helps prepare more dough in the back while the other two guys take orders in the front and make the occasional delivery. By the time darkness falls, business slows and Sal's finally able to start looking into who those people are that own the Victorian in Stoneham. He starts online with the recent real estate transactions. After he types in the address and waits for it to load, he wonders what Marco and Antonio are up to, and hopes that they've made more progress than he has today.

AFTER A COUPLE HOURS of waiting, the final light goes dark upstairs in the Victorian, and Marco sits up attentively in his seat. He looks behind him to confirm that what he sees in the mirror isn't an illusion, and when he confirms that it isn't, his stomach churns with nervousness.

"What's going on?" Antonio asks. "Is everything okay?"

"It's almost time," Marco replies.

"What do you mean?"

"All of the lights are off now, they're in bed."

Antonio takes a quick peek over his shoulder to look for himself. "We're not going in there again while they're inside, right? They probably got a gun or something this time."

"No, we're not going in yet."

"What are we doing then?"

"You'll see."

Marco starts the engine and pulls out into the street. There's not a soul in sight in either direction. He makes a couple more loops around the neighborhood before coming to a stop in front of the target's driveway again. He motions for the plastic bag that's still under Antonio's seat, and Antonio reaches in between his legs and fetches it out. They remove the gloves and masks from the bag and put them on.

"I thought you said we weren't going inside yet," Antonio says.

"We're not."

"Then what the hell are we doing?"

"Just stay here, I'll only be a minute."

"Marco," Antonio combats with a hint of frustration in his voice, "tell me what's going on."

Marco holds his finger to his mouth to quiet Antonio. "Just hang on for a minute. I'll be right back. Stay here in case we have to bail."

Marco holds out his closed fist and waits. Antonio shakes his head, seemingly in confusion, but he does eventually make a fist of his own and smashes it against the top of Marco's. It's harder than usual, as it stings Marco's hand. Marco slides out of the seat and leaves the door open.

He peers around the neighborhood landscape for any witnesses, then continues once he sees none. There are plenty of stars overhead tonight and the air isn't as cool as it had been the evening before. A gust of wind sways the tops of the tallest trees in the distance. It's a perfect autumn evening. Marco makes his way toward the driveway and walks up the concrete stairway to the front door. He's a little jittery, unsure of what to expect once he reaches the top. Once at the top, he removes one of his gloves and reaches inside his pocket for the key to the front door - the same key that he had found underneath the loose brick during their last visit. His hand trembles. He finds it, delicately pinches it between two of his fingers, and pulls it out. After putting his glove back on, he tries the key in the door.

The key jams as he pushes it into the lock, and he struggles to remove it. Being careful not to break it off in the lock, he twists it until it does finally give way. He flips the key around and tries the other end, but the results are much of the same. He suddenly realizes that things have just gotten a whole lot more difficult. He slides the key back into his pocket and scurries toward the Cadillac. He stays low, acting like a lion sneaking up on a wildebeest, and glides across the dew-covered grass.

Antonio's mask is already pulled back up above his face when Marco approaches, so Marco does the same once he gets back into the vehicle.

"Are you going to tell me what that was all about?" Antonio asks.

Marco is out of breath and panting heavily - a sure combination of the pumping adrenaline plus the impersonation of a wild animal on the hunt in the desert. "It was a test to see if the key still fits," he says.

"And?"

Marco shakes his head. "It doesn't. They changed the locks."

CHAPTER FIFTEEN

Peter wakes early, even before the sun does. He goes through his usual morning routine and is careful to make as little noise as possible. Jen hates to be woken up. He feels refreshed from a longer than usual sleep, and he's ready to tackle the challenges of the day.

Things have been difficult for him and Jen since they decided to make the permanent move to the big city, and he considers the stress that he has been putting on her. She didn't want to move, he knows that, and he thinks that maybe he's been too hard on her. Maybe she just needs time to settle in. He decides that he'll try to do something nice for her today, maybe pick up some flowers on the way home or something. Dark hydrangeas are her favorite, so maybe he'll surprise her with some of those.

Peter goes outside to start his car in the now partially risen sun, then he goes back in the house and waits for it to warm up. He heads upstairs and sneaks into the bedroom where his wife is still sleeping. He glides across the floor, trying not to frighten her, and makes his way to his wife's side of the bed. He strokes her hair and watches her sleep for a moment before leaning in to her ear. Feeling guilty from the night before, he whispers, "I love you too," before kissing her forehead and leaving for the day.

THE NIGHT IS BRUTALLY long, cold, and boring, and Marco and Antonio are out of memories to rekindle. They reminisce about all of the things that they used to do together growing up - like late nights at Fenway Park, having a sleepover and finding Marco's dad's stash of porn, and how they once got into a fistfight over a girl when they were in junior high. The laughs are frequent and the memories lucid, but ten hours of sitting in the same position without any stimulation is exhausting. Marco really just wants the show to get on the road.

They struggle to stay awake during the early morning hours, so they agree to rotate sleeping. Antonio takes his turn first and then switches with Marco every couple of hours until the morning comes. Marco occasionally drives around the block to keep himself alert, but he always parks back in the same spot near the end of the street. It allows him to have a clear view of the target house, plus a free path out of the neighborhood if needed.

The action finally starts at around 7:00 A.M. when a man - the same man that was in the bed during their first visit - emerges from the house. Marco is awake now.

"Antonio, wake up," Marco says excitedly, nudging Antonio with his elbow.

Antonio wakes quickly but is obviously still groggy. He looks confused, like he doesn't even know where he is. "Has it been two hours already?" he asks.

"No, it's been three."

"Why didn't you wake me up?"

"I tried, you wouldn't move."

"Sorry."

"Don't worry about it, it doesn't matter." Marco motions to the rearview mirror. "Look."

Antonio turns himself around, looks out the back, and watches as a man walks down the cement stairs and makes his way to his car. "Finally," he says.

"And he didn't lock the door."

Antonio's head snaps around and he looks at Marco. "Are you sure?"

"Positive."

"What do we do then?"

"Now's our chance, let's go." Marco starts the engine and jams the transmission into gear. Since the car's engine had been off for a while, Marco's hands are frozen, so his grip on the steering wheel isn't the best. Marco parks the Cadillac on the street with its rear end facing the Victorian, just a couple houses down from it. Marco puts on his mask and gloves and waits. He can feel the pounding of his heart against his eardrums.

"What if someone sees us?" Antonio asks, now also wearing a ski mask over his face and gloves on his hands, with a hint of trepidation in his voice.

"We don't have a choice. There's no other way inside. Neighbors are probably busy getting ready for work at this hour, so let's just hope that we get lucky they don't notice." Marco continues to stare at his rearview and waits for the perfect moment to act. He's on edge.

Seconds later, the man reemerges from his car and heads back toward the front door of the house. Marco bites his tongue, fearing that the man realizes his mistake and is going back to fix it.

But then everything changes.

The man doesn't lock the front door of the house. Instead, he goes back inside.

"What the hell?" Antonio says as he watches this happen through the rearview.

"Now," Marco says, "this is out chance. Let's go."

"What are we going to do?"

"We'll sneak inside and hide and wait for them to leave."

"What if they see us?"

Marco shrugs. "Let's hope they don't."

Marco makes a fist and holds it out for Antonio, who does the same. They smash them together and get out of the car. They wait for a silent count of three, then close their doors together, minimizing the sound. Marco and Antonio scurry toward the house like two professional bandits.

JEN WAKES BEFORE HER alarms suggests she does, but she takes her time crawling out of the warmth of her bed. She had a difficult time sleeping, as she had woken up two different times during the night with the same nightmare of those eyes staring at her from underneath the mask. Those eyes, dark and petrified, much like her own, will haunt her dreams forever. She just knows it. She fears that she'll never be able to get over what happened.

After sitting up and checking her email on her nearby laptop, Jen eventually drags herself from the bed and enjoys a hot shower. The steam helps to loosen her joints, which are stiffer than usual this morning. She does her best thinking in the shower, and today appears to be one of those creatively high days. She makes it quick so that she can write down her thoughts on the article she had started last night. She gives herself a few bullet points in which to continue with her momentum when she has the time to work later in the day. ADT is scheduled to arrive in an hour, so that gives her just enough time to tidy up a bit downstairs and maybe fix herself a light breakfast before they come to complete the installation of the security system.

The white van with blue markings plastered on the side pulls into the driveway in front of the house five minutes before 9:30 A.M. Jen is sitting in the chair in front of the bay window, waiting for them, and is pleased that they're on time. Two men with dark slacks and blue polo shirts exit the van and make their way toward the front door. Feeling a little anxious about two more men she doesn't know coming into her house, Jen unlocks the key lock and deadbolt and opens the door after the first knock.

"Good morning, miss, is this the Winston residence?" asks the man who had been driving. He smiles politely at Jen, and she returns the gesture.

"Hi, good morning, yes. I'm Jen Winston, please, come in." Jen steps aside and lets the two strangers into her home.

The two men introduce themselves as Eddie and Beck and explain that they'll be the ones completing the installation. Eddie is the driver and he's the veteran of the duo. He does most of the talking while Jen listens and nods her head, and they agree on which package she's interested in having setup. He tries to upsell her on the one with the camera monitoring system, but even she thinks that may be a bit of an overkill, so she declines.

Once the paperwork is signed to give the men permission to do what they do, Beck heads back to the van to retrieve the tools. He returns moments later and he and Eddie get to work. Jen goes into the other room and tries to keep herself busy while keeping one ear on her guests.

MARCO PEEKS INTO THE bay window and catches a glimpse of the man's lower legs disappearing up the stairs. He nods to Antonio, who grabs the door handle and turns until it pops out of its position in the doorframe. The door barely squeaks at all. Marco slides inside the house first, his entire body now trembling, and Antonio follows and closes the door behind them.

They stand at the bottom of the stairs, masks and gloves on, not sure what to do. Marco's heart is working overtime to keep pace with how fast the adrenaline is flowing. He knows how close they are to getting caught right now. Trying his best to concentrate, Marco quickly scans the area to see where they can hide. Things are just as he remembers them - now being able to see, while he hadn't before since it was dark - but there's no telling which closets are full and which ones are not. He doesn't remember if the man had been wearing a jacket or not, and he's worked too hard to get caught that way. Hiding in a closet is not an option.

Upstairs, a door creaks and footsteps approach the stairs from above Marco's head. Instinctually he looks up as if he can see through the ceiling and tries to measure where the steps are coming from. He can't. Antonio hits him with his hand and holds his arms open in bewilderment. Marco looks around again, but sees nowhere to hide. With the footsteps above their heads getting closer and closer to the top of the stairs where they can be seen from, he grabs Antonio by the collar and they rush down the hall and toward the kitchen. Marco walks on only his tiptoes to avoid making any noise.

Just as the front door opens and closes, Marco and Antonio scamper into the kitchen and make a quick right, crouching behind the L-shaped island countertop. Marco holds his breath. He's not sure they made it. Once the two locks on the front door engage, Marco exhales a sigh of relief and relaxes. He looks to Antonio and smiles widely, almost laughing. He knows just how close it was.

"Now what?" Antonio whispers. "We can't stay here."

Marco knows that's true. "Let's go upstairs and hide out in one of the closets in those empty bedrooms. We should be safe there until the lady leaves."

Antonio nods in agreement and he follows Marco into the open. Marco checks all of the windows and the sliding glass door in the back to make that sure no one is watching. When it's obvious that the coast is clear, he and Antonio climb the stairs and head toward the first bedroom at the top. In an all too familiarly eerie sight, the door at the end of the hallway is closed, so Marco knows that they have some more time to wait it out. The lady - Jen, if he remembers her name correctly - must still be sleeping.

Inside the bedroom, Marco cautiously steps over and around the scattered moving boxes that line the floor and pushes his way into the closet. He's afraid that if he makes any noise at all, they might be found. So he's careful not to. When Antonio joins him inside the closet, they turn their backs to the drywall and stand shoulder to shoulder, facing the door. All they can do now is wait.

IT TAKES EDDIE AND Beck a couple of hours to fully install a hard-wired security system that's equipped with a pin pad and emergency alert system. Jen spends most of the time downstairs and in earshot of them, and she finishes unpacking the last moving box just moments before they finish the installation. Eddie gives Jen a rundown of the system and gives her instructions on how to set and change the password while Beck returns the supplies to the van. He returns to put a blue decal on the window before turning and heading back to the van for good.

"Thank you so much for doing this," Jen says to Eddie when they're alone.

"It's my pleasure, miss. Thank you for your business."

"My husband and I just moved here from Maine and we had someone break in our first night here."

Eddie cringes. "I'm sorry to hear that. You can be assured that you're safe now. Anything you need, just let us know. Okay?"

"Do you mind if I ask you one last question before you leave?"

"Shoot."

"If the system is armed, what are the chances that someone can still get in the house?"

Eddie pauses for a beat before answering. "I always like to tell people, if someone really wants to get in, they can get in. We can't stop someone from tossing a rock through a window, or breaking the door down or something, but we hope to deter them from doing so by showing that the house is protected. Beck put a sticker on the window near the front door, and we can leave a stake in the yard with our logo on it if you'd like."

"Yes, please," Jen says quickly. She's a bit disturbed at the thought that she may not be as safe as she had expected, even with this system in place.

"But don't worry, miss. If someone tries to break in or tamper with the system in anyway, we'll know about it immediately and we'll dispatch the police. It's a silent alarm, so we'll be alerted before the intruder even knows what's going on. There's no need to worry anymore, you're protected with ADT. We're always there." Eddie offers a kind smile, and it helps to reassure Jen a bit.

They shake hands before Eddie leaves.

Jen watches through the bay window as Eddie says something to his partner. Beck gets out of the passenger's side and retrieves something from the back of the van. He returns around the front of the van with a stake and jams it into the ground in the front yard. He adjusts it so that it's level and faces the street, then he waves to Jen before getting back into the van. Jen waves back as the van reverses out of the driveway and disappears down the street.

CHAPTER SIXTEEN

The ADT van pulls out of sight and Jen feels a little better already. Not great, considering what Eddie had told her about someone still being able to break in if they really wanted to, but things are looking up. She walks around the house and tests out each window, ensuring that they're still securely locked. In the kitchen, she finds a notepad in the drawer and writes the passcode for the alarm system on one of the empty pages, then tosses it back in the drawer for safekeeping. Satisfied and motivated to get things done today, she makes her way upstairs to change into her running gear.

She strips and lays her clothes out neatly on the bed before changing everything from head to toe. She attaches her phone to her bicep and pumps up her best motivational workout playlist before heading back downstairs. She sets the alarm, closes the door, and locks it before stepping outside. The air is cool and refreshing, and the clean oxygen fills up her lungs as she breathes it in. She loves being outside. She waits for the alarm to beep before jamming the soft earbuds into her ears and stretching out her calf muscles. She decides that the beep signifying her safety is her new favorite sound.

Rejuvenated and feeling like a new woman, she prepares to extend her loop further than yesterday, and she plans to increase her pace too. Her knee joints start out rigid, but they quickly loosen up as she forces them to cooperate with her mindset. The first mile flies by and her belly is adequately storing enough air to help push her through the difficult moments. Her pulse is starting to level out and her rhythm is smooth. She's in for a long one today, and she loves how that feels. It's been far too long.

It was only just over a year ago that Jen was aggressively training for a marathon. Her training began just after the New Year, and she rapidly worked her way up from one mile to fifteen. She was on pace to reach the twenty-six mile mark by late summer, and she had been looking forward to participating in the local event that ran through and around the southern coast of Maine in September.

In early July, her health began to deteriorate, but she had just assumed that it was from pushing herself too hard. She hadn't been a runner before, so she just figured that her body was telling her to slow down. She listened and took a couple of weeks off, but she was never able to fully gain her stamina back. That puzzled her. By the end July, she was diagnosed with Lyme disease - which isn't uncommon for people who spend a lot of time in the woods, as she learned - and her dream of running in the marathon was shattered. Peter was supportive and sympathetic through it all, but the whole ordeal put Jen in a bit of a depression for a few months.

She has good and bad days even now, although more good than bad, it seems, but some of the symptoms still linger. Her joints do still get occasionally arthritic and she has bouts of lethargy, but she's mostly back to how she was before. She tries to take advantage of the good days when she has them, and stringing multiple of them together consecutively helps to improve her outlook on the disease. It makes her realize that it's she who's in control of her mind, regardless of how her body feels. One's mind is powerful enough to win out more often than not.

Jen hasn't yet reached the two-mile mark when her phone rings, interrupting the music thumping in her ears. She stops to look at the screen while still running in place, and picks it up curiously when she sees who it is.

GERRY DALE AND JAMAAL Harris pull into Dave Carson's driveway at 6:35 A.M. The single story house is lit up inside and a single light shines dimly above the front door. Gerry pulls his squad car in the driveway, then he and Jamaal step out onto the gravel. In front of him in the driveway is a light blue van with a faded key lock emblem on the side door. It has many similar features that Mrs. Winston had described the locksmith's van to have yesterday, and it seems to match the photo that Ben Schultz had showed to him and Jamaal as well. Gerry flashes his light on the van to inspect it further before he and Jamaal head to the front door of the house.

Gerry can hear some activity inside as they approach, but he's unsure if it's children at play or the television with the volume turned up too loud. Gerry knocks twice on the door with his knuckle, but gets no response. He wants to avoid ringing the doorbell in case others are still sleeping inside, but he feels like a fool standing outside in the cold without getting a response. Reluctantly, he pushes his finger into the illuminated doorbell light, the condensation transferring to his overgrown nail, and the chaos begins from the other side of the door almost instantaneously. A dog starts to bark, which is followed moments later by a wailing infant, then by a hollering woman.

Gerry looks to his partner, who makes a face at him. Gerry knows that face, and he knows that it's not a reassurance that Jamaal will have his back. He also knows that he has just pissed off some people, and therefore, he's on his own when it comes to dealing with those people. He thinks of what his own wife would do if someone rang the doorbell at this hour, and he instantly regrets the decision.

He clenches his molars together in anticipation of the forthcoming crusade.

The front door swings open and a woman looking like she's been hit by a bus stares at Gerry in the face. Her hair is scattered in every which direction and she wears a nightgown that hangs to the floor and shows very little of her aging body. Her face quickly switches from hatred to concern when, perhaps, she realizes that the two men at her door are police officers instead of whomever she had anticipated.

Gerry says, "Good morning, ma'am, we're sorry to bother you so early, but we were just hoping to catch up with Dave before he leaves for work. This is the Carson residence, right?"

The woman looks between Gerry and Jamaal. Gerry can only imagine what she's thinking.

"What do you want with my husband?" the woman asks. "Is he in trouble?"

"No, he's not in trouble. We just want to ask him a couple of questions. Is he still home?" Gerry asks the question, although he already knows the answer. It's a police thing.

Dave's wife shifts her eyes to her husband's van that's over Gerry's shoulder and holds the position for a while. "Wait here, I'll go get him. What did you say your names were again?"

"I'm sorry, I'm Officer Dale," Gerry says. "My partner is Officer Harris."

Dave's wife nods and disappears inside the house. She leaves the door open only a crack, but the noise from inside couldn't be clearer. The commotion reminds Gerry of what it was like when his boys were young, and he offers his sympathy. It never was very much fun, he realizes now. And with the memory making its way to the surface, he's glad that he doesn't have to go through that phase of his life again.

Moments later, a thick man in dark jeans and a white t-shirt that's too small appears at the front door. His hairline is receding and his hair is thinning, and Gerry wonders if the baby is his. His wife - assuming that was his wife, of course - looks a little old to be having a baby, so Gerry concludes that it's probably a grandbaby instead. The man with the beer gut steps outside and closes the door behind him.

"Can I help you?" he says.

"Are you Dave Carson?" Gerry asks.

"I am."

"Sorry to bother you, Mr. Carson," Gerry begins, "but we were just hoping to ask you a few questions if you have a moment."

"I have an appointment with a client in twenty-five minutes, so make it fast. What's this about?"

"You have a client whose home was broken into recently, is that right?"

Dave smiles and chuckles softly. "I'm a locksmith. Most of my clients have had their homes broken into recently."

Gerry nods, realizing that it was kind of a stupid question. "Right. There's one in particular, though, a Mrs. Jen Winston. Do you remember her?"

"The Winston house? Sure. I changed out her locks just yesterday. Is something wrong?"

"We just want to confirm with you something that she told us. She said that you had said that whoever broke into her house likely had a key. Is that true?"

Dave shifts around his weight, clearly getting a little bit uncomfortable about where the questioning is going. "Yeah, I told her that's what it looked like to me."

"Why do you think that?"

"Well, there was no sign of any lock tampering and there was no damage to the locking mechanism itself when I removed it. Usually the lock is completely destroyed or messed up real bad if someone broke in. If someone used a crowbar or something, I could tell by just looking at it. These locks, both the one on the front door and the one on the back, looked normal and had no sign of forced entry."

Gerry nods while Jamaal takes some notes on a pad that's small enough to fit in his breast pocket.

"Okay, that's all we needed to know. We just wanted to corroborate her story. Thank you for your time," Gerry says.

"You came all the way out here just to ask me that?" Dave says, sounding almost annoyed.

"I stopped by your office yesterday, but your secretary told me that you'd be out on jobs all week, so I didn't want to bother you during working hours. Thanks again for your time."

Gerry nods to Dave, who nods back, then disappears into the house. Jamaal finishes his note and puts the pad back in his pocket. Gerry waits for him to finish, then they walk back to the car together and get into their respective sides.

"What are you thinking?" Jamaal asks his partner once they get inside the car.

"I think we should send a forensics team down there to check for prints. If this Dave guy is right and it was someone who had a key, they must have been looking for something. Maybe it's someone we already know."

Jamaal nods. Gerry reverses into the street and heads back in the direction of the station. When they arrive, they immediately go see the forensics team in the basement and provide them with the details. It takes a couple hours to find time to talk with the Sheriff and convince him to arrange for a forensics team to be sent out, so Gerry and Jamaal wait around past their shifts until it's all sorted out. Once the arrangements are made, Gerry gets on the phone and places a call to Mrs. Winston to let her know what's going on.

MARCO IS STILL IN the closet in the Stoneham house, but is now sitting on the carpet. Antonio is right beside him. He listens to two men install a full home security system downstairs - he can tell by the conversation that that's what's happening - and he doubts that they'll be busted now. But he's not sure what that means for him and

Antonio yet, though, either. The air is stale inside the closet, and both of their masks are up over their heads to allow them to breathe easier. There's nothing they can but sit and wait. Still. And think.

Marco's not certain how long they've been waiting, but the boredom is deadening. Staying awake is his greatest challenge, and considering the circumstances, that's a little bizarre. When the two men downstairs finally do leave, he and Antonio get back to their feet and hide their faces behind their masks. They're not outnumbered anymore, so Marco's just waiting for the right time to make a move.

Suddenly, energetic footsteps make their way up the stairs and Marco tenses up. It's the not knowing that he doesn't like. His heart is back to racing again, and the cotton of his mask is becoming heavy from the soaking up of the perspiration that welts from his face. He's going to need a shower when they get out of here.

Just as quickly as they'd started, the footsteps disappear down the hall and fade away into the bedroom. Moments later, the footsteps reappear behind some muffled pop music and head back down the stairs. Marco doesn't recognize the tune, and he's more confused than ever. Downstairs, the front door squeaks open and then closes again, followed by a single beep. Marco turns his head and looks at Antonio.

Jen is gone.

And they're alone in the house.

Marco's eyes widen, and he leans his ear toward the closet door to listen closer. Emptiness. Their time has finally come.

"Should we do it?" Antonio whispers.

Marco pauses for a beat to think about it, just to make sure that he's not missing anything. When convinced that he's not, he says, "Let's go."

Not wanting to waste any more time, Marco pushes the closet door open and slides out. It creaks slightly, but for a nice change, it doesn't matter. No one is around to hear it. The non-recycled oxygen outside the closet is a treat too, and he takes a moment to suck it in. Quickly moving on, Marco leads Antonio out of the room without speaking. They take a left and head straight for the bedroom at the end of the hall. The door is already open, inviting them inside.

Women's clothes - blue jeans, a conservative blouse, and an unflattering and not very big cream-colored bra - are laid out nicely on the bed, and Marco notices them immediately. He finds it a little bit strange.

Antonio heads over to the window and looks outside. "The car is still in the driveway," he says.

Marco considers this, plus the music and apparent change of clothes, and comes up with something that makes sense. "She must have left on foot," he says. "Maybe she went for a walk or something."

"What does that mean for us?"

"It means that we have to work quickly."

"Shouldn't we get out of here and come back?"

"No, we can't do that. We have no way in now, not with that alarm."

Antonio nods, although reluctantly.

Marco wastes no time in getting started. He knows that the quicker they work the quicker they can get out of here. It's the only way to end this. He starts on one side of the room, Antonio on the opposite, and he slowly walks around the perimeter of the room, keeping his hands on the drywall. He knows what they're looking for, but he doesn't know where in the room it is. That's the problem. According to Sal, Bartolo had told him that it's definitely in this room, though. With that, all of their eggs have been put into one basket. Marco just hopes that his father was right.

While Antonio scans his side of the room, Marco does the same to his, in search of the soft spot, but finds nothing. He's careful to make sure that he doesn't miss anything, and it takes more time than they probably have to spend. But it has to be done. There's no coming back.

Together with Antonio, Marco pulls out the bed and slides the wooden nightstand toward the door. They slip behind the furniture and continue their search.

Marco sees it right away and kicks himself for being so diligent before. The soft spot it obvious, far more obvious than he was led to believe, and he knows now that they've wasted valuable time. The soft spot is simply a deficiency in the drywall that stands out from the rest. It's a small, rounded, unpainted section of the wall, and it's nothing more than a self-patched hole. It's really not even hidden at all.

Marco's heart leaps with excitement. After a long search and a long journey over the last few months, they've found it. Finally. And now he can relax a bit, knowing that their treasure is going to be put to good use.

STILL RUNNING IN PLACE, Jen answers the phone, "Hi, Officer Dale, how are you doing?"

"Mrs. Winston, do you have a minute?"

"Sure. Is everything okay?"

"We spoke with the locksmith that did your locks yesterday, and he confirmed what you told us."

Jen is taken aback a bit. She's not sure how she feels about Officer Dale basically admitting that he didn't believe her before. "Okay."

"We're going to send a forensics team over to your house to do some dusting for fingerprints. We'll see if they can find anything that may help identify the intruders."

Considering the officer's initial reservations, Jen is pleasantly surprised at the ever-growing interest in her situation. "When?"

"They'll be there in an hour. Are you home?"

"I will be. Will you be coming too?"

"No, actually. Neither myself nor Officer Harris will be there, but I'll check in. The team will arrive in a police van and they'll have identification on them. They'll do some quick dusting around the front door and the bedroom upstairs."

"Thank you, Officer Dale. Thanks for doing this."

"You're welcome. We'll be in touch."

Jen hangs up. The interruption cuts her run short today, which disappoints her, but hopefully she'll get some answers out of it. She puts her phone back in the armband on her bicep and restarts the music. She increases her pace and starts back toward home.

ANTONIO SCAMPERS BACK AND forth across the carpet between the wall and the window that faces the front while Marco tries to break through the wall where the soft spot is. Although just a patch, it's thick and rubbery, and Marco didn't come prepared with any tools. He's almost embarrassed at the oversight. He tries to cut through the material with a key from his keychain, but progress is slow.

"Oh shit," Antonio says as he makes his way back to the window.

"What? What's wrong?"

"She's back."

Marco bolts to his feet and runs over to the window to see for himself. Jen - who's prettier than he had remembered - approaches the front door, red-faced and breathing heavily, and holds two fingers up to her neck. In a panic, Marco rushes to the far corner of the bed and gets himself into the pushing position. Antonio approaches the other corner and does the same. An intense drum solo sounds from inside Marco's chest. It's like a band with a new sound has set up shop under his skin. He and Antonio push the bed on a count of three and it slides back into its original position.

The front door opens and closes downstairs, and footsteps begin up the stairs.

Marco's heartbeat intensifies. He's starting to worry that they're not going to make it.

Marco pushes the nightstand on his side of the bed back to its designated spot on the floor, and Antonio does the same on his side. Marco motions to the closet behind Antonio, and they hurry inside. Marco holds his breath again as Jen approaches from the hallway just as the door closes.

JEN WALKS INTO THE bedroom, her heart still working overtime from the fast pace in which she ran home with. She's winded, to say the least, and her legs feel like jelly. She turns on the light and the fan in the attached bathroom and starts the shower. Back in the bedroom and out of view of the window that leads to the front, she struggles to pull her top off as the material sticks to her. She fights it and eventually wins, then slides down her yoga pants and kicks them to the side. She snaps her underwear against her hips as she makes her way back into the bathroom and slides into the shower.

MARCO BITES HIS TONGUE, realizing how close he was to finding the goods. If only he had a simple tool, even just a screwdriver, they'd already be out of here. He kicks himself. But he must move on. He considers their options going forward, and he doesn't like any of them. If they leave now, they can't get back in the house, not without being detected. But they can't stay here and risk being seen either. He clenches his jaw and squeezes his fingers into a fist out of frustration. He doesn't know what to do.

He can see through a crack in the tri-fold closet door, and he watches Jen without blinking. Her naked backside stares at him, and the thrill of the voyeur gives him butterflies in his stomach. Realizing that he and Antonio have only one logical option right now, Marco waits until the bathroom door is pulled closed before pushing open the closet door and risk being seen. Luckily, the closet door is slightly longer than it should be, so the friction against the carpet stops it from making any sound. Marco motions for Antonio to go first, which he does. Marco follows and tiptoes out of the room, sneaking into the hallway. The stairs creak as he climbs to the bottom, but he pushes on and ignores it. Antonio whips open the front door and sprints toward the Cadillac that still rests a couple houses down on the street. Right on his heels, Marco closes the door behind him then sprints toward his friend.

He hops inside the Cadillac, starts up the engine quicker than he ever has before, and peels out of site. He doesn't even close his door fully until they're already halfway down the street. Antonio struggles to catch his breath in the seat next to him.

CHAPTER SEVENTEEN

Jen finishes drying her hair and ties it up in a loose bun above her head. The fan is working overtime from the heat of the hair dryer, and Jen is sweating already because of it. The bathroom is too small for her - it's not much larger than that on an airplane - and it warms up quickly. Peter had offered to use it as his personal bathroom so that Jen could have the larger one down the hall, but she likes the fact that she doesn't have to walk into the coolness of the hallway if she needs to relieve herself during the night. So she took the smaller of the two.

First world problems.

The bathroom was an afterthought, as it was once a small walk-in closet that was changed into a bathroom later on in an attempt to improve the resale value of the house. Jen and Peter had bought the house after it went to foreclosure, and she feels bad that the previous owner spent that kind of money to improve the house and ended up losing it anyway. Although she feels guilty, they did get a heck of a deal on the place, so it's hard to complain. It's in better condition than they could have expected for not having seen the inside prior to the sale too, so that's been a nice surprise.

There's a medicine cabinet above the sink and an enclosed shelving unit above the toilet, but it's still not enough storage space for all of her necessities. She's not big into wearing makeup and doesn't have more than a couple different hair styling products at one time, so that helps. She prefers to go all natural, and despite Peter's encouragement to splurge on herself from time to time, she rarely does. She's not trying to impress anybody.

It's been just under an hour since Officer Dale called, so Jen is expecting the visitors to arrive any minute now. As she readies herself to head downstairs, she notices that the closet door across the room is partially cracked open. It's Peter's closet and she hasn't been in there at all today, nor would she have any reason to. She surely would have noticed it earlier, she thinks, and wonders to herself why she didn't then but does now. Strange. She approaches it and looks inside. Everything appears to be in place, undisturbed and orderly. She brushes it off, assuming that Peter must have just forgotten to close it all the way this morning, then closes it.

Jen heads downstairs to wait for her visitors. She tries to turn the deadbolt to disengage it, but realizes that it's already unlocked. She tries the key lock on the door handle after, and it also opens freely. To her left, she notices that alarm is no longer armed either, and it's beeping, so she tries to retrace her steps. She remembers with clarity that she did lock the door before she went upstairs; she's certain of it. She came in after her run, closed and locked the door, then armed the alarm - in that order. She's positive she did, or at least she thinks she is. Now she's starting to doubt herself.

A feeling of uneasiness rests in the pit of her stomach, and she doesn't like it. There's no way that she left the door unlocked, not with the paranoia that she's been feeling. She considers making the rounds downstairs to see if anything is out of place, but before she can act, a car door closes outside. Her heart leaps at the startle. She makes her way over to the bay window in the living room and peeks out. A team of three - two women and one man

- walk toward the house. Each has a lanyard dangling around their neck and are carrying buckets and other small containers of supplies. The SUV in the driveway tells her that it's the local crime unit from the Stoneham Police Department, so she goes back to the front door and opens it as the forensics team approaches. Just seeing them makes her feel better all of a sudden.

THE FORENSICS TEAM COMES and goes in a matter of hours. Besides brief introductions and the occasional question - like where is the bedroom or do you mind ifs - there isn't much interaction between Jen and the team. They do their dusting and extract a handful of different fingerprints from the front door and the bedroom door upstairs, then they leave, telling Jen that either Officer Dale or Officer Harris will be in touch. That's pretty much it.

Jen's column is due in two days, so she spends much of the early afternoon working on it. She tends to submit articles to her editor on the due date and is rarely early. She doesn't require much editing anyway since she revises her own work, so everyone at the magazine is generally okay with her waiting until the last minute. After she completes the first draft over lunch, she decides to call it quits for the day.

The first home improvement project that she and Peter had decided they wanted to get done was the bedroom. Although it appears to just need a new coat of paint and maybe some new carpeting, it's their first priority. Jen has a difficult time sleeping amongst the clutter, and the dullness of the paint on the walls does something to her subconscious mind that makes her feel uncomfortable. Although having dark colored walls is said to be better for sleeping, she prefers something soft that is more welcoming, as it makes her feel like she's in a state of meditation or something. She's never been one to follow trends and rarely even listen to someone else's advice. She knows what she wants and she's not afraid to go after it, and she disregards what others may think. Maybe it's confidence or maybe it's stubbornness, but either way, it's who she is.

Behind the bed upstairs is a rough, uneven patch of drywall that seems as if it was added in or repaired relatively recently. Peter had noticed it initially during the first walkthrough after they signed the paperwork on the house. His first thought was that the previous owner had kicked a hole in the wall and repaired it, or maybe it was an accident that occurred during the horseplay of a couple of rowdy kids. Nonetheless, it's an obvious patch that might still be noticeable even when painted over, but it has to be tended to.

Jen corners the bed and wriggles it away from the wall. She rotates between the two outward-facing corners until the bed is pulled far enough away from the wall for her to slide behind and work comfortably. When she moves Peter's nightstand out of the way, she notices something unsettling. The indent on the carpet where the nightstand lays is off. Usually when a piece of furniture rests in the same place and doesn't move, a crease the size of the legs leave an obvious indentation on the floor.

Not this time.

There's a trough in the carpet where the nightstand should sit, but the wooden legs aren't in it. It's somewhat off track, like someone had bumped into it or moved it ever so slightly. The new position has yet to create a crease in the carpet, which means that it's fresh and has happened recently.

Jen doesn't remember knocking her hip against it or anything, and she doesn't think that the bed nicked it when she was moving it, but it must have been one of those things. This whole home invasion thing has got her rattled still, obviously, and it's making her see things that aren't really there. She shakes her head and brushes it off. ADT had said that no one could get in without breaking a window or something, not with the alarm enabled, and she knows that she set it when she left. She's just being paranoid, she concludes, and she approaches the wall with a sheet of sandpaper.

THE DAY HAS BEEN hectic and stressful, but it's not as bad as it had been the day before. The vacant store manager position has been posted through corporate for the inner city location that had lost their manager yesterday. The local police have already tracked down the individual who burglarized another of Peter's stores yesterday as well, and he was arrested and arraigned early this morning. All that was taken was some cash from the register due to the thief being young and inexperienced, and he panicked before he was able to get any jewelry. The youngster had been desperate for cash, apparently, although the police won't tell Peter much more than that. All of the money is being returned to the retail location this afternoon since the accused has already confessed, so things are looking up in that respect.

After dealing with all of the business that he was unaware was part of his job description when he accepted the position, Peter finally finds some time to get some real work done in the afternoon. And real work, of course, means doing nothing productive. He makes a phone call to a florist that's not too far from home and puts together a nice setting for Jen. There will be multi-colored hydrangeas in a tall rectangular vase that's made of glass, and it should be ready to pick up on his way home. Peter hopes that his wife will like it - not only the flowers, but the surprise as well - and he bets that their therapist would praise him for his efforts if she were to find out about it.

As soon as Peter hangs up with the florist, his mobile rings on his desk. He glances at the screen and sees his wife's face smiling back at him. The timing is ironic, and he wonders if it's Cupid toying with him. He picks up the device and swipes the green phone symbol to the right with a smile on his face.

JEN RUBS THE SANDPAPER over and around the patched hole in the wall and smooths away the unevenness. The center of the patch has a thin jagged line that sits further in the wall than the rest of the patch, and it looks out of place. Peter and Jen don't have any pets, but it looks like a cat has kneaded into the wall with one of its claws. Maybe it was a mouse. Jen would love to have a kitty to keep her company during the day - and to keep away the mice that appear to be roaming around - but Peter is allergic. Sometimes she thinks that she would like a small dog as a running companion too, but she's not sure that she's ready for that type of commitment. Cats are more independent while dogs are more dependent, and Jen's not really in a position in her life to be relied on. It takes a strong woman to admit to herself.

She pushes the sandpaper around the edges of the patch and uses some elbow grease to try to flatten a tough spot. She uses both hands and throws all of her body weight into it, and when she does, the wall gives way. She pushes one final time and her finger breaks through the patch, and soon the rest of her hand follows. She's able to pull back in time so that she doesn't smash her fist into the wall stud, but she scrapes up her wrist pretty good. She pulls her arm out, flicks off the remnants of drywall, and inspects the damage. The wound stings, but she can tell that it's mostly harmless.

The hole in the wall, on the other hand, is in pretty bad shape. Drywall powder has fallen on to the carpet below the hole, and surely more has fallen inside the wall. Jen tries to close the gap and pinch the severed ends together to see if it's fixable, but she quickly finds that it's not. Although she considers herself to be handy, she's never patched drywall before and wouldn't even know where to begin. She thinks Peter may know, so she reaches behind her and retrieves her phone from the nightstand.

As she waits for Peter to pick up, if he even does at all, something from inside the wall captures her attention. Something seems to be glowing at her, although she can't tell what it is. Wounded wing and all, she reaches back inside the hole for the item, grabs it, and pulls it out. Her hand hits something on the way out and a small ping sounds from below it, kind of like a tiny marble hitting a tile floor. The object in her hand is heavy and she almost drops it, so she pinches the phone between her shoulder and cheek and uses both hands to yank the item further out. Whatever it is fits nicely between her two hands, and it's cold to the touch. The hole widens some more as the object slips out, and the drywall doesn't retract until the object is freed completely. Jen holds the mysterious discovery in the palms of her hands and stares at it, not knowing what to think.

The significance of it is not clear right away, and maybe there is none, but Jen can't help but think that this is what those two guys were after the other night. She's not exactly sure what it is, but something about its shine won't allow her to take her eyes off of it. There's something almost hypnotic about it. How those two guys knew that it was here and what they had planned to do with it are the next thoughts that enter her mind, but she continues to be pulled in by the object's trance, so she pushes the thoughts aside.

Peter answers the other end of the phone and brings Jen back into the present. She stares at the item that's in her hands and struggles to come up with the right words that will adequately describe to her husband what it is that she has found.

CHAPTER EIGHTEEN

Marco and Antonio ride back toward the city in the direction of the pizzeria. The ride is mostly quiet as Marco is deep within his own thoughts. He's struggling to grasp just how things went so wrong. That, in combination with the fact that they were so close to being caught, has him feeling shaken.

Seemingly random and unprompted, Antonio breaks the silence in the seat next to him. "I don't think I can do this anymore, Marco," he says.

Marco is taken aback, not having expecting that. "What are you talking about?"

"We almost got caught in there today. Another ten seconds and we would have been busted."

Marco actually thinks it's less than that, but he keeps it to himself. "Yeah, it was close."

There's a long pause between them.

"That's it?" Antonio presses. "That's all you have you to say?"

"I don't know what else you want me to say."

"If we get caught we're both going to jail, do you realize that?"

Marco shoots a glance to Antonio from behind the wheel. "We won't get caught."

"But we almost did. You said it yourself, there's no way we can get back in that house now that there's an alarm system. It's over."

"It's not over, Antonio. It's not over until my dad is out of prison or I'm in there with him. We've come this far already."

Antonio shakes his head and stares out the window. "I just don't think I can do it anymore."

"Well, we'll be to Sal's in less than five minutes, you can tell him that yourself."

The rest of the drive to Sal's is awkward and tense, but it ends quickly. Marco pulls into the lot of the pizzeria and parks the Cadillac in its customary position next to Sal's Lexus at the far end. He and Antonio get out and make their way toward the front door. Marco presses the button to call his uncle on the buzzer, and they walk inside once the door's lock disengages. They make their way around the counter and into the backroom where Sal is waiting for them in the open doorway that leads up to his studio.

Sal greets Marco first with alternating cheek kisses, then he does the same to Antonio. After, Marco follows him up the stairs and into his apartment, with Antonio trailing behind. Once upstairs, they all sit around the table and wait for someone to initiate the conversation. Sal does.

"Okay, boys," he says. "I can tell by the look on your faces that something happened. Tell me what you saw."

Marco begins, "It's bad news, Uncle Sal. We had a chance to get the goods, but we weren't expecting it, so we weren't prepared. I think we've lost our chance."

Sal looks between Marco and Antonio, and Marco fears that he'll be able to see the tension.

"What do you mean?" Sal asks.

"We saw an opportunity to get inside and we took it," Marco says. "We waited around for a while until the guy left, then we snuck upstairs and waited for the lady to do the same."

"Did she?"

"Eventually, but it wasn't for very long. We found the hole in the wall in the bedroom, but we didn't have time to dig it out before she came back."

"Did she see you?"

"No, I don't think so."

Sal pauses. "Okay, well, this is good. Now we know where it is, so we can just go back and get it when the time is right. I don't see what the problem is. Why the gloomy faces?"

"We can't get back into the house."

"Of course we can. She can't stay inside forever."

Marco shakes his head. "It's not that."

"What then?"

"They changed the locks."

"Well, we can pick it."

"There's more."

Sal looks between Marco and Antonio again, and his face shows his concern. "How much more?"

"They had a security system installed too. We were there when it happened."

Sal suddenly slides his chair back and it grinds against the tile. The screech is piercing and it fills the entire apartment. Marco cringes. Sal stands and starts to pace.

"Yep, you're right," Sal says. "That's a problem."

Marco drops his head slightly. He was hoping that his uncle would have an idea on how to get out of this, and he's disappointed in his discouragement. "Like I said, I think we've lost our chance to get back in the house."

Sal paces for another moment before sitting back down and pulling the chair in close. "Okay, boys, it's not that bad. We can come up with something. Please just tell me that's everything."

Marco keeps his head down but lifts his eyes to look into Sal's. "Not exactly," he says. "Antonio has something that he wants to tell you."

ENRIQUE HENDERSON AND STEPHAN Cooper are partners. Partners might even be a stretch. Stephan is Enrique's driver, and that's about as far as the relationship goes. Stephan is an acquaintance of an acquaintance of Enrique's, and they were introduced when it was known that a driver would be needed for a job. Enrique has promised him a cut of the money when it's all done, but chances are, Enrique will just eliminate him and take it all for himself. That's kind of how he does business.

That's what Stephan does for a living - he drives. He's hired by all types, both legal and illegal, and he doesn't ask for many details except for the amount of the payday. He usually requires it upfront, but with the number that Enrique is talking about with this job, he had agreed to get paid after the job is done.

Enrique is a badass. He gets what he wants when he wants it and will take out anyone who stands in his way. He's been in and out of prison on multiple occasions, but he's not going back again. Not under any circumstances. He'd rather die than go back to prison, and that makes him very dangerous. He knows all about the Salazar's and what they're up to, although they know nothing of him.

Except for Bartolo. Bartolo knows Enrique very well.

Enrique also knows of Sal's relationship with Willy at the pawn shop, and he's using it to his full advantage. Willy has less than two days now to get the artifact from Sal, then Enrique is going after it himself. He doesn't need the Salazar's to get it for him, but they know where in the house it is, so it could save him some time. Plus, if he were to go inside and get it himself, it poses the risk that he may get caught. Sure, it will cost him $50,000 to do it the backdoor way, but it puts all the risk on the Salazar's and none on him. The upside is so much greater than $50,000, so he'll make that up in a second once he has the artifact in his possession.

All Enrique can do for now is wait. He and Stephan have rented out a studio apartment close to I-95 for the month, just so they're close to the action. They'll head over to Willy's early on Friday and pick up the artifact, then head toward Logan Airport and get out of town. What Stephan doesn't know is that there's only one plane ticket and he's not going to be the one using it. Enrique has left Stephan in the dark about what's really happening.

SAL, MARCO, AND ANTONIO spend the rest of the morning together in Sal's apartment. When the time comes, they move the conversation downstairs and into the kitchen to prepare for the day. Antonio shares his reluctance to continue participating in the whole thing, and Sal receives it well. He's sympathetic and tells him that he understands why he feels that way, but he basically begs him to continue to help without trying to seem desperate. He subtly reminds Antonio that he was the one who gave him a place to work and to start his culinary career, and that when the rest of his family had abandoned him and moved to Maryland, Sal was always there for him with open arms.

And it works.

Antonio cracks under the weight of the guilt and agrees to finish the job. Marco thanks his best friend and promises that this is the last job, and Antonio says that he believes him. Sal is proud of himself for being the peacemaker, but he quickly moves on and is attentive to the task at hand before Antonio has a chance to change his mind.

"So while you boys were out at the house, I did some research myself," Sal says while rolling out some pizza dough.

"What did you find?" Marco asks.

Sal wipes his hands on his pants and disappears into the storefront. He returns a moment later with a notepad and begins to read, "I looked into the real estate transactions and found out that the Stoneham house was bought by Peter and Jennifer Winston. They moved into town from Maine. It looks like Peter is some sort of district manager or something for a jewelry store chain, and Jennifer works for some magazine that's based in Maine."

"Did you find any significance to them buying the house that they did?" Marco asks.

"I don't think so. I think it's all just coincidental. Wrong place wrong time."

Marco nods. "This Jen girl, does she still work for that magazine?"

"It's unclear. There's some stuff with her name on it on their website within the last couple of months, but nothing recently. Maybe it's because of the move, or maybe she quit altogether."

"There was an office downstairs in the house, maybe she works from home," Marco offers. "That would explain why she was home in the middle of the day."

Sal nods, agreeing with the thought. "Could be. Let's say she does work at home. That means that we have to plan for her being there most of the time. Between her and the alarm, it's going to be tough."

While still preparing pizza dough for the opening of the shop for lunch, everyone is quiet. Sal's drawing a blank on where to go from here. There are less than two days left before Willy's buyer will be back and expecting the goods, so they need to come up with a plan before tomorrow night. They'll never get away with doing something in the daylight, Sal realizes, so there are just two more windows of time left before it's too late.

After a few more minutes of silence, Antonio clears his throat and begins to offer up an idea. "I've been thinking," he says.

Sal stops what he's doing and is attentive to the soft-spoken wingman. Throughout all of this, Antonio's been nothing more than the sidekick and often the lookout, and Sal is grateful for that - someone has to play the role. It's a little out of whack, considering that he's the most intelligent one of the group - and no one would argue with that statement. It's always his type - the introverts - that come up with the best ideas and solutions to the most challenging problems. Although unusual, when Antonio does offer up his thoughts for discussion, Sal listens. He desperately hopes that Antonio is on to something, because he has nothing.

"I don't know if it'll work or not," Antonio continues, "but considering all the facts, I think I may have an idea on what we can do."

Marco looks over to Sal, and they both smirk. Antonio is back, and it's just in the nick of time.

"Go ahead, my friend," Sal says. "What do you got?"

CHAPTER NINETEEN

Peter stares at the phone on his desk and waits for the call to connect. He puts it up to his ear when it does. "Hey, Jen."

"I'm surprised you answered."

"Yeah? I've been in the office all day." Peter pauses and waits for a response, but gets none. "What's going on? How did the installation go?"

"It went fine. Officer Dale called again too. They sent over some forensics people to dust for fingerprints this afternoon."

"For what?"

"I'll tell you about it later."

"Okay...was there something you wanted to talk about now then?"

"Oh, right. So I started to sand that rough spot behind the bed, but I actually made it worse and I don't know how to fix it."

"Worse how?"

"Well...I may have poked a hole right through the wall instead."

Peter pauses and bites his tongue. "Oh."

"I don't know what happened. I was just using the sandpaper and I pushed on it, and boom, there it happened." Jen pauses for a second. "Are you mad?"

"No, I'm not mad. I can fix it. We can get some supplies later when we get some paint. Do you still want to go?"

"Do you?"

Peter sighs. He hates it when she does this, but he tries to hide it. "Yes, we can go. I was thinking about leaving here soon actually."

There's a long, silent pause.

"Jen?" Peter says.

"What?"

"Did you hear what I said?"

"Uh, yeah. I heard you."

"What are you doing?"

"There is one more thing I wanted to tell you."

Peter's heart leaps, suddenly a little uneasy. "Okay. What is it?"

"I'm not really sure how to say this, but I found something."

"What do you mean? What did you find?"

"In the wall. I found something in the wall."

"What is it?"

Jen pauses again. "I'm not too sure actually."

JEN KNEELS ON THE floor behind the bed, still pinching the phone between her shoulder and cheek. The object from inside the wall is sitting in the palms of her open hands, and she studies it while trying to describe it to Peter on the other end of the phone. It's a statue of sorts, dark purple or maroon in color, and it kind of resembles a Buddha. It stands roughly six or eight inches tall and isn't much more than a couple inches wide. It's heavier than it looks, which is really only maybe five or six pounds. There are no apparent inscriptions or recognizable symbols anywhere on it, and it doesn't appear to have much value. If it has some sort of symbolic resonance or deep meaning to someone, Jen is unaware of it. She's never seen something quite like this, and it being kept behind the wall sparks her interest.

The statue has a unique characteristic that stands out above anything else, and it gives Jen the creeps. The status has a face, but its eyes are missing. There are two socket holes where they should be, but there's nothing there except for two rounded, caved in depressions. Jen is not a spiritual woman, never has been, but something inside of her is telling her that there's something sacred about what she has found. She's mesmerized by the pull of the empty face that blankly watches her, and she can't keep her eyes off of it.

She hangs up with Peter with the understanding that he'll take a look at it and the hole in the wall when he returns home. She carries the statue across the room to the dresser with a vanity mirror over it and rests it on the top. She puts it in the center initially, but quickly changes her mind and slides it closer to the edge and out of the backdrop of the mirror. Although not a believer in superstitions and spirits and the like, Jen thinks it would be safer to not disturb the omens. Before leaving the room, she turns the statue around so that its blank eyes face the wall, just in case.

In her office downstairs, Jen tries to concentrate on editing her column while she waits for Peter to come home, but she can't keep her mind off of that statue. She abandons her work for now and searches the net, trying to find something that resembles what she has found. To her displeasure, she finds nothing that's even remotely similar.

Officer Dale finally calls to check in with Jen as he said he would, and he fills her in on what to expect next. He should have some results of the forensics work by tomorrow, although he warns her not get her hopes up for anything of substance. She considers telling him about the strange things that keep happening: the unlocked front door, unset alarm, cracked open closet, shifted nightstand, strange scuff mark on the wall patch, plus the peculiar statue, of course. She considers what his response might be, and she decides to tell him none of it. She'll wait until Peter gets home to find out what he thinks they should do.

PETER ARRIVES HOME BEFORE 5:00 P.M. and the sun is actually still out. Autumn days are shorter and darkness consumes much of his waking hours outside of the office this time of year, so it's a nice treat to actually see the sun. He walks up to the front door, conspicuously holding a bouquet of flowers near his hip so that Jen doesn't see them right away. The glass vase is awkwardly heavy. He slides his new key inside the locks and pushes into his house.

Jen is waiting for him just inside the door as he enters. She tells him the code to the alarm - which is the year of their wedding anniversary - and enters it into the pin pad before the sixty seconds run out. As Jen shows him the new window locks and tells him about her day, Peter listens, kind of, while trying to figure out if there's a subliminal message in Jen's using of their wedding anniversary year for the alarm code. She knows that remembering dates is not his strength, and he wonders if she has done it on purpose to test him.

Their therapist back in Maine used to lecture them about not trying to one-up the other. They're always playing games back and forth, as if trying to test their love for one another, and now Peter knows just what their therapist had been talking about. Everything's a competition and sometimes it seems as if they're fighting against one another as opposed to working with each other. This is the first time he's realizing that.

Peter hears Jen talk to him, but he doesn't listen to much of what she says. Her lips are moving and Peter nods every few seconds to give the appearance that he's listening, but he's an awful actor. She can see right through him and calls him out on it.

"Are you even listening to me, Peter?" she says.

"Huh?"

Jen shakes her head at him in disappointment or disgust - Peter's not sure which one, not that it matters.

"That's what I thought."

Peter snaps back to reality and quickly realizes that he has fallen back into the old habits that their therapist had warned him of, and he quickly changes the subject before it starts an argument. He almost forgot about the bouquet in his hand and uses it as a distraction. He lifts the flowers in front of his chest and pushes them in the direction of his wife. "These are for you," he says.

Jen looks at the rainbow of hydrangeas in front of her, but holds out for a while before taking them. "What are these for?"

"I picked some up on the way home for you. I thought you might like them."

Peter can tell that Jen is studying him for a lie, but he knows that she won't be able to find one. She shifts her eyes back to the hydrangeas and almost starts to cry. Peter thinks that he knows what she's thinking. The vibrant purples, blues, and yellows must remind her of home. She had carried two dozen just like these when she walked down the aisle almost nine years ago. Peter can't remember another woman ever looking as beautiful as she did that day. She must be reminiscing about it.

Jen takes the bouquet from her husband and buries her face in the purple floret that sits high above the others. She closes her eyes and leans her head back - an obvious sign that she loves the scent of them. It reminds Peter of the time that she had told him all about her mother shortly after they first met. She was glowing when she told him about the two of them walking through the garden, just talking. Peter always wishes that he could have met the woman, at the very least to thank her for bringing Jen into this world.

"What's wrong?" Peter asks as his wife begins to cry softly.

Jen wipes a tear from her cheek and buries her face into Peter's upper body. The smell of her pomegranate shampoo reminds him of old times. He wraps his arms around his wife and they hold an embrace for a while.

"Thank you, they're beautiful," Jen eventually says.

She pulls away from their rare moment of romance and carries the flowers into the kitchen. She cuts the stems diagonally and adds some of the nutrients that came with the bouquet into the vase. Peter sits on one of the barstools at the island and Jen tells him more about what she has found during the day.

Peter doesn't contribute much to the conversation, but he actually listens this time, like for real. Jen is animated when she tells him everything, so he decides just to listen and to not try to tear her down. He's skeptical of much of what Jen tells him, and in his mind there are easy explanations for everything. He probably just didn't close the closet all the way this morning, she must have just forgotten to lock the front door and set the alarm during the hectic rush, one of them must have bumped into the nightstand, and the scuff mark on the patch on the wall was most likely already there. The statue, however, even he agrees that is interesting.

Upstairs, Jen shows Peter the statue. He picks it up and studies it. Like Jen, he finds nothing that makes it look anything remotely familiar. The eyes, or lack thereof, are especially eerie. It's like something is missing, like its eyeballs have been removed or intentionally left out. Peter wonders if it's trying to say something, like there's something about it that one cannot see or that there's more to it than meets the eye. Something like that. Or maybe it's just a coincidence; maybe it's just a strange statue with missing eyes.

TOGETHER, PETER AND JEN make and eat a quick supper then head out into the city to get some supplies. Peter doesn't fight Jen's desire for plum or pistachio paint, and he thinks that he may actually secretly enjoy it. Either color would be easy on the eyes, at least. The salesman at the home improvement store hooks them up with the tools that they need to patch the drywall, and they head back home with detailed instructions on how to do so.

It's close to 8:00 P.M. by the time they return home. Peter encourages Jen to finish editing her column and sending it off to her editor tonight so that she doesn't have to worry about it tomorrow, and she actually takes his advice. Peter is going to take the day off tomorrow so that they can get the wall patched and the room painted, so he stays up late watching mindless made-for-TV horror films. Halloween is approaching, so it's that time of year where the networks binge on blood and gore before the holidays arrive.

Peter climbs into bed shortly after midnight, the blankets nice and warm, and he curls up into his wife. He pulls her in close and caresses her shoulders. He whispers in her ear to try and wake her, but she stays asleep. He snuggles in closer, his growing bulge making his presence known, and tries again, but she still doesn't move. With one last effort, he lightly kisses the back of her neck and shoulder with his moist lips, but it's all for naught. It's been so long that he can't even remember the last time, and he's gotten used to the rejection. It doesn't really even bother his psyche anymore. He had thought that bringing her flowers and holding her hand in public would be enough to garner him with some type of reward, but he sees now that that's not the case. He feels foolish for thinking that it actually might. Eventually he gives up, turns over, and falls asleep, just like he's done on numerous other occasions.

CHAPTER TWENTY

Marco and Antonio head back over to the Stoneham house - which they now know is owned by the Winston's - after closing time at the pizzeria, and they take sleep rotations like they did the previous evening. Sal had liked what Antonio had to say earlier, Marco too, and they think that his plan might work. There's nothing they can do for now though, so they wait. Marco's getting used to that. He parks out at the end of the street again, ensuring that they're close enough so that he can keep an eye on the house. Once Peter Winston leaves for work in the morning, they'll make their move.

Marco wakes Antonio at 6:30 A.M. so that they can go over the details again. Peter left the house around this time yesterday, a little after, so Marco expects for him to do the same today. Seven o'clock comes and goes, and soon eight does as well with no sign of Peter or Jen. Marco takes a drive around the block and creeps past the house at 8:15 to try to get a look inside, but he can see nothing. He feels defeated. He considers the scenarios and sees nothing playing out the way they had planned, so he decides it's best if they just back out for now. Something is wrong, and they can't risk being seen, so they take the news back into the city and head for Sal's. The goods are due to Willy tomorrow, so they may have to do this in the dark tonight. Nobody wants to do that again, not with both Peter and Jen in the house, but time is running short, so they may have no choice.

THE SUN CREEPING IN through the pulled shades wakes Peter, and it's the first time that he's awoken in the light in weeks. He's not completely sure what time Jen gets up in the morning or what exactly it is that she does during the day, as he's never really asked. He fears that he may start to resent her if he finds out that she may not be pulling her weight, so it's best if he doesn't know. He works long and stressful hours and he's not so sure that Jen puts in the same kind of effort that he does. He pushes the thought out of his mind and moves on. He doesn't want to think about that today, not after the nice time they had last evening.

Jen wakes not long after Peter and joins him for coffee downstairs. After they eat breakfast, they patch the wall upstairs before they can paint. It will take a few hours for the patch to dry enough to be painted, so they decide to do something with that statue. The lack of any trace of anything similar to it online is puzzling, so they think that showing it to an expert might be the best way to find out what it is. It might be the only way.

They prepare themselves for the day and head out the front door together. Jen sets the alarm, engages both locks, and double checks them both before joining her husband at the bottom of the concrete stairs. They make their way toward the driveway and approach Peter's Audi, holding hands. They're interrupted before they can make it inside.

"Excuse me," a woman's voice yells out to them from behind.

Peter and Jen turn simultaneously and look in the direction of the voice. The woman is older. She's not elderly, but she's at retirement age at the very least. A small ankle bitter is at her feet, studying intently but not yet barking. Peter can tell that it's considering it, though.

"Can we help you?" Peter asks.

The old woman approaches and eventually makes her way toward them, then stops when she gets close. "Hi, I don't mean to intrude, but my name is Betty and I live a couple doors down." Betty points over her shoulder at the dull house two lots away from their own. "You're new in the neighborhood, aren't you?"

"Yes actually, we moved in earlier this week," Peter says. "I'm Peter Winston and this is my wife Jen." Peter holds out his hand and Betty takes it. Jen does the same when they finish.

"I don't want to be a bother," Betty offers, "but I just thought I should tell you something. It could be nothing, but it seems a bit out of the ordinary."

Peter looks at Jen curiously, then he turns back to face Betty. He says, "What is it?"

"It's just that I've seen a vehicle that's been driving through the neighborhood at the wee early morning hours the past couple of nights, and it seems to be slowing down when it gets in front of your house. I saw that the police have been by here and I see that you have a security system now, so I just wondered to myself if it might have something to do with all this. I'm sorry, I don't mean to-"

"It's okay. What kind of car was it?" Peter says.

"It was dark out both times I saw it, so I didn't get a good look. You see, I get up early with Trixie here," Betty says, referring to the dog, "so I see a lot of things that go on around here. Some of the other neighbors around call me Betty the Watchdog." Betty smiles and chuckles softly to herself.

To Peter, it's obvious that Betty enjoys the title and the responsibility. He's not used to having neighbors and isn't sure if it's common practice or not, but he finds the whole concept a little curious, especially considering that they don't have any children. Trixie the dog sits in front of her owner and waits patiently.

"It's silly," Betty continues, "but it's kind of true I suppose. When everyone is at work, I keep a lookout."

Peter nods. He pauses for a moment, considering this, before getting the conversation back on track. "About that car, did you see anything?"

"Oh for heaven's sake, I'm rambling. I wasn't able to see it clearly, but it looked like one of those new fancy ones."

"Was it a car or an SUV? Maybe a truck?"

"It was a car, black I remember now. Oh, and there's one more thing too."

"What's that?"

"There was one of those baseball stickers on the back window."

"No offense, but how could you tell there was a sticker on the back window, but you couldn't tell what kind of car it was?"

"It was here this morning when the sun came up, if you must know, and I saw the sticker as the car was pulling away."

"What kind of sticker was it?"

Betty smiles playfully. "We're just outside of Boston, what do you think it was?"

"THAT WAS STRANGE," JEN says to Peter as they climb into his Audi.

Peter watches Betty and Trixie in the mirror as they walk in the opposite direction and back toward their own property.

"Do you believe her?"

"I'm not sure yet," Peter admits. "She seemed a little bit senile to me, don't you think?"

"Maybe. I think she's telling the truth though."

"Yeah, well, I'm not sure what to believe."

Peter drives toward the city in search of an antique shop that may be able to help with their mystery find. The statue is in Jen's handbag that she holds close to her chest. It's like she's cradling a newborn. The handbag isn't fancy or expensive, and she'd really rather not have one at all.

But sometimes a lady needs extra space, as Peter had convinced her one time, and wearing a fanny pack is not going to happen. So a handbag it is.

In the city, they find a couple of shops within a few miles of one another, but neither one has any clue what the statue is. The news is discouraging and it does nothing except for further heighten the mystery of its origin. On their way back home, Peter finds and stops off at a pizza joint to grab a quick bite. It's a place that Peter has heard about from some of his buddies at the office, and the reviews are excellent. The lot is nearly full for the lunch hour, but Peter does find an open spot in the corner. The shop's location is just outside one of the many stops on the commuter rail, so it's perfect for the business people who have an hour to kill for lunch. Big Sal's Pizzeria it's called, and it's owned by some local Italian family, or so Peter has heard.

The line is long and the tables are full, but Peter and Jen decide to wait anyway. He's starving. Three men are behind the counter and running around like crazy, all of whom are wearing black t-shirts that are covered in flour from the pizza dough. The line eventually dies down and Peter and Jen make their way to the front of it.

The man behind the counter says, "Welcome to Big Sal's Pizzeria, I'm Big Sal. What can I get for you today?"

Big Sal is big alright. He's average height and grossly overweight, but he's very pleasant. Small beads of sweat cover his forehead and his belly is stretching out that t-shirt more than it should. His energy is infectious though, and Peter can't help but smile at him. Peter orders a couple of slices for him and one for Jen while she grabs an empty table in the corner next to a window.

It's not long before one of the other guys that had been behind the counter with Big Sal brings over their order, plus a couple of glasses of ice water. The waiter is young, probably no older than early twenties, but his energy level is far less than that of overweight Sal. His lack of enthusiasm for being here is obvious, and Peter recognizes it as a generational thing. Most people of similar age that

Peter has run into have the same type of motivation: none. They want to make money without working hard, as opposed to the other way around, like it should be. Quite honestly, it pisses Peter off, as he's worked his ass off to get where he is. That's one of the reasons why he doesn't hire many people who are under thirty. He finds it difficult to get past his stereotype in that respect. The waiter stops in his tracks when he sees Peter and slowly approaches the table with the pizza - Peter can smell the bacon, and his mouth starts to water. The waiter tries to avoid Peter's eyes without it seeming obvious, but Peter notices.

"Hey, you look familiar," Peter says. "Do I know you from somewhere?"

The young waiter reluctantly looks up and offers a weak smile. "I don't think so. Have you been in here before?"

"No, we haven't. We just moved into town recently actually."

"Oh, where to?"

"We live out in Stoneham."

The waiter nods anxiously. "Well, welcome to the neighborhood." He turns and leaves before Peter can say anything further.

Peter turns to his wife and says, "Do you recognize him?"

Jen shakes her head. "I don't think so. Should I?"

"I don't know, I just feel like I've seen him before. It's those eyes. I swear I've seen them somewhere."

ANTONIO KEEPS HIS HEAD down and walks quickly back around the counter before the guests figure out who he is. The line has died down quite a bit and Sal seems to be handling it okay, so he grabs Marco and sneaks into the kitchen in the back. His heart is pounding.

"What's wrong?" Marco asks.

Antonio is frantic. "I think it's them."

"What are you talking about? Who's them?"

"The people who live in the Stoneham house, the Winston's. I think they're here."

"No way, it's probably someone that looks like them."

"I swear, man, it's them. The guy asked me if we've met before. I think he recognized me."

Marco's eyes widen. "Where are they?"

"Over in the corner by the window. Go look for yourself if you don't believe me."

Marco does just that. He disappears out into the front while Antonio paces around in a small circle. A moment later, Marco returns.

"I don't know if it's them or not," Marco says. "I can't tell. Let's just wait and see what happens."

"What if they realize it's us? We're dead."

"Relax, Antonio. They won't recognize us, we had our masks on. They didn't see our faces."

THE SAME WAITER COMES back over to the table and drops off the bill for Peter for when he and Jen are ready. They finish their pizza and down the waters before rising from their seats. They agree that the pizza is just as good as advertised and that they'll definitely be back when they're in the area again. They walk over to the counter and Peter hands Big Sal his credit card. Their waiter and the other guy that had been behind the counter when they entered are nowhere to be seen.

"How was everything?" Sal asks, still sweating.

"Excellent, thank you," Peter says.

Sal smiles at them and swipes the credit card.

While waiting for the card to be processed, Jen says to Peter, "What do you think we should try then? If no antique store knows what it is, what are we going to do with it?"

"I have no idea. I really don't," Peter says.

"Looking to sell something?" Sal interjects.

"Maybe," Peter says, now looking at Sal, "you know someone?"

"I've got a good buddy who runs a pawn shop just a few blocks from here actually. He's been in business forever. He might be able to help you with whatever it is that you've got."

Peter looks at Jen and shrugs. "Why not? It's worth a shot. I hadn't considered a pawn shop."

Sal writes down the address to the pawn shop - Willy's Pawn it's called - and hands it to Peter. The credit card machine beeps, so Sal looks down to finalize the transaction. He seems to pause when he does, and Peter wonders if something is wrong. But before Peter can ask about it, Sal hands him back his card, along with a receipt.

"Here you go Mr. Winston," Big Sal says, his voice now sounding dry. "Thank you for coming. Maybe we'll see you again." Then he smiles.

Peter thanks Sal, then he and Jen leave the restaurant. Outside, Peter unlocks his Audi from a distance and makes his way toward it. Jen stops in her tracks in the middle of the parking lot once they approach.

"What's the matter?" Peter asks.

Jen points to a black sedan that rests in the spot next to Peter's Audi. "Look."

Peter steps toward where Jen points and takes a peek. All he sees is an ordinary, rusty, black sedan. "What am I looking at?"

"Look at the back. There's a Red Sox window sticker in the corner. It's a black Cadillac, which is fancy, and it has a baseball sticker. It's just like that old lady described."

Peter sees the vehicle in front of him but is still skeptical. There's nothing fancy about this Cadillac, besides its brand. It may have been nice fifteen years ago, but not any longer. "There has got to be a million black sedans that have the same sticker on it in this city. It's probably just a coincidence."

"So you don't believe her then?"

"Who? Betty?"

"Yeah."

Peter shrugs. "I still don't know what to think. She was pretty bizarre, if you ask me."

He walks over to his Audi and climbs inside. In the mirror, he watches as Jen pulls out her phone - to snap a picture of the back of the black Cadillac, perhaps, for some unknown reason - then she joins him.

AS SOON AS THE Winston's leave the restaurant, Sal bolts into the kitchen and calls out for Marco and Antonio. They're already waiting for him by the time he gets into the back.

"Uncle Sal," Marco begins with a hint of urgency in his voice, "there's something we need to tell you."

"The Winston's, they were just here," Sal says, ignoring Marco. He's suddenly out of breath. He's been that way since he saw Peter Winston's name on the credit card just a moment ago.

Antonio looks at Marco and says, sounding like a teenage girl, "See, I told you it was them."

"Go get me the phone," Sal demands. "I need to call Willy."

CHAPTER TWENTY-ONE

Antonio disappears around the corner and returns moments later with the cordless landline. He hands it to Sal, who quickly dials the number that he knows like the back of his hand.

Willy picks up on one of the first couple of rings. "Willy's Pawn."

"Willy, it's Sal."

"Big Sal, how are you? I was going to give you a call this afternoon to make sure that we're still on for tomorrow. Will I be seeing you tomorrow? Please say yes."

"I don't know yet, but that's not what I'm calling about."

"What do you mean you're not sure yet? My buyer threatened my life if I don't have the item in my hands when he returns on Friday."

"Don't worry about that, okay? I'll talk to the guy myself if I need to. We'll figure that all out later. I need a favor from you."

"I've heard that before."

Sal pauses, not sure of Willy's tone and if he likes it or not. No, he definitely doesn't like it, but he tries to ignore it. "There are two people coming your way, a man and a woman, I need you to tell me what they're trying to sell."

"A man and a woman? I'm going to need more than that, Sal."

Sal goes on to give Willy a description of Peter and Jen Winston and he tells him their names on more than one occasion. "Peter and Jennifer Winston, can you remember that?"

"I've got it, Sal."

"Okay, good. So when they leave, give me a call and tell me what they wanted. Can you do that?"

"Why are these people so important to you?"

"The less you know the better."

"This doesn't have anything to do with tomorrow, does it?"

"Again, the less you know. I wouldn't ask questions if you don't want to know the answers."

"Fine. I just hope that you know what you're doing."

"Don't worry about it. Just remember-"

"Yeah, yeah, I know. I'll call you."

PETER INPUTS THE ADDRESS of the pawn shop into his GPS and heads in that direction. Jen is fidgety in the seat next to him, which is something that she always does subconsciously when in deep thought. Undoubtedly, she is coming up with some sort of whacky theory about that car with the sticker in the parking lot and its possible connection to what the old lady saw. When she gets something in her mind she won't let it go until she finds out whatever it is she needs to find out about it, and that's one of the many reasons why Peter fell head over heels for her long ago.

Peter and Jen met for the first time nearly ten years ago. Peter was a few years out of college at the time and was bouncing around different places trying to find where he fit. He wound up in the woods of Maine after he accepted a job with a land surveying company. At the time, he had no specific career in mind and was willing to take just about anything that paid enough. He only lasted there a few months, but the experience was more than worth it. He wound up meeting Jen while she was a summer camp director during the summer between her junior and senior years at the University of Maine. Peter was sent out with his boss to do some property measurements at the camp for city taxes, and he fell hard for Jen.

He would to sneak into the camp during the night and meet up with Jen, and he would be sure to leave before the sun came up so that they wouldn't get caught. It's not that she wasn't allowed to have visitors, because she was, it's just that if they knew what they were doing with the kids around, Peter probably wouldn't be allowed back.

They both had thought it was just going to be a summer fling, and initially it was, but when Peter accepted a new job in traveling sales, he once again found himself up north. They got together for lunch one day during a week-long sales training meeting that Peter had on the seacoast, and they picked up right where they left off. They stayed together for good this time, and when Jen graduated in the spring, Peter switched jobs again to be with her. They got married the following summer, and the rest is history. Now, eight years later, they're just like every other married couple, and they find themselves drifting apart more every day.

WILLY'S PAWN IS SLOW on this Thursday afternoon, so it shouldn't be hard for Willy to pick out the man and woman that he's expecting. Sal had seemed almost frantic on the phone, and it worries Willy. He fears that the stress may finally be getting to him and that he may not be able to meet the deadline. If the buyer comes back tomorrow and Willy still doesn't have the artifact, he's a dead man. That much has been made clear. He hopes that Sal was serious about saying that he'd talk to the guy himself, because if he doesn't, everyone is screwed. Willy just hopes that Sal understands what's at stake for him here.

The door in the front chimes and Willy looks in its direction. Inside walk a man and a woman that seem to match the description that Sal had given him earlier, but he needs to find out for certain.

"Hi there folks," Willy says, then he waits for a response.

The woman smiles and waves in his direction, and the man gives him a subtle nod. They casually stroll along the perimeter of the shop and admire some of the goods in the glass cabinets. They stop occasionally and point inside a case and chat quietly amongst themselves. Willy knows a browser when he sees one, and he can tell by the way that they're walking that they have no intention of buying anything today. He suspects that these are the Winston's.

The browsers slowly make their way along the wall and eventually arrive to where Willy is standing on the opposite side of the counter. Willy leans his weight on one leg and waits for one of them to initiate the conversation. The man looks up first.

"How's it going?" the man says.

Willy nods. "Good, you? Can I help you with something?"

The man looks to the woman that's with him - his wife, presumably - and motions to her handbag. "Maybe."

She looks down and digs around for something inside her bag.

"I'm Willy by the way," Willy says as he holds out his hand.

"Hi, Willy. I'm Peter, this is my wife Jen." Peter takes Willy's hand and shakes it.

Jen fetches the statue from her purse and hands it to Peter, who places it on the counter with both hands.

It was an easy trick - getting their names like that - and once again, Willy's instincts are right. "What is this?" he says.

"That's kind of what we were hoping you could tell us," Peter says.

Willy picks up the statue and studies it. He subtly shakes his head as he turns it over, recognizing it. Peter and Jen seem to notice, as they look at each other and shrug.

"What are you looking to do with this? Pawn, sell, or trade?"

"We're not really sure," Peter begins. "We just kind of want to find out what it is and see what our options are. We might be interested in selling it."

"Where did you get this?"

Peter looks to Jen, and she steps forward. "We just moved into town, and we found it while cleaning out the house," she says.

Willy nods but doesn't say anything. He suspects that's not the entire truth.

"So, do you know what it is?" Peter asks.

"Yes, actually," Willy says. "I do. I've seen one or two of these over the years. Not one like this exactly, it's been altered, but I have a pretty good idea of what it is."

"And?"

"It's an ancient Chinese warrior replica statue. It has some philosophical significance to Chinese historians. Some of these have sold for upwards of $25,000 at auction, so they can be pretty valuable."

Jen snaps her head at Peter and smiles at this news. Peter smiles back, then turns to face Willy.

"What about this one?" Peter says. "How much is this worth?"

"Unfortunately, almost nothing. Like I said, it's been altered. I'm sure you noticed, it's hard to miss, but the eyes have been removed. Either someone never finished carving it, or more likely, someone chipped out the eyes."

"Why would someone do that?" Jen asks.

"Difficult to say."

"Is it worth anything then?" Jen says, sounding discouraged.

Willy shakes his head. "Not really. I can probably sell it to someone as a paperweight or something. I'll give you five bucks for it. That's my best and final offer."

Peter looks to Jen and frowns. He reaches across the counter and pulls the warrior statue back toward him.

Once in hand, he hands it to Jen, who jams it back into her purse, surely less delicately than she had earlier.

"We'll just hang on to it if that's all it is then," Peter says. "Thanks anyway." He and Willy shake hands, then he leads Jen out of the shop.

Willy waits until they disappear into the parking lot before calling Sal.

SAL AND MARCO WAIT next to the phone in the kitchen while Antonio tends to the front. It's been thirty minutes since Sal had initially spoken with Sal, and he's expecting a return call from him at any moment. He taps his foot repeatedly, like it's an uncontrollable nervous tic.

"What should we do, Uncle Sal?" Marco asks. "Should me and Antonio head over to the house now since we know that they're gone? It'll give us some time to poke around at least."

"Not yet, let's wait until Willy calls back."

"But we're wasting time! Now could be our chance."

Sal holds out a hand in an effort to calm his rowdy nephew. "Not yet, Marco. Let's stick to Antonio's plan. We don't even know what they're doing there yet. Just relax."

Marco throws his hands on his head and starts to pace. "I don't know about this, I still say we're-"

The phone rings, cutting Marco off.

"Shut up. Hand me that," Sal says, pointing to the ringing phone.

Marco grabs the cordless phone and hands it to Sal.

Sal answers it, "Willy, talk to me."

"They just left," Willy says.

"What happened? What did they have?"

Willy describes to Sal in detail the Chinese warrior statue that they brought in. He tells Sal that it was altered and practically worthless and that they just decided to keep it. Sal thanks his friend for the information and promises to be in touch soon about tomorrow. He disconnects the call and lets it all sink in for a while.

"So?" Marco says, anxiously, with his arms spread wide.

Sal puts the phone down on the counter and slowly looks up to his nephew. "They found it."

"That's good, right? Saves us the trouble then."

"No, they still have it."

"What? Willy couldn't make a deal?"

"It's not that."

"What do you mean? I'm not following."

"The eyes are missing."

Marco pauses. "Uh oh."

"Yeah, uh oh."

"What the hell are we going to do?"

"There's only one thing we can do. We need to get in that house, and it needs to happen tonight."

"But what about the plan? Be patient, you said."

"The hell with the plan. There's no time for that anymore. Grab Antonio and head over there now. I don't care what you have to do or how you do it, just get your asses in that house and figure out what the hell is going on. Everything we've discussed in the past is thrown out the window. Do what you have to do. And bring your guns. We need those eyes, and we need them by morning."

CHAPTER TWENTY-TWO

Peter and Jen leave Willy's Pawn with the warrior statue in hand and no extra money in their pockets. Although Jen is disappointed that it's practically worthless, at least knowing its origin is some positive news. But she's not ready to give up that easily. She's still convinced that there's more to it than Willy at the pawn shop had said.

A while later, Peter pulls into their driveway in Stoneham amidst the sunshine and kills the engine. He and Jen get out of the car and start walking in different directions.

"Where are you going?" Peter yells to her as he heads for the front door, probably just now realizing that she isn't following him.

"I'm going to talk to Betty some more, I have a few more questions."

Peter looks away. Jen knows that he's rolling his eyes, and she would slap him for it if she were close enough to him.

"I thought we were going to paint?" Peter says. "It should be dry enough to start now."

"You get started and I'll be right behind you. It'll only take a minute."

Peter reluctantly nods and heads inside. Jen makes her way across the yard and heads for Betty's, right into the direct path of the sun's rays. She's forced to shield her eyes.

Betty's front door is welcoming. It's not a cookie-cutter neighborhood, but it's close. The front steps are similar in height and style, and the front door might be identical to their own. There's a mat with puppy prints on it that asks Jen to wipe her paws, so she does just that while waiting for the already ringing doorbell to stop chiming. Moments later, Betty opens up and smiles at her.

"Hello, Jen. This is a pleasant surprise," Betty says as Trixie barks behind her.

"Hi, Betty. I'm sorry to bother you."

Betty waves her hands frantically. "No need, is everything alright, dear?"

"Yeah, everything is okay, I was just wondering...I'm sorry, do you mind if I come in?"

Betty bends down and picks up Trixie, then she pulls the door open fully. She stands to the side and allows Jen into her home. Jen walks in and takes in the orderly entrance way. There's a small dining room to the left, a long hallway straight ahead that branches off to a couple of closed doors on either side, and a carpeted staircase on the right. A well-positioned rectangular card table rests against the side of the staircase in the hallway, and a handmade knitted slip dangles from it. Photos, perfectly spaced out and all in identical golden frames, line the wall up the stairs. It reminds Jen a lot of what her mother's house used to be like. It feels very homey.

"Those are my grandchildren," Betty says as Jen admires the photos. "I have four of them, plus a great grandbaby on the way."

"Beautiful family," Jen says, noticing a photo at the top of the stairs where a much younger Betty is dancing with a man of about a similar age. Jen assumes that it was her husband, and she wonders what might have happened to him.

"Thank you, dear."

Jen stands awkwardly in her neighbor's house and tries to find the words to break the ice. She's not really even sure where to begin. "Do you have someplace we can sit? I have a couple of questions about what you were saying earlier, if you don't mind."

"Of course. Follow me."

Betty puts Trixie down and Jen followers her down the hallway. Trixie trails behind, trying to get a whiff of Jen up close, but no longer yapping. Jen is led to an eat-in kitchen at the end of the hall and sits in one of the chairs at the table. The kitchen is surprisingly updated for being that of a woman of Betty's age, and Jen is impressed.

Betty says, "What is it that you wanted to ask me?"

"About what you said earlier, about the car that you saw driving by."

"Yes, what about it?"

"Well, I was just wondering," Jen pauses as she fetches the phone from her hip pocket, "if it looked anything like this." She opens the photo that she took from the parking lot of the pizza joint and slides the phone across the table toward Betty. It's a photo of the entire backside of the black Cadillac that had been parked next to Peter, which encompasses both the license plate and the Red Sox window sticker.

Betty picks it up and studies it over the top of her glasses. "I don't know, dear. I'm not sure. Like I told you earlier, I didn't really get a good look at it." Betty puts the phone back on the table and pushes it toward Jen.

Jen leaves it there.

"What about the sticker? You said that you saw a sticker in the back window, didn't you?"

Betty picks up the phone again and takes another look. She shakes her head as she inspects it. "I suppose it was like this one here, yes." Betty hands the phone to Jen this time, who is forced to take it back. Betty looks into Jen's eyes and smiles. "You know, if there's something else you want to ask me, anything at all, please don't be afraid. I'll be happy to tell you everything I know. All you have to do is ask."

Jen sighs softly and smiles, feeling relieved that Betty was the one to say it. Then she proceeds to ask Betty all of the questions that she has on her mind.

OFFICER GERRY DALE RECEIVES a call from Jen Winston while at home, and he almost doesn't answer it. He's spoken to her enough in recent days. It's late afternoon and he only has a couple of hours left to himself before his next shift starts. Reluctantly, he does accept Mrs. Winston's call and is glad that he does, because she has something that's possibly useful for him. She doesn't share many details over the phone, which Gerry is actually pleased with, and he agrees to stop by the house in a few hours. These things are better to discuss in person, he finds. More information tends to be shared that way.

Later on, Gerry meets Jamaal at the station and they stop down in the basement to see forensics before heading over to the Winston's house. Gerry had put in for a rush in processing yesterday, and they came through for him. The results of the fingerprint dusting at the Winston residence are available, so it gives Gerry and Jamaal something to share when they arrive. It'll be a dual-purpose visit.

THE ENGINE OF MARCO'S Cadillac idles just enough to fill the cabin with warmth. The night is chilly, although not yet approaching freezing. Marco sits behind the wheel, chewing on the inside of his lip, and Antonio is next to him. They're just waiting again. They've spent a lot of time waiting over the past three days, and Marco's still not exactly sure what it is that they're waiting for. The right moment is unlikely to present itself, as there never really is the right moment for something like this. But it has to happen tonight either way, whether the opportunity presents itself or not.

The Winston's house is in view down the street, and it's mostly dark. One room downstairs is lit with a light on inside, and a single bulb over the front door outside does its best to brighten up the walkway. Once complete darkness sets in, Marco and Antonio will make their move. They can break a window or crack open the door with no problem if they're forced to, but the alarm system is an issue. Marco just hopes that Antonio's plan will work.

The nearest police station is fifteen minutes away with traffic. Considering the time to dispatch in combination with the less congested streets during the night, Marco figures that they have about seven minutes to get in, get the goods, get out, and disappear out of sight by the time the police arrive. It's nothing more than an educated guess with no basis of fact, but it makes sense to him.

Their best bet is to do this before the night gets too late. It's a Thursday night, so the streets will quiet down significantly after midnight. If this was a Friday or Saturday night it would be different, but it's not, so they need to do this before midnight if they want any chance of getting away. Before midnight means more vehicles on the streets, more vehicles mean more traffic, and more traffic means more time. Even seconds are big in a situation like this, never mind minutes, so they need to take advantage of all the help they can get. An extra thirty seconds could be the difference between Bartolo's freedom or a family reunion behind bars in Concord.

THE BEDROOM IS PAINTED and drying, and Peter and Jen wait downstairs for the officers to arrive. Jen had told Peter all about her conversation with Betty while they were painting, and she thinks that he finally may be coming around to her way of thinking. There are too many coincidences to ignore at this point, and she's hopeful that the officers can look into things a bit deeper.

Jen hears two car doors close outside, and she confirms that it's the expected guests through the bay window before unlocking and opening the door for them. Greeted with handshakes, she and Peter lead the officers down the hall and into the kitchen. Everyone sits around the table, even Officer Harris this time, and they wait for someone to make the first move. Officer Dale does.

"So, Mrs. Winston," he begins, "you said on the phone that you have some things that you'd like to discuss."

Jen looks to Peter, who nods to her in encouragement. She looks Officer Dale in the eyes and tells him everything: the unlocked front door, the unset alarm, the closet, the nightstand, the scuffed up patch, the warrior statue, Betty's warning about the car with the sticker, seeing a car matching that description at the pizza place, the trip to the pawn shop, and about the details of the second conversation she had with Betty.

Officer Dale just listens and doesn't interrupt while Officer Harris takes notes. When Jen is finished, everyone leans back in their seats and lets everything sink in. Jen looks between Officer Dale and Officer Harris and waits for a response. Neither one of them says anything or offers up any non-verbal cues initially, but Officer Dale does eventually chime in after a delay.

"Okay, is there anything else?" he says.

Jen looks to Peter again, and he shrugs.

"No, I don't think so," Jen says.

Officer Dale looks to his partner and nods. Officer Harris retrieves a small stack of folded papers from his inner pocket and hands it to Officer Dale. Officer Dale unfolds it and places on the tabletop.

"What is this?" Peter asks with a look of concern on his face, now sitting up straight in his chair.

"We got back the forensics report on the fingerprint dusting," Officer Dale says, "and the results are inconclusive."

"How can that be?" Jen asks, bewildered.

"There were a lot of partials found, but no fulls."

"Can you do anything with partials?" Peter asks.

"Not much, unfortunately."

After a brief pause, Jen says, "So what do we do from here then?"

"We can run the plate on that car you saw matching the description of the one that your neighbor mentioned seeing and go from there. It's probably a long shot, but we'll look into it."

Without hesitation, Jen gets up from her seat and walks over to the counter to retrieve her phone. She scrolls to the photo of the rear end of the Cadillac from the pizza place and hands it to Officer Harris, who jots down the details and offers his thanks. Jen walks back around the table and sits in the same chair that she had been in before.

"So that's it?" Jen says.

"For now, yes," Officer Dale begins. "We'll run the plate tonight and see what happens. You two just be on the lookout for anything unusual and give us a call if you see something. You have my number. We can do a drive-by every couple of hours if you'd like, just to make sure that everything is okay."

Jen loves the idea. "Would you? That would make me feel better. I'd really appreciate that."

"No problem."

The officers get up from their seats and let themselves out through the front door. Jen locks up and sets the alarm, then she and Peter head upstairs to bed. She has no indication if the officers believe what she had to say or not, but she supposes that's just them doing their job and not showing their hand.

Peter strips off his slacks and shirt and hops into bed. Jen peeks out the window before doing the same, minus the shirt - she keeps that on. She sees nothing outside. Just spooky darkness and some stars. Even the moon is nonexistent tonight. She slides in close to her husband and can feel the warmth of his skin on hers. She closes her eyes, feeling safe knowing that the house will be watched during the night while she sleeps.

CHAPTER TWENTY-THREE

Gerry zips his coat up to his neck to block out the cold as he and Jamaal make their way toward their squad car. Gerry gets in the driver's side, Jamaal the passenger's, and they close the doors. Gerry backs out into the street and heads toward the city.

"Are you buying what she's selling?" Jamaal asks, referring to Jen's detailed story.

"Some of it is out there, I admit that, but add everything up and I think she may be on to something. There are just too many coincidences to ignore. What do you think?"

"You know, all of that shit about the furniture being out of place and the front door being unlocked is hogwash. She's just paranoid. But everything that old lady said is interesting and might be something worth looking into."

"I agree."

"What do you want to do then?"

Gerry considers it for a moment. "There's not much we can do until morning. We'll drive by the house every couple of hours like I said and maybe we can catch up with that neighbor in the morning."

Jamaal nods. "This graveyard bullshit is really starting to piss me off. We can't get anything done at night."

"Tell me about it. Seven more weeks."

"I can't fucking wait."

MARCO AND ANTONIO STAY low as a police car drives right past them. With the lights off they blend right into the night in Marco's Cadillac, but they can't be too careful. It's not as if they're doing anything illegal at the moment, but sitting in a parked car in the middle of the night in a residential area is a bit frowned upon in this part of town. When the police car passes by without stopping and makes a left and disappears out of site, Marco sits back up and exhales a little.

"What the hell was that about?" Antonio says, now sitting up too. "They were there for a while."

"I don't know. Kind of late too, huh? Strange time for a couple of cops to be visiting."

"I don't like this, Marco. I don't like this one bit."

"I know, I know. Just relax, we're doing nothing wrong."

"I'm not sure they'll see it that way. What are we going to do?"

"I say we wait here for a while and see if they come back or not."

"And what if they do?"

Marco turns, faces his friend, and shrugs. "Let's hope they don't."

Within fifteen minutes all of the lights are killed inside of the Winston's house and the entire street is dark. Marco glances at the clock and notes the time. There are two and a half hours remaining until midnight, so they'll make their move in two. Marco leans back in his seat and rests his head against it. He thinks about his father.

Marco remembers the day that his father was arrested like it was yesterday. It was the day after Christmas, a Monday, and the family was having a Christmas hangover. His mom had made a big Italian breakfast as she always did the day after, and the entire family was there. How the tradition started, Marco doesn't remember, but it used to be one of his favorite days of the year. Aunts, uncles, cousins, and even a couple of close family friends made the trip from out of town.

It snowed three days prior, so the front yard was covered with a thin layer of the white stuff and a small snowbank was piled up on the right side of the driveway. Cars and trucks lined the street up and down, and people were arriving all throughout the morning. Marco's mom had the dining room table set festively and she had left all of the food out on the countertops for people to serve themselves like they were at a buffet. Sal had helped Marco's mom cook that day, and they found time to eat a bit themselves while the sausages were sizzling on the stovetop. The house smelt great and everyone was having a great time laughing and reminiscing about their favorite family stories. Holiday music blared from the surround sound. It was a great time.

Until the police knocked on the door and ruined everything.

There was a group of them. When Sal opened up they blasted through the front door, nearly knocking it right off its hinges. The cops ran into the dining room and found Bartolo, then slammed his face against the table, sending food flying, while slapping the cuffs on him. Marco had thought they were too aggressive in their force used against his father, especially considering that he wasn't even putting up any resistance. People were screaming and crying everywhere, and it all happened so fast. The cops wouldn't say what Bartolo was being arrested for or where they were taking him, so Sal hopped in his Lexus and followed the squad cars downtown. Marco went with him.

When Sal and Marco got there, someone finally told them what Bartolo was being charged with and that he would have to wait until the following day to be seen by a judge. A big crowd gathered at the courthouse at 9:00 A.M. for the hearing the next day, and when the judge denied bail, everything started to unravel. Marco's mom left shortly thereafter and things have never been the same since. Marco has accepted that his parents won't ever be getting back together, but he still shuns his mother for leaving the way that she did. When Bartolo needed her the most, she broke down and fell apart, leaving Marco to try to keep everything together until his dad got out.

Marco was young and juvenile at the time - and he still is in many ways - but he tried his best. The house was just too big for him to maintain and pay for by himself, and he quickly got overwhelmed by his parents' debt. He had nowhere to turn. Sal had tried to help some, but all it really did was delay the inevitable. Marco tried his best but failed to stay in the house for more than a few months. The bank took control of it and sold off his father's assets, but it wasn't enough. The house went to foreclosure and is now gone forever, and Marco hopes that his father can forgive him for that one day.

MARCO LOOKS DOWN THE street at his father's old house - the one that was taken away from him unjustifiably, in his mind - and remembers playing on the front lawn as a youngster. He remembers himself and Antonio playing football against his dad and uncle on Thanksgiving, and he remembers his mother and father teaching him how to ride a bike on these very streets. Marco looks next to him and sees his best friend nervously waiting in the seat, and he hates that things have gotten to be like this. He can't believe it's all gotten this out of hand.

Marco knows that the Winston's are sleeping in the same room that his parents used to sleep in, the same room that he was conceived in, and he's bitter about it. The more time he and Antonio spend in this neighborhood, the more memories resurface. They're memories of times that he can't get back, and they're memories that will never go away. And the longer this all takes, the longer it will be before he can start to move on with his life and create new memories.

None of this is the Winston's fault, he realizes, and they are simply the victims of being in the wrong place at the wrong time, just as Sal had pointed out. He hopes that they too can forgive him someday - like his father - and understand that this isn't personal. His greatest fear is that someone gets hurt who shouldn't, someone innocent, someone just like him and his family. But the longer this takes, the greater the chance is that someone does get hurt. Despite his reservations, though, he will do what has to be done. His life and the lives of his family are on the line here. If Peter or Jen Winston stand in the way of that, they may force his hand. Marco bets that they'd do the same thing if the tables were turned. Anyone would.

IT'S BEEN AN HOUR and a half since Gerry and Jamaal left the Winston's house. They're back in the neighborhood now and making the rounds, as promised. They had a domestic disturbance to respond to shortly after they left, so Jamaal is just on the phone with dispatch now. The dispatcher is running the plate that Mrs. Winston had taken the photo of earlier in the day, and they're expecting results shortly. Once Jamaal receives them, he thanks the dispatcher and hangs up. Then he turns to his partner.

"We've got a hit on that plate," he says.

"What do you got?"

"The vehicle is registered to a Marco Salazar of Boston. Do you know him?"

Gerry thinks about for a long second, then says, "The first name doesn't ring a bell, but the last name is familiar. Does he have a record?"

"Checking now."

Gerry slows the car down as they pass the Winston's house and he scans the property for any sign of anything out of the ordinary. He sees nothing, so he continues down the street.

"No record," Jamaal says, "but his father does."

"Who's his father?"

"Bartolo Salazar, formerly of Stoneham, current living at 965 Elm Street in Concord."

Gerry turns to Jamaal, surprised to have heard him say that. "Isn't that the correctional facility?"

"Yep, it is."

"What's he in for?"

"Homicide in the second degree. He's still awaiting trial later this year."

"Heavy charge. Where did he live in Stoneham before he was incarcerated?"

"Twenty-two West Lane."

Gerry slams hard on the brakes and stops the car in its tracks. The brakes squeal as the tires burn rubber onto the pavement beneath. The force of the sudden stop jolts Jamaal toward the dashboard, but the seatbelt keeps him from smashing against it.

"What did you just say?" Gerry asks.

"About what? What the hell is the matter with you?" Jamaal says, rattled.

"The address. What was it?"

"Twenty-two West Lane in Stoneham. Why?"

"Jesus Christ, Jamaal." Gerry shifts the transmission into reverse and moves the car backward until it's adjacent to the Winston's mailbox. He shines his flashlight out Jamaal's window at the double twos that are on the side of the mailbox. The numbers reflect when the light hits them, and Jamaal slowly turns to Gerry once they do.

"What street are we on?" Jamaal asks.

"West Lane."

MARCO AND ANTONIO SHRINK in their seats again as a police car makes its way down the street. It's impossible to tell if it's the same car as before, but Marco assumes that to be the case. The car screeches to a halt suddenly in the middle of the street, then moves backward and stops when it's across from the Winston's house. A dim light shines into the yard, as if the officers have spotted something, perhaps something nocturnal that doesn't belong. The car sits there for another moment before pulling up the street and turning around, then it stops permanently when it's on the side of the road, again across from the Winston's house. The headlights fade out, leaving only some interior illumination that Marco can barely even see.

"It looks like they're staying," Antonio says.

"Yeah, but why?"

Antonio shakes his head and says nothing. Marco turns off the headlights before starting up the car, then he re-buckles his seatbelt before pulling into the street.

"What are you doing?" Antonio asks.

"We can't stay here, not like this."

"But, what-"

"I know, Antonio. I don't know what we're going to do, but there's no chance we're getting in there tonight. Not with these cops hanging around. We have to go tell Big Sal, maybe he can work something out with Willy."

"You're probably right."

"I'm definitely right," Marco says. "It would be suicide to even try. We need a new plan."

CHAPTER TWENTY-FOUR

Gerry and Jamaal spend the night parked on the street across from the Winston's. Because of a lucky break, which is what happens most of the time, Gerry finds, Marco Salazar is now the main suspect for the home invasion that had occurred a few nights ago. But he and Jamaal don't have anything concrete on him right now, just suspicion, so that doesn't mean much at this point. They merely just want to talk to him. They'll confirm the Winston's neighbor's story in the morning, but until then, all they have is a theory.

The Winston's had said that there were two people in the house that night, and they were both certain of that. That means that Marco wasn't working alone, so who was with him? Nothing was taken from the house, no one was hurt, and there was no evidence of a break in. What were they even doing inside the house and how did they get in?

All of the information that Gerry and Jamaal have right now is that a vehicle matching the description of the one that Mrs. Winston saw at the pizzeria was seen driving around the neighborhood in recent days. It hasn't been confirmed that it was even the same vehicle yet, as it was just one matching the description. Gerry did some research and has been able to confirm that Marco did indeed reside in the house during the time that his father - Bartolo Salazar, the accused murderer - owned it, but he's not sure how much that really helps. Could it have been that Marco was just driving by to see how the house looked one night while he was out? It's possible, but the ironic timing and circumstances surrounding the whole situation makes Gerry think otherwise. Someone who used to live in the house is seen in the neighborhood the night it was broken into is just too coincidental to be ignored.

Marco Salazar had something to do with the invasion, or he knows who does at the very least, they just have no proof yet. Gerry is convinced of that. Considering the lack of evidence of a break in and the commentary from the locksmith, it seems plausible that Marco still had a key and was able to let himself in. That coincides with what the locksmith had said in terms of him finding no trace of damage within the locking mechanism itself.

Marco Salazar and an unknown accomplice let themselves into the Winston's house during the night using a key that Marco had kept from when he used to live there. They went upstairs into the bedroom where the Winston's were sleeping, looking for something, and panicked when they woke up.

What they were looking for, though, who knows? Mrs. Winston seems to think that someone was back inside the house a second time based on some strange happenings - which, in Gerry's opinion, are insignificant when looked at individually - that she discovered, but that can likely be traced back to paranoia. She's clearly a little bit unstable about it all - her having to stay inside the house all day, worrying, while her husband leaves for work. A lot of it is in her head now, and Gerry expects that she'll be calling with new discoveries in the coming days. He doesn't get the impression that Mrs. Winston is the type to give up very easily.

That statue that she keeps referring to, though, that's a mystery still. Based on what Mrs. Winston had described, the wall was fairly obviously patched at a prior time, which means that someone must have opened up the wall and put the statue inside, which does raise further questions. Someone must have put it there for a reason, more than likely the previous owner. Maybe it was Bartolo Salazar, or maybe it was Marco Salazar. It would make sense. Maybe Marco buried something inside the wall before the house was sold off, and now he's trying to get it back. That's what he was looking for that night.

That's the theory.

Gerry talks it out with Jamaal, and they agree that it's an avenue worth exploring further. Only one thing is known for sure at this point, and that's that two men were inside the house and were looking for something, but obviously didn't find it - they ran out of the house without grabbing anything, as far as the Winston's had seen. Maybe it was the statue inside the wall that they were after, or maybe it wasn't. All Gerry and Jamaal have at this point is a theory purely based on circumstantial evidence and far more questions than answers. Gerry's convinced that the answers will come, and maybe it'll be when they least expect it. He knows that they have the when and they're pretty sure that they have the how and the who, at least part of it. The key things that they're missing are the why and the what. Why was Marco Salazar in the house and what was he looking for?

As the night darkens and the hours until sunrise dwindle down, Gerry realizes that they have a lot of work ahead of them. They agree to keep the new information to themselves so that the Sheriff won't kick them off the case and put on one of the investigators. The action is slow at night, so they need something to keep themselves engaged until they go back to first shift. Although neither one says anything, Gerry knows that they both know that they're in for some extended hours while they investigate this. Their wives will hate them for it, but that's nothing new when the graveyard shift comes around, so that's not a deterrent. Gerry's determined to find out what's going on here, and he's pretty sure that Jamaal is on the same wavelength that he is.

IT'S SHORTLY AFTER MIDNIGHT and Sal is wide awake and eagerly waiting to hear from his nephew. Sal hopes that not having heard from Marco yet is good news, but that's just speculation. It could mean that a number of scenarios have come to fruition. And if he's honest with himself, very few of those scenarios actually have positive outcomes. Across the room in his apartment, which is too hot and smells of spicy sausage, the buzzer hums and jolts Sal's nerves. He jumps up from his sofa bed and hurries across the studio, glancing at the timepiece on the oven as he does. Marco's voice is timid through the speaker, and Sal knows right away that it's not good news. He buzzes Marco and Antonio in and heads down the stairs. His palms are a little sweaty with anticipation, unsure of what to expect, while he waits for the boys to arrive.

While Sal stands in the open doorway in the back of the kitchen, leaning on the doorframe, Marco walks in. The look on his face tells it all, and Sal's heart drops, along with his expectations. Antonio quietly slips in behind Marco and stands in his shadow.

"Why are you here already?" Sal asks.

"We have a problem," Marco says.

Without saying anything, Sal motions with his head for the boys to follow him upstairs, which they do. Upstairs, the three of them sit at the round table in the kitchen and shoot quick glances between one another.

"What kind of problem are we talking about here?" Sal says as he looks between Marco and Antonio.

Marco says, "Pigs. They got to the house at maybe eight or eight thirty and stayed for a while. They came back a couple hours later and don't look like they're going anywhere. They're parked across the street from the house as we speak."

"We need those eyes tomorrow, Marco," Sal says, trying to keep his voice as calm as possible. But on the inside, he can feel his blood starting to boil. He struggles to comprehend why Marco acts like he doesn't understand the urgency of the situation sometimes.

"I know that, Uncle Sal! Do you think I'm not aware of that?"

"Did I say that?"

"You've only mentioned it a hundred times. It's my dad's life at stake here, I'm fully aware."

"And it's my brother's life."

Marco throws his head in his hands and sulks. Sal thinks that he hears a sniffling sound from inside of Marco's hands. Sal can see now that Marco is distraught about this, and he feels badly for having doubted him. Sal leans back in his chair and fills his cheeks with air, then slowly exhales. To his left, Antonio sits with his hands in his lap, not showing any emotion at all.

Marco looks up and says, "What are we going to do?"

Sal's surprised to not see any tears in Marco's eyes when he does. He crosses his arms and looks into space, just thinking. Silence fills the room.

"Can we get the money another way?" Antonio asks innocently, almost naïvely.

Sal turns his head and glares at Antonio. Something can be said for thinking outside of the box, but sometimes, one just needs to stay inside the box and show some reason. Now is one of those times. "You got an idea on how to get twenty grand by Tuesday?" he mocks.

Antonio shrugs and shrinks in his chair.

Sal turns back to his nephew and says, "What are you thinking, Marco? You must have an idea. You must have come up with something."

Marco waits for a moment, then he says, "I think I agree with Antonio. We need an alternative."

Marco shoots a glance across the table to Antonio, who gives him a subtle nod, showing his appreciation for having his back. Sal scoffs at it. Now is not the time to be all buddy-buddy. Someone has to step up and be a man. He had thought that Marco was up for it, but now, watching how his nephew is folding under the pressure,

Sal isn't so sure about that anymore. He's never been so disappointed in Marco in his entire life.

Sal looks between the boys and shakes his head. "If you think this is your way of getting out of doing this, you're wrong," he says. "Both of you. I'm going to see Willy in the morning and will talk to his buyer myself. I'll set him straight and get us through the weekend. But you," Sal points a finger at Marco, now feeling himself starting to overheat, "better come up with something better than looking for the money somewhere else. This is what we talked about from day one, and we're going to finish this. Capiche?"

Marco stares at the finger in his face and is frozen with fear. Sal can smell it on him. Marco hasn't had to deal with this type of adversity yet in his life, and now's the time for him to find out what he's made of. Now's the time to find out if he's ready to be a man or not.

"Fine," Marco says, nervously, then he drops his head and refuses to look at Antonio.

THE NIGHT IS UNEVENTFUL and unexciting. The street is completely silent. No one comes and no one goes. Not even a wild animal. There's no sign of Marco Salazar or his car. When the sunrise finally jolts some awareness into Gerry, he shifts in his seat behind the wheel in anticipation. Jamaal is still next to him, semi-snoring, while he stares out the window.

Across the street and a couple of doors down from the Winston's, a door closes, the sound of which captures Gerry's attention, and he turns in that direction. When he does, he spots an elderly woman walking down the front steps, slowly, led by a small dog on a leash.

"Is that her?" Jamaal asks.

"I think it might be," Gerry says, already unbuckling his seatbelt. "Let's go."

Gerry opens his door and steps out into the street. The feel of solid ground under his feet is a nice change. He hikes up his pants and stretches out his back, which cracks a little, and inhales the cool air. It all feels so nice. As the old woman walks in their direction, Gerry smiles and waves to her. It takes her a minute, but she does eventually notice, returns the gesture, and approaches him and Jamaal, who is now out of the car as well.

"Can I help you?" the woman says in a motherly tone upon approaching. Her dog sits at her feet and waits for further instructions, its tail rapidly twitching.

Gerry clears his throat and says, "Good morning, ma'am. I'm sorry to bother you, Mrs..."

"Anderson," the woman says. "Betty Anderson."

"Mrs. Anderson, do you have a moment to answer a few questions?"

Betty looks between Gerry and Jamaal and her facial expression changes. While before she had looked jubilant, she now looks almost worried. "What's this about?"

"No need to worry, it will only take a minute," Gerry says. "I'm Officer Gerry Dale, and this is my partner, Jamaal Harris. We just have a few questions." Gerry pauses and waits for a reaction. When he doesn't get one, he proceeds by saying, "You know Mr. and Mrs. Winston, is that right?"

"That's right. Met them yesterday as a matter of fact. Nice couple."

Gerry nods. "Mrs. Winston tells us that you and she had a long chat yesterday afternoon. Do you mind telling us what that was about?"

Without hesitation, Betty tells Gerry and Jamaal everything that she had told Jen the day before, all of which coincides exactly with what Jen had said to them. The confirmation helps to validate their initial theory of what happened, and Gerry immediately feels better about pursuing their suspicion of Marco Salazar. He thanks Betty for her time and she continues down the sidewalk, telling him that it's her pleasure, with her pup leading the way. He and Jamaal get back into their squad car.

"We going to pick him up?" Jamaal asks when he closes his door.

"Not yet," Gerry says. "We still have no proof that it was actually him. Let's hang back for a while and wait for him to make a mistake. We need to catch him in the act."

Jamaal nods in agreement. Gerry starts the car and buckles himself in.

Chances are that Marco Salazar won't try anything during the day - these types of things tend to occur during the evening, where the criminals are less likely to be spotted, in their minds - so now is a good time to head home and catch a few hours of sleep. Gerry could use it, and he's sure that his partner could too. He'll call Mrs. Winston later in the day to let her know what's going on and that they're pursuing a suspect. Until then, she'll be safe during the day while her husband is at work, but Gerry will ask a colleague to drive by later just to be sure.

If Marco Salazar is anything like his father, things could get violent at any time. The trick is to catch him before he causes any permanent damage, but after he does enough to be put away. Things could get dangerous, so Gerry knows that they need to be cautious, yet aggressive at the same time. The right moment will come; they just have to be ready for it. And with a high degree of confidence, Gerry thinks that they will be.

CHAPTER TWENTY-FIVE

After a mostly sleepless night for Sal, morning eventually comes. He had sent Marco and Antonio home shortly after they arrived last night so that he could have some time to think to himself. Even with the peace and quiet, he came up with nothing but empty thoughts, and he still searches for something he can tell Willy.

His brother may never get out of prison if Sal can't come up with $20,000 by Tuesday. Today's Friday. Stan Brothers will take the case once the rest of his retainer is paid, but he'll drop it if Sal is even a dollar short. They've generated $80,000 so far, so maybe they have time to get the rest before Tuesday, but not without risk.

Getting those eyes had been the plan - the eyes that were supposed to be on the statue - and they were going to generate enough money to pay for the rest of Stan Brothers' $100,000 retainer. Bartolo had brought it up during one of Sal's visits to Concord, although he wouldn't say how the item got to be inside the wall, and Sal didn't ask. What else Bartolo is hiding, who knows, but the details aren't important. What matters is getting him out of there. Bartolo's adamant that he didn't kill that man, and Sal believes him, so he's doing everything that he can to help get him out of that place.

It had seemed like the perfect plan - to save the easiest part for last. Marco knows that house like the back of his hand, so breaking in should have been easy. Except nothing about it has been easy. Whatever could have gone wrong so far has, and now that the cops are poking around, the shit may really hit the fan soon. If they can somehow connect Marco to all those other home invasions and thefts around the city, he's toast. He'll be in Concord with his father and neither one of them may ever get out. Sal will be alone - his only true family in prison - and left to run his own business into the ground. His life as he knows it is on the line, and the stakes have increased exponentially. He has to find a way to get this done.

Marco and Antonio have spent the last few months gathering up goods to be sold to help pay for Stan Brothers' retainer. The arrangement has worked out well, although each time they do it increases the odds that they'll get caught. They've been breaking into unsecured upscale houses at random and taking their valuables. They give the items to Sal, who in turn sells them to Willy, who then sells them in his shop for a small profit. Sal and Willy have made hundreds of deals since the summer when this all began, and everyone is winning. It's not like Willy really has a choice to be involved, though, not with the dirt that Sal has on him.

Neither Sal, Marco, nor Antonio are in this for money to benefit themselves, and they'd never do anything to hurt someone else if they didn't have to. The whole thing had been Sal's idea initially, and he regrets that he doesn't have the agility to be in the trenches himself. He would switch places with the boys in a heartbeat if he could. The family has never had the kind of money needed by Stan Brothers, and Bartolo had begged Sal not to sell the pizzeria to get it, so this was all that he could come up with. He was reluctant to tell Bartolo about it, and despite knowing only bits and pieces of what's going on, he's clueless about how deep it goes. There's only so much someone can say while using the phone in prison, and speaking in code can be difficult and too obvious sometimes.

Sal tightens his belt as he steps out of his Lexus in the parking lot of Willy's Pawn. It's 8:00 A.M. and he's been waiting in his car in the lot for over an hour. He still doesn't know what he's going to say to Willy when he gets inside. He's anxious just considering how Willy might react to the news.

WILLY STILL HASN'T HEARD from Sal. He was supposed to call yesterday and confirm that everything was still a go for today, but he never did. Willy had called the pizzeria three or four times, but he was unable to connect with Sal. The buyer will be back in four hours, and if Sal doesn't come through, there will be bloodshed. That much Willy was promised. Pawn is a tough business that sometimes gets nasty, but this one might be the nastiest of them all. Willy's been threatened before, but not like this. This was no halfhearted advice that the buyer gave - it was a legitimate threat, a warning. Willy is officially worried.

If Willy finds a way out of this, whether Sal comes through or not, he's done. He's done with making deals with Sal and he might just be finished with the entire pawn business altogether. Fifty years is a good round number. Not many people can say that they ran a successful and profitable business for that long. Of course there were up years and down years, but over the course of five decades, Willy can proudly say that he has come out ahead. He can sell his business, take the money, and move out to Martha's Vineyard to spend the rest of his years in peace. His late wife would have loved the idea.

The front door chimes and interrupts Willy's daydream. He glances down at his watch - the one his wife had given to him long before she died for their anniversary over thirty-five years ago - and is surprised to see the time. It's

8:00 A.M. already, which means only one thing: this should be Sal with the item.

Willy waits behind the counter for Sal to appear from around the corner. When he does emerge, Willy can tell that it's not good news. Sal's eyes are sunken and he's as white in the face as a new set of dentures. Thick bags of exhaustion rest beneath his eyes, and he looks like he hasn't slept in a week.

With concern for his friend, Willy calls out to Sal, "You look like hell, what's wrong?"

Sal looks up but doesn't say anything. He drags his feet while taking the final few steps to the counter. "I don't know how to say this," he says when arrives. "I've been up all night trying to find a way-"

"You don't have it, do you?"

Sal drops his head. "No, Willy, I don't."

There's a long silence between the two men as they both look in opposite directions, not sure what to say.

"What are the chances I can get some more time? Just a couple of days is all I need."

"I don't think that's going to happen. My buyer was pretty clear, we had until today." Willy suddenly gets hot. "We're screwed, Sal. No, we're worse than screwed. We're fucked. We're royally fucked, do you know that?"

"Maybe not."

"What are you talking about? Of course we are. This guy was not screwing around."

"What if I talk to him? I can explain the situation, tell him what's going on, and-"

"It's too late, Sal. This guy is no joke. I wouldn't put it past him to kill us both over this."

"Let me talk to him. It's my fault that you're in this situation, so it's up to me to get us out of it."

Willy pauses and considers the offer. He's not keen about Sal grouping them together by saying it's their problem, considering how if Sal had done his part like he was supposed to, none of this would be happening. Despite his objections, Willy lets it go. He has no explanation for what to tell Enrique about why he doesn't have the item, and if Sal's willing to try to explain it directly, he sees no harm.

"Fine," Willy says, "but if he wants blood it's your ass. You got that?"

"I wouldn't have it any other way."

THE WAIT IS FINALLY over. Today is the day that Enrique Henderson gets his due and can get out of the city for good. He wakes up early and takes his time reviewing his itinerary. With a plane to catch at noon, he's on a tight schedule. Stephan Cooper, his driver, is sleeping easy on the pullout near the window, completely oblivious about what's going to happen today. Enrique will wake him up when it's closer to show time. He needs him to be well rested and sharp, if not just for a little while. Until then, Enrique runs through all of the possible outcomes in his mind. They all end with him leaving town with the merchandise.

Enrique and Bartolo Salazar were acquaintances once upon a time not that long ago. A mutual business associate had loaned Bartolo a big sum of money to help start up his brother Amelio's pizzeria, and Enrique was responsible for collecting the payments. Initially everything was fine and regular payments were being made. After a year, though, things started to change. Bartolo had come up with some bullshit excuse about an increase in rent and slowing business, so payments started coming in late. Worse, they eventually stopped coming in at all and interest was compounding on a daily basis, so Enrique had to do something. His boss was getting restless.

To pay the back owed debt, Enrique had made Bartolo a deal. The rumor around town was that Bartolo was an excellent poker player, and there were a bunch of guys down at Barry's Pub that vouched for Bartolo's game. In exchange for Enrique paying off Bartolo's back owed debt, all of Bartolo's winnings in an underground, high-stakes, week-long tournament would go to Enrique. With death threats being received against himself and his family, Bartolo had no choice but to accept the deal. He was short on cash, as usual, so he took out a home equity loan on his house to cover the tournament buy-in.

Things were going well when the tournament first began. Bartolo had outlasted twenty-four other men and was left standing with one other out-of-towner on the final day. Bartolo had one hell of a hand - three aces and a nine - so he went all in. His opponent had been bluffing all day, so when he called and went all in himself, Bartolo had thought nothing of it. When the river was an ace of spades, Bartolo and Enrique went nuts. They hollered and fist pumped and hugged, but stopped once the out-of-towner started laughing at them. The guy threw his hand on the table and spread his cards across the top of it. It was a royal flush, ten through ace, all spades; an unbeatable hand. And only one of two possible combinations that could have beaten Bartolo's nearly as impressive hand. The out-of-towner wrapped his arms around the pile of chips and pulled them in front of him. He was jubilant. And arrogant. Enrique wanted to slit his throat right there, but it wasn't his place, so he didn't. Bartolo had played the odds and lost. Just like that, nearly a hundred grand was gone. The out-of-towner took his money and left town after a successful week, and no one ever saw him again.

Now instead of owing money to their mutual business associate, Bartolo owed an angry Enrique the same original sum, plus ten percent. Payments to Enrique followed much of the same pattern as before. Sometimes payments were late and sometimes they didn't come at all. Enrique didn't give him as much time as the other lender did, though, and it wasn't long before an ultimatum was given.

ENRIQUE WAKES STEPHAN AN hour before they need to leave, and they go over the details one final time. Although Stephan doesn't ask many questions, Enrique is confident that they're on the same page. He trusts Stephan for some reason, and that's unlike him. Stephan showers and eats, then he and Enrique go out to the car and head for the pawn shop to collect.

SAL AND WILLY WAIT impatiently behind the counter inside of the pawn shop. Feeling that he has the right to know, Sal finally confides in Willy the reasoning behind all of this. He tells him about where all of the goods have come from, who did it and why, and most importantly, he explains the importance of this final transaction. Willy doesn't say much during the confession, and when Sal finishes, he takes a long swig of some Jack that he keeps under the counter. He offers some to Sal after sucking down his share, but Sal declines. He knows that he's not in the best frame of mind to drink right now.

Willy has some questions, all of which Sal answers with honesty. He feels bad for involving Willy, but he does point out that Willy has been deeply involved already without realizing it. Receiving high valued stolen goods is a felony, and Willy has done that many times over. Willingly or not doesn't exactly matter at this point, especially considering the thousands of dollars - tens of thousands, really - of goods that have come through this shop in recent months. Sal fails to mention this to Willy, but he hopes that he recognizes that his ass on the line here too.

Willy's visually upset that Sal didn't tell him what was going on at the beginning, but he's not one to hold a grudge. Not at his age. That's one of the things that Sal really loves about him. Although its presence is undeniable, Sal doesn't mention anything about the elephant in the room that's been keeping Willy loyal for years.

Sal lets Willy in on a new plan, a plan for them both to walk away from this, and Willy agrees to play along. Despite that, Willy doesn't share many details about the buyer, just his name: Enrique. Quite honestly, Sal knows that Willy isn't telling him everything that he knows about the mystery buyer, and he's okay with that. Sal would do the same thing if he was in Willy's situation. Some things are better left unsaid, even between friends. Especially between friends.

Enrique should be arriving shortly.

STEPHAN COOPER PULLS INTO the parking lot of Willy's Pawn and keeps the engine running. He waits in the car while Enrique goes inside the shop. He's calm, as usual. He positions the vehicle and adjusts the mirrors so that has no blind spots. He can see the front door to the shop, the street to his right, the subway to the rear, and the entire parking lot to his left. He keeps his hands on the wheel at five and seven so that he's ready to bail in an instant if need be.

He's in position.

The car is a rental, as they usually are, so it looks like he's from out of state and unsure of where he's going. The out of state license plate tends to give that impression, and most people on the road tend to have a little bit of sympathy because of it. It gives Stephan just that much more of an advantage. But in reality, the situation is the complete opposite. Stephan has lived in and around the city his entire life and he knows all of the back roads and alternate routes to every which direction, which is why he's working with Enrique on this particular job. If something goes wrong it's up to Stephan to fix it. If the cops put a tail on him he needs to lose them. If bullets go flying he needs to avoid them. Most importantly, when Enrique tells him to go somewhere he better damn well go there. No questions asked. Those are the conditions. He knows what his role is and he's fine with it. There's a lot of money waiting for him on the other side of this, maybe even enough for him to stop driving for good.

ENRIQUE ADJUSTS HIS BLAZER so that it sits flat as he opens the front door of the pawn shop and ignores the chime. He spots Willy right away from the other side of the shop, and he's standing with someone behind the counter. It's man, a large man, and he doesn't look like an employee. Enrique doesn't recognize him.

It was less than a month ago when Enrique had made his first visit into Willy's Pawn. It had only required a short time of schmoozing before he and Willy were in the back office, alone, and out of earshot of his other employees. Enrique had casually told Willy that he was an old friend of Amelio Salazar's brother, Bartolo, and that Amelio should be coming to Willy with something special that he wants to sell very soon. He wouldn't say anything more besides that. He had told Willy that he'd stop by again later in the week to discuss it further.

Two days later, Enrique showed up again, and this time, Willy had mentioned that what Enrique had said during his prior visit was true. The Salazar clan did indeed have something special that they were going to need to sell, and Enrique wanted it. The specifics of the item were never discussed, and they didn't have to be. It didn't matter. Enrique had promised Willy $50,000 cash for it, and all Willy had to do was hold it and not mention its presence to anyone.

At the time, Willy had said that he expected to have the goods within a couple of weeks. Two weeks quickly turned into three, and three turned into four. Enrique had started to put some pressure on Willy to set a date, so Willy did the same to the Salazar's, or at least he said that he did. And now, nearly a month after the initial date was set, today is the day that the transaction finally takes places. Enrique is tired of waiting.

"Who's this?" Enrique says to Willy as he arrives at the counter. He places his palms on top of the glass, wrapping his fingers into it, and holds the position. His boss had once told him that it's a position of dominance, and that's exactly what he's going for in this situation. Enrique flexes his biceps for maximum effect.

"Let's go into my office," Willy says as he opens up the counter for Enrique to follow.

Enrique makes eye contact with Willy's guest and it clicks. It's nice to put a face to the name, and he does see a minor resemblance to Bartolo. He smiles at the big man, who just looks back at him in confusion. The three men disappear into the back and enter Willy's office. They all stay standing. The only sound that fills the room is that of the ticking of Willy's timeless watch. It a nice piece, Enrique admits, and he may just take it from Willy if this doesn't go well.

"I'll ask again, who is this?" Enrique demands. He knows now, but he wants an explanation from Willy. This was supposed to be an anonymous deal, and Amelio seeing his face could put the entire operation at risk.

"This is my good friend, Amelio Salazar. He's the guy who's selling what you're interested in."

"You can call me Sal," Amelio Salazar says.

Enrique studies Amelio, but ignores him. He decides on the spot that he is not going to call him Sal. Amelio is not his friend. Enrique looks to Willy and says, "Why is he here?"

Willy looks to Amelio and nods subtly. Enrique notices and doesn't much care for it. He doesn't like secrets.

"If I may," Amelio begins. "There's been-"

"I asked Willy," Enrique says, still looking at Willy. "Willy, why is he here?"

Willy and Amelio glance at each other again and say nothing. After a moment, Willy finally says, "Listen, we've run into a bit of a challenge."

"Elaborate."

"Well, let's just say-"

Enrique whips his arm behind his back, grabs the pistol from his belt, and slams the weapon on Willy's desk. The sound cuts Willy off mid-sentence.

"Do not give me bullshit," Enrique says. "Was I not clear last time I was here? Tell me what's going on, and tell me now."

"Please, no one has to get hurt," Willy says, stammering a bit, fumbling his words. "Just let me explain."

"I'm waiting."

While he watches Willy's tongue tie itself in knots and Amelio getting fatter by just standing there, Enrique grows frustrated. He reaches for the gun on the desk and cocks it while it still rests on its side. He points it at Willy.

"Tick tock, tick tock," Enrique toys.

"He doesn't have the goods!" Amelio interjects, speaking quickly. "I don't have them. I couldn't get them. But I know where you can find them."

Keeping his arm steady, Enrique spins the barrel of the loaded gun so that it now points at Amelio. "Where?"

"Twenty-two West Lane in Stoneham. The owners found it, they still have it."

"And if they don't?"

"They do."

Enrique stares into Sal's eyes. Sal is sweating profusely. A bead of perspiration falls from his eyebrow and splashes against his belly. Although he tries to give the appearance of ice water in his veins, Enrique can see right through him. He can see how terrified he is. And he can also see that he's telling the truth. This guy doesn't have the balls to lie right to Enrique's face. With that, Enrique slowly reaches for the gun on Willy's desk and grabs it. He disengages the hammer and slips it behind his back and into his belt.

"If it's not there," Enrique begins, "I'm coming back for you. Both of you." He brushes past Amelio and heads for the door. Before leaving, he stops, looks back, and grins. "Say hello to your brother for me."

Enrique rushes out of Willy's office without looking back. He doesn't doubt that Willy has a loaded weapon around, but he does doubt that he'd be willing to use it. Without wanting to risk it, Enrique quickly - walking, of course - makes his way back into the storefront, around the counter, and out the front door. At any moment he half expects a bullet to be implanted into his back. But it doesn't come. It's a big mistake. That's the difference between Enrique and everyone else, he realizes. If he were in Willy's shoes, he would have trailed behind a few steps and shot him before he even made it back into the store. Enrique supposes that's why he's so damn good at his job. Still alive and well, Enrique makes it outside and walks across the parking lot toward the white sedan that's waiting for him - the one with the Utah plates. Stephan Cooper is waiting for instructions when he hops inside.

"Twenty-two West Lane in Stoneham," Enrique says without looking in Stephan's direction. "Do you know it?"

"I'll get you there," Stephan says.

"Good. And better make it quick. We have a flight to catch in two hours."

The car is already partially into the street before he can even finish the sentence.

CHAPTER TWENTY-SIX

M arco has been up for hours, just thinking. He paces the compact living room and forces himself to come up with an idea of what to do next. A once vibrant blue sofa sits lonelily on the opposite side of the room. A large flat screen television rests on top of an old bureau pretty close to it. That's basically everything that it's the room. Sal had put a real scare into him last night - he has never seen him that way before - and it frightened him. Because of it, the way Sal had acted, Marco's determined to make this right. He's determined to come up with a solution to their problem before it's too late. While still thinking to himself, Marco barely even notices when the buzzer sounds from inside the kitchen.

Without even asking who it is, he walks over to it and buzzes the guest in. He realizes a couple minutes later that the habit could be dangerous - letting people in the building without confirming who they are first - but it's too late to do anything about it now. He brushes it off. A moment later, a knock comes from the door. Marco closes one eye and peeks out the hole, then unlocks the door for his guest when he sees who it is.

"Morning, Uncle Sal. What are you doing here?" Marco says.

"Hi, Marco. Can I come in?"

Marco steps aside and lets his uncle into the apartment. The unexpected visit it puzzling. "What's going on?"

Without saying anything, Sal hands Marco a paper bag.

"What's this?"

"Open it."

Marco takes the bag from Sal and is surprised at its heaviness. He cracks the bag open and looks inside. Unable to make out what it is, he reaches inside and pulls the item out. He almost has to use two hands to do so. It's a bottle, made of glass, and he spins it to read the label. It's Jack Daniel's Tennessee Whiskey, half empty and golden brown.

"Happy twenty-first birthday, Marco. Sorry it's not full. I'll make it up to you," Sal says, half-smiling.

Marco smiles, almost touched at his uncle's effort. He had not been expecting this, especially not on today of all days, not with the importance of it for his father's case. "I thought you'd forget."

"I'd never forget," Sal says. He says nothing more.

And he doesn't have to.

Marco takes a baby step toward Sal and throws himself into his chest, the bottle of Jack jamming into his sternum as they embrace. He holds the embrace longer than usual, as it just feels right, the memory of Sal's outburst from last night long since faded away. He does release his uncle eventually, and Marco blinks away a tear when he does. "Thank you, Uncle Sal," he says. "It means a lot."

Sal brushes the sincerity away, not wanting to look weak. "Now that that's over with, we need to talk."

"Okay, let's talk."

"Where's Antonio?"

"Still sleeping."

"Well wake his ass up. I need you two back over the Winston's right away."

"Why, what's going on?"

"There should be a window of time to get inside the house today."

"How do you know?"

"Go wake up Antonio and I'll tell you. And hurry up, we have one chance left."

ENRIQUE SPINS THE BARREL of his pistol with his finger to keep himself occupied while Stephan drives through the streets of Stoneham. Enrique hopes that he isn't making a mistake by trusting Amelio and not putting a bullet in his head. Although he suspects that Amelio had told him the truth, one never can tell for certain. Only time will tell. The only reason why he didn't was to keep him honest. If Amelio gave false information and the artifact is not where he says it is, then Enrique is going back for him. And he'd make his life a living hell. Amelio would wish that Enrique would have just killed him back at the pawn shop.

Twenty-two West Lane is right near the center of a quiet residential neighborhood. The houses in the neighborhood are large but older and not really upscale, and their values are likely higher than they should be just because of the suburban feel. Stephan parks the car directly in front of number twenty-two.

"If I come running out or if you hear gun shots, you better get our asses out of here, and fast. You got it?" Enrique says.

Stephan nods but doesn't say anything.

Enrique opens his door and slides out. He takes a look around and sees no one, so he walks over the damp grass and heads up the stairs. He slides his pistol in his waistband behind his back and rings the doorbell. He's not sure what to expect, so he feels nothing. He doesn't know how many people there will be inside or if they'll be men or women, but he's determined and prepared to do what he has to do to get the artifact. He looks around one more time, just to make sure, and waits for someone to open the door.

PETER HAS BEEN GONE for hours, and Jen is hard at work herself, albeit inside the house. She had received three typed pages full of suggestions and critiques on her column first thing this morning, and her editor woke her up before 8:00 A.M. with a phone call to discuss his comments. He's always a difficult guy to please, but Jen really does appreciate the feedback - it helps to make her a better writer.

She's learned over the years to filter out most of what he has to say anyway, as he's not too particular when it comes to needing a completed article to fill the blank space. She just has to wait another week before he'll be all over her and begging for the completed article as is, as not having any white space in the magazine is the most important thing to him at the end of the day. They'll go through the same process next month, and then the next after that, and before they know it another successful year will have gone by. It's an inevitable cycle.

Jen is responsible for twelve investigative report length columns a year - one for each of the monthly magazine issues - plus a few extra special reports at various points during the year. There wasn't enough room for last month's column, though, so she'll get double the space in this month's edition. Jen had started out by doing more than fifty pieces a year, all of which were small stories that were no better than back-page material. Over time, she eventually graduated to where she is now after being one of the longest-tenured columnists on staff and gaining a loyal readership. Her big break came three years ago when she had raised awareness on some bald eagle poachers that were hanging around in the protected areas of the forest. After her report led to the eventual arrest and imprisonment of the two poachers, she became a big deal within the Maine environmentalist circles. Her editor had no choice but to feature her work going forward, unless he wanted to lose her to a rival. Sometimes all someone needs is just a chance to show what they can do. That's exactly what happened to Jen, and she hasn't looked back. She did have offers to go elsewhere, mind you, but Maine was always home. She uses that for leverage even to this day.

The chime of the doorbell interrupts Jen's concentration. Startled, she looks around the room for a clock. When she sees the time, she's at a loss. She's not expecting any visitors today. She stands up and peeks out the window in front of her desk. A white sedan with non-Massachusetts license plates rests adjacently to the front of the house, still on the street. Jen can tell that it's still running by the gray exhaust fumes that eject from the rear of it.

From the window in her office, she can see the outline of someone standing on the front step of the house, but she can't see their face. Whoever it is has their head on a swivel and is looking to their right. Jen makes her way over to the door, unlocks the deadbolt and key lock, silences the alarm, and pulls open the door.

"Can I help you?" she says.

The man in front of her stares back at her blankly and doesn't react right away. Eventually, he says, "Are you the owner of this house?"

"I am. My husband and I."

"Is your husband home?"

"No. Who are you and what is this about?"

The man continues to stare at Jen and something in his gaze sends a chill down her spine. Her internal red flag rises to the forefront. Something is off. She doesn't like the way that he's looking at her, so she reaches for the door and begins to take a step back. When she does, he grits his teeth and lunges at her, not making a sound, and wraps a hand around her throat.

ENRIQUE KICKS THE FRONT door closed with his heel as he forces the woman into the hallway. Her eyes are bulging as she desperately tries to pry his fingers away from her windpipe through gasping breaths. Enrique slams her back against the wall and releases some of the pressure from her neck. The panel of drywall rattles behind her and a framed photo threatens to fall to the floor and shatter. The woman sucks in air frantically, all the while carrying a look of panic on her face. Enrique loves the feeling of being in control, but he reluctantly releases his grip, and when he does, she immediately starts to choke on the overload of oxygen that floods her lungs.

Enrique backs up a step and retrieves his pistol from his belt. He scans the woman from head to toe, licking his upper lip and makes a sucking noise inside of his mouth as he does. Overall, he likes what he sees. Her body is tight, her breasts small, but her face is missing something. She's not a ten, not even an eight probably, but he'd still take that in a heartbeat. If only it was another day.

"I need you to listen to me, and listen to me good," Enrique begins. He waits for a moment while the six and a half massages her aching neck. She's going to be bruised and swollen pretty good, but she'll be fine in time. "Are you listening?"

The woman looks up, tears streaming out of her eyes, her trembling hand still protecting her neck, and nods. "Please don't hurt me," her voice cracks as she speaks. "You can have anything you want, please just don't hurt me."

Her legs are pinched together, really tightly, and Enrique knows what's on her mind.

"I've been told that you have something that belongs to me," Enrique says. "It's a statue, a warrior statue, left behind by the previous owner. You know it?" Enrique holds the gun in his hand loosely, his finger ready to pull the trigger at any time if need be.

The woman nods her head slowly after taking a moment for consideration. She almost looks relieved when he tells her what he's after. Enrique notices the tension loosen up in her legs.

"Where?"

"Upstairs in the bedroom at the end of the hall," she says, stammering. "It's sitting on the corner of the dresser on the left."

Enrique points his gun at Jen. "Don't move," he says, then he disappears up the stairs.

He finds the statue immediately upon entering the bedroom. It sits just where described, so he picks it up and holds it firmly in his grasp. He doesn't spend much time looking the item over as he recognizes it as soon as he walks in. This whole thing had been easier than he had thought. He should have just done this in the first place, he thinks, instead of waiting a month for the Salazar's to get it. And in the end, they didn't even end up getting it in the first place. What a bunch of losers.

Enrique bolts out of the bedroom, down the hallway and stairs, and out the front door. He doesn't even bother looking back to see if the woman is still where he left her as he sprints across the lawn, artifact in hand, yelling to Stephan, "GO! GO! GO!"

Stephan kicks the transmission into gear and peels off immediately upon Enrique hitting the seat.

JEN SLAMS THE FRONT door once the monster of a man leaves and flips the deadbolt before dropping to the floor and wailing. Her neck is pulsating and her heart is pounding, and she screams profanities at the hardwood. She lets herself go while thinking about what the hell just happened to her. Everything happened so fast.

Those eyes, the way that he was looking at her, that monster, it was pure evil. She can say with certainty that this was a different man than either one of the two that were in the house the first night. Both of those guys looked just as scared as she and Peter were, but not this guy. This guy was ruthless, heartless, and she wonders if he's the second coming of the Devil himself. This is proof: evil really does exist.

This has got to end. Every day gets worse in this house, and Jen doesn't think that she can last even another single day. Once she's composed enough to pick herself up off the floor, she reengages the alarm and finds her phone.

She calls Officer Dale at home and tells him what has happened. He sounds personally defeated on the phone and tells her that he'll get changed and be right over.

Peter has a similar reaction. He answers his phone on the first ring, believe it or not, and he actually offers up some sense of empathy for once. Jen screams at him and tells him that she's not spending another night in this house, and he waits until she finishes her rant before responding. He promises that he'll be home right away and that they can talk it out with the police. Jen apologies for screaming at him and says that it's not his fault, and Peter reassures her that he'll be home soon. But he doesn't say that he forgives her.

Jen triple checks the alarm before heading upstairs. She strips her now perspiration-soaked clothes off and tosses them to the floor. She's not sure that she'll ever be able to wear that outfit again, not after that monster had touched it. She'll never be able to get his scent off.

In the bathroom, she turns on the water in the shower and heats it up until it steams over the top of the curtain. She sits on the acrylic floor of the shower with her knees pulled up to her chest and lets the water pour over her damaged body. She puts her head down and weeps, hoping that the water will boil the hatred right off of her. The more she thinks about it, the more hopeless she feels. She's tried everything that she can think of to keep herself safe, and nothing has worked to stop the madness. If anything, it just keeps getting worse. She doesn't know where else to turn, and she's close to giving up.

CHAPTER TWENTY-SEVEN

Marco turns right around the bend on West Lane and is nearly met head on by a speeding sedan. With his heart pumping rapidly and his muscles tensing up, he thrusts the wheel to the right, slams the pedal to the floor, and whips the car off the road until it comes to a stop among the leaves. Another few feet and they'd be in the ditch. Antonio bounces around wildly in the seat next to him, making noises that Marco doesn't recognize. Marco grips the steering wheel, white-knuckled, and tries to catch his breath.

"What the hell!" Antonio yells and he spins his head around to watch the white car scream out of sight. "That son of a bitch is going to get someone killed!" Antonio pauses for a second, takes a deep breath, and exhales heavily. "You think that's him?"

Marco gathers himself and jams the Cadillac into reverse. "It might be," he says. "We'll find out soon enough I guess." Marco looks over his shoulder, his hands still shaking, and reverses the Cadillac back onto the street. The damp leaves and thick mud beneath the car spit from the rear wheels, forcing it to sputter. With a good kick of the engine, Marco gets the Cadillac back onto the street, where they continue toward the opening near the

Winston's house. He spins the car around so that he and Antonio can see the house through the windshield and around the bend in the mirrors.

Now they wait.

Marco isn't crazy about Sal's new plan, and he had let him know about it back at the apartment. With those eyes being as valuable and important as they are, being willing to give the statue away makes no sense to Marco. What if the guy notices that the eyes are gone? Sal had tried to convince him that the guy - Sal had said that his name was Enrique - would be in too much of a rush to even notice. But Marco's not too sure about that. Sal is banking on it, but it's not something that Marco would have done. He doesn't like it. But the damage has already been done and there's no going back now, as Sal has already given Enrique the Winston's address. He gave up the only hope they have left of getting Bartolo out of prison, and it potentially offers nothing in return. While Marco disagrees, he trusts that Sal knows what he's doing. All Marco can say is that Sal better be right about this.

Marco and Antonio have the tools necessary to get into the house once vacated this time, although they don't know for sure if it'll actually work or not. In case of failure, Marco has already made up his mind on what he's going to do. He hasn't told Antonio, of course, as he would never agree to go along with it if he knew the possible end result. Although he's prepared to do what's necessary, Marco really hopes it doesn't come down to that.

If Sal is right, the cops should be showing up shortly to pick up Jen. They'll likely bring her down to the station for her to give an official statement about what happened. It's known that she's already in contact with the cops as evident by two of them spending last night hanging around outside the house, so there's no doubt that she'll call them again. When they arrive and take her away, that's when Marco and Antonio have their chance. The house will be empty and they can concentrate on finding those eyes, plus taking care of that alarm.

"What if she's dead?" Antonio says.

"Who?"

"Jen. What if Enrique killed Jen when he broke into the house?"

Marco hadn't considered this, and he doubts that Sal did either. The more he thinks about it, the more he realizes that Antonio is so right. What if Jen is dead? What if she didn't call the cops and they're never coming? They can't go into the house and find out for themselves either - imagine if their DNA was found near the crime scene. Never mind not getting those eyes, what if they were charged with her murder? It wouldn't be the first time, Marco realizes, thinking about his father. On the other hand, what if she is alive still and wounded? What if Enrique left her for dead and she's suffering? What if she needs their help? Marco suddenly has a lump in his throat as he considers the scenarios.

"We can't think like that," Marco says, pushing the thoughts away the best that he can. "Let's just wait it out and see what happens. Let's assume that she's fine and has already called the cops and that they're on their way as we speak." Marco says it, but he's not sure that he believes it. Antonio has raised a valid concern, and Marco tries to ignore the doubt that has crept into his mind. And in the end, he just really hopes that Sal has made the right decision.

OFFICER GERRY DALE SITS across the table from the Winston's and listens as Jen tells him and her husband what has happened to her. Peter had arrived home from work just before Gerry got the house, so Peter is hearing this for the first time too. He looks stunned. His pupils are dilated and he's shaking uncontrollably. Gerry wonders if he might explode. Jen is crying as she speaks and is difficult to understand at times, so Gerry asks her to repeat herself on more than one occasion.

It all seems very bizarre. It's not that Gerry doesn't believe Mrs. Winston's story, because it's clear that she's telling the truth based on her reaction. She's obviously disturbed by what has happened to her, and the shiners on her neck do help to corroborate her story. Gerry can't help but think how convenient this all is, though, as everything that Mrs. Winston has reported in recent days has taken place when she's been alone, aside from that first night. When she finishes describing everything that she can remember, Gerry jots down some notes on his notepad so that he doesn't forget to fill in Jamaal later on. Jamaal was unable to come right away, so he'll meet them back at the station.

"I know this is hard," Gerry begins, "but it's really important that you answer some questions while the memories are fresh. Is that okay?"

Peter puts his arm around Jen's shoulder and caresses her wounded skin. She leans in toward him and puts her head on his chest. She looks up to Gerry and nods.

"It's okay," she says.

Gerry flips his notepad to a blank page and finds Mrs. Winston's eyes. "This guy, your attacker, have you ever seen him before?"

"No."

"So it's no one you know then?"

"That's right."

"Could it have been the same person who broke in during the night earlier this week?"

"No, I don't think so."

"And you're sure about that?"

"I'm not one-hundred percent sure, no. But his eyes were different this time. This guy was more...evil than the other guys. Plus there were two guys before, remember?"

"Yes, I remember," Gerry says. "I'm just trying to put the pieces together here, that's all."

It's a partial truth. Jen's description of the guy today, although vague, is close to that of Marco Salazar, so he's prying. Gerry knows that he's close to blowing the cover off the lid of this whole thing.

The motive makes sense. Marco was in the bedroom the other night, obviously looking for something, but he didn't find it. Might it be a coincidence that the statue was found behind the wall in the bedroom - the same very room that Marco had been creeping in? Gerry thinks not. Marco was unable to get what he was looking for that night since the Winston's were in the bed, so he came back for it during the day, when he knew that Jen would be alone.

"The getaway car, you said it was white?" Gerry continues.

"Yes, it was white. And from out of state."

Gerry nods. Initially, this throws a wrench in his theory. Marco drives a black vehicle, a fifteen-year-old Cadillac, according to DMV records. The white vehicle is a problem.

Then it hits him. Marco was with someone that night, someone who is unknown up to this point. Gerry knows nothing about this partner - male or female, black or white. And he doesn't know whether they live in state or out. That could be it. Marco's partner in all of this is the driver of the white sedan.

Maybe Marco is more intelligent than Gerry had given him credit for. Crime does run in his family, after all. He couldn't risk that someone may have seen his car that night, so he used his partner's this time. It's a good plan, Gerry will give him that much. He probably thought that no one would catch on to the tactic, but he probably didn't think that someone with Gerry's experience would be on the case either. Gerry has always felt that he's underemployed - he should be a detective, he thinks, and not a lousy patrol officer - and this case has further proven that. He smiles to himself, confident that he has his guy, and that this will propel him to bigger and better things professionally. But he tries to hide his satisfaction so that the Winston's won't notice and get the wrong idea.

"Did you happen to see the license plate?" Gerry says. "Maybe the number or what state it was?"

Jen shakes her head. "No. I only saw it from the window from an angle."

"If you only saw it at an angle, how could you tell that is was from out of state then?"

"Colors. There were colors on it. It wasn't like the mostly white Mass plates."

Gerry shakes his head, satisfied with her explanation. "Would you be willing to come down to the station with me? Officer Harris will meet us there and you can give your official statement then."

Jen looks to her husband for approval, and he shrugs. "Sure, why not?" she says. "It'll get me out of this house for a while at least."

"You can both ride with me if you want. I can drop you back off on my way through later."

Peter smirks. "That's okay," he says. "We'll drive separately."

IT'S NOT LONG BEFORE Marco and Antonio get some action. First comes a black Audi flying around the bend at a high rate of speed. Its tires squeal as it spins into the Winton's driveway and stops suddenly. A man gets out and rushes to the front door. He fumbles around on the top step before disappearing into the house.

"Peter?" Antonio says.

"Looks like it."

Less than ten minutes later, a squad car appears from around the bend going at a much lower speed than the Audi had been. Its sirens are off and it casually pulls into the Winston's driveway and parks behind the man's Audi. A uniformed officer gets out, climbs up the stairs, and knocks on the front door. The door opens just a moment later and he disappears inside.

Less than a half an hour later, three people emerge from the house: a man and a woman - Peter and Jen Winston, presumably - and the uniformed officer. The officer gets into his squad car and pulls out of the driveway. Peter and Jen pile into the black Audi and do the same thing. Antonio sinks in his seat a bit as the two vehicles drive past.

It's just how Sal had thought it might happen.

After both vehicles disappear around the bend and out of sight, Antonio relaxes. Then he starts to prepare himself mentally for the moment he and Marco have been waiting for.

Marco looks around the area and motions for Antonio to retrieves the plastic bag from under his seat. He does and hands Marco his gloves and mask. They dress in their disguises. Before getting out of the Cadillac, Antonio opens the glove box and pockets the multi-tool that Marco keeps on hand for emergencies. The tool has everything that he should need.

Once outside and on a silent count of three, they close their doors. There's almost no sound. Then they smack their fists on top of one another's and head for the Winston's.

"Let's do this," Marco says.

Antonio nods.

With Marco leading the way, Antonio trails behind as they sneak past the ADT sign in the lawn and approach the house. He's feeling confident. To no surprise, the front door is locked, but that shouldn't be much of a problem. Not this time. Over the past few months, Antonio has become a near expert level lock picker, so he takes the lead. He removes the multi-tool from his pocket and isolates the metal file from the rest of the tools. The deadbolt is the more difficult of the two locks, so he starts with that one.

With a surprisingly steady hand, he jams the sharp end of the file into the deadbolt and lifts it to its maximum. To help his concentration, Antonio closes his eyes and leans one ear toward the locking mechanism. He gets in the zone, freeing his mind of any doubt. It's just business as usual. Using a hex wrench, he inserts the long shaft into the bottom of the lock and pushes toward the pins. He slides the file back and forth until the pins inside click and the steel makes contact. When the pins do click, he slowly pulls the file out while wiggling it up and down, and waits until the pins release before turning the hex wrench. The deadbolt disengages with a snap.

Antonio opens his eyes and grins. It's like stealing candy from a baby, if you know what you're doing. He likes feeling needed. He moves down the door and uses the same tools on the key lock. He fidgets around with the file until it grips the pins, then he slides the hex wrench into the opening and spins it until it unlocks. Antonio looks to Marco and they make eye contact. Marco nods, grinning. With no turning back now, Antonio pushes the door open, and holding his breath, he and Marco step into the house.

Now comes the hard part.

Antonio is starting to feel the pressure already. And it's damn heavy.

The alarm starts to beep as soon as the door opens. There's no telling how long they have until the unarmed alarm notifies the ADT call center, so Antonio has to hurry. The alarm panel is on the wall right next to the door, so Antonio tends to that while Marco heads upstairs.

Antonio uses the multi-tool to remove the one screw on the underside of the panel, then he uses the file to get underneath it and pry off the cover. It pops off and falls to the floor with a clang of plastic against wood, leaving Antonio staring at a web of multi-colored wires. He removes his mask to air out his sweaty face, then he wipes away the beads with his sleeve.

He's read up on this. One of the wires will kill the system, one will set off the alarm, and all the others will cause various malfunctions within the specific electrical components in which they're connected to. Clusters of red, yellow, blue, green, black, and white wires are everywhere, but Antonio can't remember which one is the right one. Now is not the time for a mental blockage. He closes his eyes and tries to think, to push past it. All he can hear is the beeping of the alarm and a loud, repetitive banging coming from upstairs. It's distracting. He clenches his eyes tighter and tries to clear his mind to get back into the zone.

Come on, he tells himself, think.

How long has it been? Thirty seconds maybe. He doesn't know. The alarm is still beeping, and he finds it getting louder and louder, although he knows that it's just an illusion. But he can't ignore it. The sound doesn't dissipate. He reaches into the cluster of wires and separates the colors. His hands are trembling. He makes a crease on the wires near the connections that are wide enough to fit the scissors from the multi-tool, but he struggles to steady the scissors. He pulls his hands back and shakes them as if to flick away water, then he goes back in. He can feel himself getting lightheaded.

Is it red or is it yellow? Or is it black? He can't remember. The alarm continues to beep. He has to make a decision. He's running out of time.

Red? Yellow? Black?

Beep...beep...beep.

Just seconds left.

Red. He chooses red. He goes with his gut. Earlier, he had made up an acronym to try to remember the one that he needed to cut based on the research that he did this morning. Acronyms or catchy jingles had always helped him to memorize things growing up. That's basically how he made it through high school. RR BB was this one: red is right, black is bad.

He thinks.

He bites his tongue and waits for something to happen. He half expects a whirling alarm to sound overhead like it does in the movies when the thief tries to steal from a bank vault. But it doesn't. The screen on the panel fades away and the beeping stops. No alarm.

No alarm!

Antonio weakens in the knees and nearly falls to the floor in relief.

UPSTAIRS, MARCO LOOKS AROUND the bedroom at the end of the hall that used to be his parents'. He tosses the Winston's stuff everywhere, looking for what he and Antonio came for. Just in case the Winston's had found the eyes and took them off the statue and put them somewhere, Marco wants to make sure that he knows about it. To his displeasure, he doesn't find anything. He slides the bed out of the way and looks for the hole in the wall. The walls are freshly painted, so he can't tell exactly where the hole was. He feels around on the wall for the soft spot, but it's gone. Someone must have patched it up. He starts to panic. He looks around the room for something to use, something solid, but he finds nothing. Realizing that he's wasting too much time, he starts to kick the wall.

If the hole had been recently patched, chances are that it will give out fairly easily. He kicks around where he thinks the hole was and the drywall starts to crack. Paint chips fall to the floor and all over the toe of his shoe, but he makes progress. He slides to the left and kicks some more, and he almost falls backward when the panel of drywall gives way and his foot breaks through to the other side. If the headboard on the bed wasn't there to support his weight and break his fall, he would have gone down for sure.

Antonio enters the room just as Marco tries to pull himself free. He rushes over to the wall and crouches down beside his friend. Marco uses Antonio's shoulder to balance himself while Antonio pulls on his leg. It comes free with two good tugs.

"What the hell happened?" Antonio says with perspiration covering his face.

"Found the hole."

"I see that. And I took care of the alarm, the beeping stopped."

"Which one did you cut?"

"Red."

Marco whips his head in Antonio's direction. "I hope you're joking. Tell me you're joking."

"I'm not joking, I cut the red one."

"Oh shit."

Antonio's face turns white, like he's seen a ghost. "What? What's wrong?"

"The black one cuts out the system. The red one is the silent alarm."

"How do you know?"

"Because you told me! In the car, remember? RR BB. Red is run, black is beep. That's what you said."

Antonio leans his head back and closes his eyes, and if trying to recall the conversation. A moment passes, then he seems to remember. His eyes shoot open like a bullet from a gun. "Run if red is cut because that will set off the alarm. Black will turn off the beep," he says.

"That's right. That's what you told me."

Antonio leaps to his feet. "We've got to leave then, now, Marco! The cops will be here any minute."

"We're not leaving until we get those eyes. It's our last chance. Help me look."

"But, Marco-"

"Help me look!"

Marco kneels down in front of the hole and tears more of the drywall until it's large enough to fit his head inside. He leans in and scans the area, but sees nothing right away through the blackness. He starts to back his head out so that he can make the hole even bigger, when something steals his attention. A twinkle emerges from underneath the wreckage like the sun reflecting against the face of a tiny wristwatch. Marco pulls his head out, reaches his hand inside in the direction of the shine, and tosses some drywall to the side. He feels around on the ground until his fingers roll over something hard and out of place. His heart leaps.

This might be them.

He backs his arm out of the hole and grabs a chunk of the wall. Antonio grabs a corner himself and they both pull it toward them. In one big motion, a chunk of drywall the length of a femur breaks away and the wall is open to the floor. Marco tosses some of the broken pieces to the side until he sees what they came here for. Both missing eyes from the statue - glassy and smooth, shiny and perfect - lay next to one another under a pile of loose drywall on the floor. They're blue diamonds, rounded at the top and shaped like a pyramid on the bottom. Light can be seen shining through them when held in the air like a rotating kaleidoscope. They must have fallen off the statue when it was pulled out of the wall.

Marco studies them in amazement as they rest in the palm of his hand. They're not much bigger than a pair of marbles, but they're his lifeline. These are what may save his father. And after all they've been through to get them, here they are. Finally. This is all going to be over soon.

Less excited about the prospect of the find, Antonio is standing in the doorway and yelling to Marco, "Come on, Marco! We have to leave!"

Marco closes his hand firmly around the treasure and pops up to his feet with fresh energy. He feels like the kids from *The Goonies* who have just found One-Eyed Willy's treasure. He chases Antonio down the hall and meets him at the bottom of the stairs. But he pauses before opening the front door. "Do you hear that?" he says.

Antonio looks all around with a sense of paranoia overwhelming him. "What? Hear what?"

Marco walks over to the bay window in the living room and peeks out. The sound of police sirens are getting closer. Then, right on cue, the first of three squad cars speeds around the bend. "It's the cops!"

Antonio panics. He's bent at the knees and standing on his toes, acting like a squirrel who's stuck in the middle of the street with an oncoming vehicle approaching at full speed. "What are we going to do?"

Marco pauses and thinks. Without much hesitation, he grabs Antonio's hand and spreads open his fingers. "Here, take these." He slides the eyes into his hand and forces it closed. "Whatever you do, do not lose these. Let me see that tool."

With his free hand, Antonio removes the multi-tool from his pocket and hands it to Marco. Marco stashes it in his hip pocket.

"What are you doing?" Antonio asks.

"Wait five seconds, then sneak out the back door."

"No, I can't let you do this."

"Please, Antonio. Just do it."

"I can't do-"

"If we both go to jail those eyes are gone forever and my dad's never getting out. Please."

"Marco..."

"Go! Now! Give them to Sal and tell him what happened. He'll know what to do."

Antonio stares at his friend with desperate eyes. He closes his hand around the diamonds and turns away. He runs down the hallway and approaches the sliding glass door in the kitchen. Marco turns around and nods, then waits until Antonio disappears outside before opening the front door.

Marco steps out onto the front stoop. Police sirens rip through the air like thunder. Marco raises his hands above his head and starts walking down the steps. He can sense his life flashing in front of his eyes. Three squad cars pull into the driveway simultaneously and screech to a stop. All six doors open and each of the men point a loaded gun at Marco.

One of the officers yells out to him, "Don't move! Keep your hands above your head and don't move!" he says, his voice bellowing in the open sky. "Lay on the ground! Face first!"

Marco stops moving and does as he's told.

Within moments, the multi-tool is pulled out of his pocket and Marco is on the bottom of a seven-man pileup and is being crushed by the weight. He struggles to breathe from the pressure being put on his lungs, his ribs threatening to fracture. His wrists are twisted behind his back and cold handcuffs are tightened around them. With his heart pumping too fast and the adrenaline oozing out of his pores, he's dragged to his feet by the steel on his wrists. One of the officers starts to recite Marco his Miranda rights as he's led to the police car.

All Marco can think about is Antonio and how badly he needs him to get out of here. He wants to shoot a quick glance to where his Cadillac should be, but he thinks better of it. He can't risk it. Instead, he looks straight ahead. Luckily, the keys to the Cadillac are still in the ignition, so Antonio can make a run for it once the coast is clear. Marco's forced into the back seat of the police car and the door is slammed in his face. The six officers wipe sweat from their faces and shake hands before heading their own separate ways. One of them says something into the radio that's attached to his collar, but Marco can only see his lips moving.

As the police car pulls out into the street, Marco catches a glimpse of something in the yard. It only takes him a moment to recognize it. Laying belly down under one of the bushes in the side yard is Antonio. He's hiding. The sight of his friend is refreshing, and Marco knows that everything is going to be fine. Antonio will tell Sal everything that's going on and Sal will figure out a way to get him out of this.

"You better wipe that smile off your face, boy," says the cop in the passenger's seat in the front.

Pig.

Marco hadn't realized that he was even smiling, but he stops. The cop rolls his eyes and mumbles something to his partner, the driver, and turns back to the front. Once his back is turned, Marco knowingly smiles this time.

They did it.

They outsmarted a professional criminal and now have enough money to pay Stan Brothers, the man who's going to get Bartolo out of jail.

IN THE POLICE STATION downtown, Peter and Jen Winston are in a private room giving their official statement to Gerry. Jamaal is in the room too, as is their boss. Gerry knows now that they'll have to tell the Sheriff everything, and he hates that. He had hoped to wait until all of the loose ends were tied up before doing so. But things have spiraled out of control and lives may be in danger, so it changes things. Jamaal had filled Sheriff Henry Collins in on some of the details while waiting for his partner to arrive, so the whole crew is involved with the case now.

Sheriff Collins gives Gerry the stink eye, although Gerry pretends not to see it. While Jen is in the middle of her statement, a knock comes from behind the door.

Ben Schultz, the young research specialist, slides his head in. "Excuse me, Officer Dale," he says. "Can I steal you for a second?"

"Not now, Schultz," Gerry says.

"You're going to want to hear this."

Gerry sighs and excuses himself. Jamaal takes his place so that Jen can continue with her statement without interruption. Gerry steps out into the hallway and closes the door behind him.

"What is it?" Gerry says.

"That guy you were asking about, Marco Salazar."

"Yeah, what about him?"

"He was just arrested during a home invasion."

"Where?"

"Where do you think?" Ben hands Gerry a file. "He's on his way in for processing now."

Gerry nods. Ben takes that as his cue, so he exits down the corridor without saying another word. Gerry reviews the file and tries to hold back a smile before reentering the room. Everyone looks at him when he does.

"Is everything okay?" Jamaal asks.

Gerry looks between his partner, Sheriff Collins, and the Winston's. They all have the same blank looks on their faces. He holds the manila folder that Ben had given him into the air for everyone to see and says, "We got him."

CHAPTER TWENTY-EIGHT

Marco sits alone, his hands free, behind a wooden desk in a tight empty room at the police station in downtown Stoneham. It takes nearly an hour for him to be processed upon arrival, and another twenty minutes before he's brought into the room that he's in now. It's an interrogation room, he assumes, as there's a one-way mirror to his right and a small video camera in the upper corner to his left. He's being watched and he knows it, but he's actually quite relaxed.

Some detective had come in to ask him some basic questions when he had first arrived, but he's been alone for a solid thirty minutes since. Marco told him nothing. He has a game plan and he's not going to intimidated or pressured into incriminating himself or Antonio. He was caught in the house, so it's pretty clear that it was him, but the cops don't have a clue about how far this goes. If Marco has anything to do with it, they'll never find out what's really happening behind the scenes. And if they do, it's going to get a whole hell of a lot worse than it already is.

Marco knows how this is all going to go. There are some people on the other side of the glass and looking in, and they're just waiting for him to show some sign of weakness or anxiousness before coming back in. They want to wait until Marco has softened his position before grilling him some more. The longer they wait the better, they think, but Marco knows that they're wrong about that. He's not like the others who have been in this seat before him. No, it doesn't matter what they say or what they do, he's not going to cave. He knows his rights and he's going to take full advantage of them, and he knows that it's going to frustrate the hell of out them. He finds some pleasure in knowing that.

GERRY DALE'S MANILA FOLDER on Marco Salazar is full now, thanks in part to Ben Shultz and his twenty-first century technology skills. Everything that's available on Marco's past is in the folder and Gerry has spent some time reviewing it. Nothing stands out besides what he and Jamaal had already learned. Marco still doesn't really fit the typical profile of someone who might break into the same house over and over again, even if he used to live there. Something is off.

Before Gerry confronts Marco, he reviews what he knows one more time. He knows about the invasions of the Winston place and the purpose for them, and he also knows that he had a partner. The troubling thing, though, is what happened earlier today. Jamaal is still gathering up more details down the hall with Jen and Peter, but if Marco was caught breaking into the Winston's house this afternoon, who was it that attacked Jen this morning?

The white car with the out of state plates that Jen's assailant was in this morning was originally thought to be Marco's partner's car, but based on this new information, Gerry is unsure about that now. Maybe there was a dispute between Marco and his partner which led to Marco being left on his own. That could explain what happened today. Marco's partner went behind Marco's back and stole the statue himself, then Marco went back later to try to...

To try to what?

Gerry doesn't know. There are still a lot of unanswered questions. If not that, who was it in the white car and how are they connected to this? Gerry has two key items on his agenda for now: one, he needs to find out who Marco's partner is; and two, he needs to find out what the significance is of that statue that everyone seems to want to get their hands on.

STILL SHAKEN FROM THE close call, Antonio hurries into the pizzeria. His shirt is muddied with soil and is covered in small holes from the rocks and pointed sticks that were underneath the bushes. He can smell himself, and it reminds him of a gardener after a long day's work. He whips open the door and runs inside the pizzeria and immediately looks for Sal. One of Sal's other employees tells Antonio that Sal is cooking in the back, so Antonio heads in that direction. He can feel the sharpness of the diamond eyes still wrapped in between his fingers.

Sal notices Antonio as he enters, and he drops everything. The wooden pizza roller hits the counter with a bang, and Sal wipes his hands using a hand towel from next to the oven.

"Well?" Sal says as he walks toward Antonio.

Antonio holds out his open hand and lets the circulation return to his fingers. The eyes have left diamond shaped indents in his hand from the pressure of his closed fist around them. There was no way that he was going to let them go. Sal reaches for them and peels them away from Antonio's skin, leaving some dough powder residue in Antonio's palm. Sal inspects the diamonds.

"They're perfect," Sal says, now suddenly with tears in his eyes. "They're absolutely perfect."

Sal closes his hand around the diamonds and pulls Antonio in toward him. He embraces him tightly and kisses him on the cheek, but Antonio just stands there with his arms dangling to his side. He can't get help but worry how Marco is holding up. After holding the position for a moment, Sal finally lets him go.

"Go grab Marco," Sal says. "I want him to come with me to Willy's to get our money."

Antonio doesn't react. For the first time, Antonio recognizes that Sal can tell that something is wrong. He eyes his shredded shirt and flares his nostrils. Then he frowns.

"Big Sal, something happened," Antonio says.

"What are you talking about?"

"It's Marco."

"What about Marco? Where is he?"

"It's the cops. They got him."

Sal puts a hand to his chest and forces himself to take deep, slow breaths. He wheezes more than he should, and Antonio is worried that he might have a panic attack.

"Antonio," Sal says as he finds a seat, a hand still on his chest, "I need you to tell me everything that happened. I need to know what we're dealing with here."

Recognizing the choppiness in Sal's breath, Antonio says, "Are you okay?"

Sal holds up his hand as if to encourage Antonio to move on. "Marco. Tell me about Marco. I need to know everything."

Antonio nods, then he tells Sal absolutely everything that happened while at the Winston's house.

IN THE INTERROGATION ROOM, Gerry sits across the table from Marco. He tells Marco everything that he knows and everything that he thinks he knows, but Marco neither confirms nor denies anything. He stays mostly quiet actually, choosing to invoke his Fifth Amendment right. He confirms basic information about himself with a quick yes or no, but he refuses to go into any details about what happened. His stubbornness frustrates Gerry, but he's well within his legal rights, so there isn't much that Gerry can do about it. An expert interrogator is on his way to see if he can get Marco to crack, but even that isn't looking very promising.

"Mr. Salazar, Marco. Do you mind if I call you Marco?" Gerry says.

Marco shrugs. "Okay."

"Marco, I want to help you here, I really do. But I need you to help me help you. If you just tell me who you're working with and what you did with the statue from the house, maybe we can work something out."

"I already told you. I did it alone and I don't know where that statue is that you keep asking about. I don't even know what statue you're talking about."

Gerry stands and starts to pace the perimeter of the compact room, frustrated. He switches gears and tries a different tactic. "It doesn't have to be like this you know. I know that you know where it is - the statue I mean. And I know that you were in that house a few nights ago and that someone was with you. The homeowners saw two of you, so stop bullshitting me, okay? I just need the truth."

"I told you the truth."

Gerry walks up behind Marco and slams his open palms onto the table in front of him. He can feel Marco jump. With a little effort, Gerry could latch onto Marco's head with his armpits and squeeze until Marco talks. Instead, Gerry towers over Marco as he sits, leans forward, and speaks softly into Marco's ear.

"I'm going to give you one more chance," Gerry says. "If you don't start talking I'll see to it that you don't see a judge until Monday. You can spend the entire weekend in a cell with the drunks and really think long and hard about this. Is that want you want?"

Marco says nothing and stays calm, which just infuriates Gerry further.

"Maybe they'll take advantage of you sexually, or maybe they won't. I hope you brought some Vaseline with you, just in case. I'll tell the judge everything that we have on you and show her that you have violence in your family history. You'll never be able to afford the bail that she sets, not a scumbag rat like you. This is your last chance. Now talk!"

Gerry backs away from the table, wipes his brow, and walks around to the other side so that he can look into Marco's eyes. He looks frozen, almost stunned, but he stays firm to his story. Gerry's blood is boiling, and for the first time, he questions if he has this in him - this detective stuff. Marco's stubbornness gives him a different type of appreciation for those detectives that can put up with this type of intolerable behavior. He didn't realize it would be so difficult.

"I would like to make my phone call now," Marco says without emotion.

Gerry grits his teeth and makes his hands into fists. He wants to throw them at Marco's face, but he doesn't. Instead, he turns around without saying anything further and leaves the room. Jamaal and Sheriff Henry Collins are waiting for him on the other side of the door.

"Damn," Jamaal says, almost smiling. "I didn't know you had that in you."

"He's lying to my face!" Gerry says. "We caught him red-handed! Why won't he just talk?"

Sheriff Collins places a hand on Gerry's shoulder to try and soothe him. "Relax, compadre. You did the best you could. We got a guy on the way and he'll be here in a bit. He'll talk to him some more then, alright? This is never easy."

Gerry brushes Henry's arm away and heads down the hallway to go get some fresh air. He kicks a chair to its side out of frustration when turning the corner.

"FEISTY TODAY," JAMAAL SAYS to the Sheriff as he watches Gerry stampede down the hallway like a madman.

"Good, I like his passion," Sheriff Henry Collins says, then he pauses. "Listen, while we're here, I just want you to know that there needs to be some discipline handed down for all this."

Jamaal looks to the Sheriff with unanticipated concern. He had been expecting some sort of accolade or a raise or something instead. "What do you mean?"

"What you and Officer Dale did, handling this case under the radar on your own, is a problem. You should have informed me of the situation immediately."

"We filed a report that first night."

"That's not what I'm talking about. You know what I mean. There's certain protocol that needs to be followed in scenarios like this. It should have been handed over to one of the investigators right away."

Jamaal nods in understanding. "I guess you're right. It won't happen again."

"Some people are going to be calling for your jobs, you know that don't you? Lucky for you, that decision is mine to make, and I understand why you guys did what you did."

"I understand. I guess that means we're off the case then, huh?"

"Off the case? The suspect is in custody, caught in the act. There isn't much of a case anymore. The guy has been caught, and that's the most important thing. But I can't just brush this under the rug though either. Do you know how that would make me look? I can't have that. Be prepared for a suspension, Harris. Dale too."

"But-"

Sheriff Collins holds up his hand. "With pay. You both have families, I know that. We're understaffed too, so we need you out there patrolling the streets."

Jamaal is relieved. "Thank you, Sheriff. Really."

"Don't thank me yet. The show ain't over until the fat lady sings, am I right?" Sheriff Collins says, half-joking, half not.

"I guess so."

"You just better hope that nobody else gets hurt, or worse. Don't screw this up."

It's a warning to Jamaal from Henry, and Jamaal completely understands the message. Henry nods and heads down the hallway toward his office, leaving Jamaal standing alone to ponder his next move.

The Sheriff is so right. Jamaal had tried to tell Gerry that they were out of place by not telling Henry about what they were working on, but Gerry wouldn't listen. He's stubborn like that. Gerry never thought that it would get to this point, and Jamaal supposes that he can't blame him for that. He had felt the same way at the time. Though sometimes he wishes that he had a partner who wasn't so persistent in sticking his nose where it doesn't belong, he supports Gerry. Jamaal could have said no and told the Sheriff anyway, but he didn't, so he's just as much to blame as Gerry is.

Although there are still some unanswered questions and some details that need to be cleared up, this case is as close to being black and white as you'll find. Marco Salazar was caught in the act and has admitted to breaking into the house. How much simpler could it get than that? Marco isn't talking yet, but he will. Once he's threatened with serious jail time if he doesn't spill his guts, he'll talk. They all do. And when he does, everyone will find out what really happened and why, as well as who the mystery man was that had been helping him. Jamaal and Gerry will serve their one week paid suspensions and everyone will soon forget all about it. They'll just tell their wives that they're on a surprise vacation - use it or lose it should suffice - and soon enough they'll be off the graveyard shift and back to working days. Everything will go back to normal. What could go wrong? It'll all play out like it's supposed to in time.

IN THE KITCHEN IN the rear of the pizzeria, Antonio explains all that had happened at the Winston's house to Sal for the third time. Feeling better and chewing on some chalky antacids, Sal flattens some pizza dough while he listens.

"He handed me the diamonds and told me to run out the back," Antonio says. "He told me that it wouldn't do us any good if we were both in jail."

"Then what happened?"

"How many times are we going to do this?" Antonio complains. "I've already told you what happened."

"Just tell me, Antonio."

Antonio sighs. "Fine. Marco opened the front door and put his hands over his head. When the door closed, I slipped out the back and waited. I heard some yelling around the front and I got worried. And before you ask, no, I couldn't hear what was being said. The sirens were too loud. Anyway, so I figured that I couldn't just be standing there if someone came around the back, and I certainly couldn't go back inside the house. There are some hedge bushes lining the side of the house, so I got on my stomach and crawled underneath to hide."

"Yes, I remember those," Sal says, nodding. "Then what happened?"

"Then after a while, when nobody came around the back, I crept toward the front, army crawl style, to see what was going on. That's when I saw Marco being shoved into the back seat of the police car. Then-"

"Hold that thought," Sal says as he reaches for the ringing phone. "Big Sal's Pizzeria, this is Big Sal." It takes a moment for him to realize what's going on, but when he does, he nearly drops the phone in the pizza dough that is starting to resemble a crust.

"What's wrong?" Antonio says.

Sal ignores him. After a few minutes of just one word responses, Sal slowly hangs up the phone and can feel himself getting flush. He turns to Antonio and says, "That was Marco."

Life springs into Antonio, and he straightens his posture. "Is he okay? When is he getting out?"

"Monday."

"Monday! He can't stay in there the entire weekend. What about bail?"

"He's scheduled to see the judge at nine o'clock Monday morning. Bail will be set then. They're talking a big number, Antonio."

"How big?"

"We won't know until Monday for sure, but it's looking like thousands."

"Thousands! Why?"

Sal shrugs. "It sounds like they have a lot on him. They seem to think that he was Enrique earlier today, the guy who broke in and got the statue. They're convinced that he has the statue stashed somewhere."

"So?"

"So something must have happened when Enrique was there. So on top of breaking and entering, burglary, and damage to personal property, they've tacked on first degree assault."

"They can't go that, it's not true! Nobody was even in the house!"

"They just did." Sal drops everything and makes his way across the kitchen. He grabs the light jacket that hangs from the back of the door that leads up to his apartment and puts it on.

"Where are you going?" Antonio asks.

"To see Bartolo. I need to tell him what's going on with Marco."

"I should turn myself in and tell them everything. Marco shouldn't be alone in there."

Sal walks over to Antonio and puts his finger close to his face. "Don't you dare do such a thing. What are you going to tell them, that you know that Marco didn't assault anybody because you were the one who broke into the house with him? Don't be stupid. We can't do anything rash right now, capiche? Marco was right, it doesn't do us any good if both of you are in jail. I just need some time to figure this out." Sal puts his sweaty hand on Antonio's face and taps it lightly a few times. "Just stay here and relax. Let Big Sal take care of this."

CHAPTER TWENTY-NINE

Enrique Henderson and Stephan Cooper are back in their studio apartment near the interstate, the statue now in hand. Enrique tells Stephan nothing of what had happened inside the house, and he doesn't ask. Stephan's role is to drive. That's it. Whatever Enrique is doing, Stephan knows none of it. Now that he's had some time to think about it, Enrique is having second thoughts about letting that lady live. That's twice now that he regrets something that he hasn't done, and he wonders if greed has made him a little bit lazy. He hopes not.

Enrique's flight leaves from Logan in an hour. He's been careful to keep the plane ticket in his possession at all times so that Stephan doesn't notice that there's only one of them. Who knows what he might do if he were to find that out. A fight to the death seems plausible, and Enrique doesn't want to take that chance. Stephan thinks that they're supposed to be at the airport to check in already, but Enrique insists on waiting until it's closer to boarding time. He simply just doesn't want to wait in the lines. Plus, there is still something that he has to take care of first.

Stephan won't get his money until they land. That's the agreement. He hasn't been told where they're going, which he doesn't like, but he has nowhere to be, so he's up for the adventure - he's told Enrique as much. The two men have lived in close quarters for the last month, so Enrique feels like he knows the man. Stephan could get his next call for a job at any time and it could be for anywhere across the globe, so he doesn't ever expect to stay in one place for too long. He's done work in forty-two states, fifteen countries, and on three continents. He knows four languages and has made close to a million dollars in the last five years alone. And with all that said, he still wants more, and that's why he's here. This job is paying more than he has ever made at one time, and it's not even close.

Enrique has shared nothing about himself.

Across the studio, Enrique opens the one closet that's near the front door and reaches inside. He pulls out a heavy-duty compact toolbox which contains everything that he needs to break through the statue. The statue itself is practically worthless - it's what inside that he's looking for. He places a drill equipped with an eighteen inch long and super thin bit, a clamp, and a flathead screwdriver onto the kitchen table. He cranks the clamp around the statue until it holds it snugly. One thing he's missing, he realizes now, is a way to keep the statue firmly attached to the table so that it won't move around when he drills into it. The bit is oversized and requires him to stand over the top of the statue to drill into it, so he reluctantly asks Stephan for help.

Without hesitation, Stephan slides into position and wraps his hands around the base of the statue. He applies downward pressure to keep it as steady as possible on the table. If Enrique didn't need his assistance right now, now would be the perfect opportunity to jam the drill bit into Stephan's brain through his earhole. It almost disappoints him that he can't. But the time will come, he just has to be patient. Using the electric drill for what it's designed for, Enrique lines up the bit head with what he estimates is the center of the top of the skull of the warrior statue. Keeping a slow and steady pace, he pulls the trigger and watches as the hole starts penetrating deeper and deeper. It's a delicate process that cannot be rushed for fear of damaging what's inside, so he takes his time. As the drill bit slowly starts penetrating the solid frame of the statue, a minuscule crack starts to spread across the top. Every so often, Enrique reverses the direction of the drill and tries his hand with prying away pieces of the splitting statue with the flathead, but it's still too soon.

Enrique can feel the difference in the rotation of the drill bit when he breaks through the top layer of protection, but the crack isn't wide enough to allow him to separate the front and back halves pieces quite yet. Even with the pressure of the clamp stressing the statue and providing extra leverage to spread the crack, he's forced to rotate it and re-clamp multiple times. He does it to ensure that the top, bottom, left, and right sides have all been drilled to the core. The cracks have spread around almost symmetrically, but it takes one final clamp right on top of the drill holes on the left and right sides of the statue to finally split the figure. Enrique uses his entire body weight to torque the crank of the clamp to the right while Stephan goes against the pressure to the left. With the help of the flathead being used as a wedge from deep inside one of the cracks, the statue finally separates and breaks into two individual pieces.

With the sound of glass on glass clanking on the table, tens of millions of dollars in the form of hundreds of small but perfectly conditioned diamonds burst out from inside the statue and scatter across the table. The Cha-Ching sound of green being passed from one hand to the other resonates in Enrique's head as the diamonds cover the top of the table. They sparkle like a clump of a hundred stars trapped in a glass bottle. And with that, all of the work thus far has been worth it.

"Holy shit," Stephan says as he leans back in his chair, looking completely bewildered by the scene developing in front of him.

With a slight grin on his face, Enrique retrieves a dark sack from his pocket and funnels the diamonds inside. When the last of the diamonds are in and the sack is secured, Enrique looks to Stephan and says, "Okay, we can go now."

Stephan gets up and heads for the door. Enrique follows, the sack of diamonds firmly clenched in his hand. He feels for his gun with his other hand, and finds it in his belt. The last thing that Enrique has to take care of is to ensure that he's the one who's going to use the single plane ticket that's in his pocket. Although he doesn't have a plan yet, he just needs to wait for the right time to make his move. The right moment will present itself, he's certain of it. The plane should be off the ground in forty minutes, so he has no more than twenty to get it done, and even that might be cutting it close.

JEN REFUSES TO GO home. She convinces Peter to hang around the station for a while until they find out who the police are suspecting is responsible for all of this. A short time ago, Officer Harris had confirmed that a suspect is in custody, but he wasn't able to provide his name yet. He said that he didn't want to sway them either way in regards to identifying him, so that's why it's being held back. Jen's not so sure. He also said that they think it's the same person who had attacked Jen earlier today and who broke into the house earlier in the week. Officer Harris also confirmed that they're still working on who the second intruder was during that first night. Jen suspects that they don't have a clue who it is.

Until Jen can identify the suspect, she's not going anywhere. Peter finds them some coffee from the Keurig machine in the hallway, and they sit in silence while they sip on their drinks. The combination of pumpkin spice and mocha fills the room, the warm aromas warming Jen's core. It smells and tastes and feels like autumn. It reminds her of home. She and Peter are in an interrogation room, but it really has more of the feel of a meeting room. Not a whole lot of interrogation has gone on as far as Jen can tell.

Jen doesn't think that Peter believes all of her story. The bruising on her neck is hard to explain, but she can tell that he's not buying it by the way he refuses to look into her eyes when she talks to him. It hurts. She's been through a lot this week and things only seem to happen when she's alone. Aside from that first night, Peter has seen none of what Jen has. And worse, when she thinks about it, nothing even happened that night. Everything has gone down while Peter's been at work, and he just doesn't understand what she's going through. He never has. He wasn't even sympathetic when her father died, which was only a year into their marriage. She should have seen the signs of how things were going to be then. To say that Peter is heartless is too hostile, but sometimes Jen thinks that it's an appropriate way to describe her husband. She just doesn't understand the way that he thinks sometimes.

A light knock comes from behind the door moments before it opens. Jen springs to her feet and nearly spills her coffee all over the table.

"How are you holding up?" Officer Dale says as he walks in the room. He sounds genuine in his concern.

Jen shrugs. "Okay, I guess."

"We're ready for you now."

Jen takes a deep breath and follows Officer Dale out of the room without looking to her husband, who trails behind them. Officer Dale leads them to the end of the hall where Officer Harris is waiting outside of another interrogation room.

"You're sure you're up for this?" Officer Harris says to Jen when the group approaches. "We can do this another time if you'd rather. He'll be here all weekend at a minimum, probably longer, so you can come back later if you'd like."

Jen nods anxiously. "No, it's okay. I want to do this."

Officer Harris nods. "Okay then."

Officer Dale puts his hand on the back of Jen's shoulder, his touch making her shiver, and leads her to the one-way mirror on the wall. Jen crosses her arms and rubs her sleeves with her chapped hands. Peter stands close and tries to offer his support, although Jen hardly even realizes that he's there.

Inside the interrogation room are two men. One has his back to the window and is dressed in dark slacks and a button up. Jen can see what appears to be a police badge hanging from his belt. He must be an interrogator or something, she assumes. The other man sits in a chair directly across from the interrogator, and he looks up and into the mirror when prompted. Jen stares at him and studies his face.

She flashes back to the face of her attacker from earlier in the day. Those eyes, she'll never forget them, as evil as they were. He had a well-developed jaw line and a symmetrical face, and she may have actually considered him to be handsome if they had met under different circumstances. She'll never forget his face for as long as she lives. His hands were strong and he showed no emotion while standing in front of her with his fingers wrapped around her throat. He had seemed to be getting some sort of sexual arousal from the entire experience. He could have killed her without much effort, and she knows that. Why he didn't is the thing that bothers her most.

The man who seemingly stares back at her through the glass is young - far too young, in fact - to be her attacker. He looks so innocent sitting there, and she almost feels bad for him. Then she remembers that he was caught inside of her house when she and Peter left to come to the station, and she suddenly doesn't feel so bad for the kid anymore. Jen takes a step back and looks away. Her emotions are suddenly pulled to the forefront, and she has to fight to stop the tears from falling. Peter puts his arm around her and pulls her in close, but she's distant. She's feeling overwhelmed.

Jen thinks back to the night this all began, the night when the two guys were standing next to her bed while she and Peter were sleeping. Despite there being a light on at the time, her eyes had struggled to adjust to the darkness of the room. The two intruders were both wearing dark ski masks and holding guns, but she didn't get a good look at much else. She remembers dark eyes, brown probably, but that's about it. This guy does brown eyes - the one in the interrogation room, staring back at her - but so does fifty percent of the population, so that doesn't help much. Nothing else on his face rekindles any memories, and that disappoints her. She knows that this is far from over.

"Is this the man that attacked you today, Mrs. Winston?" Officer Harris asks.

Jen looks between the three men that surround her with care, and it kills her to say it. She knows that this means that her attacker is still on the loose and that he might just come back to try and finish the job. He left a witness, which may have been a mistake, and the reality of that sends a chill down Jen's spine. Whatever his endgame was, whatever he wanted with that statue, she hopes that he found what he was looking for. With all her of being, she just hopes that he won't be coming back for her. Despite having three strong men by her side and there to protect her, two of them with guns, she has never felt so alone in her entire life.

"No," she says, "that's not him."

THE TRAFFIC THIS TIME of day is light in the city, despite the rush to make it to the terminals on time. The ramp to Logan is on the right-hand side, so Stephan Cooper forces his way across three lanes to exit. Enrique rides in the back seat, still trying to figure out how he's going to end this. They should be at the airport in only minutes.

"About those diamonds," Stephan says, peering into the rearview mirror.

"What about them?" Enrique says without looking. He stares at the white lines that scream past him on the street.

"What's the deal?"

"It doesn't matter. Just drive."

"I say we split them."

Enrique finally looks up and into the reflective eyes of his driver. He says, "That wasn't our arrangement."

"Well, to be fair, I didn't know then what I know now."

"Okay."

"Okay, what?

"Okay, what's your point?"

"My point is that I deserve to split those with you. I put myself out there to help and I did everything you asked, plus some, so I think I'm entitled to my share."

"You're not getting greedy, are you?"

"Of course not, it's just-"

"You know what? Do me a favor. Pull over."

"Why?"

"Just pull over. You're right. I'll split them up."

"Are you serious?" Stephan switches his eyes between the rearview and the windshield with rapid fire, his eyes attentive and unblinking. He looks shocked.

The car pulls off to the side as much as it can and comes to a stop.

Enrique waits for Stephan to turn around and face him before shooting him in the throat. Stephan's neck snaps back and his eyes roll back in his head immediately upon impact. Blood sprays out of the back of his neck and covers the dashboard like a fresh coat of wet paint. Fluid pours out of the hole in his neck like a swaying firehose on full blast. Enrique wishes that he had a poncho. Stephan falls to the side and is kept in the sitting position only by the seatbelt across his chest. He seizes in place before bleeding out and falling limp in about a minute.

Done. Problem solved.

Enrique slides across the back seat and waits until there's a break in traffic before opening the door. He wipes the gun free of his prints and tosses it in Stephan's lap. He's all business. He feels nothing. If anything, maybe just relief.

The body will be found within the hour, but Enrique will be long gone by then. The gun has had the serial number removed and the barrel has been intentionally tampered with, so the gun is untraceable. The car is a rental and under Stephan's name, as was the studio apartment. All things considered, the police will find no evidence of Enrique even existing, so they'll have no choice but to rule it a suicide.

Stephan Cooper isn't Enrique's first victim, and he probably won't be his last. Greed gets the best of people sometimes, and if Stephan had been satisfied with his agreed upon reward, Enrique may have let him go. He was never getting any of the money, of course, and he wasn't getting on that plane, but he may have made it out alive. Maybe. May that be a lesson for him to remember during his next life, if there is such a phenomenon.

Enrique pops the trunk and grabs his carry-on from the way back. He throws the bag over his shoulder and starts walking toward the airport. Cars fly past him, the passengers inside more than likely cursing at him for being in the road and holding up traffic, but he carries on. No one seems to notice the blood-soaked car that he leaves in his wake, or maybe it's that nobody cares. Most people would rather not get involved, and that's exactly what he's counting on.

The entrance to Logan Airport appears as Enrique makes his way around the bend. A giant analog clock hanging on the overpass tells him that he has less than ten minutes before his flight boards. As he approaches, he checks in on his mobile phone, ensuring that they'll hold the flight for him.

The sack of diamonds rubs against his thigh as he walks, and it serves as a reminder that it's only a matter of hours before he can finally collect his big payday. He smiles and silently thanks Amelio Salazar for giving up the location of the statue so easily. He wouldn't have killed him. That was never part of the arrangement. The old man, maybe, but not Amelio. Not after all that Enrique and Amelio's brother, Bartolo, have been through together.

Enrique thinks about that woman again, the one who had looked so frightened earlier today, the one who had begged for her life and had been willing to give up anything for it. Enrique wishes that he had that moment back. He wishes that he would have taken what she was offering before he grabbed the statue. Maybe she would have even liked it, he dreams. She was so helpless and weak, but Enrique fears that he may have let his guard down too easily on that one. He should have had her, taken the statue, and killed her on the way out - in that order. What he can say with confidence, though, is that she won't talk. He's seen the faces of those who will talk and those who won't, and that woman was definitely a non-talker. If she only knew what she was up against, she wouldn't even dare.

CHAPTER THIRTY

Sal sits in his Lexus in the parking lot of the correctional institute in Concord, just pondering. Visiting hours end in thirty minutes and he has no idea how he's going to face Bartolo. He had made two promises to his brother when he first got incarcerated: first was that he wouldn't sell the pizzeria under any circumstances; second was that he would look over Marco and keep him safe. He has clearly failed at the most important of the two.

Bartolo is largely invested in the pizzeria financially, but it was never his dream like it was Sal's. Bartolo actually technically owns the pizzeria, as it was he who had provided all of the capital in the form of a personal loan. Sal didn't have the required credit profile or personal assets to be used as collateral, so Bartolo stepped up to help when Sal needed it. He had a solid credit score and a large house to put up, and he didn't hesitate to do so.

Now that the house is gone, Sal has always wondered why his brother is still adamant about keeping the pizzeria. Maybe it's a pride thing. Or maybe it's the only thing that gives him a chance at a normal life when he gets out. No bank will loan money to someone with a foreclosure on his credit report, so that pizzeria is the only asset that Bartolo has left. Maybe that's what it is, or maybe it's something else completely, but Sal can't help but be curious about it.

Sal eventually works up the courage to head inside the facility. His palms are sweaty and the hair on the back of his neck is soaked. He feels like his t-shirt is suffocating him. He goes through the usual security check upon signing in with the clerk, and he's ushered to the waiting area for one of the correctional officers to retrieve his brother after the notification page is sent out across the system.

When everyone is in place, Sal is led to the room that he's becoming all too familiar with. Despite his regular visits, Sal still gets jittery every time he sees the phone bank and all of those orange jumpsuits sitting on the other side of the glass. He finds an empty booth and waits for Bartolo to arrive. He nervously taps his heel against the tile.

Bartolo appears from around the painted brick wall in his usual getup. Ankle chains and handcuffs restrain his mobility, and he shuffles his feet across the cement floor as he approaches. He keeps his head facing downward until he sits in front of the glass and is forced to look at his brother. He fumbles with the phone.

"What the hell happened to you?" Sal says, referring to the black and blue shiner that covers his right eye. It looks fresh.

"Just prison," Bartolo says, then he shrugs.

"It looks bad. Does it hurt?"

"What do you think?"

"Sorry, that was a stupid question."

There's a tense silence between the two brothers. At one time they could speak so freely and openly, but things have changed now. That's what this kind of stress does to people.

"What are you doing here?" Bartolo says in a low, saddened, hushed tone. "I wasn't expecting you until Tuesday after you paid Stan Brothers. What's going on?"

Sal looks away and tries to find something to stare at, but his little brother's unblinking, pained eyes are all that he can find. They're hard to ignore. "I don't know how to say this."

"Please just cut out the bullshit. Just give it to me straight for once. What's going on, Amelio? Why are you here?"

Sal sighs. "It's Marco. He's in trouble."

Bartolo's entire body stiffens, his face looking strained because of it. What happened?"

"The boys got what we need, but-"

"Be careful, remember? They could be monitoring this conversation."

Sal nods. "As I was saying, they got what we were looking for, but Marco got busted. Only Marco. I can't really get into details right now, but the...item is safe."

Bartolo nods a few times, telling Amelio that he understands and that he wants him to say no more. Looking relieved, he exhales. "Okay, good. What about Marco then?"

"He can't get in front of a judge until Monday at nine. He'll be held for the weekend."

Bartolo clenches his fists and Sal can see the anger starting to build up within his brother.

Sal continues, "They've got a bunch on him, although most of it is wrong. But we can't do anything until bail is set on Monday."

"Are we going to have enough?" Bartolo sounds almost panicky. "What are you hearing?"

Sal shrugs. "Not sure. They told Marco is could be thousands."

"Thousands! What the hell happened?"

"I told you, it's all wrong. They think he was someone else."

"Who?"

Before Sal can answer, the uniformed correctional officer taps Bartolo on the shoulder and tells him that his time is up. Another inmate waits his turn a few feet behind the booth, chained up similarly. Sal kicks himself, knowing that he shouldn't have wasted so much time in the parking lot, dreading the conversation. Bartolo pleads with the guard for another minute, but is denied.

Before hanging up the phone, Bartolo says, "I'll call you Monday afternoon after Marco sees the judge. We'll figure it out then. I get some free time shortly after nine, so I'll call you then."

Sal nods. He watches the guard drag his brother away and out of site. Nothing is worse than watching a family member being treated like that, like a monster who needs to be chained up. What's even worse than that, though, is having two. Sal cringes at the thought of Marco being treated the same way.

Still clammy, Sal leaves the jailhouse and heads back to his car in the parking lot. He doesn't have to walk far, which is good, because he's not sure that his blood pressure can handle it today. Despite the cool autumn air, the cloth seat of his Lexus is warm from resting directly in the path of the sun. There are no clouds overhead, allowing the rays to do their thing without interference.

Before starting up the engine and heading back to the pizzeria, he opens up the glove box and pulls out a pen. He twists the cap off and flips the now open end over and pours the contents into his open palm. The two diamond eyes fall softly into his hand and sparkle luminously when the sun hits them just right. Satisfied with the self-modified contraption, Sal slides the diamonds back into the hollowed out pen and puts the cap back on. He returns the pen to its designated position under the user's manual and closes the glove box. He starts up the Lexus and heads back into the city.

PETER HOLDS HIS POSITION on the front stoop and takes a deep breath before fully turning the door knob. Jen timidly stands behind him, breathing on his neck. They've been warned that their home is a wreck, but he's not quite sure what to expect. Reluctantly, Peter turns the knob and pushes the door open. The first thing that he notices is that the alarm doesn't beep.

The house looks like a crime scene. What once was the front panel to the alarm system is now on the floor, and a knot of colored electrical wires hangs from the wall. One of them is cut. That must have been what had triggered the alarm company to dispatch the police, Peter assumes. The intruder must not have known that the way this system is set up, any tampering of the system is a direct alert. The wires can't be cut without the cops coming, not even the one to disable the system. They won't even bother calling to confirm that everything is okay, they'll just send the police over right away. It's a way to safeguard the homeowners without alerting possible intruders, and it did exactly what it was designed to do. Even Peter can admit that Jen has made a wise decision by having the system installed. He'd never tell her that, though. That would mean that she won.

Jen brushes past her husband and makes her way down the unlit hallway and into the kitchen. Peter follows and looks for any signs of anything missing or out of place, but everything appears to be in order at first glance. Ahead of him and in the kitchen, Jen checks the slider, which opens freely. She gasps.

"What is it?" Peter says as he approaches her from behind.

"The slider is unlocked."

"Safe to say it wasn't from you?"

"No. You?"

Peter shakes his head. "The front door was unlocked too."

"What does that mean?"

Peter puts his hand on his head and scratches while he thinks. "Maybe he came in through the back, cut the alarm, and then left out the front door. He got caught out front, so that would make sense."

"Or?"

"Or...there was someone else with him. Someone who left out the back during the commotion in the front."

Jen nods as she wraps her arms around herself. "I wonder what they wanted."

Peter shrugs. "Is there anything missing?"

Jen scans the room and says, "It doesn't look that way."

"Let's go check upstairs."

Jen makes sure that the slider is fully closed, then she locks it before following Peter upstairs.

Upstairs is worse. The bedroom is destroyed. Drawers are pulled out of the dressers, clothes are scattered across the floor, and the freshly patched hole in the drywall is caved in and wide enough to expose the wooden studs behind. Jen starts to cry when she takes in the scene. Peter is also troubled by what has happened, but he's far less emotional than Jen is. He doesn't know how to react. He does know that he's going to need to paint over that spot again after he patches it for a second time, though. That annoys him.

Peter kicks a pair of Jen's underwear to the side and pulls her into his chest and lets her weep. He looks around the room and is completely disturbed at what has happened. The intruder, or intruders possibly, was looking for something - that much is clear. What he couldn't find hidden away in the drawers, he searched for in the wall. It must have been that statue. Whatever its purpose, people want it. The old man at the pawn shop wasn't willing to give them practically anything for it, saying that it was worthless, which seems strange now. Either they're all missing something, or there's something that they don't know about it. Regardless, it's in high demand, apparently, and people are willing to go to extreme lengths to get it. What that means exactly, Peter doesn't know.

Peter looks down at the top of his wife's head and has a feeling of hopelessness. There's nothing that he can say that will make her feel any better about what has happened, and he thinks that he understands now what she's been saying all along. He admits to himself that he didn't fully believe everything she had said before, but now seeing the condition of the house, he realizes that he has severely underestimated the situation. He wants to apologize to her for that, but he doesn't think that he can muster up the courage to admit that he was wrong. Instead, he kisses the top of her head and caresses her hair. The once powerful scent of pomegranate has since faded. It now just smells dull and tired, if that's even possible. Within himself, Peter makes a promise that he'll make it up to her - he'll make up for everything that he's done, and more importantly, all that he hasn't - and he just hopes that she'll stick around long enough to let him.

GERRY CAN'T SLEEP, HIS mind running rampant with all of the action of the day. He lies alone in the bed that he and his wife share and tries to ignore the daylight that creeps its way around the thick darkened curtains. The Winston case is consuming his every thought. A case has never taken over him like this before - and for good reason, since he's just a patrolman - but for now it's all that he can think about, even though the finish line appears near. Something still isn't adding up.

Mrs. Winston saying that Marco Salazar - the main suspect behind all of this that is in police custody - was not the man who attacked her earlier in the day is a setback. Without this known threat of violence, his bail might be manageable, which is bad news. If he posts bail, Gerry and Jamaal lose all of their leverage. The threat of him being jailed gives them the best chance of getting information out of him. He wouldn't talk today, not even to the veteran expert interrogator, so it's clear that he's not going to make this easy.

Marco Salazar knows more than he is saying. He does admit to breaking into the Winston's house, but he won't say for what purpose and is adamant that he was working alone. He hasn't asked for a lawyer yet either, which Gerry finds peculiar. Gerry's not totally sure what to make of that. It's like Marco is just buying time and waiting for something.

But what?

Thanks to Jamaal's summary of his conversation with Sheriff Collins from earlier, Gerry can add the looming suspension to his list of sleep distractions. Tomorrow is a new day, but Gerry hasn't yet decided where he'll even begin. He and Jamaal have just the weekend to find out more about Marco Salazar and his motives, and Gerry worries that that's not enough time. They have to come up with something that will show the judge that he's a threat to the community before leaving the courtroom on Monday.

Marco is the guy responsible for all of this and Gerry knows it. He just has to make sure that the judge sees it that way too. The Winston's lives may be in danger if Marco's back on the streets, and who knows what else he might be up to aside from what he's already been caught doing. His father has a violent criminal past, which will help their case a little bit, but it may not be enough in and of itself. Gerry's career may be at stake here too, the same with his partner, so it's becoming about more than just the Winston's and their safety. It's becoming personal for Gerry and he's a man who doesn't like to lose.

CHAPTER THIRTY-ONE

Sal sleeps with the hollow pen under his pillow and the diamonds still inside. When he wakes before sunrise on Saturday, the first thing that he does is check that the diamonds are still there. They are. The diamonds are Bartolo's lifeline, Marco's possibly too, and he refuses to let them out of his site. He wouldn't have slept if he could have gotten away with it. Sal throws on the same pants and t-shirt that he wore the day before and heads down the stairs and into the kitchen. The pizzeria isn't going to be opening for a few hours, so it gives him time to take care of what he needs to today before that takes precedence.

He leaves out the front and sets the alarm, then heads over to his once new Lexus. The car's in bad shape. It always starts and seems to run okay once it gets going, but it's on the back nine for sure. If it were a housecat, it would probably be on life six or seven by now. The back seat has a hole from a cigarette burnt into it, which, strangely enough, Sal doesn't know how it got there. It wasn't there when he bought the vehicle, and he's never allowed anyone to smoke while in it. It seems to be one of those mysteries in life that can't be explained, and he cringes every time that he sees it. He's always wondered how it even got there in the first place.

Sal's first stop is Willy's Pawn. Inside, the shop is empty and Willy is nowhere to be found. Sal makes his way around the perimeter of the store and calls out for his friend, but gets no response. He opens the break in the counters and heads into the back room. He calls out again, his voice bellowing in the openness, but still gets nothing in return. Around the corner, a light shines from the inside of Willy's office, so Sal heads in that direction. Inside, he finds Willy with his head flat against the desk, and his heart drops.

Sal immediately fears the worst. He fears that his good buddy has been killed for something that Sal had gotten him involved with, and Sal starts to shudder. The guilt would be too much for Sal to handle. Under his breath, he pleads for Willy to be alive. Standing across from Willy's desk, he looks for blood and doesn't find any. Then he walks slowly around to the other side and approaches the old man. He reaches down, his hand trembling, and touches Willy's shoulder with the intention of flipping him over to inspect the damage. Sal jumps back when Willy reacts to his touch.

Willy grumbles and his body jolts at the touch of Sal's unsteady hand, and he whips his head up to see who's interrupting his power nap. "Who's there?" he says, groggily.

Sal puts his hand to his chest and breathes a heavy sigh of relief. He leans his backside against the corner of Willy's desk and almost laughs. He's starting to get paranoid. "It's me, Sal," he says.

Willy rubs his eyes and sits up in his chair, then glances around for something. "Shit, I must have fallen asleep," he says. "What time is it?" Willy's attentiveness suddenly spikes, and he frantically studies the TV monitor for activity in the storefront.

"It's okay, the store's empty," Sal says, trying to settle his friend. He knows that it won't ease Willy's mind in regards to if anyone had been in the store before Sal and if they took anything, but Sal hopes that Willy will let it go.

He does.

"I'm getting too old for this," Willy says, obviously embarrassed. "What are you doing here, Sal?"

Not wasting any time, Sal says, "Marco got arrested yesterday."

"I...I'm sorry, Sal. What happened?"

Sal tells him.

When he finishes, Willy waits a moment before mustering up a response. He says, "So what are you doing here then? Is there something that I can do to help?"

Sal retrieves the hollowed out pen from his pocket and removes the cap. He pours the contents into his open palm. The two mint diamonds stare Willy in the face.

"Do you remember that statue that those people brought in to you the other day? The Winston's." Sal says.

Willy nods as he removes the diamonds from Sal's palm. He analyzes them for imperfections under a handheld microscope that he removes from the top drawer of his desk.

Sal continues, "These were supposed to be on that statue. These were the eyes. They must have fallen off before the statue was found. This is what the buyer was after."

Willy turns one of the diamonds over and inspects its underside. He looks up to Sal and nods like it all makes sense. He puts the diamonds back into Sal's hand and says, "Enrique was going to give me fifty grand for these. He never told me what it was that would be coming in, but he said I'd know it when I saw it."

"Would you have known?"

"I would hope so. Where did you get these?"

Sal bypasses the question. "Hold on, fifty grand? He was going to give you fifty grand for these? I thought you said you'd give me twenty-five?"

"That's right."

"But they're worth fifty grand!"

"It's a business, Sal. I need to make a living here too. You're a businessman, you know what that's like."

"I'm not in the business of screwing people."

Willy stares back at Sal but doesn't say anything.

Sal continues, "I thought we were friends?"

That strikes a nerve with Willy. "I don't want to hear that shit! We are friends, but this is my life. Don't you get that? If I don't make money I don't eat. It's as simple as that. If I wasn't your friend I would have turned your ass in already."

Sal looks away. He wants to remind Willy that he's deeply involved here too, being that he's been in possession of tens of thousands of dollars of stolen goods, but he doesn't.

"After all that I've done for you," Willy continues, "I can't believe that you have the balls to question my friendship." His Santa-like beard bounces as he speaks. "I've been nothing but loyal to you, Sal. Do you think I'm stupid? Do you think I didn't know something was up when you kept coming back week after week with more stuff? You live in a fucking studio apartment above your pizzeria for Christ sakes."

Sal refuses to look into Willy's eyes as he knows that he's right. Sal had thought all this time that Willy was oblivious to what was going on, or maybe that he just didn't care enough to ask any questions. As it turns out, Willy has known all along. He knew that everything he had agreed to buy from Sal was stolen, and he didn't care. He didn't ask questions because he was trying to be a good friend, not because he was blind to what was happening right in front of him. Willy has been more than a good friend; he's been the best of friends.

Now overcome with guilt after realizing this, Sal forces himself to meet Willy's eyes. He can sense the deep hurt within him, and Sal knows that he was the one who put it there. Sal wonders to himself how many of those grays in Willy's beard have been a result of his actions. "Willy, I'm sorry. You're-"

"What do you want from me, Sal?" Willy says. "Why are you here?"

"I'm here to collect," Sal says as he places the diamonds on Willy's desk. "I need that money."

Willy gazes at the diamonds on his desk and stays quiet. Sal thinks that he knows what Willy's thinking about. He remembers that time that Willy had told him the reason why he doesn't typically purchase fine jewelry and stones. He had said that it's just too easy to miss an imperfection in something and lose money. Sal bets that's what Willy is struggling with now.

"I'm done, Sal. I'm out," Willy says.

"What are you talking about?"

"I can't do this anymore. What happened yesterday really got me thinking. Life is too short, you know? I'm selling."

Sal takes the blow right in the gut. "When did you decide this?"

"Last night, but I've been thinking about it for years. I'm seventy-two years old. It's time for me to move on before it's too late. I need to do this while I still can."

"One more. I just need this one last favor from you, can you help me?"

Willy scoops up the diamonds and shakes his head. He hands the diamonds back to Sal and lowers his head. "I'm sorry. I just can't do this anymore."

"Please, Willy. My brother and my nephew are in jail. They're counting on this money. They're counting on me."

Willy refuses to look at Sal. He stands firm. "I can't."

"Please," Sal says, his voice filled with desperation. "Please don't make me beg."

JEN AND PETER SPEND the night in a hotel. Jen refuses to stay in the house another night, especially with the alarm system now destroyed. First thing in the morning they head back to the house to meet ADT for an emergency repair. They'll pay double because it's a Saturday, but Jen couldn't care less. It's late morning by the time ADT finishes.

Shortly after, Officers Dale and Harris stop by the house to photograph the damage to the alarm panel and the mess upstairs. They leave, promising to contact Jen after court on Monday and assuring her that an officer will drive by the house every couple of hours during both weekend days.

Not much can be done over the weekend with the case, so Peter and Jen spend the rest of the morning cleaning up the house. They have enough supplies remaining to re-patch the hole behind the bed and are able to repaint the back wall. The constant reminder of what has happened is torturous for Jen.

Peter tries his best to distract his wife by keeping them busy and talking about everything but the case, but she's distracted. The effort doesn't go unnoticed, though, and she really does appreciate that he's trying. They go for a walk after dinner and Peter shows some sensitivity for the first time in months. Jen flashes a smile at him for doing so, and they walk arm in arm for nearly an hour. Thanks to the Lyme disease that won't go away, Jen's joints are sore today, so their progress is slow.

Wherever rock bottom is, they've already hit it and are on the back way up, Jen thinks. She hopes that Peter senses it too. Despite all that they've been through since moving to the city, Jen for the first time feels the support and love from her husband that she has desired. She's willing to forgive and forget everything that has happened between them, and he's finally showing signs of being the man that he used to be, the same man that she married so long ago. She had thought she'd lost him.

Peter's not a strong man physically, but his tight grip around her waist makes her feel secure. She gazes up at her husband and tells him that she loves him. Peter stops, turns his wife to face her, and pulls her face toward his. It's sensual and romantic, and the way in which he massages her lips with his makes her melt. It's been a long time since she's felt this way. Her knees tremble with the butterflies of a teenager before her first time, and it's a feeling she's long desired. The feeling makes her forget all about the pain, even if it just may be temporary.

"I love you too," Peter says, "and I promise that we'll make it through this."

Jen can't help but smile at his reassurance. But the best part, the part that keeps the smile from disappearing from her face, is that she actually believes him. Her loving husband is back.

WILLY HOLDS FIRM INITIALLY, but Sal all but forces his hand. Out of desperation, he threatens to tell the police about all of the stolen goods in Willy's possession, plus about the secret that he's been keeping to himself for all these years. Willy had tried to forget about it.

Ten years ago, Willy got himself in a heap of trouble. It was three years to the day that his wife had passed away, so he was depressed. It was a Thursday. He closed up shop early that afternoon - which is something that he almost never does - and went down to the pub around the block. He spent nearly four hours hopping from pub to pub and drinking away his sorrows until he was cut off from each.

He tried to drive home that night, but he didn't make it very far. In retrospect, he realizes that it was stupid and he'd do just about anything to go back and change it. Less than a mile from the pawn shop, Willy hit a pedestrian with his truck. The guy just jumped in the middle of the street from nowhere and Willy was unable to avoid him. It probably didn't really happen that way, but that's what Willy firmly believes occurred that night. He was heavily impaired and knew that he'd be going straight to prison if the police ever found out about it, so he did something even dumber than driving in the first place.

Instead of reporting the accident and taking responsibility for what had happened, Willy did the unthinkable. The pedestrian wasn't dead from the collision, but he was in need of critical medical attention.

It had been obvious. But instead of doing the logical thing - which, undoubtedly, he would have done if he wasn't impaired - Willy panicked and threw the man in the back of his truck and drove for another mile in the opposite direction.

The man had begged him to let him go, but Willy wasn't in the right frame of mind to comprehend what he was doing. He managed to pull the man from the bed of his truck, drag him across the pavement, and push his back up against the side of the bridge. That in and of itself was a near miracle - that Willy was coherent enough to even get the guy in that position. The man had screamed in pain from all of his injuries, but Willy was too drunk to care. He stared at the man's agonizing eyes with tears in his own, and apologized for doing it, then he pushed him over the side of the bridge and into the Charles River. The man had a broken arm, severely sprained ankle, and a dislocated hip, so Willy knew that he'd be unable to swim. Willy watched for two minutes while the innocent man batted his good arm and tried to stay afloat before eventually succumbing to the current and sinking to the bottom of the river.

Willy somehow made it back to the pawn shop in one piece and slept it off. When he sobered up the following day, he washed out the bed of his truck, cleaned himself of the blood, and waited for the cops to come.

They never did.

Willy saw the man's face on a missing person flyer a couple of weeks later, and he almost threw up all over it. The man, apparently, had a family. He still has never been found and he remains a cold case to this day. And in the end, presumably, Willy got away with his murder.

It took Willy months to tell anyone after it happened, and it was Sal in whom he decided to confide his deepest secret to. The guilt had been weighing him down like an anchor - kind of like that innocent, undeserving, disadvantaged pedestrian that had no chance against that current - and he needed to confess what he had done to somebody, so he chose his good friend. Neither one of them spoke of the incident until today, when Sal brought it up in the ultimate betrayal. Willy has always feared that it would come back to haunt him one day, one way or another. He just never thought that it would be Sal who be the one to threaten to reveal the secret.

REGRETFULLY, SAL LEAVES WILLY'S Pawn with $25,000 in cash. He's confident that he has made the right decision by doing what he did, but he's still not at peace with it. He knows that there's no turning back now and that Willy will no longer be there for him if he ever needs help in the future. Sal wouldn't have really told the police about what Willy's hiding, he doesn't think, but he had to use the only leverage that he had. It was the only way. He's desperate.

Sal now has the money that he needs to save his family, but it's at the expense of his dearest friend. Willy will never speak to him again, and although he hates that, he understands it. But family comes first - it always has and always will. All that Sal can do now is hope that his personal values will help push him through the loss of the best friend that he's ever had. And now he just has to hope that Marco's bail will be set at $5,000 or less, or this will all have been for nothing. They're at the mercy of the judge now.

CHAPTER THIRTY-TWO

Stan Brothers readjusts his necktie in the mirror as he cleans himself up. His face is red and his hair gel has faded to dust. He fixes it the best he can, but concedes the fact that he'll have to re-do it before he heads home later. Linda, his youthful secretary and mistress, buttons her blouse using her reflection in the window on the other side of the room. Stan puts his wedding ring back on before turning to her.

"Have you heard from my brother-in-law?" Stan says. "They should have landed yesterday afternoon."

Linda pops in the last of her buttons and flattens the fabric before turning to Stan. "He hasn't called, no," she says.

"Will you let me know when he does, please?"

Linda walks toward Stan and stands up on her toes, trying to kiss him. He turns his head and holds his hand up in front of her face.

"Uh, uh, watch the face," Stan says. "I just put lotion on. I don't want it to dry out."

Linda holds up her hand and flips her wrist toward him, which makes her look all too young and sophomoric. It's a firm reminder of just how youthful she is, which is exactly what Stan prefers.

"Whatever," Linda says. "I'll let you know if he calls." She leaves and heads back to tend to the front desk.

Stan rinses his mouth out with mouthwash and spits into the trash can. He straightens the photo of him and his wife on his desk and opens up his calendar. His next appointment isn't for an hour.

Stan has been sleeping with Linda for six months. Linda has been working for Stan for seven. Stan is ten years her senior. He had hired her with the worst of intentions, and it has worked out just the way that he had planned. He pays her well above market value, but that comes at a price. She seems to accept the extracurricular duties of the position, but to be fair, all the others did at first too. She'll get tired of it like the others and will just stop coming into work one day. Sometimes money isn't the only thing that matters, as Stan's learned, and he's always on the lookout for his next prospect should she be needed.

Stan loves his wife and has no plans to leave her, but she's not twenty-two anymore, and her body looks it. He does hope to have children with her one day, but he's too selfish to bring another life into the world right now - he knows that. He's at a point in his life where he'd rather spend his money on expensive booze and high fashion. And young women too, of course.

To the best of his knowledge, his wife has never known about his indiscretions, and Stan can't imagine that she'll ever find out. If she has, she's never said anything about it. Maybe she wouldn't even care. She hardly ever stops by the office, so he'll never get caught in the act. Plus, Linda will never say anything, not with the money that she's making. Even if his wife did find out somehow, Stan knows that she'd never leave him. He has given her everything that she's ever wanted in life, and she's unable to support her lifestyle without his paycheck. She'd never give that up, so Stan feels like he can do whatever he wants, and he does. In his mind, it's the ideal setup.

SAL STANDS AROUND AND leans against the desk in the reception area for the receptionist to reappear from the hallway. He's in Stan Brothers' office and the experience is all too familiar for him. The same blonde bimbo from last time sees him and makes her way down the hallway with no sense of urgency.

"Can I help you?" she says as she readjusts the bottom of her blouse.

"I need to talk to Stan," Sal says. "Is he in?"

Blondie sits behind the desk and tosses her hair over her shoulder. The leather chair swivels as she plops down gracefully. "Do you have an appointment?"

"No, but I really need to see him."

She makes a few clicks with her mouse on the computer in front of her. "It looks like he's free on Friday."

"Friday? That's almost a week from now. I need to see him now."

"I'm sorry, but without an appointment, I can't help you."

"Will you page him or something? Tell him that it's Amelio Salazar. He'll fit me in, trust me."

Blondie rolls her eyes, but she does call into Stan's office as suggested. When she hangs up with her boss, she looks to Sal and says, "He said you can go on back."

Without saying anything, Sal claps his hand on the top of the chest-high desk and darts toward Stan's office. He carries a polyester bag near his hip. Stan is waiting for him in the doorway of his office when Sal arrives.

"What do I owe this pleasure today, Amelio?" Stan says with a lot of energy. "I wasn't expecting you until Tuesday."

They shake hands.

"Can I come in?" Sal asks.

Stan steps to the side and lets Sal walk past him and into his office. Stan walks around to the other side of his desk and sits. Not really impressed with the view of the city this time, Sal sits in the client chair across from Stan and waits for an invitation. The room smells an awful lot like latex.

"What can I do for you?" Stan asks.

"Bartolo's son, Marco, also my nephew, got arrested yesterday."

"Oh. Listen, if you're here to hire me, don't bother. I don't think you can afford me. My retainer-"

"I'm not here to hire you."

"You're not?" Stan lifts his legs and drops them on the top of the desk. He crosses his ankles and shifts his weight around. "Why are you here then?"

"We owe you $20,000 on Tuesday for Bartolo's defense, right?"

"That's right."

"I have the money." Sal lifts the bag and presses it against his belly.

This catches Stan's attention. He slides his feet off the desk and corrects his posture. "That's great. So you're here to pay early then? It's wise of you, Amelio, it really is. The more time I have to prepare Bartolo's defense the better. I'll be honest with you, I didn't think you'd be able to come up with the rest, I really didn't."

"I'm not here to pay you."

Stan moans. He intertwines his fingers in the shape of a pyramid and places them in front of himself on the desk. The shoulders of his suit jacket rise up, giving the appearance of Stan being swallowed. "I see," he says. "Please enlighten me then, Amelio. Why are you here?"

"Marco's bail will be set on Monday. Depending on how that goes-"

Stan sighs and slouches back in his chair. "Will you please just get to the point? What does any of this have to do with me?"

"If you'd let me finish...I tried to say that depending on how the bail hearing goes, I may need to use some of the money that we owe you to get Marco out. I don't know yet, but depending on what the judge says-"

"You're asking for an extension again, aren't you?"

"Like I said, I don't know yet. But there's a possibility that we may be a little short."

"Get out."

"What?"

Stan jumps to his feet, red in the face, and thrusts a pointed finger toward the door of his office. "Get out of my office, now!"

"Stan-"

"If I don't have a check in my hands for $20,000 by five o'clock on Tuesday, I'm out. I don't care if you're a penny short, and I'm not kidding about that. No more extensions. Now get out!"

Sal stands, taken aback, and subtly shakes his head in disapproval in Stan's direction before leaving. Although not having expected that response, he doesn't have the energy to argue with him today. He walks down the lonesome hallway and exits Stan's building without so much as acknowledging blondie's presence behind the desk.

"GET IN HERE!" STAN yells into the intercom on his desk as Amelio Salazar storms out of his office.

"Coming," Linda says, like an obedient child.

While waiting for Linda to arrive, Stan walks across his office and grabs a glass from the card table. He removes the lid from the crystal pitcher and pours himself a third of a glass of straight bourbon. It burns his throat as he guzzles it down, but he loves it. He needs it to keep him sane.

How dare Amelio think that he can try to screw Stan out of money? He's just trying to push it off until something better comes around, Stan thinks, and he's having none of it. Stan Brothers is a hot commodity in this town, or so he tells himself, and he will not be played by a lowlife like Amelio Salazar. There are lines of people just waiting to become Stan's clients, and he can have any case that he wants. He's in high demand.

The truth is, Stan's not in high demand anymore. He just refuses to accept it. Three or four years ago it was the case, but now he's lucky to have one new client a month.

After he had won a few big cases and made some quick cash, he got complacent. He started to think that he couldn't lose in court, that he was invincible, and he got exposed. His track record has gone from superb to mediocre, and it's dropped even lower than that in recent months. He hasn't actually been in a courtroom since July.

The $80,000 that Amelio had given him is already gone. Every penny of it. Stan was able to pay some delinquent rent to the landlord of the building and catch up on some utilities. His personal finances are a mess too, as the foreclosure process is about to begin on his house in less than thirty days. He can't support his lifestyle anymore, never mind his wife's, and he's pretty sure that she's sleeping around too. Although he's no better, it still hurts. It hurts bad. The bourbon and the meaningless sex with Linda are the only things that keep him going. But even that may end soon. If Amelio Salazar doesn't come up with the rest of that money by Tuesday, Stan won't be able to make payroll and Linda will be gone too.

"Is everything okay?" Linda says, suddenly appearing in the doorway.

Stan pours himself another drink before turning to her. "I need you."

"Is everything okay?"

Stan takes a swig and walks over to his desk. He sits in his chair and leans his head back. He closes his eyes and tries to remember what his life used to be like. He does have a way out of all of this, but he's still waiting for that phone call from his brother-in-law to confirm that everything is still a go. Until then, all he has is Linda.

Linda makes her way across the room and nears Stan. She drops to her knees and unzips his pants, sighing slightly, all the while Stan still holds a firm grip around his warm glass of inspiration.

CHAPTER THIRTY-THREE

The photographs that Gerry and Jamaal were able to snap at the Winston's house don't really do them any good. All they really do is confirm what they already know, which is that the statue is what Marco Salazar stole from the house and that he wasn't working alone. The damage upstairs - the hole in the wall, specifically - combined with the timeline of the disabling of the alarm tells the whole story. Plus, Marco wouldn't have had time to dump the statue, and it wasn't on his person when taken into custody. There's no way that one person could have done it all alone before the police arrived. Stumped on where to go next, Gerry and Jamaal prepare to go their separate ways after their shifts.

"How did he say it?" Gerry says.

Jamaal looks at his partner, puzzled. "Who?"

"Sheriff Collins. About the suspension, what was his tone?"

"You're still worried about that?"

"You aren't?"

Jamaal shrugs. "Not really. It's not that big of a deal. We'll still get paid."

"When my wife finds out, man, she's going to flip."

"Don't let her find out then."

Gerry makes a face showing his dissatisfaction of his partner's comment. Jamaal should know better than that, Gerry thinks. It won't be that easy.

"There's nothing that we can about it now," Jamaal continues, "the damage has already been done. We did the right thing." Jamaal says it, but he doesn't sound like he really believes it.

Gerry sighs. "I guess you're right. I just wish there was a way around it, you know?"

Jamaal grabs his jacket from his locker and heads for the door. "I feel you. But I don't know what to tell you. Goodnight, Gerry."

"Night," Gerry says. He cringes as he says it, hating the fact that it's not even noon, yet they're both going home to get some sleep. "Enjoy the day tomorrow."

Jamaal leaves.

Gerry sits on one of the faded wooden locker room benches, shirtless. His once flat stomach has slowly turned to chub over the years - a sure sign of his aging body; no one has beaten Father Time. Although he never understood it as a youngster, Gerry now completely understands why Ponce de Leon spent his life's journey looking for a way to keep himself permanently young. Gerry would do the same thing. He stares at his uniform hanging up in the locker in front of him, feeling dejected, hoping that he didn't make a mistake that will cause him and Jamaal their careers. The stench of warm, stale man fills the room. It's his fault and really isn't fair that Jamaal has to suffer the consequences of his actions too, but he doesn't have the balls to tell the Sheriff that. If he would have just listened to Jamaal when he had suggested that they tell Sheriff Collins about the Winston case early on, they wouldn't be in this predicament. The guilt weighs heavy on his conscience.

Gerry and Jamaal have tomorrow off, as they do on most every Sunday, but Gerry doubts that he'll be able to get his mind away from work. Some much needed quality time with his family is in order, but it might be difficult to enjoy knowing what looms on Monday.

He and Jamaal have gathered nothing further to incriminate Marco Salazar, and they have no way to prove that he has violent tendencies. Without any further evidence that Marco is a threat to the community, the judge could do just about anything. A flight risk isn't a plausible argument either as all of Marco's direct family is in town, so he has nowhere to go. He does have a mother out in Montana, but there doesn't appear to be any strong connection between them, so that's out of the question.

The best that Gerry can hope for is that the judge has a rough weekend and that she wants to make an example out of Marco come Monday. He did admit to breaking into the house and there is physical evidence to support that, so they do have that much going for them at least. Where the trouble arises, though, is that he has no prior criminal history. That, combined with the fact that Mrs. Winston has ruled him out as her attacker makes it far less than a sure thing that he'll be held on a high bail amount that he won't be able to come up with. Worst case scenario is that Marco is able to post bail and go back home until the trial. If that happens, Gerry fears that they'll never find out what really happened. More details will come out in the trial for sure, but Gerry doesn't think that he can have that hanging over his head until then.

Gerry forces himself up from the bench. He puts on his shirt and buttons up the chest, leaving the last one under the collar free. His grayed chest hairs burst out from the top. He doesn't much care for the look, but it gets his wife hot, so he does it. What husband wouldn't? He tosses his changing bag over his shoulder and lays his uniform across his forearm. His phone buzzes before he gets to the door. Despite struggling to retrieve it from his deep pocket, he manages to pull out the phone and glances at the screen.

It's Jen Winston. Again.

FORT WORTH IS HUMID at this time of year, which isn't much different than the other eleven months of the year. The Texas sun beats down on Enrique as he fingers the sack of diamonds in his pocket while he waits. Downtown is bustling and the sidewalks are filled with busy cowboys and cowgirls getting in some weekend shopping. Enrique has spent most of his life in the northeast, so the culture differences in the south are a big change for him, and he's not too sure that he likes it so far. He fits in better with the hard-nosed, tough-minded crowd, and the kindness and slower pace of the southerners that he's encountered so far is out of the norm for what he's accustomed to. If only they knew why he's here, he thinks, maybe then they wouldn't be so friendly.

Despite his reservations about his geography, Enrique might end up somewhere in the south when this is all over. He may be better off relocating to a small town and trying to blend in with the locals and maintaining a low profile. He fears that he won't be able to leave the country if anyone finds out what he has done, so he may have no choice but to blend. He could buy himself a cowboy hat and some boots and look just like the rest of them. No one would even think twice. In fact, he would look out of place if he didn't equip himself with that silly getup.

Surely he won't be on the no-fly list, but his name and face could get around if the police are looking for him. It will take him some time to find someone who can hook him up with a fake passport and a new identity, so he'll hang low until then. Money, at least, is one problem he knows that he won't have.

His contact should be arriving any minute. The meeting was arranged by an associate of Enrique's superior, so all he has is a first name. The contact has Enrique's mugshot, so he'll be approaching him directly upon arrival.

"Enrique?" says a man's voice from behind Enrique, right on cue.

Startled, Enrique turns and faces the man. "Yes. John?"

John nods, and the men shake hands.

"Shall we go inside and sit?" John says, motioning to the coffee shop at their backs.

Enrique nods once and follows him inside.

The shop is full of mostly overweight woman, all seemingly with men by their sides. The employees behind the counter appear to be overwhelmed at the size of the line as they fill the to-go cups with ice. Enrique grabs an empty table near the window while John finds a spot in line by the door. A couple of minutes later, he brings two iced coffees to the table and hands one to Enrique. Enrique knows how this all works and will play nice, he decides.

"Glad you made it," John says.

"You too."

"I was expecting two of you."

"There's been a change of plans. You'll be dealing directly with me now, and only me."

"Is that so?"

"Is that going to be a problem?"

John takes a long drink through his straw. "Do you have the item?"

Enrique taps on his pocket that holds the sack of diamonds. "I got it right here."

"Good. Then no, there won't be a problem."

PETER MAKES JEN AN early lunch and they sit at the table and eat together. It used to be a habit but has since become a sparse activity that only occurs on a rare occasion. Peter's been doing his own thing in recent weeks while Jen has been doing much of the same. Not today, though. Things are finally looking up for the two of them, and he's encouraged about that.

"I'm sorry," Peter says mid-bite.

"For what?"

"Everything. I'm sorry for how things have been between us recently, and I'm sorry for not being there for you during all of this."

Jen takes a bite of her sandwich and chews slowly, trying to come up with an appropriate response. She just stares at her sandwich and refuses to look into Peter's eyes.

Peter waits awkwardly for Jen to say something. Anything would be nice, good or bad. Just say something. He has put himself out there for her, which is not something that he does on a regular basis, so some feedback would be appreciated. He suspects that she's trying to figure out what the right thing to say is, but she's conflicted between her mind and her heart. Based on her lack of anything, verbal or non, Peter fears that there may be irreparable damage that she just cannot get past. All he wants to do is rekindle their relationship and save their marriage. He'd even be willing to go back to couples therapy if that's what it takes, but he'd never admit that to Jen. Not yet anyway.

"Jen?" Peter says. "Did you hear what I said?"

"I heard you, yes."

"Will you say something?"

"I don't know what you want me to say."

"I want you to tell me how you feel. I'm opening up to you here, Jen. That's what you want, isn't it?"

Jen looks away. Peter knows that she hates it when he recites dialogue from their old therapy sessions, but he just can't help himself sometimes. She's obviously looking for a distraction to move the conversation in a different direction. She gets bailed out when the doorbell rings.

Jen's face drops. Peter notices that her color lightens and her wheels are spinning. He wonders if she's having a flashback to her attacker. She takes slow sips of her water, which she always does when her belly aches. The doorbell rings for a second time.

Peter stands up and starts toward the hallway. "Are you expecting anyone?" he asks.

Jen gets up and prepares to follow her husband. "I don't think so. Will you go first?"

With Jen close to his hip, Peter makes his way down the hallway and approaches the door. He disengages the alarm and unlocks the door.

As he opens it, Peter is curious who it could be. Thoughts of another attack do cross his mind, but it all just seems too soon. He's almost relieved when he sees who it is. Standing on the stoop with a kind smile on her innocent face is Betty, the neighbor, and her pup Trixie sits patiently in front of her.

"Hi, neighbors," Betty says, still with a smile on her face. A sliver of lettuce is stuck between her two front teeth. She reeks of moth balls and hand soap.

Peter can sense the tension release from Jen's body as she exhales and steps forward.

"Hi, Betty," she says. "How are you?"

"I'm fine, dear." Betty gasps when she processes the look on Jen's face. "Oh my! Are you alright? You're very pale, are you ill?

Jen offers a half-hearted smile. "Me? I'm fine. It's just been a long week is all."

The smile fades from Betty's face and she waits for a moment before continuing. She says, "I don't mean to be a bother, but I was just hoping that you may be able to help me with something."

Peter looks to Jen and raises his eyebrow slightly, asking her if she knows what Betty's talking about without actually saying anything. Jen shrugs with her eyes.

"What is it?" Peter says.

"That young man police officer that you've been talking to...his name has seemed to escape me."

"Officer Dale?" Jen says.

"Yes, that's it I think, Officer Dale. Would you happen to have is telephone number?"

Peter looks to Jen again, suddenly unsure what to think of this Betty woman that he doesn't know much about. He wonders how Jen feels about her. He realizes that he's never actually asked.

"Do you mind if I ask what you need to talk to him about?" Peter asks.

Betty looks between the attentive eyes of Jen and Peter. She bends down and scoops up Trixie and brings her up to her chest. "May I come in?"

CHAPTER THIRTY-FOUR

It's been four more hours and Stan Brothers still hasn't spoken with his brother-in-law. It's completely out of character for him, so Stan's officially worried. It's been over twenty-four hours since his flight should have landed, and Stan still hasn't heard a peep from him. Stan has booked the next flight out of town and will be heading out there himself to find out what's going on. He can't risk this not going well. Everything is riding on this.

"Linda, get in here," Stan says as he buzzes the intercom up front. He sits in his chair and waits for her to arrive. She knocks twice before popping her head in.

"Everything okay?" Linda asks.

"Come in."

Linda pushes the door open fully and steps into Stan's office. She looks tired. She sighs as she starts to unbutton her blouse.

"Already?" she says.

Stan stares at her and shakes his head in disgust. She's always thinking about sex. "What are you doing? Keep your clothes on. Have you received any phone calls for me today that I should know about?"

"Just clients."

"My brother-in-law didn't call?"

"No. You still haven't heard from him?"

Stan shakes his head and sighs. "No."

"Is there anything that I can do?"

"Do I have any appointments tomorrow?"

"No, tomorrow's Sunday."

"Good, let's keep it that way." Stan gets up and puts on his jacket.

"Where are you going?"

"I should be back on Monday. If I'm not, push everything out a day." Stan walks past Linda and heads for the door.

"Where are you going?"

Stan stops and turns to face Linda before leaving. "Go home, Linda. See you Monday."

Stan swings by his house to change clothes and put together a small travel bag before heading to the airport. He catches his wife at the house and explains to her the situation. She hasn't heard from her brother either, so she's supportive of the idea. Without offering any details of the arrangement between her brother and himself, Stan gets his wife's blessing to go track him down. He was going anyway, whether she approved or not, so the agreement just makes it easier and avoids an argument that he doesn't have the time for.

The traffic is backed up as Stan nears Logan Airport. He has left extra time to account for the weekend rush, but this is more than the usual airport traffic. When he finally makes it around the bend, he sees why. Two squad cars, two unmarked squad cars, an ambulance, a fire truck, and a tow truck line the right side of the road less than a mile from the entrance to the airport. The emergency vehicles surround something covered in a tarp, another vehicle, presumably. It must have been a really bad accident for the tarp to be involved, and Stan is naturally curious. Whoever the idiot was that wasn't paying attention and got himself killed, Stan hopes that he knows that he has caused a lot of people a lot of wasted time today.

After nearly missing his flight due to the holdup on the freeway, Stan settles into his seat in line with the wings of the plane. He buckles up at the direction of the stewardess over the loudspeaker and prepares for lift off. Once in the air and steady, he closes his eyes and leans back while the overhead fan blows cool air on him. It's a straight shot to his destination, so he has almost four hours of flight time to get some rest. He plans to take full advantage of that.

As he's close to drifting away in part due to the vibrations and rhythmic sounds of the purring engines, the passenger next to him leans over and says, "So, what are you going to Fort Worth for? Business or pleasure?"

Stan angles his head and just stares at him.

ENRIQUE RIDES WITH JOHN to the transfer location, which is less than two miles away from the coffee shop. John pulls into a residential townhouse community and parks in the driveway of the unit toward the end of the cul-de-sac. Internally, Enrique commends them on the choice of location. If something goes wrong and Enrique tries to turn on them, there will be a lot of witnesses. It works the other way around too, which provides Enrique with some comfort. He likes his chances of getting out of this alive and with his money.

John leads Enrique into the single story unit and into the kitchen in the back. Waiting inside is another man, his hair slicked, dressed in all black, and casually spinning a gun on the table. Enrique recognizes him right away. It's Duke Franco.

"Mr. Henderson," Duke says to Enrique as he approaches, "it's good to see you."

Enrique nods in appreciation. "Good to see you."

They shake hands.

Duke turns to John and says, "Where's the other guy?"

"I'm told that there has been a change of plans and we are to work with Mr. Henderson only," John says.

Duke turns back to Enrique and makes a face. "Is that so?" He waits a beat for Enrique to say anything, which he doesn't, before continuing, "Okay then. Let's get down to business so that we can all get out of here, shall we? Do you have the diamonds?"

Without saying anything, Enrique reaches into his pocket and pulls out the sack of diamonds. Reluctantly, he places the sack on the table in front of Duke. His hand is a little bit less steady than he had expected it would be. Perhaps that's because of the lie that he's about to tell. Duke motions to John, who grabs the sack and disappears down the hall with it.

Duke and Enrique go way back. They have been doing business together for years and have both been extremely successful. To say that Duke Franco is a mob boss would be inaccurate as he isn't affiliated with any organized crime group, but he does have the power of a mighty kingpin. He is essentially the CEO and President of an all-powerful multi-million dollar underground criminal enterprise. It's a complicated business model, but it's one in which has made Duke one of the wealthiest men in the country, and very few people know about it.

Duke has made his living by being an intermediary to all types of contract crime, including bank heists, hate crimes, homicides, and everything in between. Duke is hired through the proper channels to coordinate the desired act and find the right people to put the plan into action. It's a methodical way to get things done and it takes some extra time, but Duke has found it to be highly lucrative. By having multiple support channels and lines of communication all across the country, it makes it more difficult for the crime to be traced back to its roots. The front line men do sometimes get caught in the act, and many of them are in prison now, but there's an understanding within the organization that rats will not be tolerated. Those who have been caught are guaranteed another job once released from prison, if they want it, as a way to keep them quiet. Even still, some have decided to talk. Those who have made that decision have learned the hard way as all of them have mysteriously died before they could testify on the witness stand. Duke has eyes and ears everywhere, and he's always watching and listening.

He is Big Brother.

Duke has men and women in all facets of life playing some part in keeping the organization under wraps. There are inmates all over the country, Wall Street executives, members of local and federal governments, police officers, judges, and even some lawyers that are connected. And of course, there are everyday people, like Enrique, and those who have been designated smaller roles, such as being a driver or providing a distraction - men like Stephan Cooper, for example. Duke charges a steep price for his services in order to weed out the weaklings, and also as a way to cover his tracks. He's found that money seems to help keep everyone quiet.

Duke pays each of the connected individuals a hefty sum of cash for each of the events in which they participate in, so he has no shortage of workers. He funnels the money through the individual in charge of the specific job, so not many people actually know of Duke's existence. Duke insists on getting all of the money up front - paid for by the ones who initiate the conversation - and he has a close team of accountants who keep track of it all. There's no paper trail, ever, unless you count the crisp, green one hundred dollar bills that are passed around. Duke, of course, keeps a nice royalty for himself before paying his team leaders, who then, in turn, pay the individuals that have been assigned to their specific job. Duke has the final say on who can be involved in a specific job, although he does allow input from some of his most trusted team leaders. Some people go years without being needed, while others are regulars. Enrique Henderson is a regular. He's one of Duke's go-to guys for the northeast region, although most of the work comes out of Boston and New York City.

When Duke and Enrique are alone, Duke motions for Enrique to sit, which he does.

"How come I was not made aware of the change in organizational structure for Operation Salazar?" Duke says.

Enrique takes a moment to gather himself before answering. He had been expecting this sort of questioning, but he's still tense. "It was an unexpected change in plans," he says. "It all happened last minute."

"I need you to provide details. I need to know what we're dealing with here."

Enrique, becoming uncomfortable, shifts in his seat. "As you know, my driver for the job was a Mr. Stephan Cooper."

"Ah, yes, Coop. He's a good egg. Go on."

"Everything went to plan...well not exactly actually, but I got it done."

"Stop stalling. Tell me what happened after you retrieved the diamonds. That's all I care about."

Enrique is suddenly sweating. "Right, okay. Well, Mr. Cooper didn't know how high the stakes were and how much money was involved until late in the game. He saw the diamonds after the job was done, and he got greedy."

"I see. So he demanded more money then?"

"Essentially, yes. Greed is not permitted, those are your own words."

Duke nods, seeming to recall all of the times when he has in fact said those words. "Remind me again, what was his expected payout?"

"A million five."

"Steep price for a driver."

"He's the best, or, was the best. Plus, he had to pay someone too."

"Excuse me?"

"He was working with someone behind the scenes to conspire to embezzle some extra money from the victim. I thought you already knew."

"No, I know nothing of this. This is the first I'm hearing of it. Who is he?"

"He's a lawyer from Brookline. Stephan's brother-in-law if I remember correctly."

"Is he clean?"

"Yes, according to Stephan."

"Is there any chance that he'll blow the whistle on us?"

"No chance. He doesn't even know that Stephan is dead."

"But if he's family, chances are that he'll find out sooner rather than later."

"Not soon enough."

Duke considers this and nods repeatedly. "What's this lawyer's name?"

"Stanley Brothers, but he goes by Stan."

ENRIQUE HAS TAKEN AN enormous risk by lying to Duke Franco's face. Despite their longtime business relationship, Duke will not spare any feelings when it comes to dealing with those that have betrayed him with untruths. Things didn't happen with Stephan quite the way Enrique said they did.

The part about Stephan's greed is true, and in Enrique's mind, it's a good justification for what he did. But the part that he didn't share was that taking Stephan out of the picture was part of Enrique's plan all along. Despite what he told Duke, Enrique had never planned to bring Stephan with him to Texas to collect the payment for the diamonds. Stephan should have known better, as secondary players hardly ever join the team leaders for payment collection. Stephan, in Enrique's estimation, must have thought that he was an exception since Duke had approved the accompaniment ahead of time. It had surprised Enrique even then, and he never did find out why Duke made an exception. By fabricating a story and taking out the middle man, that means that Enrique gets to keep more of the loot for himself.

It's not a big falsehood that Enrique has told, especially considering that Stephan's payday was coming out of his own cut, but it's about more than that. Simply said, Enrique has had enough of the game. He's been to prison one too many times and risks going back with each day that he's on a job. He just wants out. The problem is, like with the mob, there's no getting out of Duke's labyrinth of deception. Some people have been able to separate themselves from it, but always with the threat of being taken out at any time looming over their heads. For someone like Enrique, someone who knows much of the ins and outs of the operation, he won't just be allowed to walk away. He knows too much.

Fully aware that if Duke finds out his plan his head will be on a bounty, Enrique's prepared to disappear. Faking his own death seems to be the easiest route to do so, and it would help to keep Duke off his back. Nothing positive can come from someone trying to recoup money from a dead guy, so Duke would never risk the exposure.

John summons Duke down the hall, and they reappear into the kitchen a few moments later. John has a loupe and a microscope in his hands - which, Enrique assumes, were used for inspecting the diamonds for imperfections - and Duke carries a thick steel briefcase near his hip. He places the case on the table, opens it, and spins it to show the contents to Enrique.

"Congratulations," Duke says. "Each of the diamonds checked out fine. Here is your payment in full. Six million dollars, just as discussed."

Enrique picks up and fingers through some of the stacks of cash on the top row, the smell of greed leaving its stain on his fingertips, but he doesn't count it. His heart drums with excitement. Duke's word is his bond, and Enrique has yet to see him try any funny business or try to screw someone out of their hard earned payday. Pissing your people off isn't the best way to run a business, and Duke knows that. Most people who get paid won't talk, that's just how it is. Enrique closes the case and snaps the hinges closed. He stands up and faces his boss.

"We'll be in touch," Duke says. "John will give you a ride back."

Duke and Enrique shake hands again.

Enrique knows better than to object, so he accepts the ride and follows John back to the car. John drops him back off at the coffee shop and leaves without saying anything. A firm handshake confirms a job well done, and that's all that's needed. Enrique is left alone with a case full of cash and nowhere to go. He piles into his rental car and puts the case on the seat next to him.

Now it's time to disappear.

CHAPTER THIRTY-FIVE

Betty, Jen, and Peter sit around the Winston's kitchen table while Trixie the dog lays under Betty's chair. Betty accepts Jen's offer for a cup of tea and sips it politely while Jen and Peter wait for her to start talking. She eventually does so without being prompted.

"I may have some information that you and that policeman may like to hear," Betty says. She takes a sip of her steaming tea and waits.

"Please," Jen says, "continue."

"There are two things actually. First, I had just returned home from walking Trixie here yesterday morning, and I just happened to look over before I went inside the house, and I saw some commotion. I saw a man running and hollering toward a vehicle that was parked at the end of your driveway, which seemed odd. At first, I didn't think much of it, but then when the police came by later...well, you know."

Betty pulls out a yellow notepad from her apron pocket and slides it across the table toward Jen. Jen picks it up and glances at it.

"What is this?" Jen says.

"It's the license plate number on the car I saw."

Jen looks to her husband and gives him a look. He has the same reaction. They've been through this before with Betty, and her memory seems to be less than trustworthy. Jen decides to test her.

"I thought you said that you didn't think it was a big deal at the time? Why did you write down the plate then?"

Betty smiles. "That's what I do, dear. It's my job to watch over this neighborhood and make sure that everyone's safe. You never can be too sure."

Jen's not satisfied with the answer but doesn't press further. Peter fidgets in his chair, looking unconvinced.

"What else can you tell me about the car?" Jen asks.

"It was white, dear. And the license plate was from out of state. Utah I think it was."

Jen whips her head around to face Peter, then quickly back to Betty. Suddenly she starts to shake and her palms moisten with nervous perspiration. Based on that comment alone, she knows that Betty is telling the truth. "Did you see anything else? Did you see the guy's face or anything?"

Betty shakes her head. "No, not very clearly. The man ran out of your house with something in his hand and leapt into the passenger's side of the vehicle. The other man drove in the other direction and they left."

Jen nods. She knew that there were two people, there had to have been, so that's no surprise to her. She doesn't think that it'll be a surprise to Officer Dale either, when he hears it. Jen grasps the paper with the license plate written on it firmly in her hand and places her other on Betty's wrist.

"Thank you, Betty," she says. "This will be so helpful."

"What was the second thing?" Peter says, suddenly sounding interested again.

"What's that, dear?"

"The second thing. You said that you had two things to share with us."

"Oh for heaven's sake, I nearly forgot. Yes, of course. After you left with the police, I sat in my living room and watched over the house. You've had nothing but trouble, so I was hoping I could help by making sure that everything was safe. Anyhow, I must have fallen asleep, because I awoke to the sound of sirens and saw some more commotion out front. While all of the policemen were surrounding a young man and putting him in the police car, they missed something."

"What do you mean?" Peter says.

"While all of this was happening, someone else was hiding in the side yard."

"Hiding?"

"That's right. He was crawling underneath your bushes on the side, and he waited there until everyone cleared out. When everyone left, he got out of the bushes and walked down the street. Then he left in that same black car that's been around here recently. I hadn't noticed it hiding behind the trees down the street - the car that is. It's a clever hiding spot, if I don't say."

Jen listens intently to make sure that she tells Officer Dale everything and doesn't miss something. He's been adamant that there have been two people working together, and this confirms that. She asks the obvious question, "Did you see his face? Do you know who is he?"

Betty crosses her arms and leans back in her chair. "I did, and yes, I know exactly who he is. And I know who the owner of that car is too."

WHILE STILL IN THE locker room at the police station, Gerry answers Jen Winston's call. After a quick chat, his interest is piqued and he knows that going home to enjoy the next day and a half will have to wait. He rushes out of the station and heads toward the Winston's. He tries to ring Jamaal on the way but gets his voicemail. That's no surprise to him, as Jamaal frequently turns his phone off when not on duty to avoid distraction from his family time. Gerry had been hoping that it wouldn't be off quite yet though, as he really wanted to share the news. They may have found their second guy.

Gerry makes a conscious effort to dial down his excitement as he approaches the Winston's. Despite feeling a huge sense of relief for catching this break, he realizes that he has to tone it down and act like a professional. While in the driveway, he takes a moment to himself before heading for the door.

Mrs. Winston greets him as he climbs up the top step and he follows her into the kitchen. Mr. Winston, the neighbor Mrs. Anderson, and her dog are all waiting for him. Gerry sits in the open seat at the head of the table and pulls out his notepad.

Jen briefly summarizes what she had told Gerry on the phone, and Betty and Peter fill in any details that she misses. Gerry keeps up with a steady pen and just lets everyone else do the talking. When the recap of the arrest is outlined from Betty's perspective, Jen encourages Betty to repeat what she had told her and Peter before about what else she saw.

Betty begins, "Do you remember our conversation from a few days ago, officer?"

"Why don't you recap it for me?" Gerry says.

"I told you then about how long I've been in the neighborhood, and that I know what goes on around here better than anyone else, remember? I've seen a lot of things and a lot of different people come through here."

"I'm sorry to interrupt," Gerry says, "but what does this have to do with what you saw?"

"I'm getting there, just wait. Anyhow, I lived next door to Bartolo Salazar and his family for fifteen years. I used to babysit his son when he was younger from time to time actually, so I know them fairly well."

"His son being Marco Salazar?"

"That's right. To say that I was a little hurt when I saw how he was being treated by your colleagues is an understatement. He's a good boy, you know."

Gerry sighs. He didn't come here to get lectured to by this old lady, and he desperately hopes that she gets to the point sometime soon. "Mrs. Anderson, now is not the time for this. Will you please just tell me what it is that you saw?"

Betty crosses her arms and shoots Gerry a disgruntling glance. "The boy that I saw crawling around in the bushes was Marco's best friend, Antonio. He used to come around all the time when the boys were little."

"Antonio what?"

"Antonio Esposito."

Gerry jots down the name, underlines it, then stands and thanks everyone for their information. He has to fight the urge to smile. He tells Jen that he can show himself out. But before he can leave, Betty stops him.

"For what it's worth," she says, "I think that you're making a mistake here."

"And why's that, Mrs. Anderson?"

"I know that family and those boys, and they would never do anything to cause any harm. They must be in a heap of trouble to have got caught up something like this."

Gerry ponders Betty's advice for a moment, but he quickly turns dismissive. "Thank you for your thoughts, Mrs. Anderson, but Marco Salazar is not who you think he is."

"Or maybe it's the other way around. Maybe he's not who you think he is, his father too. Maybe there's more to this than you realize. Things aren't always as they seem, you know."

"Would you like to expand on that?"

Betty pauses and gathers her thoughts. "I'm just saying that perhaps you should look into this more. There might be something that you're missing."

"If that's how you feel, then why did you want to talk to me? Why did you tell me what you saw?"

This captures the attention of Jen and Peter too, and they both look to Betty and await an explanation.

"Despite what you may think of me, officer, I do have morals. I'm a strong, independent woman and I do what I think is right." Betty rubs Trixie's head calmly as she speaks. "And although I don't agree with what you are trying to do to those boys, I have an obligation to this neighborhood to report what I see, so that's what I'm doing."

Having nothing to say in response, Gerry thanks Peter and Jen again for the call and shows himself out. He gets into his car and sits for a minute. The information he has just received is bittersweet. The more he seems to find out about the case, the cloudier it all becomes.

Marco Salazar is seemingly a good person with no criminal past, and Mrs. Winston has already confirmed that he was not the one who had attacked her. His assailant is finally known and can be tracked down, but Gerry is starting to doubt what he thinks it is that he knows. Maybe Betty was right, he concedes, maybe there's some larger scheme at play here. He wonders if he's turned a blind eye to the facts while trying to find the evidence to incriminate Marco.

Under most circumstances, Gerry would be looking up Antonio Esposito and finding out where he lives and going to pick him up, but not today. He tries to call Jamaal again to get his thoughts on the new developments, but he gets the same recorded message as before. Marco Salazar's hearing is on Monday, and Gerry suddenly doesn't know what he wants to come out of it.

Sickened with himself for thinking that way, Gerry forces himself to remember the fact that Marco was caught red-handed breaking into the Winston's house. He's not as innocent as Betty thinks he is, and the case against him is pretty solid. But on the other hand, Mrs. Winston's attacker is still at large and is in possession of that statue that was stolen from the house, as Gerry has since learned. One question still digs at Gerry though, and it's one that may break this whole case wide open: what is the significance of that statue, and what does it have to do with all of this?

CHAPTER THIRTY-SIX

Stan Brothers arrives in Fort Worth in the dark of night. He was able to catch a couple hours of sleep on the plane, so the one hour time difference doesn't bother him much. He leaves the airport in a rental car equipped with a GPS and knows what he has to do. He had hoped that it wasn't going to come to this, but here it is. It's the worst case scenario.

His brother-in-law is Stephan Cooper. Stephan is Stan's wife's older brother, and they have become close through the years. Out of desperation, Stan had approached Stephan a few months back about some financial trouble that he was having. Stephan has made good money for as long as Stan has known him, although Stan never has been able to fully understand where his money comes from. All he knows for sure is that Stephan leaves for days or weeks at a time and always comes back wealthier than when he left.

When Stan had learned what Stephan does for a living, he was hesitant at first to get in on it. But when Stephan offered Stan a way to get himself out of debt completely, Stan had no choice but to listen. His mortgage was a couple of months behind even then - worse now - and he was about to lose his office space due to overdue rent too, so it was that or lose everything that he'd worked for. For Stan's participation, Stephan had offered him a third of his payout. $500,000 is enough to cover all of Stan's debts, plus some extra. The dollar amount was high, but Stephan had told Stan to consider it a favor for his sister. The security of a clean job was worth the money, Stephan had said. And the last thing that he wanted was to see his sister have to change her lifestyle because of Stan's reckless mistakes, or to find out what he did for a living. She would never approve.

The guilt that Stan feels about the whole situation is intense, but he knows that there's no other way to save himself. Filing for bankruptcy won't help as he'll lose everything anyway, and the banks surely won't give him any more money after that, so getting involved in Stephan's doings is the only way. Doing it the legitimate way - representing new clients and winning cases - would have taken too long. Time is something that he didn't have the luxury of having, not with debt collectors screaming in his ear. His affair with Linda only makes things worse, he realizes, but he just can't help himself. Sometimes a man has to get what he needs elsewhere if he's not getting it at home. If Stephan knew what Stan really does behind closed doors and behind his sister's back, he would never forgive him. And he would tell him to figure out a way to get out of debt on his own.

Stan's role in this whole setup is rather simple. According to Stephan, he had been summoned for duty and was just waiting in the wings until it was time to be called into action. It had all started almost a year ago now, and it took that long for phase one to be implemented. When the time was right, Stephan had given Stan the go-ahead to approach a man in prison and offer his legal services. Bartolo Salazar was that man.

At the time, Stan didn't know who Bartolo was or what he had been accused of, but he did as he was instructed to do. The fear was that if another defense attorney took the case they would dig into it and find out what had really happened, which would undermine the whole operation.

That made Stan's role crucial to the success of the project. With Stan in place to keep the investigation under wraps and not push it too far, Bartolo would stay in prison and Stephan and Stan would get their money without encountering any resistance from outside parties. That way they would be able to control everything and significantly lower the risk of getting caught.

To keep things appearing to be as normal as possible, Stan insisted on still receiving his usual retainer for his legal expertise. The money was just a bonus to help Stan stay afloat while awaiting the big payout, and he had been genuinely surprised when Bartolo and his family started to pay him in increments. He had set phony deadlines to keep the persona up, plus it allowed him some more time to keep the creditors away.

WHILE SITTING IN THE rental car in the parking lot of the airport, Stan retrieves two phone numbers from the back of a business card that's in his wallet. Stephan had given them to him in case of an emergency, and Stan now considers this an emergency. Stephan doesn't fully trust the man that he's working with, so he had made alternative plans in case things didn't go the way they were supposed to. Stephan is a wise man.

The first number that Stan calls is an emergency line that dials directly into the apartment that Stephan had rented out in Fort Worth. Stephan was to have the line transferred to his mobile phone so that it would ring in both locations. If he doesn't answer the phone that all but confirms that something has gone wrong, especially since Stephan's phone doesn't leave his sight. Plus, it's now approaching thirty hours since Stan should have arrived in Texas.

Something's definitely not right.

The emergency line goes unanswered and into a blank voicemail box, confirming Stan's greatest fear. He has already confirmed that the flight that his brother-in-law was supposed to leave on did depart Boston on time and did arrive in Dallas/Fort Worth on time, so something must have happened along the way. There's no way to tell for sure at this point, so that's what the second phone number is for.

Stephan had given Stan the second number to use as a last-ditch effort to try and track him down. It's close to being a guarantee that the guy on the other end will answer as he's not one to miss out on a potential job opportunity, Stephan had explained, so it gives Stan hope. He reads the name written on the back of the card as he dials the number.

"Yeah?" says a man's voice from the other end of the phone after the first ring.

"I'm looking for Enrique," Stan says.

"Who's asking?"

"My name is Stan Brothers. I was told to call this number if there was some trouble."

ENRIQUE FEELS HIS HEART rate pick up as he listens to the man on the other end of the phone. Despite knowing exactly who Stan Brothers is, he probes him for information. He was told by Stephan that Stan knows only the bare minimum about the operation, but this trick obviously says differently.

"Is Stephan with you?" Stan Brothers asks through the phone.

Enrique wasn't prepared for this, so he tries to come up with something quickly. He draws a blank. "No, he's not with me."

"Where is he then?"

"I don't know."

"Well, did he come with you to Texas?"

"Who said I'm in Texas?"

"Just stop with the games, alright? I'm in Fort Worth and I know that you are too. Maybe we should meet up."

Enrique is taken aback. How does Stan know that he's in Fort Worth and how is he here already? If he still thinks that Stephan is alive, that means that the highway patrol must have cleaned up that mess near the airport in Boston. Stan would have seen it otherwise. Despite his instincts telling him not to, Enrique decides that it may be in his best interest to meet with Stan and find out just how much he knows. He needs to find out if this guy is going to be a threat once he finds out what has happened to Stephan.

"Fine," Enrique says, then he gives Stan the address to his current location.

Enrique had decided to find a place to stay the night before heading out of town. Instead of trying to maneuver around a foreign place in the middle of the night, he had thought that it was wiser to wait until morning. That way, he'd have a clear mind, rested body, and daylight to guide him. Now in hindsight, knowing what he does about Stan Brothers, he regrets that decision. He could run now, but he's best served to deal with this head on and get it over with. There's no telling what this Stan Brothers character is capable of.

In almost a half an hour exactly, a knock comes from the front door of Enrique's hotel room. The knocking makes him jump, but only initially. He quickly gathers himself and puts his game face on. Enrique opens the door, meets Stan Brothers for the first time, and invites him inside.

RESTING IN THE DARK outside of the Southern Belle Hotel, John dials his boss. He's been trailing Enrique since he dropped him off at the coffee shop earlier in the afternoon, and he finally has something to report. An unidentified man knocks on the door and enters the room that Enrique is in, and John knows that he's on to something.

Duke had a feeling that Enrique was up to no good and demanded that John find out what it was. It's not like Enrique to change the plans of an operation at the last minute, so Duke had seen right through his deceits. As usual, Duke's intuition was right. Duke's always right.

"Duke here."

"Hey, it's John."

"What do you got?"

"Someone just joined our guy in his hotel room. A man, unknown identification."

"Is it Stephan Cooper?"

"No, definitely not," John says as looks at the photo that he has of Stephan Cooper. Stephan had been short and overweight during this particular shot, while the man entering Enrique's room is tall and thin, maybe even a little muscular.

"Okay, so he probably wasn't lying about that then. Might it be the third party that he mentioned? Stanley Brothers?"

"It might just be. I'll go find out on your command."

"Go now," Duke says, "and bring them both back here. Alive."

John hangs up with Duke and waits for a moment. He waits for any commotion inside the hotel room - yelling, love-making, gun shots. When he sees and hears nothing, he pockets the photo, checks the barrel of his .38, and gets out of the car. The parking lot is nearly empty aside from two cars at the far end, Enrique's rental in front of his room, plus the mystery visitor's. John puts the weapon in his belt and walks toward the door to Enrique's room. He gives two firm knocks with his knuckle and waits. He steps to the side so that he can't be seen through the peephole. It's time to get to the bottom of this.

STAN AND ENRIQUE STAND across from each other in front of the queen size bed in Enrique's hotel room. They stare one another in the eye.

"Where is Stephan?" Stan demands. "Where is my brother-in-law?"

"He didn't make it."

"What do you mean he didn't make it?"

"He had an accident."

"Meaning?"

"Did you not see the mess on the street near the airport back in Boston?"

Stan thinks back to his ride to Logan. At first, he had just assumed that there was traffic, but then he recalls the emergency vehicles surrounding the car with a tarp over it. No, it can't be, Stan thinks, suddenly feeling ill. His heart drops to the floor. "What happened?"

"Someone got greedy, so someone got hurt," Enrique says without any emotion.

Stan clenches his fingers together and makes two fists. He can't understand how someone can be so cold. His blood is boiling. "You son of a bitch! What did you do to him? Tell me what you did to him!"

"Use your imagination."

Two knocks come from the door. Enrique looks in its direction and starts toward it.

"Ignore it!" Stan says. "Tell me what happened to Stephan."

"And what if I don't?"

Stan pauses. He didn't bring a weapon, but he should have. It's a major mistake. He sits down on the end of the bed and tosses his head into his hands. What has he gotten himself into? How is he ever going to explain this to his wife? He can feel her wrath already.

Two more knocks come from the door. Enrique starts in that direction again, but is stopped suddenly when the door is blasted open with a forceful thrust. The sound frightens Stan so much that he actually falls to the floor and covers his head with his hands. For some reason, his first instinct is that it's an explosion. A man enters, screaming obscenities and waving a gun around, and he's staring right at Enrique.

"John? What the hell are you doing here?" Enrique says with his hands raised.

"Shut up," John says as he points the gun directly at Enrique's face. He motions to Stan. "Who is this?"

Enrique looks to Stan just as he climbs to his feet.

Stan looks into the gunman's eyes and says, "I'm Stan Brothers. Who the hell are you?"

John grabs one of Enrique's arms and pulls it down by the wrist. "Both of you come with me, now."

"I'm not going anywhere," Stan says.

"Just listen to him," Enrique says. "Trust me."

Stan looks to Enrique and can see the fear in his eyes. That worries him. Now concerned, Stan walks toward Enrique and the man named John. John slides his gun into the back of his pants and grabs one of Stan's wrists with his free hand.

"If you don't resist you won't get shot. If you do, then you will. Understood?" John doesn't wait for a response before continuing, "You both have some explaining to do."

Enrique drops his head and walks without resistance to John's car across the parking lot. Stan is more timid, but he doesn't try anything either. He's intimidated by John's persistence and conflicted by Enrique's sudden apprehension. Enrique and Stan slide into the back seat and John shuts the door behind them.

John slides into the front and dials a number on his phone. He waits for a second, then says, "Duke, I got them. We're coming your way."

CHAPTER THIRTY-SEVEN

Betty leaves the Winston's house not long after Officer Dale does. Still at the kitchen table, Peter and Jen sit silently while trying to put all of the pieces together. They're both at a loss for words. Betty speaks like she knows something that others are missing, but she insists that's not the case.

While Peter disappears into the other room to try to find something to keep himself busy, Jen thinks back to her conversation with Betty from a couple of days ago. It was on Thursday, two days ago, when Jen went next door to Betty's to talk after she and Peter went out to get some opinions on that mysterious statue.

Jen didn't realize it at the time, but considering it with what Betty has just said to Officer Dale, she wonders if Betty was giving her a warning during their prior conversation. Betty had said some of what she told Officer Dale, mostly about her seeing and knowing everything that goes on around the neighborhood, but there was something more. Jen remembers it well. Betty had said that the people who used to own their house were good people. The owner, who Jen now knows only by the name of Bartolo Salazar, and his wife had lived in the house, although it was always a mystery how they paid for it. The wife didn't appear to work and Bartolo used to leave for weeks at a time, but it seemed that there never was a consistent job. Despite that, they had lived in the same house for more than twenty years.

Betty had always assumed that Bartolo was into some shady business, but she never saw anybody sketchy go by the house or never saw anything out of the ordinary. Whatever he was doing, he was hiding it well, and all appearances were that he was making a decent living. He would go months without leaving the house for more than a few hours at times, but then he would have stretches where he would only be home for one day in a month too. Betty had always wondered what he was up to, but she was never able to coax it out of him or his wife during casual conversation.

Despite all of that, Betty had carried on about how nice the family was and that they were always willing to help her around the house if needed. After her husband died, the Salazar's were more than neighbors to her; they were like family, and she'll always be grateful for that. Perhaps that's why she's defending them the way she is. Betty did provide a chilling detail to Jen though, and it was something in which she had said so nonchalantly. Without any restraint, as Jen was getting ready to leave, Betty had said that she always thought that the Salazar's would be back. She noted that they weren't the kind of people to just let their house be sold off without a fight, and that they would do whatever it took to get it back. They loved the house and it had fit their family perfectly.

Jen didn't think too much of it at the time, but now knowing what she does, she's terrified. What if the thieving of the statue is just a cover? Although she knows that his name is Antonio Esposito from Betty, Marco Salazar's accomplice is faceless to her right now, and she wonders if he was the one who had attacked her. The attack could have easily just been the prelude to the main event that was to follow. Is that why he waited to kill her? He must have gone to get his buddy and brought him back to the house so that they could do it together. Antonio

Esposito and Marco Salazar are going to come back and kill her. She just knows it.

The theory gives Jen anxiety, and something inside of her tells her that it's real. She can just feel it. She walks over to the sink and splashes some water on her face while she tries to steady her breathing. She tries to drink some too, but neither helps to ease her panic. She thinks that she might vomit. There's only one thing left for her to do at this point, and she knows it.

She hasn't told Peter about what Betty had said before, but she thinks that now is the time. She goes looking for him and finds him browsing the web in her office. To her surprise, he recognizes the fear on her face and actually listens to what she has to say. He holds her hand and doesn't say anything while she tells him about her theory. She wishes that he would say something this time, even if it's a lie; anything to make her feel better.

"I can't do this anymore, Peter," Jen says. "I don't know how much longer I can live like this."

"It's been a rough start, I'll admit that," Peter says.

Exhausted tears fill up Jen's eyes, and she lets them fall down her cheeks. Peter looks at her and it almost seems as if he can feel her pain.

"I'm sorry," he says. "I'm sorry for not believing you before."

Jen lets that sink in for a moment before responding. She's not sure how she feels about that comment. She wipes her cheeks dry with her sleeve. "I didn't know that you didn't believe me. You think I would lie about this?"

"I never said that."

"Actually, you kinda just did."

"That's not what I meant. I'm just saying that at first I thought that maybe you were...I don't know, exaggerating maybe."

Jen rips her hand from Peter's grasp and crosses her arms, now defensive. She knew that her husband was a fraud, and this confirms that. "Exaggerating?" she says. "Were you not there the other night? Did you not see those two guys in our bedroom in the middle of the night, pointing guns in our faces? Remember that?"

"Of course I remember. That's not what I meant."

"What did you mean then, Peter? I'm not really feeling your support right now. That's a big surprise."

Peter puts his head down mercifully.

"I'm going to make this really simple for you, okay?" Jen continues. "I'm not staying here anymore, not in this house. You're welcome to come with me or you're welcome to stay. Do whatever you want, but I'm leaving."

Peter snaps his head up and looks at his wife. "And where are you going to go?"

"Home."

"This is your home. This is our home."

"No, it's not. It's your home. My home is in the woods up north. I did this for you and I'm the one who's had to deal with all of this while you're away at work. This isn't me and you know that. I tried, I did, but I just can't deal with this anymore. I'm sorry, Peter, but I just can't live like this."

"Jen-"

"No, Peter, just stop. You have to pick. It's me or this house."

DISPATCH COMES BACK WITH the results of the license plate gathered by Betty Anderson, but they're inconclusive. The vehicle that Betty claims that she had seen outside the Winston's on the day of the attack had Utah license plates. Dispatch is able to confirm that the plates were indeed from Utah, but the car is registered to Enterprise Rent-A-Car. That means one of two things: one, someone from in-state rented the vehicle to cover their tracks; or two, someone rented the vehicle out of state and brought it in. Regardless, the name of the person who rented the vehicle is unknown at the present time.

Although not yet able to fully answer the question of who it was in front of the Winston's house, Gerry knows what his next logical move is. He'll be making a trip to one of the local Enterprise branches to find out who it was that rented the vehicle. There's one not far out of the way on his way home actually, so that'll work out well. First, though, he has another stop to make.

Having visited his partner's home hundreds of times over the years, Gerry knows the quickest route to Jamaal's house, so he takes it. The house sits back off the road in a residential area in the nice part of town, and Gerry has always envied the prized location. He knows right where the blind driveway hides off the main strip, and he pulls in amongst the row of tall oak trees when it appears.

Jamaal's truck is in the driveway, along with his wife Shawna's minivan, but there are no signs of anyone through the windows in the front of the house. Gerry gets out of his car, walks up the steps, and knocks on the front door. He hopes that Jamaal is still awake. Moments later, while Gerry observes the children's plastic play sets in the yard, Shawna opens the door and greets him with a hug.

"What are you doing here, Gerry?" Shawna asks with her usual jubilant enthusiasm that Gerry has grown to adore.

"I hate to just drop in like this," Gerry says, "but there's something important that I need to talk to Jamaal about. He hasn't gone to bed yet, has he?"

Shawna crosses her arms and frowns a little. "Is everything okay?"

"Everything's fine. It's just about a case that we've been working on. Work stuff."

Shawna nods. "Come on in, I'll go grab him."

Gerry walks in and closes the door behind him. Although he can't see the children, he can hear them down the narrow hallway seemingly arguing about how to properly assemble a peanut butter and jelly sandwich. Gerry can't help but smile. He remembers those days when his own kids did the same thing. It seems like it was just yesterday.

Jamaal walks into the living room and greets Gerry with a handshake. Regardless of the informality of the situation, Jamaal always insists on being polite. He looks so different without his uniform on. Baggy sweatpants fall from his hips, big floppy slippers drag under his feet, and his well-toned upper body fills out a long-sleeved thermal shirt nicely. Even now, looking at his most vulnerable, he still has the aura of respect surrounding him.

"What do I owe this pleasure?" Jamaal says as he sits onto the leather couch. "I've got to be honest with you, partner, I'd rather be sleeping right now. We see enough of each other."

"I'll be quick," Gerry says, now sitting too. "If you would have answered your phone..."

"Yeah, yeah. Get on with it."

Gerry smiles. "Right after you left the station earlier, I received another call from Jen Winston."

"Again? What's the matter with her this time?"

"Remember that neighbor of hers that we talked to a few days ago?"

"The old lady?"

"Yeah, Mrs. Anderson."

"Betty, that's right. What about her?"

"She went back over to the Winston's today and had some pretty interesting things to say."

"Oh yeah? Like what?"

Gerry tells him.

"And so I spoke with dispatch on the way here, and they tell me that the car is a rental," Gerry says. "So I'll be stopping at the rental car place near my house on the way home. You want to come with?"

Jamaal leans back and ponders the offer. "Are you sure about this?"

Shawna suddenly appears from around the corner and leans against the doorframe. Jamaal sees her and shrinks. He must realize that she's been listening to everything, and he knows better than to work on his day off.

"No, you go," Jamaal continues. "But I want you to call me if you need anything, alright?"

"You sure?"

"Yeah, I'm sure. I've got to hit the hay anyway, I'm toasted."

Gerry and Jamaal get to their feet and shake hands again. Gerry waves to Shawna before turning toward the door and heading in that direction. He can still hear the kids down the hallway, but the conversation has since moved away from peanut butter and jelly. Jamaal opens the front door and holds it for him.

"Last chance," Gerry says before he walks out.

"I'm good, really."

"Are you going to at least turn your phone on this time?"

Jamaal laughs. "Yeah, yeah. I'll turn it on. Now get the hell out of my house." He playfully pushes Gerry out the front door. "I'll see you in court on Monday."

CHAPTER THIRTY-EIGHT

Inside Duke's townhouse, the four men are at a standstill. Enrique and Stan sit across from Duke at the table while John stands behind them with his .38 on his hip. Neither Enrique nor Stan is restrained in any way, but they're stuck frozen in fear, especially Stan. Although he did willingly agree to participate in this whole event with his brother-in-law, he was clueless about the extent to which the operation reached. He knows now that he has made the biggest mistake of his life by coming to Texas.

Admittedly, Enrique had never thought that it would come to this. He had thought that he was clever enough to outwit Duke and his closest men, and he almost was. His only mistake, he realizes, is that he shouldn't have stuck around in town for the night. It was one simple mistake, and it may be fatal. He's comforted with the thought that if John was following him like he apparently was, he wouldn't have gotten very far anyway. It might be better this way actually so that John doesn't find out where he's going to hide and report it back to Duke. If Enrique can find a way out of this, he still has the chance to start over and disappear the right way. That would give him the chance to finally get out for good.

"I never thought I could be so disappointed in you," Duke says in Enrique's direction. "I thought you were one of the good ones."

"This is just a big understanding," Enrique says, confident that he has come up with an elaborate lie believable enough to allow him to walk away from this.

"Is that so? What about you, Mr. Brothers? Why are you here?"

Although Stan loves nothing more than being called Mr. Brothers, the tone in which Duke says it sends ripples of apprehension down his back. "It's like I told you, I hadn't heard anything from my brother-in-law after the allotted time, so I just followed the instructions that he gave to me."

"And what were those instructions?"

"If I didn't hear from him, I was told to call the number that he gave me."

"And that number lead to Mr. Henderson here, is that your story?"

"That's the truth."

Duke turns to Enrique. "Now, why would Stephan Cooper give his brother-in-law your personal phone number if he ran into trouble?"

"I don't know," Enrique says.

"What I think is going on here is that you are lying to me. I think that you and Mr. Brothers are working together and that you conspired to kill Stephan so that you two could split the money. Am I getting warm?"

"No, no. This is just a big misunderstanding," Enrique pleads. "You have to let me explain."

"I don't have to do anything. I don't know what it is that you two are up to, but I'll figure it out. And when I do, you'll have to suffer the consequences."

"Please, Duke. Let me explain."

Duke crosses his arms and leans back in his chair. "Fine, humor me. Let me hear it."

Enrique is relieved at the chance to finally tell his side of the story, and he jumps at the opportunity without hesitation. "All due respect, I think you actually have it backward. I had never worked with Stephan before, so all he had to go by was what people told him about me. I'll be honest, we didn't really click, but we did the job we were hired to do. No one said that you have to like everyone you work with, right? I think what actually happened was that Stephan and Stan were conspiring against me. Stan came to Texas to meet up with Stephan so that they could gang up on me and take all of the money for themselves. That's what really happened."

"That's not true!" Stan combats.

John comes up behind Stan and wraps his talon-like fingers around the back of Stan's neck. "Shut up," he says, then he presses his thumb into the pressure point on Stan's neck until he tenses his shoulders and is forced to settle down. "Keep the noise down. Are you calm?"

Stan nods and immediately massages his neck when John releases his grip. Duke gets up from his seat and walks around the table. With the backs of Enrique and Stan facing him, Duke nods to John and leaves the room. John slowly removes the .38 from his hip and cocks the hammer. A single bullet slides into the chamber.

Enrique starts to smile. He knows how this all works. When someone has betrayed Duke, the participating parties tell him their side of the story and he makes his decision from there. To his credit, Duke does consider past experiences when deciding who to eliminate, so Enrique likes his chances. He has told a convincing story, he thinks, and he could tell by the look on Duke's face while he was talking that he believes it too. Enrique leans his head down, leaving his neck freely exposed for John.

John again grabs the back of Stan's neck and pushes his head forward.

"What's going on?" Stan says, his voice stammering.

John forces Stan to look down at the table by applying more pressure to the back of his neck. Almost giddy with anticipation, Enrique steals a glance through his peripheral vision at Stan's face one last time before he's taken out. It's sick, Enrique knows, but seeing the fear of death in someone's eyes is euphoric for him. That's probably why he's been so successful in this business.

John pushes the barrel of his weapon into the back of his target's skull and pulls the trigger. A loud yelp echoes through the room as the face of the now lifeless man slams into the table.

Stan shrieks at the snap of the gun and almost gets sick when he sees Enrique's obliterated face lying on the table next to him. The blood has already started running off the table and onto the floor. Stan suddenly has the urge to vomit.

Stan braces for his turn and waits for his lifetime epiphany to arrive. He has always expected images from his life to play through his head like a slideshow just before death, but it doesn't come.

"Get up," John says from behind him.

While unable to keep his eyes off of Enrique, Stan hesitates for only a moment. Being impatient and not wanting to repeat himself, John yanks Stan to his feet by his collar. Stan nearly stumbles as he tries to avoid the blood on the floor from staining his shoes. John leads Stan out of the room and toward the front door. Duke meets them there.

"I expect you know what happens now if you lie to me, don't you?" Duke says as puts his arm around Stan's shoulder.

Stan opens his mouth to speak, but no words come to him. He just shakes his head as he covers his belch with his hand just in case chunks are upchucked.

"I believe what you told me, so I'm going to let you walk out of here," Duke says.

John opens the front door and stands to the side. Duke releases Stan from his grip and nudges him toward the open door. Stan steps into the sunlight and basks in his freedom, the fresh air helping to push away the need for heaving.

"I don't ever want to see your face again, do you understand me?" Duke continues.

"That won't be a problem."

"Good. Don't make me regret this."

STAN WASTES NO TIME in leaving town. Duke insists that John drives Stan to a location of his choice, so Stan chooses the airport. The next flight back to Boston isn't until tomorrow morning, so Stan will stay close by until then. He finds a hotel near the airport with a vacancy, so he spends the night there with just his thoughts.

This has been a wake-up call for him. Two people are already dead plus who knows how many others. Stan can't imagine that there aren't any others. John had acted like it wasn't his first time. He didn't even seem bothered by it. The wise thing to do would be for Stan to forget everything and just get back to his life, but he knows that he can't do that. Without the money he had been expecting, it's only a matter of months before everything is gone. And that's if he's lucky; it could be sooner than that. He'll be evicted from his office and his home will be taken away from him by the bank. It's only a matter of time before his wife finds out what he and her brother were up to, and she'll never forgive Stan for what he did. She will undoubtedly shift some of the blame for Stephan's death onto Stan, and she'll live a life of resentment. Or worse, she'll divorce him outright. His life as he knows it is over.

Despite being terrified of Duke, Stan sees only one way out of this. He's going to lose everything either way, but maybe at least he can do something that's morally right for once. He decides that he can no longer accept any more money from the Salazar family. They've been put through hell and played like fools, and they have no idea. Worse than that, they've been taken advantage of while counting on Stan. For the first time, he feels guilty about that. He suspects that they'd understand the situation better if they knew what was at stake for him, but that's a moot point. It starts with them. Stan needs to separate himself from the case completely, then he can do the right thing. One step at a time.

WHEN JOHN RETURNS FROM dropping Stan Brothers off at the airport, he cleans up the mess made at the townhouse. He wraps up Enrique's body, scrubs the kitchen floor with bleach, and gets rid of all the evidence in case anyone comes looking, although unlikely. After darkness falls, he single-handedly carries Enrique's body - which is wrapped in a sheet - out to the car before taking off again.

John drives out into a wooded area miles away from anything and dumps Enrique's body there. He might be found, or he might not be. It doesn't matter. John considers burning the body so that even dental records are unobtainable, but he decides that it isn't worth the effort. Enrique had no known family alive, so the odds of someone looking for him are low. A hiker may come across him down the line, but his body will likely decompose beyond any recognition by then anyway. Best case scenario is that he's removed from the face of the earth completely by the hungry mouths of the coyotes. John sees the possibility as a realistic one.

After John takes care of the body, he backtracks to the hotel. He uses the keycard from Enrique's pocket to let himself in and he rummages through the room until he finds the case of money - the case that Duke had given to Enrique earlier after receiving the diamonds. He finds it under the bed and checks the contents before leaving. A stack of cash is gone, but the rest is there. It's not about the money, it never was, so that doesn't matter much. What does matter is trust and loyalty. Duke is a loyal man who puts his trust in the people he has working with him, and he expects the same in return. The extra money will go to those people when the time is right. When Duke's betrayed by someone through lies and deception, he does all he can to preserve his name. John willingly buys into the message and is happy to do the dirty work to carry it on. Everyone needs a role in the scheme, and John's is well-defined.

CHAPTER THIRTY-NINE

Sunday morning. Sal had a dream last night which was vivid and detailed, and it has given him an idea. He rings Antonio first thing and asks him to come over to his apartment, which he agrees to do. The pizzeria isn't open for as long on Sunday's, so Sal is confident that his other employees can handle the load today. He's going to be out of commission.

When Antonio arrives, Sal greets him with the customary kisses on each cheek and sits him down at the round table. Antonio has dark bags under his eyes from the obvious lack of sleep and it's clear that he's been up all night thinking about Marco. Sal isn't much different.

"What did you bring me here for, Big Sal? Antonio asks. "It sounded urgent. Do you have some news on Marco?"

"No news yet. We'll find out tomorrow. Are you going to come to the courthouse with me? The hearing is at nine o'clock."

"For sure, I'll be there."

"Good."

After a brief pause, Marco says, "So, what's this about? Why did you ask me to come here?"

"I had a moment last night."

"A moment?"

"Yeah, a moment, a realization. You know, it's like I had a perfect moment of clarity in my subconscious. The lack of sleep does that to someone, you know."

"If you say so."

"It's like I had an epiphany or something. It's like when I woke up this morning I knew actually what we have to do."

Antonio makes a face at Sal, looking almost disturbed at the way that Sal's talking. "Are you okay?"

"I'm good. No, I'm great. I know how we can get out of this, Antonio."

Antonio is cynical, but he leans his back against the chair and pretends to listen. "And how's that?"

Sal tells him.

By the time Sal is finished, Antonio is up and anxiously pacing the room. "I don't know about this, Sal. I don't like this."

"You said you wanted to help, didn't you?"

"Well, yeah, but not like this. I don't think that this will solve anything. We lose all leverage if we do this."

"That's a risk we have to take."

"Is it though? Marco hasn't told the cops anything yet, what makes you think that he'll start now?"

"How do you know that he hasn't told them anything?" Sal asks.

"I'm still here, aren't I? I'd be right in there with him if he told them."

Sal nods, conceding the argument. "Maybe they're just buying some time, waiting for right moment."

"For what?"

Sal shrugs. "There's no telling what Marco might say once he gets in front of a judge."

"You think he'll talk?" Antonio says, suddenly nervous.

"I don't know what Marco will do. Nobody can say for sure. All I know is that he's being accused of some serious shit."

"But most of it's not true."

"You think that matters? He has to prove that it wasn't him."

"Doesn't it go the other way around? Innocent until proven guilty?"

"Come on, Antonio. You don't really believe that I hope. You can't be that naïve."

Antonio looks away. After a moment of silence, he says, "You really think this is the best way to go?"

"I don't see any other alternative, do you?"

"But what if they don't see it your way? What if they just call the cops? This whole thing would be over and everyone would be in jail. You too."

"We don't have a choice."

Antonio drops his head. He shakes it a couple of times before looking back up to Sal. "Fine," he says. "I don't like it, but I'll do it. When are we doing this?"

"Now's good."

SUNDAY'S ARE SUPPOSED TO be for spending time with family, but Gerry is just as distracted as he thought he'd be. His trip to Enterprise yesterday yielded disappointing results, and he's struggling to shut his mind off.

Although he was able to discover who it was that rented the vehicle with the Utah plates, the results were not what he had been expecting. It wasn't Marco Salazar or Antonio Esposito who rented the car, but a new name: Stephan Cooper. What his connection is to the Salazar's has yet to be determined. The net just keeps getting wider.

During the night while everyone in the house is sleeping, Gerry wakes up after tossing and turning for most of the afternoon. Since his wife is sleeping, he takes the opportunity to get some more work done on the case before tomorrow's hearing without getting any grief from her. He makes good use of the time and is able to learn quite a bit about Stephan Cooper.

Stephan has a couple of non-criminal misdemeanors on his record, but nothing that stands out as alarming to Gerry. He's a professional driver it seems, and he travels all over the globe doing so. Special projects mostly, most of them secretive, only known by the W-4s linked with his social security number. Besides living in the area, there appears to be no direct link between Stephan and the Salazar family. Or the Winston's for that matter.

What baffles Gerry are the seemingly large, although sporadic sums of money that Stephan pulls in every few months or so, all of which have gone unaccounted for on the federal tax level. The deposits into Stephan's account are all in cash, and not much of it ever goes back out. Gerry doesn't work for the IRS and would rather not get involved in that mess, but it does raise some red flags. Stephan is making big bucks doing something, and it's not something that he wants the government to know about.

Obviously, Gerry would like to talk to this Stephan Cooper and find out what his connection is to the Winston's or the Salazar's, but he won't get his chance to do that. While having Ben Shultz do what he does best without distraction, Gerry receives the news. Ben isn't thrilled about working during the night, but what he discovers in his research is a major blow to Gerry's momentum.

There was an unidentified man found dead in a car by Logan Airport on Friday afternoon. The victim had suffered a single fatal gunshot wound to the neck and had bled out by the time police found him. The scene was a bloody mess, Gerry is told, and it was a call from a passerby that tipped off police.

There was a gun found in the vehicle, and initial ballistics reports confirmed that it was the gun that killed the man, so the lead investigator on the case is convinced that it was suicide. There were no prints on the weapon and no other obvious signs of DNA found in the vehicle besides the victim's, so a suicide was the most logical explanation. The victim shooting himself in the neck is peculiar, but the investigator has seen stranger things. As of now, no one has come forward admitting to having seen anything, so the investigator can only go on what he has in front of him. Everything points to suicide.

From the few details that Gerry knows, he doubts that it was a suicide at all. The combination of the victim having no identification on him and driving an out of state vehicle leads the lead investigator to assume that it was a tourist. When Ben Shultz tells Gerry that the Utah State Police were contacted about any missing persons matching the victim's description and said there were none, Gerry immediately suspects that it's his guy.

There aren't too many Utah plates driving around Massachusetts, so there's no way it's a coincidence in Gerry's mind. Ben is able to confirm through the filed police reports that the license plates do match the car that Gerry is looking for, and that's all that Gerry needs to know that Stephan Cooper is dead. Stephan is the one who rented the car that was seen in front of the Winston's house, and how he's dead. But, why?

Taking full advantage that Jamaal is on the same sleep schedule as he, Gerry phones his partner at around midnight to share the news that he has found out. After a long discussion, they formulate a new theory.

They know that Marco Salazar was the one who broke into the Winston's house looking for that statue. Based on the tip from Betty Anderson, they can conclude that Antonio Esposito was his accomplice. They must have been the two people that broke into the house that first night too, probably to try and find the location of the statue. The second time around, something had gone wrong when they tried to disable the alarm system and they tore up the place trying to find the statue. They were probably unaware that it was already gone by the hands of Stephan Cooper and Jen's mystery attacker. They wouldn't have made such a mess and risked getting caught by putting their DNA all over the place if they already knew that it was gone.

Jen Winston's attacker was after the same statue, and he's the one who has it now. Jen had previously ruled out Marco as being her attacker, so he's definitely out. It still could have been Antonio Esposito who did it though, but the motive is unclear if so. If Marco and Antonio were looking for the statue together, which Betty Anderson claims they were based on seeing them both at the scene at the same time, there would be no reason for Antonio to have attacked Jen previously. Whoever attacked her has the statue already, so that all but rules Antonio out too. It will take Jen Winston eliminating him once Gerry and Jamaal track him down to be certain though.

That leaves two people: Jen's attacker was either Stephan Cooper or his mystery partner. Considering Stephan's track record as being a driver, it only makes sense that he was the one driving the getaway vehicle and not the one who had attacked Jen. Not only was the car with the Utah plates rented under Stephan's name, but he has no history of violence, so him being the attacker doesn't seem to fit the profile. Based on Jen's statement, the attacker was calm and collected as if it wasn't his first time, so that just further decreases the likelihood that Stephan Cooper was the guy - a guy with no experience with violent crime wouldn't be very calm. That conclusion leaves Jen's attacker - who's also the guy who has the statue - as being the one person left that Gerry and Jamaal don't have the identity of. If they find him, they find that statue, and they get the answers that they still need.

What makes the most sense, Gerry and Jamaal agree, is that whoever had attacked Jen and has the statue is also the one who killed Stephan Cooper. Maybe there was a disagreement on what to do with the statue, or maybe it was a business deal gone badly. Who knows? They were clearly on their way to the airport, so whoever the attacker was has already left the state and possibly even the country too.

With Stephan Cooper out of the picture, Gerry and Jamaal may never find out who the mystery man is. If Marco Salazar continues to be unwilling to talk about what he knows, the case may never be fully solved. As Jamaal points out, there may still be some hope though. If Antonio and Marco are as good of buddies as Betty claims they were growing up, Antonio may show up at Marco's hearing on Monday. That may especially be the case if he's feeling some guilt for getting away while Marco takes the fall for everything. That's their best chance to track down Antonio without alerting him that they're on to him. The last thing they want is for Antonio to leave town and disappear without talking to him first. Between the two of them, Marco and Antonio, one of them is bound to talk. Considering how stubborn Marco has been thus far, Antonio seems to be their best hope.

Gerry feels a sense of relief knowing that he's prepared to move forward with the case when he goes back to work next week. When his wife wakes up, he does his best to put everything out of his mind and enjoy the day off with his family. He treats his wife to some romance while his two teenage sons do whatever it is that teenagers do.

His eldest son will be heading off to college in the fall, and his youngest will be following the year after. Gerry knows that his time with his family is winding down and that the nest will soon be empty. The years have passed him by in a flash, like a blink of an eye. He takes a moment to reminisce with his wife about how great their lives have been up to this point, and he knows that everything will be different in just a few short months.

He's had a dream for a while now, a mid-life aspiration of sorts, and he finally decides to tell his wife about it. She's taken aback at first, but quickly offers him her full support. He takes great comfort in knowing that his wife will be there to catch him if he falls, regardless of what the end result is. It gives him the confidence that he needs to pursue his dream when this is all over.

CHAPTER FORTY

It's a good drive to the suburbs from Big Sal's Pizzeria. Sal has driven the route hundreds of times, but today seems like the longest that it's ever been. Like Antonio, he also has doubts about how this is going to go, but he's desperate to try something. Anything. He's out of ideas otherwise. With the unknown of how Marco's hearing is going to go tomorrow and the deadline for the remainder of Stan Brothers' retainer looming on Tuesday, time is precious.

Sal still has the $25,000 that he had coaxed out of Willy hidden away. It's all cash. There's a loose wall panel in his studio that serves as a hidden compartment, so the money is stashed in there for safe keeping. For its safety, no one else knows where it is, not even Antonio. Sal doesn't trust very easily sometimes, and Antonio knows better than to even ask. Sal won't make it to the bank before court tomorrow, and he's okay with that. It takes time for the bank to process the funds once deposited anyway, so having cash readily available for tomorrow is best. He'll deal with writing a check out to Stan Brothers later.

The window is tight, which is the main cause of Sal's anxiety about the whole situation. Stan Brothers is still owed $20,000, which does leave some extra to pay for

Marco's bail. The charges are heavy though, and that does deeply concern Sal. If it takes more than the extra $5,000 to get Marco out, that won't leave nearly enough time for them to come up with the extra money for Stan. Especially now that going back to Willy's for help isn't an option. Plus, Stan had made it very clear on Sal's last visit that anything less than a full payment was unacceptable. The stakes are the highest that they've ever been.

If things don't work out the way that he hopes, Sal knows what Bartolo will tell him to do. Bartolo will say to spend the money on bailing Marco out and to forget about him, but it's won't be that easy to do. Sal's already dished out $80,000 to Stan Brothers that he can't get back, so it would be difficult to just walk away from that. He hopes that it won't come down to making that decision.

Sal pulls into the driveway of their destination and stops the car. He leans back in his seat and takes a long, deep breath. Antonio does the same thing. There are so many ways in which this could go, and it's all so unclear.

"Are you sure about this?" Antonio says.

"No, I'm not sure about anything," Sal admits. "But there's no backing out now, we've come this far."

Antonio nods in agreement, although he had been hopeful that Sal would change his mind at the last minute. He waits to open his door until Sal does first. Coming back to this place - his brother's old house - gives Sal an unsettling feeling, and he would rather be just about anywhere else besides here. There are too many memories for him, and most of the negative ones make their way to the forefront of his mind. He can't forget about how it all ended so abruptly the day after Christmas last year. In what should have been one of the best, that day turned out to be one of the worst of Sal's life. The memory just won't fade away. It's like a lingering cough that refuses to go away, or a pestering stray cat without a home. Sal tries to steady his nerves as he walks with Antonio up the steps, but he struggles. His forehead is suddenly covered in nervous perspiration, his neck too.

"Here goes nothing," Sal says as he and Antonio approach the door, then he presses his unsteady index finger into the doorbell.

APPARENTLY, JEN IS SERIOUS about moving back to Maine. Luckily for her, a good majority of the moving boxes were never unpacked, so it won't be a big effort for her to get her stuff ready. She has already begun packing up her office, leaving her laptop for last, and is making good progress. Despite Jen being adamant about proceeding with the move, Peter doesn't think that she'll go through with it. She's playing games with him and waiting for him to stop her, he thinks, and he's just waiting for her to give in and forget it. It's a stalemate.

Peter didn't choose the house over his wife when she had asked yesterday, but he might as well have. He had paused before saying anything as he was trying to figure out if Jen was serious or not, but she took it the wrong way. Go figure. She took his delay as him having to think about it, which told her all that she needed to know about how he feels. She's pissed off at him again because of it, and they haven't spoken a word to each other since. Peter can't win.

Peter stands in the doorway of Jen's office, arms crossed, and watches her fill boxes. He has no plans to offer his help. She doesn't turn to look at him although Peter knows that she can feel him supervising over her shoulder. How could she not? He's been observing and chewing loudly on his tongue for the last ten minutes. Finally unable to stand it any longer, she drops everything and turns to him.

"Why are you hovering?" she snaps.

"Just watching."

"Nice to know you can still talk."

"I can say the same thing for you."

Jen sighs. "Do we have to do this?"

"You tell me. You're the one who's packing."

A chime sounds from the doorbell, breaking up the tension that's leading nowhere constructive. Jen shrugs in Peter's direction and follows him to the front door. Peter disables the alarm system and opens the door. Standing on the other side are two men, one young and one old, one big-boned and one slim. Peter recognizes them, but he can't place from where. Jen is silent behind him.

"Can I help you?" Peter says.

The older, big-boned man with a dirty shirt steps forward and says, "Hi, do you remember me?"

Peter bites his lip and tries to place the faces. He can't. "I'm not sure. Should I?"

The man in front of him takes a deep breath and exhales loudly. His breath smells of pizza sauce, which is actually quite pleasant. "My name's Sal," he says. "You were a guest at my pizzeria a few days ago."

The memory resurfaces. "That's right, I remember now. And you were our waiter," Peter says as he points to the younger guy who's standing behind Sal. "I'm sorry, though, I don't remember your name."

The young man clears his throat and says, "The name's Antonio."

Peter nods, now remembering. He feels around for his wallet, thinking that he may have forgotten it at the pizzeria or something. He has no other explanation to why they'd be here. "What can we do for you guys?"

Sal shuffles his feet in place and looks away for a moment. When he looks back to Peter, Peter notices how sweaty he is.

"I'm here to talk about my nephew."

Peter looks over his shoulder to his wife, and she shrugs again. Peter has an obvious question, but is unable to get it out.

"Marco Salazar is my nephew," Sal says.

Just hearing his name makes Jen gasp aloud. Peter stiffens up too. He squeezes the open door firmly with his hand until it hurts.

"How dare you show your face here?" Jen blurts, now suddenly in the forefront. "I should call the cops and have them drag your ass to jail with your scumbag of a nephew!"

Sal puts his head down and shakes it. He looks hurt. "Please, if you'd just let me explain."

"Give me one good reason why I shouldn't have you both arrested?" Jen demands as she crosses her arms.

Sal doesn't hesitate in saying, "I want to tell you why everything has happened to you the way that it has."

Jen, still with her arms crossed, glances at Peter. He can tell by the look on her face that her interest is piqued.

"Why?" she asks.

Sal sighs. "May we come in?"

Jen looks to Peter again, and he returns the glance. They make eye contact and they both know that they're on the same page, even despite of their crumbling relationship. Peter steps back and holds open the door. Jen backs behind her husband cautiously as Sal and Antonio walk into the house.

"Should we sit?" Sal asks once inside.

"I think it's better if we stand," Jen says.

"Okay then. Standing it is."

Tense silence fills the hallway like a wildfire that threatens to spread.

"Go ahead," Peter says. "Say what you came here to tell us."

"There's no easy way to say this, so I'm just going to come out with it," Sal begins. "My nephew, Marco, was one of the two guys that broke into your house while you were sleeping the other night. The other guy," Sal motions to Antonio who sinks beside him, "is Antonio here. I suspect that you already knew that. I know you both have been working with the police through all of this, but I don't know how much they've told you. My brother, Bartolo, Marco's dad, used to own this house before you. He's in prison right now, but he's innocent."

Peter laughs under his breath. Everyone in prison thinks they're innocent.

Sal ignores Peter's subtle insult. He continues, "The house was taken by the bank after a few missed payments, which is why you're here. Anyway, my nephew didn't know that anyone had moved in yet, but when he and Antonio saw the commotion inside, they had to check it out. There was something hidden behind the wall, something that we needed in order to pay for Bartolo's lawyer."

"The statue," Jen says.

"That's right," Sal says. "That first night, they were just trying to find out if it was still in the house. That was all. They didn't know that your bed would be in front of the wall where the statue was until they got into the room. You see, they were just going to grab it and go if they could find it."

"Why bring guns then, huh?"

Sal winces. "Sorry about that. That was a mistake. They weren't loaded, I can assure you."

Jen falls back on her heels, clearly not having expected an apology. "So, what, they didn't expect that we'd wake up?"

Sal looks to Antonio and shrugs. "They didn't think it through I guess. When you woke up, they panicked."

"How did they get in?"

"Huh?"

"How did they get in the house?" Jen repeats. "The locksmith we hired said that there was no sign of forced entry."

"Jen," Peter says, trying to shush his wife. He doesn't want her giving away too much information. For all they know, this could all just be a trap.

"It's fine, Peter," Jen says, waving off her husband. She turns her attention back to Sal. "You were saying?"

"My brother always kept a spare key under one of the loose bricks outside. Marco had checked up on it a few different times so he knew that it was still there."

Peter nods. It all makes perfect sense to him, and the story does seem to fit with what the locksmith had said.

"But why didn't they just come earlier?" Jen asks. "Why wait until we moved in?"

Peter too is interested in the response to that.

"They didn't know at first. Once the bank took the house, they put one of those locks with the pin pad on the doors, so there was no way in. We had to wait until the locks were removed, but we didn't know when it was going to happen. One day Marco drove by and it was on, and then a couple days later it was gone. By the time we were able to get out here again, you had already moved in."

"I'm not buying it," Peter says, suddenly unimpressed with the tale.

"I'm telling you the truth," Sal says.

"No, you're not," Peter challenges. "The statue that you claim was worth money, it wasn't. We checked around. It was nothing more than a paperweight."

"You're right about that part," Sal admits. "The statue itself is worthless. What was on it, though, wasn't."

"What do you mean?" Jen says. "There was nothing on it."

"That's where we got lucky."

"I'm not following."

"The statue's two eyes were both diamonds when it was put into the wall, but they weren't there when you came across it. If they were, we'd never be here and you'd have sold that statue for a nice chunk of change."

Peter is suddenly intrigued again, being in the jewelry business himself. He says, "Diamonds? What kind of diamonds? I don't remember any diamonds. I would have seen them."

"I don't know what kind, that's not really my thing."

"That's not your thing?" Peter mocks. "You broke into our house on more than one occasion to get them, but it's not your thing. Stop screwing around with me. What did they look like?"

"Just diamonds, blue diamonds. I really don't know anything about them."

Peter shuts out the world and tries to recall what the statue had looked like. Its face was small, he remembers, and there was something unusual about it. He had thought at the time that the eyes were just caved in intentionally to symbolize something, maybe a symbol of

Chinese mythology or something. He wasn't sure. Now knowing what he does, he can see how diamonds could have fit in the slits. They'd have to have been small diamonds, though, likely no more than a carat each.

"How much?" Peter asks.

"How much for what?"

"The diamonds. How much are they worth?"

"Were. They were worth $25,000."

"$25,000 each!"

"No, for both of them."

"Oh." Peter's excitement dials down a bit, but that's still one hell of a find. For a one carat diamond to be worth that amount of money still is impressive. Although they couldn't have been flawless at that price, the flaws were likely internal. A true diamond expert could confirm by magnifying it, but Peter suspects that they would have nothing more than a few small cavities or minor chips.

"Wait," he says, "you said were. Where are they?"

"Gone," Sal says. "We got them and I sold them. They were still in the wall, they must have become dislodged from the statue at some point."

It all clicks for Jen, her face now lit up like a Christmas tree. "So that's why they came back? To find the diamonds. That explains the mess upstairs, they were looking for them."

"That's right."

Jen turns her attention to Antonio, who despite being present for the entire conversation, has not contributed a word. "What about the guy who attacked me? I know it wasn't you, I would recognize his eyes anywhere. Was that part of your plan to make sure that we were out of the house so you could come back? Did you arrange that?"

Sal looks ashamed. "It wasn't supposed to happen like that."

"So you do know who he is then?"

"Yes, but it's not what you think."

Peter watches as the dagger of Sal's truth twists deep within his wife's gut. He knows that Sal's admission is causing her a great deal of pain. He feels it too.

"He was supposed to be the buyer of the diamonds," Sal admits, "but he threatened violence when we didn't have them when he wanted. He was going to kill me, so I told him where I thought he could find the statue. At that point, I already knew that you hadn't found the diamonds and that you still had the statue."

"How'd you know that?" Jen asks.

"The pawn shop. Willy's a friend of mine."

Jen shakes her head in disgust. "So, what, you were willing to sacrifice me instead of yourself? You were willing to let me die over this whole thing?"

"I had no way of knowing that you were in the house, you have to believe me."

"Then why did you come back? If you told this guy where to find the diamonds, you knew that they'd be gone already. You had to be in on it!"

Peter puts a hand on Jen's shoulder to try to calm her. He notices her legs starting to shake, which does happen to her weak joints sometimes when stressed. He finds Sal's eyes and says, "Maybe you should be going now."

"We had nothing to do with it, I swear! I told him where the statue was, not the diamonds. We didn't know for sure where the diamonds were, but we knew that they weren't on the statue."

Jen relaxes a bit, but stays on high alert.

Sal continues, "I was hoping that he would just grab the statue and leave without realizing the diamonds were missing. And he did."

"Then you came back and found them yourselves," Jen offers, now mellowed.

Sal nods.

Just as the tension fully releases from Jen's joints, she appears to have a realization. The tension returns with a vengeance, and she starts to panic. "What if he comes back?" she says. "What happens when he finds out that the diamonds are missing? He'll come back!"

"That's why we're here," Sal says. "We want to help you. That's why we're telling you all of this."

"You want to help us?" Peter says. "Now you want to help? Don't you think that you've done enough damage already? You have your money for your brother's lawyer, so what are you really doing here?"

Sal sneaks a glance to Antonio, who offers no support. "Marco, my nephew, has spent the entire weekend behind bars."

"Am I supposed to feel bad for him?" Peter says. "He broke into my house. Twice."

"He sees a judge in the morning to determine how much his bail will be. We have enough to cover my brother's lawyer's fee, but not much else. But if Marco's bail is too high-"

"So that's what this is about?"

"All I'm asking is that if you help us out, we can help you in return. We'll talk to the police and tell them everything that we just told you. We'll do what we can to help them track down your attacker and keep you safe. I just want my family out of jail. You'll never hear from us again once this is all over."

"I've got a better idea," Peter says. "Why don't you just tell us who the attacker was, and we'll do you a solid by not having both of you thrown in jail too. How's that sound?"

Sal looks defeated. He puts his head down and says, "Enrique, that's his first name."

Antonio, finally showing some signs of life, huffs and shoots Sal a look of disapproval.

"Enrique what?"

"I don't know. Just Enrique."

Peter pauses for a moment, then he says, "Get out of my house. I don't ever want to see you anywhere near my property again. We know that you've been wandering around the street recently too, but it ends now. Do you understand me? Now get out before I call the cops."

Sal turns for the door and motions for Antonio to follow. He turns back one last time before leaving and says, "Please, just think about it. This has all just been one big misunderstanding. No one was supposed to get hurt."

"Get out, now!"

Sal and Antonio step outside and Peter slams the door behind them.

CHAPTER FORTY-ONE

The door slams behind Sal and Antonio as they descend down the stairs. Sal wants to look back, but he knows that he's pushing his luck if he does. Peter and Jen are more upset than he had thought they would be, but he supposes that he can't blame them for that. It went even worse than he had thought possible. The best that he can hope for is that they'll sleep on it and come around to seeing things from his perspective. But based on their reaction, that seems like wishful thinking.

"What the hell did you say that for?" Antonio says as he and Sal get into Sal's Lexus.

Although he knows exactly what Antonio is referring to, Sal plays dumb. "What? What did I say?"

"Enrique's name. Why would you tell them that? They have no use for us now that they have everything they need. You just gave away any leverage we had in there."

Sal sighs. "You're right, but I didn't know what else to do. The best we can hope for is that they appreciate the information and understand the position we're in."

"And you say I'm naïve. You don't really think that's actually going to happen, do you? We've made their lives a living hell, why would they trust us?"

Sal shakes his head as he starts the car. "It's all I have left."

Antonio crosses his arms and looks out the window in disbelief. He stays that way until they pull in the parking lot of the pizzeria. Once there, Sal turns off the ignition and reaches for the handle of the door.

"Am I going to jail, Big Sal?" Antonio says, solemnly, before Sal can open his door.

Sal releases the door handle and repositions himself in his seat. He takes a moment to find the right words before turning and facing Antonio. He says, "If you want me to be honest with you, I don't know."

Antonio drops his head. "I can't go to jail, my life will be ruined."

Sal's first reaction is to ask Antonio how he thinks he feels with both his brother and his nephew being behind bars, but he holds back. Instead, he offers support. "I know, Antonio, I know. We just don't know what's going to happen with any of this. But don't worry, I'll-"

"You'll what, come up with something? You'll think of another master plan, is that it?"

"Antonio-"

"No, Sal. You have to hear this. Throughout this whole thing you've just been sitting back and watching everything happen while me and Marco were out there doing all the work. You've been barking orders and coming up with ideas, but you haven't done a damn thing yourself. Now, because of you, my best friend is in jail and I'll probably be joining him before long. I tried to back out of this a long time ago, but you wouldn't let me. You made me feel guilty about everything that you've ever done for me to sucker me in. I've had it."

Sal is taken aback. To him, this is all coming out of left field. "I gave you a job, Antonio. You should be thanking me."

"So what? It's just a job. You were the one who convinced me that I was better off with real world experience instead of a college degree. You just wanted me to stay so you could make me your slave."

"Don't be ridiculous." Sal scoffs. "Excuse me for trying to help you out."

"You never wanted to help me. You were just doing it to benefit yourself. It's always been about you." Antonio opens his door and gets out of the car before Sal has the chance to respond. He gets into Marco's Cadillac and screeches out of the parking lot.

Sal is left alone with wounded feelings, wondering how he got so involved in this mess. He never knew that was how Antonio had felt about him. He had thought that he was doing him a favor by offering him a job after high school, but he never did consider things from Antonio's perspective. On top of everything else that Sal is going through, Antonio's words leave him hurting.

Sal stares at the illuminated sign hanging above the entrance to the pizzeria and can't help but feel shameful. If it wasn't for him and his own selfish dreams of owning a restaurant, none of this would have ever happened. Everything is his fault and he's deserving of all of this. He remembers how Bartolo had told him everything shortly after the pizzeria opened.

Sal always knew that Bartolo didn't have the kind of money that he offered him to open up the restaurant, but Bartolo had insisted. All he wanted in return was to be a part of it, which Sal was hoping that he'd want to do anyway. Business was good initially, but once the buzz went away after being open for a while, things started to slow down. Since Bartolo had handled the books, Sal never knew that there were financial troubles, but he had suspected that may be the case. Bartolo's attitude began to change and he was becoming easily stressed and temperamental over every dollar that was being spent, but he would never share the specific details with Sal.

Sal didn't get confirmation of the trouble the pizzeria was in until after Bartolo was arrested. For this first time, Sal was responsible for his own accounting, and that's when he discovered the issues. The shop was more than a few months behind in rent and the expenses had far exceeded the monthly revenue. Sal had confronted Bartolo about it during one of his early visits to Concord, and Bartolo reluctantly told him all about it. When asked why he never said anything, Bartolo had simply said that he didn't want to Sal to worry about it. His dream was to make pizzas and interact with customers and not to deal with the stress of running a business. Sal never understood that, as dealing with the finances was part of running a business, but he admired his brother's heart and good intentions, even though he was so very wrong.

Bartolo had confirmed that he borrowed some money from someone that he had done business with in the past, and that things were getting nasty when he started missing some payments. The lender started making threats if Bartolo didn't pay up, so when he was approached by a third party about a refinancing-type opportunity, Bartolo jumped at it.

It was supposed to be simple. In exchange for this mystery third party to cover his debts, Bartolo just had to play poker. He was to enter a tournament and give his winnings to this guy - who, by the way, Sal has never found out his name - which should have been easy enough. Bartolo would be debt free and the third party would make his money back, plus some, if and when Bartolo won. Bartolo was a regular in underground tournaments, and he won more often than he lost. But when things went terribly wrong on a calculated gamble at the final table, things went from bad to worse for Bartolo.

Not only was the rent money for Sal's pizzeria past due, but now his house was underwater due to the equity loan that he had taken out to cover the buy-in for the tournament as well. Worse than that even, the third part financier had wanted his money back and was willing to do whatever it took to do that. A few months later, the same guy - the third party financier - had come across another opportunity to get his investment back, plus some, and he all but forced Bartolo to help him.

According to Bartolo, it all went down on Christmas Eve. Understandably so, Bartolo couldn't get into too many details over the monitored prison phone system, but he had told Sal enough that mattered. Bartolo and his creditor broke into some guy's house during the night in search of something very specific. The owner was an ancient artifact collector, and he had apparently recently come across a rare Chinese warrior statue at an auction. Bartolo's creditor had never said why he wanted it so badly, besides the obvious diamonds that were used for eyes, and Bartolo didn't ask. All of Bartolo's debts were promised to be forgotten if he helped to get the statue that his creditor was looking for, so he did.

Bartolo had to do all the work. They had found the statue right away without disturbing the homeowner. But instead of grabbing the item and leaving quietly, that was when the financier turned his back on Bartolo. He went into the old man's room and shot him once through the forehead, then he told Bartolo to stash the statue for a few days. Two days later, after Bartolo had hidden the statue behind the wall in his bedroom until he was to receive instructions on how to proceed - which, wisely, he didn't confide the location of to anyone, until he told Sal about it after he was arrested - he was arrested at his home. He was told that an anonymous tip connected him to the slaying of an elderly man, so he was brought in for questioning. After having his fingerprints taken, they had matched those that were found all over the house of the slain man, and his nightmare began.

He didn't wear gloves and neither did the real killer - Bartolo's nameless creditor - but he didn't think that it would be a problem. The financier had insisted that they would just be in and out and had no need to touch anything besides the statue. What the issue was, which Bartolo didn't realize at the time, was that the financier literally didn't touch anything - not the door handle, not the statue, not anything. With only one set of foreign prints and a slain body, the whole thing was easily pinned on Bartolo.

It was all a carefully planned setup.

The diamond eyes of the statue weren't worth nearly as much as Bartolo had owed, but his creditor had insisted that he had a bone to pick with the collector over some past disputes, so they were even. In hindsight, Bartolo came to the conclusion that the bone to pick was probably with himself for not coming through at the poker table.

Now, still staring at the illuminated sign hanging above the door of the pizzeria, Sal wishes that he never even had the dream. He wishes that he had never accepted that money from Bartolo and opened the restaurant. But more than anything, he wishes that all of this would just be over.

PETER AND JEN STAND with their backs to the closed door in silence. Jen wraps her arms around herself, frightened, and doesn't know what to think. Her hands are quivering from the thrill of the confrontation, so she tries to shake them out to calm her jitters. Peter walks over to her and pulls her into his chest. She throws her face into it and lets herself go for a while.

It's been an emotionally exhaustive week, and Jen has reached her breaking point. She has already called her best friend in Maine, and she'll be staying at her place until she can find an apartment or a cottage of her own. Whether Peter comes with her or not, she doesn't know, but she's going either way, with or without him. Peter mumbles something in her ear while trying to offer some comfort, but she only faintly hears it. After a moment of release, she pulls free from his grasp and looks up to him, her eyes red and swollen.

"I feel so violated," she says.

"I know...I know."

"I'm leaving tonight, Peter. Are you coming or staying? I just can't be a part of this anymore."

"How about what he was offering, huh?" Peter chuckles to himself, pushing off the question. "Crazy, right? How about the nerve of that guy?"

"Will you answer the question, please?" Jen says, not finding his delay at all cute.

"Why don't we wait until tomorrow? We can sleep on it tonight, go and talk to Officer Dale tomorrow, then we can figure out what we want to do."

"I know what I want to do, and I'm doing it. Whether you come with me or not is up to you."

"Please, let's just wait until tomorrow, okay? Please. I need some time to wrap my mind around everything."

Jen considers this for a second and decides that it's not the worst idea that's she's ever heard. It would probably make the most sense to get a fresh start in the morning. "Fine," she says. "But I'm leaving tomorrow with or without you."

HIS CELL IS BITTERLY cold and the food has been awful. It smells mostly of mold and filth. A leaky faucet echoes from somewhere down the cell block, which is blocked out occasionally by a yelling inmate. Other than that, it's on a torturous repeated loop, like a bad infomercial. There's a small window in the corner of Marco's cell that doesn't have bars through it, but it's too small for even a child to crawl through. The fall to the ground below would certainly kill him if he somehow made it through, so the thought of trying to escape has never seriously entered his thoughts.

Marco has spent the entire weekend by himself for the first time in his life. The one bed in his cell is firm and stained with urine, and the lone pillow is flat and practically useless. Marco has had a lot of time to think. He stands just tall enough to see out of the corner window, so that's how he has spent much of the past two days - just looking down at the people below.

The county jail is fenced in, but is otherwise right in the middle of a busy street. People walk by without even noticing that it's there most of the time, and Marco doesn't blame them. Prisoners inside the jail are outcasts and do nothing positive for society, and people hate that their tax dollars fund the lives of the lowlifes that are housed inside. Marco had felt the same way about jails and prisons and prisoners until his father got arrested. His perspective changed then. Sometimes good people do bad things, or in his father's case, sometimes good people get framed for doing bad things. Marco is the former, although he has spent a lot of time questioning whether he can be considered a good person anymore. He doesn't think that he is.

Marco had always heard that the best way to survive in jail was to either beat the hell out of someone or to become somebody's bitch on the first day, but it didn't happen like that for him. Surprisingly, nobody has bothered him. He hasn't spoken a word since he was arrested on Friday - not literally, of course, but it feels that way to him - and he has spent all of his chow and free time sitting alone. He's gotten looks from other inmates, and he was sure that people were talking about him at one point, but no one has approached him. Not one. And he's okay with that. He's just been buying time until his hearing on Monday, when he can finally see his uncle again.

He has replayed what has happened in his mind a thousand times over since Friday, and he still struggles to comprehend what went wrong. It's almost as if Antonio cut the wrong wire deliberately so that Marco would be busted, but deep down, he knows that can't be true. Antonio is his best friend, his only friend really, and he would never sell him out like that. He would have nothing to gain by doing so anyhow, so it just doesn't make sense that it could even be a possibility. Marco can't help but wonder, though. He has concluded that it's these walls that make people have crazy thoughts that they normally wouldn't have, which is why he's even considering that this as a possibility. Monday can't come soon enough.

The thing that has been on Marco's mind the most is those diamonds. He did see Antonio sneaking around the front of the house while he was being thrown in the back of the police car, but he doesn't know for sure if Antonio gave them to Sal or not. Sal would have said something when they spoke on the phone earlier, wouldn't he have?

Unless Antonio wasn't there yet, then he wouldn't have known. Marco refuses to let himself think like that, so he pushes that to the side. Using the presumption that Antonio did indeed give Sal the eyes and didn't run off with them for his own personal gain, did Sal get the money from Willy? Without a buyer lined up for the diamonds, was Willy still willing to pony up the cash? Finally, how much did Sal get for them, and is it enough to still cover that lawyer's retainer? Will there be enough left over to get Marco out of jail too? With so many questions and no answers to any of them, Marco is completely in the dark, and he hates that. Maybe tomorrow he'll have a chance to talk to Sal and find out the answers to some of these things.

Marco knows exactly what he's going to do once he's out of here. His uncle still owes him a full bottle of Jack Daniel's, and he's going to hold him to that. After all, he's been of legal age for thirty-six hours and he's yet to enjoy a drink. Not even a swig. He can almost taste it now, it just dangling there on the tip of his tongue, waiting for him to lick it away. Although Marco is determined to make it happen, he's realistic in knowing that there's a possibility that it won't.

CHAPTER FORTY-TWO

Marco is allowed a quick shower and served breakfast before he's dragged off to the courthouse. By not having a lawyer of his own, he's been assigned a court-appointed public defender. Shelley Washburn had visited him yesterday briefly, mostly just as an introduction and to confirm the details of the hearing today.

Upon arriving at the courthouse, Marco is escorted to a private room where Shelley is waiting. A single armed officer waits in the corner of the room near the door while Marco and Shelley discuss their options. Shelley is young and not very attractive, but Marco likes her so far based on their brief interaction. She has a certain confidence about her that draws Marco in.

"So I've reviewed your file," Shelley begins, "and I've spoken with the prosecutor this morning. They're willing to offer you a deal."

"And what would that be?" Marco asks.

"If you give up the name of your accomplice, they'll recommend the minimum bail to the judge for misdemeanor breaking and entering."

"Who said I had an accomplice?"

"They have a witness who is willing to testify. If you don't give up the name, they plan on charging you with second degree robbery and conspiracy to commit robbery. Both felonies. Plus whatever else they can tack on as this drags onward. This is a no-brainer, Mr. Salazar."

"But they have no proof that anything was even taken, why would I plead out?"

"There's plenty of time for them to collect further evidence before the trial. Why are you even debating this?"

"Remind me again," Marco says, not liking Shelley's attitude, "are you my mother or my lawyer?"

Shelley looks away and clears her throat, embarrassed. "I'm sorry. I'm just trying to give you the best advice that I can, as your attorney. You can trust me. I'm here to help you, but I just need to know the truth so that I can defend you properly. Everything that you say to me will be in confidence."

Marco doesn't say anything about the cop that's standing in the corner, but he suspects that whatever he hears will be unusable in court. "When can I talk to my uncle?"

"What?"

"My uncle Sal, when can I talk to him?"

"I think there are more important things to worry about right now, Mr. Salazar."

"I'm not doing anything until I talk to my uncle."

Shelley sighs and almost rolls her eyes, but stops herself before she does. "Fine," she says. "I'll see what I can do."

PETER WAKES UP A couple hours after Jen does with a clear mind. He didn't sleep well, but he knows what he has to do. It's going to be a difficult conversation to have with his wife, he realizes, but it's something that has to be done. If it means the end to their marriage then so be it, but he can't just walk away so soon.

He fabricates some lame excuse about why he can't go to work again, and although he knows that his boss doesn't buy it, he doesn't protest. Peter feels awful for missing so much time already, especially considering the mess of a week that was last week with the robbery of one of the stores plus the resignation of the manager in another. Not to mention all the time that he had taken off to move into the new house. He's not making a very good first impression.

He finds Jen downstairs moving the last of her boxes into the crevices of the back seat of her Subaru. All of her clothes, office supplies, and bathroom toiletries are packed, with the rest being left for Peter if he decides to join her. If not, it's his to keep. He pretends not to see her so that he can avoid helping. He waits until she comes back into the house before approaching her.

"Morning," he says.

"Morning," Jen replies in passing. Her face is already covered with sweat.

"Sleep well?"

No response. It was a stupid question.

Peter continues, "Do you want to talk?"

"There's not much to talk about. You know where I stand. It's really all up to what you want to do."

"I'd really like you to reconsider."

"So that's your answer then? You're staying?"

Peter explains his stance to Jen, including everything about needing to be around for the new job and the fact that they likely won't even be able to sell the house since they'll be underwater with their mortgage. They'll lose money if anything.

"Rent it out then," Jen says in response to the argument about the house. "You're just making excuses."

Peter shakes his head. He knows that there's no pleasing her. "I'm just trying to be logical here."

"Logical is getting out of a toxic situation. Logical is moving away when someone is trying to kill you."

"We don't know that."

"Were you not listening to what Sal said yesterday? When that Enrique guy finds out that the diamonds are missing, he's coming back."

"You can't run for the rest of your life, Jen."

"What do you suggest then, huh?"

"He said he'd help us."

"You can't be serious. I can't believe that you even remotely trust that guy. He was just telling us what he thought we wanted to hear so that we'd fall right into his trap. He even admitted it, this is about money."

"So what? If he can help us out by telling the cops everything he knows, maybe they can catch the guy."

"What's the difference if we just tell them what Sal told us ourselves? Either way, they're going to know who to look for. Why should we let them off the hook for what they've done?"

"What if he doesn't talk? The other guy, Marco, isn't talking. That's what the cops said. If he's not talking, what makes you so sure that Sal will?"

Jen glares at her husband. "What is wrong with you? What has happened to you?"

"What do you mean?"

"I don't even feel like I know you anymore, Peter. This is so unlike you."

"I don't know what you want me to tell you. I'm just trying to be reasonable."

"More like reasonless. What you're suggesting makes no sense."

"I guess we just think differently then."

"I guess so. It's becoming pretty clear that we're no longer anything alike." Jen brushes past Peter and storms out of the room.

Peter's left alone, again, wondering what else there is that he can do to save them.

AFTER THEIR SHIFTS END, Gerry and Jamaal drive over to the courthouse together. They discuss any additions or subtractions to their most recent theory about everything that has happened, and they come up with nothing additional. Sheriff Collins had met with the state's prosecutor over the weekend and gave him all the details about what they had found, so it's out of their hands now. They've been told that they might be called to testify during the trial about how things went with Marco Salazar, so they're prepared for that possibility.

Earlier in the day, Jamaal had asked Ben Shultz to track down and print out a headshot of Antonio Esposito when he arrived at the office. Antonio, who, according to Betty Anderson, is Marco's accomplice, so Jamaal and Gerry suspect that he might show up to the hearing. When they had arrived back to the station after their shifts to go over the final details with Sheriff Collins, Jamaal had grabbed the photo from Ben.

When Gerry pulls into the already packed courthouse parking lot, Jamaal retrieves the photo and they study it together. It's a blown up photocopy of Antonio's license and a bit pixelated, but it's clear enough to get a distinct picture of his key features.

"You recognize him?" Jamaal asks.

Gerry studies the photo further before shaking his head. "No, I don't think so. You?"

"No. Do you think he'll be here?"

"I guess we'll find out soon enough. We'll see if he's as good of a friend as Marco is or if he's away in hiding."

Jamaal nods. "Moment of truth."

Both men reach for their door handles and step out onto the pavement. With the sun warming them, they start toward the wide stairwell that precedes the entrance in unison. It's time to find out how good their detective work is.

CHAPTER FORTY-THREE

Dressed in his best and only suit that barely fits, Sal arrives at the courthouse right as it opens. Even he admits that he hasn't looked this good in years, clean shaven and not smelling of pizza, but he couldn't care less about that today. He just wants to be there for Marco. He has the cash with him, just in case, and it's inconspicuously hidden in a bag under his seat in the Lexus. It makes him a little restless to let it out of his sight, but he has little choice. The hearing doesn't start for another hour, so Sal stands outside the courtroom and waits. For what, he doesn't know, but he's there in case he's summoned for any reason.

Sal hasn't heard from Antonio since their blowout yesterday afternoon. He expects that the stress had just finally gotten to Antonio and that they'll make up at some point today. Although the words still hurt, he's not that concerned about it. Marco is priority number one.

In the corridor of the courthouse, Sal finds a chair and sits. He watches as well-dressed men and women alike make their way up and down the halls carrying folders and briefcases. Compared to what he's used to, Sal feels like he's in a foreign country; a fish out of water so to speak. He catches the eyes of a plump brunette as she exits one of the closed doors at the far end of the hallway. She looks like she's on a mission to find something or someone. As she approaches where he sits, Sal fights the urge to look around to see if anyone is near him, as he knows that there's not. Their eyes meet up and the brunette stops in front of him. Her perfume is overpowering.

"Excuse me," she says, "are you Amelio Salazar?"

"Who's asking?"

"My name is Shelley Washburn, I'm representing your nephew, Marco."

Sal pops out of his seat like he's in shape and is flooded with emotion. Suddenly the perfume isn't so powerful anymore. "Where is he? Is he alright?"

"He's fine. He's asking for you, though. Will you come with me?"

Without hesitation, Sal follows Shelley down the hall. He wonders how she had known that he was the one that she was looking for, but he lets it go. He doesn't care. She leads him into the conference room where a man sits, his back facing the doorway. Sal immediately knows that it's Marco from the shape of his head - it's much like his own. He's never been happier to see his nephew.

"Marco!"

Marco pops up from his seat and turns toward the door. "Uncle Sal!"

Sal runs toward Marco and wraps his big arms around him. Marco tries to return to gesture, but the handcuffs around his wrists restrict him.

"Are you okay?" Sal whispers in Marco's ear with a heavy heart. He can feel Marco nodding, but he doesn't actually verbalize anything.

Shelley makes her way around the table and sits across from them. Feeling her waiting, Sal releases Marco, then Marco sits again. Sal finds a chair from against the wall and pulls it next to Marco's, then he sits too.

"Okay," Shelley begins, "we're running out of time here. Mr. Salazar has been offered a plea bargain from the state, but he refuses to agree to the deal until he talks to you."

Sal makes a face. "Please, call him Marco. Mr. Salazar is confusing."

"Fine," Shelley says. "Marco, your uncle is here now, so talk."

"Tell me about this plea deal," Sal says.

Shelley does. When she finishes explaining to Sal exactly what she had told to Marco, Sal has only one question.

"How much would the bail be for both options?"

"You're worried about bail?" Shelley snaps. "Marco could be facing serious time in prison if he's found guilty. His best bet is to take the deal. Being a misdemeanor, he's looking at a maximum of six months, probably less, maybe none."

"And if he doesn't agree to the deal?"

"Years."

"If he's found guilty."

"Of course."

Sal pauses. "How good are you?"

Shelley leans back in her chair and dramatizes an exhale so that her frustration would be obvious to even the most oblivious of people. "You should take the deal."

Sal looks to Marco, then back to Shelley. "Can you give us a minute?"

Shelley looks to Marco for confirmation, and he nods. She gets up and leaves the room. Her high heels click on the tile floor and fade out into the hallway along with her full figured frame.

"Did you get the money?" Marco asks as soon as the door closes. He keeps his voice low so that the police officer in the corner can't hear.

"I have the money."

"How much?"

"$25,000."

Marco nods, looking satisfied, as if his approval was needed. "So, what do you think?"

Sal wastes no time in telling Marco about the trip he and Antonio had taken to the Winston's house yesterday and everything that came of that. Admittedly so, he never would have gone over to the Winston's if he knew what he knows now about the plea deal that the state is offering. When the Winston's tell the police about the stolen diamonds, Marco will be screwed. They'll drop the plea deal and elevate the charge from a misdemeanor to a felony, for sure. There's no other way out. They just have to hope that the Winston's don't talk to the cops before the deal is agreed to. Sal explains all of this to Marco.

When in agreement on how to proceed, Sal grabs Shelley and brings her back inside. She again sits opposite Sal and Marco and waits.

"Okay," Sal begins, "what are we looking at for bail if we accept the deal?"

Shelley rolls her eyes without holding back this time. "Why are we still talking about bail? We're talking about zero to six months of jail time versus years. That's where the conversation should be had."

"We're still talking about it because you haven't answered it," Sal says. "Will you just answer the question? How much are we looking at?"

Shelley shakes her head in disbelief. Sal is starting to think that she's stalling.

"I can't answer that for you," she admits. "It's up to the judge."

"Ballpark."

Shelley pauses. "I don't know. I've seen five hundred bucks for similar cases, and I've also seen ten thousand. Every case is different. It really depends on what the state has to say. The judge will listen to their recommendation and my objections, and she'll make her decision based on that."

Sal doesn't know what to think, but the uncertainty is killing him. Even if Marco does agree to the plea deal and gives up Antonio, they still may not have enough money to get both he and Bartolo out. Add Antonio's possible incarceration next and they'll be out of money for sure. It's a near certainty. And even despite Antonio's seemingly sudden displeasure with Sal, Sal's still not comfortable with selling him out like that. He can only imagine how

Marco feels about it. He might have to take one for the team here, though.

"Is that what we're going with?" Shelley asks. "Should I tell them that we accept their deal?"

"Yes, we accept their deal," Sal says.

"I'm sorry, but I need to hear it from Marco's mouth directly."

Marco looks to Sal with uncertainty. Sal nods. Marco turns to Shelley and says, "I accept the deal."

ANTONIO IS GLAD TO have gotten what was bothering him off his chest, but he does feel guilty about the way it went down. Although all truths that he spoke, he didn't mean to attack Sal the way that he did yesterday, but he just couldn't hold back any longer. Some of those things just had to be said. It was only a matter of time.

Although he does consider not going to Marco's hearing so that he doesn't have to face Sal quite yet, he knows that he needs to be there for Marco. He knows that Marco would do anything for him, even in the most difficult of times, so he needs to do the same. He wants to do the same. That's what friends do.

He finds a seldom worn blazer in the closet and throws it on over his shirt and tie before heading downtown to the courthouse. When he pulls into the parking lot, he notices Sal's Lexus right away, which is parked in the front row. Antonio finds a spot near the back, close to the exit.

Antonio is blown away by the overwhelming feeling of authority that lies within the walls of the courthouse, and it makes him extremely uncomfortable. He learns from the clerk which room Marco's hearing will be held in and waits near it. He passes a couple of uniformed police officers on his way, and they both give him a strange, condescending look. He keeps his head down and waits around the corner until the clock strikes nine.

GERRY AND JAMAAL SIT quietly in the hallway just outside of the courtroom that will soon be home to Marco Salazar's hearing. The pixelated image of Antonio Esposito's face fills Gerry's mind as he and Jamaal sit and wait. When the door opens at the end of the hallway, both of their heads turn to investigate.

Gerry sees it first, sees him first. Just as expected, Antonio Esposito, dressed in an amateurish getup, walks in. He looks like a child in a man's world, and he walks directly toward them. Gerry nudges Jamaal's leg.

"Are you seeing this?" Gerry whispers.

Jamaal's eyes are stuck on Antonio as he walks past them with his head down. "I don't believe it."

"Good call, partner."

"Damn, I didn't actually believe he'd show up, but I was hoping."

"Same here."

"Want to go talk to him?"

"No, not yet. Let's wait to see what happens during the hearing. We can stop him on the way out if we need to."

Jamaal nods in agreement.

Less than ten minutes later, Gerry and Jamaal stay back while everyone else waiting in the hallway is ushered into the courtroom. Gerry watches intently as Antonio appears from around the corner and sneaks his way into the courtroom like he doesn't want to be seen. Once the hallway clears, Gerry and Jamaal go in last and wait in the back. Despite there being multiple rows of empty seats available, they stay standing against the back wall near the door, all but ensuring that Antonio won't make it out without getting through them. Gerry knows that they have him trapped.

CHAPTER FORTY-FOUR

Court is in session. With a giant knot in his stomach, twisting at his guts like a corkscrew, Marco finds his seat at the defendant's table next to Shelley while the prosecution fills in the table on the opposite side. A faded wooden podium separates the two tables. Marco can only imagine the types of people who've stood behind it, pleading their innocence. He doesn't feel like he belongs here. Shelley's instructions are clear: Marco is not to say a word unless specifically called upon to do so. He can handle that. Marco can feel the walls closing in on him as people begin to fill the empty seats behind him. He's tempted to turn around and look who's in attendance, but he's been informed that it's not wise to do so. He is to sit there and do or say nothing.

Everyone in the courtroom stands as one when the back door opens and the judge makes her way inside. Judge Fawn, dressed in a bulky black robe and wearing glasses around her neck, climbs up to her bench and instructs the crowd to sit. She slips on her glasses and debriefs herself on the details of the case before reciting her required spiel to the courtroom. When finished, she officially calls the case. Marco is intimidated by her aura of dominance, even from a distance.

"The Commonwealth of Massachusetts versus Mr. Marco Salazar. Defendant, please rise."

Hearing his name said aloud makes Marco's heart leap. Shelley gives him a nod and they stand up together. Marco sneaks a peek behind him as he does, subtly so that Shelley won't notice, and he quickly finds the face that he's looking for in the crowd. About half way across the room and sitting by himself near the end of a row is Antonio. He only catches a quick glimpse, but he thinks that he recognizes Antonio's blazer as his own. His dad had given him one of his a few years back, and he thinks that may be the one that Antonio is wearing. Although he doesn't see Sal in the crowd, Marco can feel him behind him in the first row. He would recognize his heavy breathing anywhere.

"Mr. Salazar," Judge Fawn continues, "it has been brought to my attention that there has been an agreed upon arrangement with the state, is that correct?"

Before Marco can respond, Shelley steps forward. "That is correct, Your Honor."

Judge Fawn nods her head. She turns her attention to the prosecution. "Does the state agree?"

The lead prosecutor - a short man whose black hair has a strategic touch of gray, just as the television commercial glorifies - confirms and explains the terms of the agreement to the judge. "Assuming we receive the accurate identity of the accomplice," he says, "the state recommends the minimum sentence, Your Honor."

Judge Fawn turns back to the defense. "Mr. Salazar, considering the terms of the agreement, I would appreciate it if you would now provide the court with the name of the said accomplice for the record."

Marco starts to sweat.

ANTONIO IS LIVID, INFURIATED, enraged; pick the adjective, they all mean basically the same thing. That's how he feels. Is Marco really going to sell him out to save himself?

He had thought that they were friends, but now, Antonio is learning that they're not as close as he had thought. It sounds like Sal's work to him - influencing Marco to turn his back on his friend - but that may just be him being overly sensitive to the situation. Despite their blowout, Sal wouldn't do that to him either, he doesn't think. There wouldn't have even been enough time to work something like that out anyway, unless they were planning on this all along. It would explain why Marco didn't request a lawyer.

Antonio looks across the courtroom in Sal's direction. Sal is sitting in the front row just behind Marco, and he's suddenly infatuated with his shoes. He refuses to look up or turn back to face Antonio.

Antonio considers leaving the building while he still can. If Marco gives up his name, he'll be detained before he can even leave the courthouse. At least he'd get a head start if he leaves now. He could start running, although he doesn't think that he's cut out for being a fugitive of the law. Being as subtle as he can, he scans the room, looking for an escape route. Unfortunately, the only way out is the same way that he came in if he excludes the fire exit and judge's door, both of which aren't truly options. The same two police officers that were staring him down as he entered the courthouse now stand on either side of the only exit. They seem to be staring right at him.

It's blocked.

Antonio knows now that he has no choice but to stay. He interlocks his fingers, clenches his teeth, and says a little prayer. All that he can do is expect the worst and hope for the best. He needs a miracle.

WITH ALL EYES ON him, Marco can't speak. His mouth is dry and he feels like he's being gagged with cotton balls. He's completely frozen, barely even able to breathe. Shelley whispers him some encouragement, but he ignores her.

"Mr. Salazar," Judge Fawn says from behind her bench, "I repeat, please provide the name of your accomplice to the court."

Marco desperately looks for a distraction but finds nothing. He knows that this is the right thing to do, the only logical thing to do, but he can't do it. Antonio has been his best friend since they were kids, and he's not willing to give up that relationship. There has to be another way.

Judge Fawn sighs. She's becoming frustrated. "Mr. Salazar, this is your final chance. If you do not provide the name of your accomplice I will hold you in contempt of this court."

Marco can feel Shelley burning her eyes into him. A similar heat comes from the prosecution on his right. Giving in to the pressure, fearing that he may engulf in flames, he finally says, "There was no accomplice."

A frustrated murmur fills the courtroom. Shelley slams a notepad on the table, then quickly regrets it once the judge shoots her a look of discontent.

"I see," Judge Fawn says, calmly, then she removes her glasses. "You do realize the consequences of your statement, do you not? By not accepting the state's deal, you'll be charged with a felony. Two actually. Are you sure that you don't want to take a moment to discuss this decision further with your legal representation?"

"Yes, he does, Your Honor," Shelley says.

Marco ignores her. "No, that won't be necessary. I've made up my mind."

Shelley throws her hands in the air and turns her back to Marco.

"Because you're young and may not realize the magnitude of the situation, I will give you one final opportunity to change your mind then, Mr. Salazar. I would strongly advise that you take a moment to speak with your attorney. I hate to see young people throw away their lives over stubbornness. I've seen it a thousand times. Please keep in mind that your bail will be at my sole discretion and that I do factor in courtroom antics when making that decision. Do you understand that?"

He hears what the judge is saying, but he doesn't care. He won't be a rat. "I understand."

"And?"

"And I'm not going to accept the deal."

The crowd murmur increases in intensity.

"Alright then, Mr. Salazar. I gave you ample opportunity to do the wise thing here," Judge Fawn says, now sounding annoyed at Marco's disrespect. "Due to the nature of the charges against you and your actions here in the courtroom today, I am setting bail at $10,000. If you are unable to come up with that, you will stay in police custody until the completion of the trial." She bangs her gavel on the tabletop. "Court is adjourned."

Just like that, Marco sees the writing on the wall. The judge didn't even give him or his lawyer an opportunity to say anything in response, and Marco knows that's because of what he pulled. Shelley knows it too, and she lets him know it.

"I hope you're happy," she whispers. "I don't know what you're trying to pull, but you're lucky that's all she did to you. You've made me look like an idiot in front of my peers. I've got to be honest with you, I think that you deserve everything that's coming to you."

Suddenly, Marco doesn't like Shelley so much anymore. She whips her hair behind her head and storms out of the courtroom before Marco has the chance to respond, although he probably wouldn't have anyway. He wonders if he can request a new attorney even though she had been appointed by the court. He might try that. Before he can think any further, a uniformed officer surrounds him and forces him toward the side exit, which is also a fire exit, that's designated for the defendant.

SAL STANDS UP IN the front row and leans over the railing. He's crushed. What's going on inside of Marco's head? Sal

316

had thought that they were on the same page. But now, realizing that they're far from it, his worst fear has been realized, as he'll be forced to choose between his brother and his nephew. He doesn't have a clue how he's going to make that decision. Especially considering that one is innocent and one is not.

Marco turns to Sal before being dragged away by the police officer. Even after all that they've been through in the past few months, Marco has never looked so frightened. Sal tries to stay strong so that Marco won't see the panic behind his eyes, but he's not sure that he's very convincing.

"It's okay," Sal says. "I'll talk to your dad and get this all figured out."

Marco nods, then he's forced to walk out the side door of the courtroom. Sal tries to not think of where Marco is off to. A weekend is bad enough, never mind six months to a year or more by the time the trial is over. Marco will never survive in there.

Sal rushes out of the courtroom and heads outside to get some air. He desperately needs some relief. He stands with the smokers, leans his back against the brick wall, and inhales the poison that floats all around him. He searches for a sliver of hope or a silver lining in all of this, but he draws a blank. Nothing positive can be taken from this result. It truly is the worst possible case scenario.

It takes only a few minutes for Bartolo to call, right on schedule. Sal recognizes the number and moves away from the smokers so that he can speak with his brother in private. He answers the call right away, knowing that Bartolo will only have a few minutes before the next inmate in line gets his turn.

ANTONIO WATCHES IN SHOCK as Sal hurries past him without looking in his direction. His best friend has just lied to a county judge in front of everyone, and he knows it. Based on the reactions of the attorneys, police officers, and court personnel, Antonio suspects that many of them know it as well. And Marco did it all for him. Antonio feels terribly guilty for having ever doubted their friendship.

Antonio waits until the courtroom clears out before leaving himself. He's not sure what to make of what has just happened, so he takes a moment to reflect. He may not see Marco for a while, he realizes, and the thought of that kills him. Worst of all, he never even got a chance to say goodbye. And now, he fears that the friendship will never be the same as he'll never be able to repay Marco for what he has done. He just hopes that Marco doesn't resent him.

After wasting as much time as he can before finally facing his new reality, Antonio decides to leave. Sal will need his support more than ever now, so he decides to go find him and make amends. Sal must be distraught about this. First his brother and now his nephew; how much worse can it get? Antonio slides off the bench and makes his way toward the exit. The thought of Marco in that prison orange consumes his every thought. When he looks up and sees the same two police officers that he'd seen earlier, still standing there, guarding the door, Antonio's heart drops even further.

GERRY AND JAMAAL WAIT for Antonio Esposito to finally do something. He's the last one left in the courtroom and no one is left to support him. Although it makes their jobs easier, Gerry almost feels bad for the kid. When he does eventually slide off the bench and start walking toward them, his face shows his angst.

"Excuse me, are you Antonio Esposito?" Gerry says as Antonio approaches.

"Yes."

Gerry nods to Jamaal, who walks around Antonio and pulls out his handcuffs.

"Mr. Esposito," Gerry begins, "you're under arrest for robbery and conspiracy. Please put your hands behind your back. We can all leave quietly if you cooperate."

Antonio drops his head and obeys orders. Jamaal slaps the handcuffs on his wrists while Gerry recites him his Miranda rights. When legally prepared to move forward, they all walk out of the courtroom together with Gerry on one side and Jamaal on the other. Gerry holds his head up high, proudly, knowing that they got him. It was damn close, but they got them both.

CHAPTER FORTY-FIVE

Jen has thought a lot about it, and she's ready to move on. She's prepared to forget about everything that has happened and get out of this town forever. She had never wanted to be here to begin with, so this gives her a golden opportunity to get out. Marco Salazar's bail hearing should have already started by now, so she fears that she might be too late.

She finds Peter and tells him her thoughts - not just about the Salazar's, but about the entire situation. Her decision is final as she's convinced that it's the only thing left to do. Nothing else has worked. Peter agrees to go along for the ride and to talk to the police with her, although he's somber about it.

They arrive at the courthouse, Jen drives, and they hurry inside. Jen covers her face as they pass a group of smokers near the entrance on the way in. Peter asks her if she's sure about what she wants to do, which she tells him that she is. Nothing will change her mind at this point. Inside, they pass through a second door which leads to an open corridor where a few scattered suits and uniforms are standing around.

Jen spots Officer Dale immediately and heads toward him. Officer Harris is with him too, and they appear to be restraining someone. The detainee's head is down, so Jen is unable to see who it is. Officer Dale gives her a look of uncertainty when he finally does notice her approaching.

"Mrs. Winston?" he says. "What are you doing here?"

Officer Harris looks up when he hears his partner's voice. The man being restrained looks up too, and that's when Jen sees his face. She almost gasps out loud.

"Am I too late?" she says.

"Too late for what?" Officer Dale sounds almost concerned.

"The hearing. Did I miss it?"

Officer Dale looks to Peter, like he might be able to offer up some sense of reason. "What's going on here?"

"Let him go," Jen says.

Officer Dale laughs. "Why would I do that?"

"I'm dropping all charges."

Antonio is suddenly alert and staring right at her. His eyes pool and he doesn't even try to fight back the smile. The two officers, on the other hand, are anything but smiling. Officer Dale turns to his partner and makes an awkward face. Officer Harris seems to understand the message somehow and pulls Antonio off to the side, leaving Officer Dale alone with Jen and a mute Peter.

"What's going on you guys?" Officer Dale says. "Is everything okay?"

"Antonio and his uncle came to see us at home yesterday," Jen says.

"His uncle?"

"Yeah, his uncle, Sal."

Officer Dale gives Jen a blank look.

"You know," she continues, "Big Sal's Pizzeria. Sal. Big Sal."

Officer Dale shrugs, the name not seeming to ring a bell. Jen doesn't understand how they could have possibly missed that connection during their investigation of Marco Salazar.

"They told us everything," Jen says.

"Everything?"

"It wasn't Antonio who attacked me."

"I was afraid of that," Officer Dale admits. "But we do know that he was involved. We have Mrs. Anderson's eyewitness account that he was on your property during the same time that Marco Salazar was being apprehended. The robbery charges probably won't hold up, we know, but we can still charge him with conspiracy at least."

"Forget about it, all of it," Jen says. "Marco Salazar too. Just forget about it all."

Officer Dale scratches his head, looking confused. "But, why? After all that you've been through, why give up now? We have them both in police custody."

"I think you need to talk to this Sal guy. He's promising to tell you everything that he knows if you release these two."

Officer Dale retrieves his notepad from his breast pocket and uncaps his pen. "Okay, tell me about this Sal character."

"You can't miss him. He's huge, probably close to three hundred pounds."

Officer Dale scribbles down the note.

"Here he comes now," Jen continues, pointing to Sal as he makes his way in through the second door. He looks pissed.

JUST AS SAL HAD suspected, Bartolo is insistent on Sal spending the money to bail Marco out instead of paying for his own defense. Despite Stan Brothers already having received $80,000 of the $100,000 that he had required, it's a no-brainer for Bartolo. There isn't even a single moment of hesitation in Bartolo's voice, which does make Sal feel more at peace with it. After only a few minutes of back and forth, Sal hangs up with Bartolo and marches back inside with firm instructions.

The clerk's desk is near the entrance to the courthouse, but Sal moves right past it, the bag of cash now in hand - Sal had taken a little detour to retrieve it after he hung up with his brother. Although Antonio had refused to look at him during Marco's hearing, there's no time to hold a grudge. Sal is determined to be the bigger man and apologize to Antonio, then he'll try and convince him to come with him to the jail to pick up Marco after his bail is paid. Marco will be glad to see them both.

Sal spots some chaos ensuing down the corridor.

It takes Sal a moment to put the pieces together once he approaches, but when he does, he freaks out. He knows what's going on here. Despite Marco staying true to himself and not saying Antonio's name in court, Antonio is still in handcuffs. One officer hovers over him while another is a few feet away chatting with a man and woman. The woman points at Sal as he approaches, and he recognizes her face right away.

Jen and Peter Winston are here to tell the police everything that he had laid out to them yesterday, and now Antonio is going to jail because of it. They're going to tell the cops all about the diamonds too, and the charges against the boys are going to skyrocket. If Antonio was mad at Sal yesterday, he's probably going to hate him now. Sal had completely misjudged the situation yesterday and overplayed his hand. Antonio was right, Sal had given up too much information while demanding nothing in return. This is all his fault.

"Here he is," Jen says, talking to the officer. "This is Sal. This is the guy that came over to our house yesterday."

"Sir," the officer says, "are you Sal?"

"Yes, I'm Sal."

"What's your real name?"

Sal sighs, ready to face this like a man. He has failed. "Amelio Salazar."

"Are you Marco Salazar's uncle?"

"I am."

The officer nods to his partner, who then removes the handcuffs from Antonio's wrists. Sal is confused.

"What's going on here?" Sal asks.

"It seems as if your gamble has paid off."

Sal looks to Jen, then to Peter. Jen looks right at him and almost seems to smile. Peter won't stop staring at the ground.

"Were you telling us the truth yesterday?" Jen asks.

"Every word."

"With that being the case, this is Officer Dale and that's his partner, Officer Harris," she says, motioning to the uniformed officers. "They know more about this case than anyone. When you tell them what you know, maybe together you can find the guy who attacked me."

Sal can't believe it. He had completely misjudged the situation and he could not possibly be happier about that. He almost feels guilty for rushing to judgment so soon. He bites his lower lip so that he won't cry. He nods his head, just to do something.

"Amelio," Officer Dale says, "I think you better come down to the station with us."

"I'm not going anywhere until my nephew is released."

"No, that's not how it's going to work. Mr. Esposito won't be arrested yet, but Mr. Salazar stays in custody until after we talk. If we find your information to be useful, then maybe we can work something out."

"That's not what I agreed to."

"You weren't making a deal with the police before, were you?" Officer Dale points out. "This is the new deal. Take it or leave it."

CHAPTER FORTY-SIX

Sal is in a small interrogation room in the police station downtown with the whole crew. He accepted the deal. Officer Dale and Officer Harris sit across from him at the table and take notes while he talks. Antonio is next to Sal, although mostly staying quiet. Peter and Jen Winston are waiting outside the room, but they can hear everything that's being discussed.

The police officers say very little and let Sal do the talking. He tells them everything from the very beginning and leaves nothing out, except for that little thing about where the first $80,000 came from. When he finishes, Officer Harris steps out and confirms the details with the Winston's. When he returns moments later and tells his partner that the Winston's agree that Sal has left nothing out from what they were told, Officer Dale has only one question.

"If what you are saying is true then we should be able to track down this Enrique guy," he says. "Where can we find him?"

"I don't know," Sal says. "That's all that I know about him."

"I see."

"So what now?" Sal says.

Officer Dale looks to his partner, who nods to him. "Well," he says. "I guess you're free to go."

"Free to go as in..."

"Yes, both of you."

Sal and Antonio make eye contact and smile, their fight yesterday all but forgotten.

"Marco too?"

Officer Dale looks to his partner again and sighs. "Marco too."

Sal rejoices and bursts out in tears. He throws his face in his hands and sobs. He's not a crier, so it even surprises him. But the emotion of everything has finally gotten to him, and he just can't help it. A man can only keep it hidden for so long. Between his brother being in prison for a crime that he didn't commit and his nephew risking his life to save him, it's just all too much. When Sal regains his composure, he does the only thing that feels right. He pulls Antonio into an embrace and wraps his arms around him. Although initially resistant, Antonio eventually does give in and returns the gesture.

After the rare display of emotion, Sal stands up and shakes the officer's hands. He offers them free pizza for life at the pizzeria - which they both have to decline, they say - and agrees to testify once they track down Enrique. Sal is promised immunity to any related conspiracy charges. Officer Dale tells him that he will make a call and get Marco released but notes that it might take a couple of hours for it to be processed. Considering the circumstances, even the delay is music to Sal's ears.

The four men walk out of the room together and shake hands again. Officer Harris takes down Sal's contact information while Officer Dale heads down the hall to make the call. Once alone, Antonio agrees to go with Sal to pick up Marco. But before leaving the station together, they seek out the Winston's. They find them in the parking lot outside.

"Hey," Sal hollers, trying to get their attention as they pile into their car. When they don't respond, he runs over to them. "Hey," he repeats.

Jen turns around.

"I'm glad you're still here," Sal continues. "I just wanted to say...thank you."

Jen nods. "Yeah, well, let's just hope that it was the right decision and that they get the guy."

ALONE, JEN CRIES ALL the way back to Maine. It's not because of her decision to drop all charges against the Salazar's though, it's about what's happening between her and Peter. She doesn't sob for the entire five hours, but every time she calms down enough to relax, a love song comes on the radio that reminds her of how things used to be, and it starts up again.

Although ultimately her decision, it's not easy to leave Peter behind. She realizes that he has a legitimate argument about the mortgage, so she didn't force him to make that decision. She made it for him. He is to stay behind in Stoneham while she goes back to Maine. Although Peter insists that they can make it work, she knows better than that. This is the first step to a legal separation, she knows that, but there's no other way. She refuses to stay in the city and Peter has no desire to leave, so they're at a standstill. Peter has sacrificed once for her already, so she can't in good conscience expect him to do it again. Although Jen knows that Peter is upset about it too, he didn't put up much resistance to the idea, so that gave her more than enough information to know what's really going on inside of his head.

What single life is like, Jen has no idea, but she'll soon find out. For the past eight years - nine if she includes the summer before she and Peter were married - she's been loyal to the same man, but it's clear that they've drifted apart. Not only is Peter the only man that she's ever truly loved, but he's the only man that she's ever been with. Peter doesn't know that, of course, as she once told him that she was intimate with her boyfriend from high school, but that was a lie. She didn't want to put that kind of pressure on Peter at the time, and she's never regretted that decision. He wouldn't have been able to handle that kind of emotional responsibility. She even knew that way back then.

Her mother had always told her that fifty percent of marriages end in divorce, but Jen had always refused to accept that she'd be another statistic. If she was still alive today, Jen would have had someone in whom she could pour her heart out to, but she's one of the unlucky ones. Although she's going to stay with her friend for a while, no one can comfort you like your mother. Especially for daughters.

The stress of the past week has taken a toll on Jen's body. The Lyme disease rears its ugly head when Jen is feeling her worst, and today is no exception. All the while trying her best to deal with the emotion of the inevitable breakup with her husband, she can feel her joints swelling under her jeans as she drives. The pain has gradually gotten worse since she left the city, and she sees it as a reminder of what her new life is going to be like.

She'll have to suffer through the physical and emotional distress of ending a failed marriage, not to mention the constant fear that she'll carry with her until Enrique is behind bars. This new life is going to take her to the limit, and she's not sure that she's ready for that. But maybe it's for the best. If two people no longer want to be with each other, or if they're no longer capable of being with each other, then they should move one. That's what she's doing. She still loves Peter and always will, but they're different people than they once were. The honeymoon phase has long since passed, many years ago in fact, and they can no longer coexist as husband and wife.

Peter will find someone perfect for him who will undoubtedly be prettier than Jen, she thinks, and he deserves it. He deserves to be with a woman who cares about the same things that he does and wants to live the same lifestyle. All that Jen hopes for is that he'll never forget what they once had together. Many people would consider it to be eight years wasted, but Jen sees it as quite the opposite. She sees it as eight years of life experiences and memories that can never be taken away from her. She sees it as sharing eight years of her life with someone in whom she cares deeply about. And someone in whom she once was madly in love with. Her one hope, her only hope, is that Peter sees things the same way.

SAL AND ANTONIO HAVE reconciled. All is forgotten, now seeming unimportant. After Antonio follows Sal to the pizzeria so that Sal can change out of his suit, they ride over to the jail together in the Lexus. Sal lets Antonio know that his intentions were always pure and that all he had ever tried to do was offer him an opportunity to succeed. Antonio admits that he may have overreacted yesterday and that he would have left if he really wanted to. Nobody was forcing him to help Sal and Marco and he did it on his own. His best friend was in trouble, so he did whatever any good friend would do. As nothing is left to be said, they speak nothing of the Winston's. Sal knows that Lady Luck was on his side in that regard, and he doesn't want to jinx it.

The jailhouse looks like a castle up close, so big and extravagant. So protected. It has everything but the moat of alligators around the perimeter. Or the cannons, although there are armed guards sitting high above the walls in their watchtowers and just waiting for an excuse to fire their weapons. It's practically the same thing. The sun is starting to fade behind its brick walls, and Sal is getting chilly.

Waiting is the worst part. Sal feels like he and Antonio have been standing outside the gate for close to an hour, just waiting for Marco to appear from behind the barricade. He glances down at his seldom worn wristwatch and confirms that to be the case. Marco was supposed to be released at 2:00 P.M., but there's no sign of him yet. It's already after three. It makes Sal nervous.

He can't help but wonder if something has gone wrong, or if the Winston's have changed their mind.

Twenty long minutes later, Marco finally emerges from the side door of the jail, and Sal can breathe again.

Marco looks disheveled and confused from a distance, and that's likely the fault of everything that had happened in the courtroom earlier. The barbed wired gate slowly opens as Marco makes his way toward it. The imagery reminds Sal of a drawbridge that's laid on its side, not that he's ever seen that before. But if it were a possibility, he imagines this is what it might look like, albeit made from a different material. The escorting correctional officer goes no further than the exit and waits until Marco crosses the threshold before turning and heading back. The gate closes almost immediately, the metal on metal clanking as it does.

Marco's shirt is torn up pretty good, which shows the unnecessary force that was used to detain him, especially considering how he had been giving himself up, according to Antonio. That's no surprise to Sal, as he's seen it a thousand times. Exhibit A is how they had treated Bartolo, and now Exhibit B is Marco. All of that is water under the bridge at this point, though, as there are more important matters at hand. Without saying a word, Sal walks toward Marco and throws his arms around him. Sal's big belly separates them a bit, pushing Marco's torso back, but it's good enough. They cry together.

"It's over, Marco," Sal says as he squeezes his nephew. "It's finally over."

Marco only shrugs upon his release from Sal's bear hug. "For now," he says, half-heartedly, "only until the trial. We're not going to have enough money for my dad, are we?"

Sal almost smiles, now realizing why Marco is being a sourpuss. It's clear that nobody has told Marco that the charges against him have been dropped, and he thinks that he's just out on bail. Sal is more than happy to do the honors.

"They didn't tell you?" Sal says.

"Tell me what?"

"All charges against you have been dropped."

"By who?"

"The Winston's."

Marco looks between Sal and Antonio in search for a fib. They both just smile back at him. It takes Marco a while to process the information, but once he does, he jumps for joy, literally, and lands right in Antonio's arms. They hop around in celebration like they've just won the state championship while Sal watches with pride like the coach would. Sal can't help but belly laugh at Marco's youthful excitement. He's happy to see Marco acting like someone his age should for once.

When all jumped out and breathing heavily, Marco finally says, "Hold on. Why would they do that?"

"Me and Antonio," Sal begins, "we went over there yesterday. We told them everything."

"Everything?"

"Well, just about everything. I left out the part about the other houses that you've hit." Sal smiles.

Marco does too, then he wipes the sweat from his brow. "Okay, so what now?" he asks.

"I've still got $25,000 in cash under my seat," Sal says. "I say we get the hell out of here before someone steals it."

CHAPTER FORTY-SEVEN

Stan Brothers was right, his wife hates him. Upon his arrival back into town on Sunday, he goes straight home and tells his wife everything. She doesn't believe him, of course, saying that her brother would never be involved in something like that. Stan notices with irony that she only says her brother wouldn't do that, and not that her own husband wouldn't either. Stan has always come second to Stephan, and his wife's reaction just confirms his feelings about that. As one might expect, she blames him completely for her brother's death.

She's going to leave him and take everything - she tells his as much. Stan isn't surprised and would have expected nothing less from his fiend of a wife. She's beautiful, yes, but she's nothing more than a trophy wife. He sees that now. That's all she's good for, and now that the going is tough, off she goes to find her next sugar daddy. He spites her so.

What gives Stan pleasure out of the entire situation is that when his wife finds out how few assets they actually have, she's going to blow a gasket. Not only will she make a scene in front of whoever gives her the news - her personal attorney or a judge maybe - but she's going to flat out embarrass herself. She's going to look like a greedy, materialistic, egotistical, spoiled bitch, and Stan hopes that he's there to witness it. Although hopeful, he highly doubts that he'll get that pleasure. He'll be long gone by then.

Stan has been kicked out of his own house - the one that he pays for, in theory, although it has been a while since he's written a check to the bank - so his office is his new residence. But that's going to end soon too. He spends the night there and wakes up early to start packing up his files. When he's discovered to have been involved in what he was, he'll never be able to practice law again. Not in Massachusetts, not in the United States, not in the northern hemisphere. Not anywhere. What he plans to do with his client's files, he's unsure, but he owes it to them to keep them intact at least. Integrity and honesty are his new things, he decides, although it's not working out too well so far. Just ask his wife.

Linda, Stan's administrative assistant and one-time sex puppet, arrives at the office fifteen minutes early. Dressed in her Monday best, she bursts through the door to Stan's office without knocking. "What the hell is going on?" she says. "This place is a shit hole. How do you expect me to open the door with the lobby looking like that?"

Stan turns from his packing and faces Linda, surprised to see her. "Good morning to you too."

"Seriously, Stan. What the hell is going on? What has gotten into you?"

"I have to let you go, Linda. I'm sorry."

"Excuse me?"

"I'm sorry, I am, but we're going to be evicted from here by the end of the month. Pack up your stuff and go."

"Are you kidding me? After all that I've done for you, you just want to kick me to the curb like that? I've fucked you on command, Stan. Do you know what that does to a girl?"

"Well, now you don't have to anymore. Consider this your lucky day."

Linda scoffs. "Where's my last paycheck?"

"I'll mail it you."

"Bullshit. I want it now."

"I don't have it. You're going to have to wait."

"I need it."

"You do not need it. You're the only secretary in this state who's making $100,000 a year. You can wait a week."

"Administrative assistant, not secretary. Don't degrade me."

"Whatever lets you sleep at night."

Linda walks over to Stan and gets right in his face. "I'm going to call the cops and tell them what you made me do for you."

Stan smirks. "Don't waste your breath."

"I bet you'd like that, wouldn't you?"

"What are you going tell them? That you accepted cash under the table in exchange for sexual favors? That's called prostitution, babe. I'd think twice about opening that mouth of yours if I were you. You don't want your stupidity to get in the way of that pretty face."

Linda leans her head back, winds up, and spits in Stan's face like a llama. "Fuck you, Stan," she says, then she turns and walks out.

Stan clenches his teeth together while he finds something to wipe his face off with. He finds an old handkerchief in the bottom drawer of his desk and does just that. He almost gags as the stringy mucous separates from his face. He was too hard on her, he realizes, but what's done is done. He might have deserved that. He rinses his mouth with bourbon and lets the fire cleanse away the spite. Based on another negative reaction, he admits that he really needs to work on this whole honesty and integrity thing. He sucks at it so far.

It doesn't take long for him to get another chance, as just minutes after Linda leaves, Amelio Salazar pokes his head inside his office and smiles. He's accompanied by two younger guys, neither of whom Stan has seen before. Amelio also has a bag in his hand, and it's bursting with green. Stan notices it right away and knows that this is his opportunity. Now's his chance to start becoming a better man.

SAL, MARCO, AND ANTONIO take the elevator to the third floor and get out on Stan Brothers' level. Stan has the entire floor to himself, which surely costs him an arm and a leg each month. Stan can afford it, though, Sal thinks, especially considering the notable victories that he's had in the courtroom in recent years.

The lobby is a mess. Boxes are stacked to the ceiling in each corner, furniture is piled up in one spot, and to fit right in with always, no receptionist is behind the desk. Sal ignores the lack of courtesy and heads right down the hall toward Stan's office. Marco and Antonio follow closely behind.

Sal pops his head into Stan's office and smiles. Stan doesn't return the gesture. Stan looks like a walking nightmare. His face shines with oily grease from his skin, his hair is in desperate need of washing, and his office is in the same condition as the rest of the place. Something isn't right here.

"How are you doing, Stan?" Sal says.

Stan does nothing for a moment, then he says, "What are you doing here, Amelio?"

Sal walks all the way into Stan's office and drops the bag of cash on Stan's desk. The whole thing is like déjà vu for him. "Here it is, the final $20,000. That makes it an even hundred. Count it if you want." Sal crosses his arms and smiles. The remaining $5,000 is hiding under the seat in his Lexus.

"Who are they?" Stan asks, motioning to Marco and Antonio.

"This is my nephew, Marco, and his buddy, Antonio. They helped me get this money."

"And Marco is Bartolo's son?"

Marco nods.

Stan says, "I can't accept your money."

Sal is taken aback, shocked, and almost falls to his knees. "Why the hell not? It was due by tomorrow, so we're early. What's the problem?"

"It's not that."

"Then what?"

Stan sighs. "I can't take this case anymore."

"What the hell are you talking about?"

"I'll explain everything at a later time, I promise, but just trust me when I tell you that I can't."

"Not good enough. I need answers."

"Amelio, listen. You've done everything that I've asked of you, and I appreciate that, but I'm no longer going to be practicing law."

Sal shakes his head, not understanding. "But you promised if-"

"I know, and I'm sorry. Your family doesn't deserve this."

"Doesn't deserve what? You're not making and sense."

"I'm sorry, but I have to go now. Call Barry Crimestein, he can take care of you."

"Who the hell is that?"

"He's a defense attorney, and a good one. Not as good as I am, or was, but he's good. I'll tell him where he can pick up my files for the case. Trust me, Bartolo will be in good hands. He'll be fine. You'll all be fine. And $20,000 will be more than enough to cover his fees."

"What about the $80,000 that I already gave you? I want it back then."

Stan grabs a stack of papers and walks around the desk. "I'd give it to you, I really would, but I don't have it. It's gone. It's all gone. Everything I've ever had is gone."

"You son of a-"

"I'm sorry, Amelio. I really am. Tell your brother that too. I hope someday you'll understand why I did what I did."

"But, wait-"

But Stan doesn't wait. He brushes past Sal, Marco, and Antonio and leaves the building without turning back. They watch him as he disappears out the doorway and fades around the corner. Sal is speechless as he watches his brother's savior walk right out of their lives.

"What just happened?" Marco asks after a long moment of silence.

Sal shakes his head. He can feel himself sinking into oblivion. "We just got screwed, Marco. That's what happened. Royally screwed."

"What are we going to do now?"

Sal grabs the bag of cash from Stan's desk. "There's only one thing left to do. We go find this Barry what's-his-face and get your father's name cleared once and for all."

CHAPTER FORTY-EIGHT

Six months later.

Bartolo's trial began in December as expected and lasted for four weeks. Barry Crimestein did indeed take the case with open arms and had worked harder than anyone could have expected for $20,000. After reviewing Stan's notes, he had believed wholeheartedly that Bartolo was innocent and he fought his hardest for him. Despite his passion, the physical evidence was overwhelming against Bartolo, and without any witnesses to say otherwise, it was a near certainty that Bartolo would spend the rest of his life in Concord.

But that all changed in the final days of witness testimony.

Barry had called a surprise witness that came forward, and nobody was more shocked than Sal to see who it was. Nearly two months had gone by and no one had heard anything from Stan Brothers until that day. He sat on the stand for ten hours over two days and told everything that he knew and answered the same questions with the same responses each of the ten times that he was asked. He had explained to the jury all that he knew about the operation behind the scenes, which wasn't much besides what Stephan Cooper had told him. He had provided bombshell details about his involvement with his brother-in-law, about Stephan's involvement with a man named Enrique Henderson, and about their involvement with two men who he only knew as Duke and John.

When Gerry Dale and Jamaal Harris had heard Stan's testimony, they approached Bartolo Salazar's defense team and told them what they knew. They had agreed to testify their findings in court as well, as it helped to get answers to some of the questions that they had too. Since Stephan Cooper is already dead, Stan Brothers served as his voice in court and everything was taken to be factual. No one was able to track down Enrique Henderson, Duke, or John, so the trial went on with just the information at hand. Stan was guaranteed immunity for his testimony, and he disappeared again right after the trial.

It took the jury less than a day to decide on a verdict. Since the facts of the case that were presented by the defense team lined up with the details as testified by Stan, Gerry, and Jamaal, the decision was clear. Despite the seemingly overwhelming physical evidence, the twelve jurors came to the conclusion that the state had failed to provide proof beyond a reasonable doubt that Bartolo Salazar was guilty. Bartolo was acquitted of all charges against him and was set free that day.

Although the Winston's were never called upon to testify in the case, Jen Winston did attend the trial as a spectator during the final week. She was initially resistant to go back to the city to do so, but Bartolo's acquittal did make her feel more comfortable with her decision to not press charges against Marco and Antonio. Peter never made an appearance in court.

GERRY DALE AND JAMAAL Harris served their one week suspensions right after the charges were dropped against Marco Salazar and Antonio Esposito. Sheriff Henry Collins had used them as an example for the rest of his men, but he did praise them for their efforts behind closed doors.

Shortly after the suspension, Gerry had approached the Sheriff about the career aspiration that he had. His wife had still been supportive of his dreams, despite the suspension, so he went for it. The Sheriff put in a good word for Gerry at a neighboring department, and Gerry soon transferred there. He took over for a retired detective and finally became one himself. His wife is happier now too, although the late nights do still get old sometimes.

He still hasn't been able to find Enrique Henderson. He has no idea that he's been dead for months.

It was difficult at first, but Jamaal adjusted to having a new partner and started to thrive without Gerry's shadow hovering over him. He was assigned a new partner who was right out of the academy and he quickly became a mentor for the young officer. He's never been happier.

Keeping the tradition alive, Gerry, Jamaal, and their families spent the holidays together. They're still the best of friends. Never closer, really, now that they don't have to spend every day together.

IT TOOK OLD MAN Willy six weeks to sell off his pawn shop. He didn't have much trouble selling the inventory, but the building itself took a little longer. He didn't ask what his once beloved pawn shop was going to become, but he thinks he remembers the guy telling him that he was going to make it into a bowling alley. Willy couldn't care less.

Once his pawn shop was officially sold, Willy fulfilled his lifelong dream and moved to Martha's Vineyard with the profits. His old friend, Sal, had tried to connect with him a few times over the months, but Willy never took his calls. He's doing his best to separate himself from Sal and the old life that he used to have. Sal did leave him a voicemail telling him that both Marco and Bartolo were acquitted of all charges, which Willy was thrilled to hear.

He wasn't thrilled enough to call his old friend back, although he was tempted.

Despite the falling out, Willy is confident in knowing that Sal would never tell his secret to anyone, regardless of the threat that he had made. Willy is content to live out the rest of his years on the island with limited contact to the outside world. He does hope to someday forgive Sal enough to reach out to him. But for now, he's forced to live with the recurring nightmare that still haunts him in his sleep. He hopes every day that the innocent stranger that he took the life of so many years ago won't ever wash up on his beach and resurface old memories.

JEN AND PETER WINSTON have officially begun divorce proceedings. Peter had stayed true to his word initially and tried to make it work, but driving ten hours round trip every weekend was too exhausting. He had pushed Jen to try counseling again, which she agreed to, but Peter wasn't able to make the four o'clock sessions every Wednesday. He tried, he really did, but it just became impossible.

He lost his job in January for missing too much time and was never able to fully recover. He lost the house in Stoneham shortly thereafter. He's back in traveling sales and cruises all around the country doing so. He and Jen have agreed to meet for coffee the next time that he's in the area, but it will just be as friends. Everything they once had together is long gone.

Jen still works for the magazine. Her Lyme disease is still a hindrance at times, but the good days are finally starting to outweigh the bad days, and she thinks that it's because the stress level in her life has been reduced to almost zero.

She had only lived with her friend for a month, then she found a small place in the woods for herself. It's quiet and isolated, just as she likes it, and her writing is thriving. She's even started running on a regular basis again.

SAL, MARCO, AND ANTONIO are all right back where things started: twenty-two West Lane in Stoneham. When Bartolo was released from prison, he and Sal had a nice long business discussion regarding the pizzeria. Considering the debts owed to Barry Crimestein and the recurring losses being suffered by the pizzeria, they had to sell it. Neither one of them wanted to, but it was the only way to stay afloat. Sal was able to sell all of the equipment too, so between that and the actual property itself, they broke even on the sale. Sal is managing without it okay, although he does miss it.

Bartolo was awarded $150,000 in a settlement with the state for his false imprisonment. Barry Crimestein had pressed Bartolo to go to court for more, but Bartolo just wanted to be done with it all, so they settled. Without hesitation, he gave all of the money to Sal to be used for a good purpose. As if it was meant to be all along, Bartolo's old house went to a foreclosure auction within a month of him being released and after the Winston's separated. Realizing that his credit had taken a major hit when he got foreclosed on himself, he had no chance to buy it back.

But Sal did.

Using the money from Bartolo's settlement, Sal won the auction and bought the house back in cash. He had offered more than $20,000 more than the next highest bidder. It's under his name instead of Bartolo's now, but the end result is the same. The four of them live there now.

SAL, MARCO, ANTONIO, AND Bartolo sit around the breakfast table, relaxing, enjoying life. Eggs and orange juice and buttered toast cover the table, and it's great. Even the simplest of things are easy to enjoy now that Bartolo is free again. The arrangement is still new, but Bartolo can feel the bond returning with his son. It will take more time to fully repair the damage that has been done, he knows, but it couldn't have worked out better from his perspective. He couldn't be happier to have his old life back.

Bartolo's phone rings in the midst of a quiet breakfast, and it surprises everyone. Bartolo recognizes the number immediately, but he tries to hide his concern. "I've got to take this," he says, then he steps outside through the sliding door. When outside, he answers the phone, "Who is this?"

"I think you know who this is," says the familiar voice from the other end of the phone.

"How did you get this number? I told you that I'm done."

"No such thing, Bartolo. You know that. Did you not get the message before? You're lucky that you got saved."

Bartolo walks around the front of the house and into the driveway to ensure that he's out of earshot. He waves to his longtime neighbor, Betty, as she walks her pup down the street. She waves back.

"What do you want, Duke?" Bartolo asks.

"I've got a job for you," Duke Franco answers.

"I'm not interested."

"And I'm not asking. This is personal for me, and I want you to take care of this. He's a witness to a murder that's on our hands, Bartolo. Enrique Henderson of all people. And he doesn't seem to get the message. If you talk, you die. That's how it works. You know that."

"Are you talking about Stan Brothers?"

"You bet I am."

"But he was the one who got me out of prison. I can't do that to him."

"He betrayed me. He betrayed the entire operation, put it all at risk. I don't know how much he knows and he needs to be stopped. If this whole thing is blown, you'll be taken down too. I hope you know that. You'll be right back where you started - in prison."

"What's in it for me?"

"Besides your freedom, you mean? You know that statue that got you in this whole mess?"

"How could I forget?"

"It was full of diamonds."

"What? I thought it was just the eyes."

"Do you actually think I'd go through all this trouble for two small diamonds? You know better than that. I did my research."

Bartolo considers this, and realizes his boss's point. "What about them? The diamonds, I mean."

"They're yours. Well, Enrique's portion anyway."

Then it hits Bartolo. This whole thing, the setup, was about him wanting to get out. He has worked for Duke for more than twenty years, but when he tried to get out he was penalized for it. Enrique's job was to frame him, and he almost did. If it wasn't for Stan Brothers' testimony, it probably would have worked. The diamonds inside that statue, the diamonds that only Enrique and Duke even knew existed, were his payout. It all makes sense. He'll never know how Duke and Enrique had known about the diamonds inside, so trying to figure that out will keep his mind busy for the rest of his life, he figures. Duke is just smarter than everyone else.

"How much?" Bartolo asks.

"Six million bucks. That should take care of your little family for a while, wouldn't you say?"

"And if I don't?"

"Let's just say that I would hate to see all of the work that your son and brother did go to waste. Wouldn't you? That'd be a real shame."

Bartolo sighs. He knows that Duke isn't one to blow smoke without there being fire. He's left with no choice. "Fine," he says, "but I need details. Where and when?"

"Seattle, he's been spotted there. Take the first flight out. John will meet you at the airport. Oh, and there's one more thing."

"What's that?"

"Welcome back." Duke hangs up.

Bartolo feels defeated, conquered yet again by Duke Franco. He had thought this was over. He should have known that when he joined Duke all those years ago that this would happen eventually. Duke is simply too powerful to defeat on his own.

Bartolo walks around to the back of the house and walks into the kitchen through the slider. His energy is depleted and he tries to wipe the concerned look off his face. But it doesn't work. Everyone looks at him.

"Who was that?" Sal asks.

Bartolo pauses and looks between his three favorite people. He feels terrible for what they've all been through to help get him his life back, but he knows that it's just the beginning. Whether they want to or not, they're all now part of this. All three of them are just like Bartolo, and there's nothing that they can do to stop it. They work for Duke now too, one way or another, but they don't even realize it. Bartolo had tried to separate himself from Duke once before, and it almost got him a life behind bars. It will only be worse next time. And now, his family is going to find out who he really is, what he stands for, and the lie that he's been living. He's no better than Duke or Enrique or John. In fact, he's one of them.

But what Sal and Marco and Antonio don't know, what they may not ever understand, is that he doesn't have a choice. At least not anymore.

With a heavy heart full of regret, Bartolo sighs once, looks into the eyes of his protégés, and says, "What do you guys think about going to Seattle?"

About the Author

While writing has always been his passion, Dan began to pick it up as a serious pursuit after completing both a Short Story Workshop and a Scriptwriting course while in college.

After more than three years from inception to finished product, his first novel, DECEPTION, was published in May 2015. The first draft of his second novel, OPERATION SALAZAR, then took him only three months to complete, followed by four months to finish the first draft of his third.

Dan currently resides in New Hampshire with his wife and daughter.

For more information, please visit:
www.danlawtonfiction.com

Or contact him directly via: info@danlawtonfiction.com

Author's Note

Dear Reader,

I want to pass along my most sincere appreciation to you for your interest in OPERATION SALAZAR. My goal is to entertain, excite, and hopefully satisfy you as a reader with a combination of mystery, suspense, and thrills. I hope I did. As an author, I'm most grateful for readers like you and I wholeheartedly want to thank you.

If you enjoyed my work, I encourage you to please write a review to help other readers, like you, discover it. Also, please check out my first novel, DECEPTION, which I hope that you'll enjoy as well.

If you'd like to stay up to date with future works, I encourage you to visit my website for all the ways in which we can connect.

Best Regards,

Dan Lawton

www.ingramcontent.com/pod-product-compliance
Lightning Source LLC
Chambersburg PA
CBHW020222180626
46810CB00006B/2020